34/4

Connolly

I hope you
enjoy the story

10/18/13

34/4

Jonathan Gunger

iUniverse LLC
Bloomington

iUniverse books may be ordered through booksellers or by contacting:

iUniverse
1663 Liberty Drive
Bloomington, IN 47403
www.iuniverse.com
1-800-Authors (1-800-288-4677)

Because of the dynamic nature of the Internet, any web addresses or links contained in this book may have changed since publication and may no longer be valid. The views expressed in this work are solely those of the author and do not necessarily reflect the views of the publisher, and the publisher hereby disclaims any responsibility for them.

Any people depicted in stock imagery provided by Thinkstock are models, and such images are being used for illustrative purposes only.

Certain stock imagery © Thinkstock.

ISBN: 978-1-4759-9326-4 (sc)
ISBN: 978-1-4759-9328-8 (hc)
ISBN: 978-1-4759-9327-1 (e)

Library of Congress Control Number: 2013909827

Printed in the United States of America.

iUniverse rev. date: 07/10/2013

CHAPTER 1

JANUARY 7, 1976
NO SCHOOL

There is a magical sixth sense in children when it snows at night, especially a school night. Unlike most Thursday mornings, Isaac and Peter Taylor eagerly opened their eyes and were instantly full of energy. They leapt from their beds and bounced to the window, where, shoulder to shoulder, they looked out and saw the limbs of the tall pine tree bowing with the weight of a fresh blanket of heavy white snow; there was a new and wondrously white world just outside their window. Their hearts raced and they were full of excitement. Pete quickly moved from the window, bounced over his twin bed, and turned on the clock radio that sat on the nightstand between their beds.

There was a commercial playing for polyester pant suits that were on sale at Woolworths. The sound of the radio quickly drew Isaac's attention from the fresh snow, and he too, left the window and moved over to his bed and sat facing his brother and began listening intently. When that commercial ended, Pete let out a huge sigh when it was followed by the seemingly unending "Coke adds life" jingle. Once the song ended, he and Isaac leaned their heads closer to the radio with anticipation of hearing the school closing list, but when Pete heard the top of the hour network news begin he groaned loudly and fell back onto his *Six Million Dollar Man* bedspread with his arms outstretched and his head ready to explode.

The newsman had a very serious and professional tone as he dourly reported on a dangerous and threatening Chinese nuclear test that had been conducted the day before. He followed that with a horrific report about a mini bus carrying ten Protestant workmen who had been ambushed and killed as they were returning home from work in Northern Ireland. The newsman's tone quickly changed as he shifted to the world of sports and joyously reported on the exploits of Dave Cowens and the Boston Celtics, who had defeated Kareem Abdul-Jabbar and the Las Angeles Lakers the night before.

It seemed to take forever for Bob in the Morning to come back on and start talking, but when he finally did, the boys forgot their frustration, and again crowded around the radio. Bob soon began telling them what they wanted to hear.

"Well folks, nothing's open, and nobody's working expect for the snowplows and yours truly." There was a self-congratulatory laugh, and then Bob started talking again. "I guess we can give out the official list as I have it now. Should I start with the business closings or the school closings? *Theeese* are the important decisions that *I* have to make...."

"I wish he would just shut up and read the stupid list," moaned a frustrated Pete as he lowered his head between his hands. He was the older of the two brothers, tall and strong for his age, he weighed nearly one hundred and thirty-five pounds and stood close to five-foot-eight inches tall. He had light brown skin, and confident dark brown eyes that were now full of anguish. His normally stylish light brown hair that he meticulously kept feathered back and long enough to cover his ears, was now being twisted between his fingers.

Isaac sat across from his older brother wearing his Green *Incredible Hulk* pajamas, and watched him intently. He was a typical pain-in-the-neck little brother, and there was no mistaking what family he belonged to because, he too, had light brown skin, hair, and eyes, along with the same little upturned button nose as his older brother, but his hair was still short and parted on the side, like most of the boys in his fifth grade class. He was though, small for his age, standing four-foot tall, and only weighing a little over seventy-pounds. He followed, or tried to follow, Pete everywhere. He got into all of his personal things and generally made a nuisance of himself at every opportunity. He was quick with a comment and knew how to get under his older brother's skin, but deep down he worshipped his brother. Pete was everything Isaac wanted to be, he was stronger and more athletic than the other boys his age in the neighborhood, and all the girls followed him around giggling and looking at him funny.

Though the boys fought and argued constantly, they truly loved each other. Pete dominated, corrected, and complained about Isaac at every turn, and tried to hide and deny it, but there was no doubt that he loved his little brother; he just didn't want anyone to know, especially Isaac.

"Ansonia High School, Ansonia Middle School…"

"It's going to take forever to get to Mohegan School," whined Isaac.

"Shut up or Mom will make us start getting ready for school. You know how she is. Until its official, she's going to make us start getting ready. I swear, she does that just to make us crazy."

"Look outside. There ain't gonna be no school today." Isaac raised his voice in protest at being told what to do by his bossy older brother.

"Peter, Isaac, start getting ready for school; the bus will be here soon." When they heard the voice of their mother yelling up the stairs, Pete gave Isaac a glare that told him that he was treading on thin ice; he refrained from punching his little brother only because he knew it would draw more attention to them.

Isaac saw the look on his brother's face and knew he was in trouble, so he lowered his eyes and refocused on the radio in an effort to diffuse the situation and avoid getting beat up. Pete stared at his brother with clenched teeth and slowly shook his head, but soon stopped glaring and turned his attention to the radio as well. They were both hoping that their truce and ability to remain silent would buy enough time to hear if their school would truly be closed before she yelled up the stairs again.

"Masuk High School, Mohegan School." The words they'd longed to hear finally came out of the radio.

"No school!" The shout rose from the Taylor household, as well as every house with school age children in the valley.

The day was going to be difficult for adults with responsibilities, but for the children, it was paradise. Their day would be spent sledding, skating, and building snowmen, and some of the older boys were, no doubt, going to have fun throwing snowballs at cars or making extra money shoveling driveways.

ANNE TAYLOR WAS SITTING AT her old kitchen table comfortably wrapped in a fluffy white bathrobe, sipping her coffee and looking at the snow outside her window with a wry little smile on her face. She was a New England girl and loved the snow as much as her children. She had short brown hair with warm brown eyes and a glowing complexion that made her look much younger than her thirty-six years. Her smile and sense of humor were infectious and she believed it was her God given responsibility to keep everyone in her home operating with an optimistic and upbeat attitude. When she had woken up and looked out the window, she knew that there wouldn't be school, but she was in a good mood and thought it would be fun to tease and torment her boys as revenge for the gray hair she had recently found, and the sleepless nights they had caused over the years.

She grasped her cup with both hands and enjoyed its warmth as she brought it to her lips, but her peaceful moment was short-lived and she shuttered when she heard the pounding of the boys hurriedly stomping down the stairs. She lowered her cup and watched in amazement as they excitedly raced around the house getting ready for their day. An ordeal that normally took close to an hour of nagging, yelling, and prodding to accomplish was done in mere minutes. The boys were downstairs, dressed, and ready to go in record time. She had to force them to sit down long enough to eat a bowl of oatmeal and drink a cup of hot chocolate before she allowed them to run out the door thirty minutes before they would normally leave for the bus.

"Be home for lunch."

The two boys stopped dead in their tracks, turned around slowly, and looked at their mother with the saddest puppy dog eyes they could conjure. Their mouths were hanging open in shock, and heartbreak was written on their faces. "Mooooom."

The whines and pitiful looks on their faces were too much for her resolve. "Be home before dark," she conceded as she watched them dash towards the door.

"We love you, Mom," they both proclaimed as they sprinted out the door and on their way to adventure. Mornings like this were a treasure to behold for the young boys. They jumped off the front stoop and trudged to the driveway, enjoying the crunching sound of the snow beneath their feet. They paused silently and immersed themselves in the beauty that surrounded them. They were in a winter wonderland and they knew it. Fresh, virgin snow covered rooftops, trees, bushes, and cars. The air was crisp and snow continued to leisurely fall from the sky.

It would be quite some time before the plows would make it to their neighborhood, and, knowing this, most of the residents of Shelton were still wrapped in the warmth of their blankets, enjoying the rare chance to sleep late on a Thursday. Meanwhile, the Taylor family, and a few other snow-loving souls, eagerly immersed themselves into the wintery delight.

"Where do you want to go, Pete?" Isaac asked his older brother.

"We're going to Thompson's. I told James and Andy we'd meet there if school was cancelled. Come on; let's grab the toboggan and the two fliers out of the barn. We'll probably be the first ones there, so we'll have to make the path to the river with the toboggan. But once we get that snow packed, we're gonna fly down that hill."

The new snow was perfect for sledding. It was wet and heavy, and after they went over it a few times with the toboggan, it would pack hard. As the snowfall ended a little later in the morning, the sky was forecast to clear and the temperatures to drop steadily, and that was going to make their paths turn to ice in the afternoon. The boys knew they had perfect snow and perfect weather to have fun all day long.

The hill at Thompson's Tree Farm was a long walk from the Taylor house, but the hill was the best in the area. The tree farm was located on the banks of the Housatonic River. Old Mr. Thompson kept a service road that was about fifty feet wide from the top of the hill to the riverbank, and when it snowed, this service road became sledding heaven. The terraced slopes of the hill, five terraces in all, were made up of thirty feet of steep bank followed by ten feet of level ground. It was a long, steep hill that made for an incredible ride. People of all ages came to this hill from near and far, as they had probably been doing for as long as there had been people living in the valley.

Most of the older people with young children went about halfway up the hill and positioned themselves a little to the side of the main area, joyfully riding down the bottom few terraces, but the young and daring riders would start on the top of the hill. They would stand back from the edge, run as fast as they could, and dive onto their sleds. In doing so, they could reach incredible speeds before reaching the bottom of the hill. By the time they came off the third terrace, the boys would pull hard on the front of their sleds and fly through the air. The ride down was fast and furious; unfortunately, the walk back to the top was long and arduous.

On the bottom of the hill was the Housatonic River, and when it was covered with ice it was a great way to end the ride. The sled rider would reach maximum speed at the bottom of the hill, hit the ice, and spin the sled in circles, or see how far out on the ice he could travel. The river was far too wide for one to ever make it to the other side, but for countless generations, boys had tried.

PETE AND ISAAC MADE IT to the top of the hill and took a moment to take in the view of the valley and the beauty that surrounded them. Their cheeks and little noses had grown red and their lips began to dry out after the long walk, but for the most part, they weren't cold. Isaac was dressed in a dark blue snowsuit that covered him from head to toe and had matching mittens clipped to the suit which made him virtually impenetrable to the cold. He had two pairs of socks, long johns, two shirts, and insulated boots on. Pete was more interested in appearance than function. He wore a denim jacket with a *Lynyrd Skynyrd* iron-on patch on the back that he had to have after he heard "Free Bird" for the first time. Beneath that he wore a hooded sweatshirt, a flannel shirt, two tee-shirts, and long johns. Upon his head was a small black knitted cap that barely covered his ears. Snow was still gently falling and before them was a landscape that was more picturesque than any artist could replicate. The hills on the other side of the river were dotted with old Victorian houses adorning snow-covered roofs and chimneys that puffed a steady stream of light blue smoke. The trees that only yesterday were brown and bare were now full, clean, and comforting: even the streets that had yet to be cleared looked like perfect white lines written into the hills.

"Isaac, look down there at Johnson's; there's Dad pulling into the shop. He wouldn't miss a day's work if the world was ending. Check out the parking lot; there's quite a few cars buried from the nightshift. I don't think they're going anywhere anytime soon," Pete said to his little brother.

From the top of the hill the boys had a great view of the area. Johnson's was on the opposite side of the river and only a couple of hundred feet upriver from where the boys were sledding. They could clearly see about a dozen cars that had not been moved since the snow had started falling. They were covered with a thick layer of fresh snow, and there were only four vehicles that looked as if they had arrived that morning.

The river was lined with old brick buildings, many of them empty and sporting broken windows and faded paint, which championed an earlier thriving manufacturing community. Johnson's Metal Works and a few others were still in business, but the days of heavy manufacturing in the valley were coming to an end. The nation was getting ready to celebrate the Bicentennial in a few short months, but in this community, many of the people were nervous because they didn't know what was going to replace what they had always known.

The men and women of Johnson's Metal Works were very dedicated people. Several of the employees who had worked the night shift had been given the opportunity to leave early because of the storm, or to stay and wait it out. Most had stayed over for the day shift, knowing that the company would be short-handed, and also knowing that their Christmas credit card bills would be coming due and the overtime pay was extra money that would go a long way to help alleviate the pain associated with those bills, and so, snow or not, steel would be forged, shaped, and made into something useful in Shelton today.

"I don't see Andy's dad's car anywhere, do you? That whole family is probably still lying in bed sleeping. I bet Andy won't show up 'till afternoon," Pete commented. He was very proud of the fact that his father was one of the men that could always be counted on.

The snow was heavy and unpacked, and it was more like work than play the first few times down the hill. Isaac and Pete kept riding the toboggan down the hill, starting off slow and not going very far, but each time they went down the hill they packed the snow a little harder and went down a little farther and a little faster. The boys, being ten and thirteen years old, were almost oblivious to the work and the effort, but as they trudged back up the hill, they dreamed of the one improvement that would make Thompson's Hill perfect: a ski-lift.

After several more trips down the hill, they had the makings of an excellent path and were basking in the exhilarating effects of the fresh cold air that began biting their at their uncovered faces, and the excitement of having to hold on tight to the sled as they bounded down the hill and reached the speeds they craved. The snow had packed wonderfully; just as Pete knew it would, and the boys began to enjoy the rewards of their efforts and soon found themselves sliding onto the river.

When Pete was convinced that the snow was properly packed he decided to stop using the toboggan and started riding his *Flexible-Flyer*, and when he did, he wasn't disappointed. The newly waxed thin metal rails slid across the top of the snow like it was ice and after the second terrace, he was airborne. He pulled hard on the front of the sled as it came off the edge of the terrace and was rewarded with a long flight and a smooth landing. He repeated the process over the next three terraces and finished by smoothly gliding another thirty feet on the river. When his sled hit the ice he momentarily picked up speed, but when he hit the unpacked snow farther across the river, it worked as a brake and slowed him down quickly. He got up from his sled, still basking in the rush from his ride, and watched as Isaac come down the hill right behind him. He had to jump out of the way as his little brother, trying to be funny, almost ran him over as he went ten feet past where Pete had stopped. The two boys cheered their epic rides, grabbed the ropes on the front of their sleds, and started the long walk back up the hill together, energized by the prospects of the day to come.

When the boys reached top of the hill they were breathing hard and their legs were burning from the long climb. They looked at the glistening, but empty, hill below them and were surprised that by 9:30, nobody else had shown up. They began to wonder if they were missing something and quickly reassured each other that they really had heard the school cancellations. The boys didn't dwell on the missing people for too long, because they didn't care what the rest of the world was doing; they were having the time of their lives.

As the morning wore on, the snow tapered off as the wind picked up and the temperature dropped rapidly. The air was now cold and crisp and biting viciously at their exposed faces. Both boys were colder than either wanted to admit, but neither would think about stopping. Pete looked down from the top of the hill and was relieved to see Andy pulling his sled up the street, heading towards them. He elbowed his little brother and pointed him out. Andy looked almost comical as he trudged along in his oversized red snow suit, clumsily dragging his sled behind him.

"Come on, Pete, we can race down the hill one more time, and I'll bet we'll be back up here before Andy walks his fat butt up the hill," Isaac challenged his brother.

"Nah, you go ahead. I'm going to wait here for him; James can't be far behind." Pete was content to wait on the top of the hill for his friends. He didn't want to walk back up the hill with his little brother again because, while it was fun for a while, he was getting bored with only having Isaac to talk to; after all, a ten year old doesn't know much about football, southern rock, or girls, the three things that Pete had recently become preoccupied with.

"All right, watch this. I'm going to the other side of the river," Isaac said with a smile. He took four running steps and launched himself onto his sled and down the hill. He gained speed rapidly. He wasn't trying to fly in the air the way his older brother loved to; Isaac was keeping low and hanging on tight. He loved speed and Pete loved air. Pete watched Isaac move down the hill at amazing speeds, and when he hit the ice, he went further than Pete had ever seen anyone go. He was almost to the middle of the river, where, unknown to them, warm water flowed from the cooling system at Johnson's. When Isaac finally came to a stop, he rolled off the sled, rose to his feet, and jumped up, punching his fist in the air while he yelled to his brother. When he came back down, the thin ice beneath him gave way.

ISAAC PLUNGED INTO THE ICY water, his look of joy replaced by one of sheer terror. Everyone, even a young boy, knows what happens when you go under the ice in the river. His thick, warm snowsuit instantly soaked up the cold river water and became heavy. He felt the icy water hit his face, and reached out and up for something solid to grab onto. He knew that he had to keep his hand above the water or he would lose the hole, and he knew that that hole in the ice separated life from death. With incredible determination and effort, his mitten covered hand remained above the water, and after searching frantically; his little fingers did find and clamp tightly onto the edge of the thin ice. He fought his way to the surface and gasped for air, and then quickly heaved himself up and out of the icy water. Once he was laying safely on the surface, he felt an incredible sense of relief wash over him.

He rolled over onto his back and was overwhelmed by the reality of what had almost happened to him and he began to weep. A moment later he regained control of his emotions, wiped the tears from his tiny cheek, and rolled onto his knees and sat up to look for his brother. He was reassured when he saw Pete racing down the hill towards him; but his assurance was short lived. As he began to stand, his heart skipped when he heard the ice crack loudly, and then it disappeared from beneath him, and he was, once again, under water and grasping for the edge of the ice. The cold and the current were quickly sapping his strength, and his heavy clothes were pulling him down. He was terrified, but he fought valiantly for his life. He kicked his legs and arms and fought with the strength and determination usually reserved for someone many years his senior. Isaac Taylor was not going to allow himself to die today.

WHEN PETER WAS STANDING ON top of the hill and saw his baby brother fall through the ice he was instantly on his way down the hill. What he witnessed shocked him, and his mind was filled with terror. He moved swiftly and with a purpose he had never felt before. He jumped on his sled and willed it down the hill faster than he had ever gone. It took mere seconds for him to get to Isaac, but that time seemed like an eternity. His sled stopped ten feet from the hole and by then, his brother had brought his head above the water again, and was holding tightly to the edge of the ice and crying weakly. Isaac's lips were blue, and he was scared, wet, cold, and exhausted. Pete got on his belly and hurriedly crawled to his little brother, knowing that the thin ice could take them both to their deaths in an instant. When Pete reached Isaac, he stretched out his arm and Isaac latched on. Pete pulled him onto the ice, beginning to cry himself, having realized how close he had come to watching his little brother die. They lay flat on the ice for a moment and just breathed, feeling as though a huge weight had been lifted from their shoulders. They closed their eyes and appreciated the moment and each other. After the moment passed, Isaac sat up, looked around, and took a deep breath. As he turned his head to gather his bearings, the ice beneath them gave way again.

ANDY SAW PETE FLY BY him as he trudged up the hill, but didn't pay attention to him and never looked down the hill until he reached the top. When, finally, he reached the summit and looked down, he saw the boys sitting together. And then he saw the boys flail their hands in the air as they disappeared under the ice. He immediately jumped on his sled and repeated the actions that Pete had done moments before. He was panicking as he raced down the hill. As it had for Pete minutes before, the short ride down the hill seemed to take forever. Andy began saying every prayer he had ever learned in catechism. The prayers became a monotone chant of, "Oh God, oh God, oh God, please help me, Jesus, please, please, please." Andy kept repeating the words over and over. He wanted those boys to rise out of the ice, but there was no movement where the frozen river had swallowed them.

ISAAC WAS EXHAUSTED. THE ONLY thing he knew for sure was that he had to grab hold of his brother and never let go. Pete felt the icy water hit his face for the first time. The terror of what was happening slapped him and he opened his eyes under the water. He looked through the water with blurred vision and tried to make out the broken ice from the solid. Isaac was holding on tight and Pete was fighting to get them both to the surface before the current pulled them away from the hole. When he got to the top of the water he reached for the light, but the ice was solid. He frantically fought to hold his breath and get the two of them to the hidden opening. He reached up again and again, but found nothing but solid ice. Despair and panic began to overtake him. His lungs began to burn with the need for oxygen.

INVOLUNTARILY, ISAAC GASPED FOR THE air his juvenile lungs demanded. He felt the cold water enter his mouth and his tiny lungs filled with the icy water of the Housatonic River. His body convulsed and then went limp as the will to fight on left him. He no longer felt cold, or scared; he felt nothing as consciousness faded away.

PETER TAYLOR WAS FIGHTING HARD to find the opening when he felt Isaac release his grip and saw him start to float down and away with the current. Pete immediately turned in the water and swam hard towards his brother. When he reached Isaac his lungs were burning with pain. He grabbed Isaac and thrust him toward the surface. Isaac's limp body hit solidly on the thick ice above them.

ANDY DIDN'T WANT TO SEE his friends die, and as he got closer to the edge of the broken ice, he knew that he didn't want to die either. His two friends were under the ice, and by now they could be a long ways from the hole.

"Oh God, oh God, oh God, please help me Jesus please, please, please." Panic was close to taking over the young boy, but he carried on. Andrew Kennedy would not abandon his friends to the river. He looked over his shoulder and all around him, hoping to see someone coming to their rescue, but there was no one. Andy began to cry as he got to his knees and approached the hole.

He saw blurred shapes and colors thrashing about in the water. They were there. He felt an incredible sense of relief at the sight and it enflamed his sense of purpose. He no longer worried about his own safety, and reached into the water to grab at anything he could get his hands on. They were slowly moving away from him and seemed to be facing the wrong direction. He reached farther and farther until his shoulder was almost submerged in the water. His fingers finally found the hood of Pete's jacket and he immediately pulled as hard as he could.

Pete was searching for a break in the ice with one hand and holding Isaac in the other. His hand began cramping badly and he adjusted his grip in an attempt to get a better hold of Isaac and momentarily held him only by his fingers. He was shocked when, at that very instant, he felt his jacket pull against his shoulders as he was sharply yanked away from his brother. Pete's face cleared the water and his lungs filled with the air they demanded, but terror filled his heart. He thrashed about to break free of the grip that had pulled him away from Isaac. He swung his arm wildly, broke Andy's hold, and went down in the water again. He opened his eyes and looked around. His vision was blurred by the murky water; the river was dark and the current swift. Isaac was gone.

Again, he felt the pull, this time at his feet. He fought hard to stay under and tried kicking his assailant away so that he could find his brother, but Andy was not letting go and pulled him to the surface. This time the ice was solid and it supported their weight.

"No, oh God, no!" Peter screamed out loud because he knew Isaac was gone, and with him went the very core of his soul. He rolled to his stomach and attempted to crawl back in the water, but Andy, crying uncontrollably, would not let him go. Pete clawed at the ice and screamed with the anguish that very few will ever understand.

"No, No, No!"

CHAPTER 2

EMERGENCY ON THE RIVER

Bill Taylor was in the shower preparing for another day at work when the boys ran out the door.

"Bill," Anne shouted through the closed door, "you can't go to work this morning. The roads are covered with six inches of snow."

"Oh, I can make it, my beautiful wife." He was amused by her concern, but he loved snow days. He felt like a kid again when he drove his jeep in weather like this. Hell, the reason he'd bought the jeep was for the few days a year, like this one, when he could play in the snow like a kid.

"You're crazy. Nobody will care if you don't make it in until later."

Bill was a loving husband and father. His family was his pride and joy. They were his anchors and they were the main reason he pushed himself so hard to succeed. He loved his boys, and they idolized him. Bill Taylor worked hard at the Johnson's Metal Works, just like his father had done for thirty years before him. Bill's dad had shaped and cut steel on a lathe; Bill was an engineer, and he planned for his sons to be doctors.

Bill was a good engineer and proud of the changes being made at the Metal Works. Johnson's Metal Works was one of the few companies that had adapted to the new reality of manufacturing in America and had, so far, been able to survive. Many things had changed at the plant from its glory days in the fifties and sixties. New technology, better equipment, and more efficient production techniques meant higher production, but fewer jobs. The union fought tooth and nail to protect jobs, but the reality was that the company had to increase production and reduce costs or there would be no jobs at all.

Dumping waste into the Housatonic River had been common practice since there had been industry on the river, and that preceded the American Revolution. Johnson's had stopped dumping waste products into the river years before, and with other changes in the area, such as the explosion that permanently shut down the tire plant, the river was slowly coming back to life. Johnson's Metal Works used the river water for cooling metals in process, and then ran the water through a filtering system that actually let out cleaner water than it took in. Johnson's was trying hard to help with the restoration of the river. Bill had been the engineer who had designed the new cooling system and he was deservedly proud of how clean and efficiently the system worked.

Bill got into his new Cherokee, the seats of which were stiff and cold, and soon started on his way. He truly loved winter and enjoyed hearing the crunching of the snow under his tires as he began to move. He cherished the rare opportunities he was given to drive on empty roads covered with untarnished snow, and relished the calm and quiet that hung in the air after a good storm. The ride into work was slippery and slow, but sadly, uneventful.

He entered the office and stomped the snow from his feet, made his way to the break room where he said hello to a few friends, poured himself some coffee, and then went to his office to start his work. After sitting down and getting immersed in his work for an hour or so, Allen Hale burst into his office waving his hands frantically.

"There's an emergency on the river. Some kid's fallen through the ice." Without any hesitation, Bill leapt from his desk, grabbed his jacket and, like everyone else, parent or not, was on his way to help in any way he could. Bill had grown up near the river, and had heard this before, and unfortunately, he knew what this meant. A child falling through the ice on the river rarely turned out to be anything but a horrific nightmare with a tragic ending.

He climbed down the small hill to the river and started toward the crowd of people gathered a safe distance from the emergency site. He looked over toward the hole in the ice and could see the black diving hood of a diver in the water, and another diver sitting atop the ice in his wet suit assisting him. They didn't look like they were hurrying. He looked toward the top of the hill, and saw emergency workers frantically working on someone while carrying a stretcher up the hill to the waiting ambulance. He felt good for a moment, thinking that perhaps a rescue had been made and everything would be okay, but when he looked back toward the divers, he noticed the small black bag.

His heart fluttered and his stomach twisted. It got worse when he saw two of his friends hurrying towards him with a horrified look on their faces. Bill felt his stomach turn and his knees buckled. They came to him and put their arms around him in an attempt to get him away from the scene before him. "Bill, we need to call Anne and get to the hospital. They're taking Pete to Griffin."

Bill did not want to ask the next question. He looked toward the black bag, and felt faint and nauseous. His knees wanted to give out beneath him, but he kept walking toward the bag. "Where's Isaac?" The words came out weak and barely audible. Everyone knew the answer. Both men looked to the ground, and each held an arm and gave him a gentle squeeze in a vain attempt to comfort him. Bill wanted to fall to the ground. He wanted to run towards the bag, he wanted to scream loud and curse God, but he just stood there.

Allen, a friend for many years, ushered him away and told him that he would give him a ride to get Anne and then to the hospital. Bill couldn't think or move. He was turned by the men and led away. His mind went blank and he followed them as directed; at that moment he was barely breathing. His eyes were open, but he didn't see; there was talking and noise around him, but he didn't hear. His mind kept replaying the sight of the bag over and over. A realization came to him and hit him like a sledge hammer to the chest; he knew why the ice was thin and had broken. It was the warm water from the plant. It was his design.

"I killed my son."

CHAPTER 3

A MOTHER'S WORST NIGHTMARE

When Anne heard the door open, she was delighted to see Bill. She thought he had decided to come home and spend this snowy day with her. But when he walked in the door with Allen right behind him, she immediately recognized that they were shaken in a way that she had never seen before. Bill was pale and in his eyes she saw nothing but pleading, for what she did not know, Allen's eyes were evasive and covered with a glassy sheen. Instinctively she sensed impending doom and knew it had to do with her boys, felt the same emotions that Bill had felt earlier; the room started spinning, her stomach turned, and her knees got weak. Bill rushed to her and embraced her tightly, tighter than he ever had. He struggled to speak, his breathing was extremely labored, but after a moment he began to speak.

"Pete, uh, Peter's been taken to….taken to the hospital. We, um…., we need to get your coat and get down there."

"What about Isaac, where's my baby?" She pleaded on the verge of hysterics.

The tears that flew uncontrollably from Bill's eyes told her everything. Isaac was gone, and Anne was devastated. Her legs gave out and she collapsed. She cried and she wailed out loud to God himself. Bill knelt beside her in an attempt to comfort his wife. She felt him put his arms around her and her first impulse was to push him away, but after a moment or two, she buried her face in his chest and wailed.

After a short time she began to quiet down and her breathing slowed; somehow she pulled herself together enough to rise to her feet. She had to get to the hospital and take care of her living son. She was not going to let him go, not now, not ever. When they were ready, Allen gently ushered them into his car and drove as fast as he dared on the snow covered roads.

When they arrived at the hospital, Pete was unconscious and suffering from hypothermia. They hurried into the emergency entrance and were directed to ICU. Anne was frantic and felt completely helpless. When she saw her baby in that bed, with the tubes and wires and monitors, she had to momentarily stop. She brought her hand to her face to cover her quivering chin and just looked at her boy. She turned to and held tightly onto her husband, overwhelmed with emotion.

Anne regathered herself a short time later and continued on to her son. She sat in the chair next to his bed and held his hand. She vowed to Pete, to God, and to herself that she would not move from his side until he walked out of this hospital.

He woke once briefly during the night and Anne was right there to hold him. When he opened his eyes, she began crying uncontrollably. She leapt from her chair and squeezed him to her bosom and rocked back and forth muttering and moaning with a pain that only a grieving mother can understand. Pete's consciousness didn't last long, but it was enough to let her know that he was still with her, and once he was back asleep she reluctantly released her hold on him and allowed him the rest he so desperately needed.

After two days of sobbing and mourning, Anne was in the hospital bathroom getting ready for another day of misery. She looked into the mirror above the sink and, with tangled hair and bloodshot eyes, said, "I need your help Mom. I didn't tell him I loved him. They ran out the door and they told me they loved me, but I didn't say anything. I didn't tell them I loved them; and now Isaac's gone. How did you do it? How did you carry on after Dad died? I need your strength... no... I need you, Mom... Please help me. Oh God, please help me."

Anne's father had died suddenly and unexpectedly from a heart attack when she was thirteen. He'd left them nothing but great memories, and somehow her mom had managed to take care of her and her two little brothers. They hadn't had money or new clothes and toys, but they'd been happy and had always felt loved. Her mother had passed several years before, but while Anne looked in the mirror, she had the strangest feeling that her mother was with her, and it comforted and strengthened her.

She pulled herself together, took a deep breath, stood up straight, and decided that life must go on. She took an extra moment to rinse her face and straighten her hair. She looked at the face that was staring back at her in the mirror; it was her turn to be strong. She didn't know why God kept doing this to her, but the loss of her father, and the strength of her mother, gave her the courage to accept that death and loss are part of the price one must pay for living. The pain was there and would never leave, but it would subside some. It became clear to her that she must take care of her family now, as her mother had done for her and her family then.

CHAPTER 4

LIFE GOES ON

In the days that followed the accident Bill was in a constant daze, fed by a steady diet of whiskey. He sat in his oversized living room chair with a bottle of Jack Daniels on the side table, and a half empty glass in his hand, examining the issue of the warm water and thin ice over and over in his mind. He designed the system that killed his son; *his* negligence killed his son. When he had gone to the hospital the day before and had seen Pete lying unconscious in the bed and his mother weeping as she held his hand and rested her head on his tiny chest, Bill was overcome with such a powerful sense of guilt for what he had done, that it took all of his self-control to keep from going outside and putting a gun in his mouth at that very instant. He had killed Isaac, and had probably caused irreparable damage to the psyche of Peter. He knew that he had done this to his wife and children, and he became angry and frustrated because no matter how much he begged God to let him die; he kept on breathing. He soon decided that God killed his child just make him suffer.

Allen called or came by every day to offer any kind of assistance he could, but Bill didn't want to see or speak with anyone, so he sat motionless in his chair clutching his glass of pain-relieving elixir and blankly stared at the TV while the phone rang or Allen stood outside knocking on the door. Mr. Johnson made sure that food was brought to Bill's home every day. But again, he never answered the door and the food was left on the porch.

He didn't bathe for several days and was barely able to draw enough strength to put on clothes. When he finally found the courage to call Montero's Funeral Home, the conversation was short. He was barely able to keep from breaking down while on the phone, and refused to go to the funeral home or to make any selections. He told Mr. Montero, a kind man who'd taken over the business from his father, to do whatever he thought was right, send him a bill, and let him know when the services were to take place.

After Bill had been told by Mr. Montero what the schedule was to be, he went to see his wife. He didn't care that he stunk or that his hair was disheveled and greasy and his face was covered with several days of beard growth. He sat in a chair next to his wife holding her hand and avoiding her eyes as he fought valiantly to hold back the tears. He explained to her that she would have to leave the hospital briefly for the services that were scheduled for a couple of days before Pete was to be released.

Anne was torn and hesitant; she did not want to leave her son, even for an instant, but she knew she had to, and so she reluctantly agreed to leave for the funeral after Bill assured her that she would return to the hospital as soon as the services were over.

WHEN THE FUNERAL FINALLY CAME, the support from the community was overwhelming. People came from all over to pay their respects, offer help, and attempt to help the family in any way they could; but the only thing they wanted was to be left alone. Anne tried to remain strong and stoic throughout the services; Bill had started drinking as soon as he'd woken up. He was polite to the well-wishers, but not friendly. The several hours they spent at the funeral home and then traveling to the small, freshly dug grave for their youngest son was the longest day of their lives.

When, finally, they'd watched the casket lowered into the grave and had said their final good-byes to their child, they went back to the hospital to attend to their living son. Mr. Montero had made arrangements to take them from the cemetery to the hospital and Allen had brought Bill's car to the hospital and dropped it off. He spoke briefly to Bill and Anne, again offering help that was politely refused.

The hospital stay was over two days later, and while Anne and Bill were happy to bring Pete home, everyone was melancholy and silent. Pete was regaining his strength, but didn't want to go back to school because he knew the students would be staring at him and whispering, and the teachers would be feeling sorry for him and trying to protect him. He decided that he hated them all.

Bill and Anne talked about what to do and decided that he had to go back to school, and a week after he was released from the hospital he returned to school, where everything was as he anticipated. As Pete walked the halls, he could almost hear the kids in the halls and cafeteria: "There he is, the kid whose brother died at Thompson's." He could see it in his two best friends at school. They didn't know what to say to him, and he had nothing to say to them. He began drifting away from the people he had always known and loved. He wasn't mean; he just kept to himself and did as little as he could to get by. He wanted to become invisible.

Eventually the snow melted and spring came to the Valley. Anne insisted Pete play Little League again. He had been a good ball player and had played every year since he was eight. She convinced herself and Bill that the return to normalcy and the involvement with other kids would help him get past the loss of his brother. As always, Bill and Pete complied with her wishes. Pete did his job and played, but without emotion or enthusiasm. He talked to the kids on his team as little as possible, and never with excitement or friendship; he didn't want friends anymore.

The school year ended and Pete was promoted, mostly out of

sympathy and grade inflation. He didn't care about school anymore. He brooded constantly, rarely, if ever, did homework, and barely passed his tests. Andy had tried to resume their friendship, but Pete was unresponsive and evasive. Andy thought Pete should be grateful that he had saved his life, but Pete looked at Andy and thought of him as the person who'd pulled him away from Isaac. He didn't blame or hate Andy, he just didn't want to look at him, and eventually Andy gave up and drifted away. When summer vacation arrived, Pete wanted nothing more than to spend the whole vacation in his room, lying on his bed and listening to music while staring into space.

Unfortunately for him, his mother was not going to tolerate that attitude. She had always told him that idle hands were the Devil's workplace, and Pete had recently become convinced that she was doing battle with the Devil through him. She continually assigned him tasks and chores, and when she ran out of things for him to do, she would yell at him to go outside and play, or go fishing, or do anything except lay around and mope. She knew that activity, whether wanted or not, was good for the mind and the body. Moping in self-pity was an all-consuming pit that she was not going to allow her son to fall into.

Her nagging usually prompted him to get his fishing pole and head to one of the local streams to wander through the woods for a few hours, and that is precisely what he did one July morning. She wouldn't stop harassing him until he got up and out of the house, and when he finally walked out the door, he knew exactly where he was going. He and Isaac had discovered a secret place last summer and was sure that nobody else knew about it. He relished the fact that he was going to be gone for a long time; he was going through Bobby Wilson's cow fields.

THE STREAMS AROUND THEIR HOME in Huntington, a rural suburb of Shelton, were small, shallow, and plentiful. They wound through the rolling hills and farmer's fields and into the many swamps that populated the area, eventually coming together at the far mill reservoir.

All the good fishermen knew that the best spots were the ones that were hardest to reach. They were the hidden gems that were surrounded by swamp and briars and provided the most fish because they allowed the fewest people to access their treasure. Stealth and patience were required to get to the water's edge without spooking the fish and rendering the effort futile. A simple mistake, such as a shadow cast upon the water or a broken twig under a foot, was enough to scare the trout. Pete found that he loved the solitude and challenge of the hunt.

To access Bobby Wilson's hidden piece of paradise, Pete had to be willing to walk though a fifty acre pasture, make his way past the cows, and trudge through a soupy combination of mud and cow pies that was six inches deep. Once through that, he had to weave his way through a patch of briars and undergrowth that scraped, scratched, and cut the skin. After fighting through fifty feet of this mess, the ground rose onto a moss-covered rock outcropping that overlooked a bend in the slow-moving stream. This natural barrier dutifully protected the native trout that were hidden in the seclusion provided by wash-outs under tree root mats and fallen logs. The bank was lined with a variety of full and lush trees that included willows, red maples, silver ash, and black gum. In the shallows and along the bank grew water lilies, cat-tails, sweet pepperbush, and clammy azaleas.

This was a special place that few people knew about and even less made the effort to reach. It was a lost piece of Eden that rewarded the determined traveler with its secret beauty. The sun beamed through an opening in the canopy, which providing a ray of warmth on a rocky outcrop that sat about three feet above the water; it was large rock with a semi-flat top and patches of soft green moss growing on it and dark green marginal woodferns growing around it. The rock was close to twelve feet wide and eighteen feet long, and the stream below had smaller, moss covered rocks scattered about and rising slightly above the water which made a tempting, but slippery path to the other side.

WHEN PETE ARRIVED AT WILSON's pasture after a long walk from his house, he stopped at the fence and looked out. "Crap, look at all those cows," he thought to himself. The cows usually grouped together and grazed in a variety of places throughout the day. They now grazed right in his path. He took a deep breath, climbed the fence, and started across the pasture. There were about sixty cows between him and where he was going. He hated cows; they were big and unpredictable and they scared him. The mindless creatures could stand in mud and shit, barely moving all day, and then they could be spooked by something as simple as a shadow and all hell could break loose. As he gingerly worked his way through them, he thought about the scene in the movie *The Cowboys* where the boy, looking for his friend's glasses, got trampled. He hated this walk, and he hated his imagination as well.

As he worked his way across the field, he kept one eye on the cows while the other eye watched where to step. The pasture was full of small islands of semifirm earth topped with grass as short and green as a well-manicured putting green. The grass was always kept short by the constant grazing of the cows, whose life endeavors consisted of eating, crapping, and giving milk. Everywhere the ground was wet, and as cows walked, the pasture became littered with water-filled holes that were formed by their hooves as they broke through the surface mat and sank into the mud below. Stepping in one of their holes could result in something as minor as getting wet and muddy to something as severe as twisting or breaking an ankle and having to crawl out of the pasture.

Pete watched the cows as he nervously approached within a few feet of them. Some of the large animals lifted their heads and observed his movements while the others remained oblivious and continued to eat. Pete walked slowly and carefully; he wanted to do nothing that would startle them. As he made his way through the animals he wondered if they were as nervous as he was. He doubted it, since he was a thirteen year old boy who weighed a hundred and thirty-five pounds and they weighed close to a thousand. He spoke softly and calmly to them as he continued undeterred, and after a few minutes of this terror, he made it safely past them and walked on higher and firmer ground.

That pleasant area of the pasture was quite small, and soon the ground began to get lower and wetter again. The vegetation turned from short grass to hardwood trees, mud, rocks, brambles, and wide-leaved ferns. Pete stepped in the mud and felt his boots sink. He quickly leapt for a rock, but slipped off and into the mud. When he looked down, the mud was up to his ankles and rising; he was resolved to the fact the he was going to get nasty, so he didn't bother looking for a dry place to step. He worked his way forward another twenty feet to the underbrush and the game trail.

Pete pulled apart his fishing pole and held the two pieces in his hand as he squatted down and entered the briars. He slowly and quietly worked his way through. The brush was thick and made it hard for him to see more than a few feet in front of himself. The briars caught his shirt and the thorns scratched his arms, but he continued and soon saw light ahead. He quickly emerged from the brush and instantly felt the sun on his skin and its light in his eyes.

He quietly climbed on the rock and looked around. He heard the babbling brook, and watched a couple of dragon flies bounce around a lily pad for a minute or two and then he settled in. He reached into his can of worms and found a nice juicy one, baited his hook, and tossed it out. He was almost hoping no fish would bother him so that he could lie in the sun for a while. The moss on the rock was thick and almost felt like a velvet carpet. He laid down and felt the warmth of the sun envelope him. Soon the woods started coming back to life; red-winged black birds, warblers, and other birds started chirping and squawking, and in the trees the squirrels started moving about again. He listened as the stream babbled against the rocks and a gentle breeze blew and rustled the leaves above him. Pete closed his eyes and felt peace. There was no happiness, just an unfamiliar feeling of peacefulness that he allowed himself to indulge in. He soon felt guilty for enjoying himself in this spot without Isaac, but he pushed those thoughts out and allowed himself to listen to the sounds around him.

CHAPTER 5

WHAT'S A FATHER TO DO?

B ill Taylor was having a hard time. There wasn't a moment that went by that he wasn't blaming himself for what had happened. The thoughts that went through his mind were deep and dark. He wanted nothing more than to trade places with Isaac. His reason for living was gone; his drive and desire were a thing of the past.

He constantly brooded over the solution to the warm water problem in the river. It was so simple, it was right there: a settling pond. That was all he needed. The land was there, and the costs were minimal. His son hadn't needed to die, but he had; and that was because his father hadn't thought about the effects of the warmer water going into the river during the winter. It didn't occur to him that everyone else had overlooked it too. It wasn't something that had been neglected to save money; they'd just never thought of it.

Bill started to question all his work. Projects that should have taken hours were taking days. He tried to plug in every possible variable. The mathematical possibilities were endless. What else had he overlooked? How many other times had he overlooked something that had caused a family somewhere to lose someone? He was losing his mind in the never ending negative possibilities. He no longer thought with a can-do mindset and instead took the mindset of why we can't-do. He spent endless time thinking about why a project wouldn't work, why it would fail, and how someone was going to be harmed by his work. His thoughts were negative, and he became negative as well.

"Bill, let's do lunch," Charlie Bidwell yelled through the door.

"Nah, I've got to finish this. I'll be here another hour or two. Fabrication needs these revisions."

Charlie shook his head. Bill had eaten lunch alone since he had come back to work. The guys took turns trying to get him out of his fog, but they were getting tired of Bill feeling sorry for himself.

Charlie walked over to Allen Hale and let him know they would be dining alone.

"Listen, Al, I am not wasting any more time with him. If he doesn't want to help himself, why should we bother? I feel for the guy. I really do. I can't imagine how much it hurt, but damn, it's been almost a year."

"Come on Charlie, ease up. It hasn't been anywhere near a year. He's okay, he just needs more time. Let's go eat. Let's do the Pizza Palace. I could do with a good grinder."

The men left work and went to enjoy their lunch. Bill had, of course, overheard the conversation and had to agree with Charlie.

"Just leave me the hell alone," he thought to himself. When he had given them enough time to leave the building, he grabbed his jacket and headed for Doc's, the bar up the street. He was having lunch with his new best friend Jack Daniels. Food and sobriety were two things that Bill had lost all interest in.

CHAPTER 6

SO CROWDED
AND SO ALONE

They were finally gone. Pete had grabbed his pole and gone fishing, and Bill had gone to work, twenty minutes late, as had now become the norm. She walked to the kitchen sink and braced herself with both hands on the white double sink and took a deep breath. She looked out the window of the old farm house they had bought when the boys were small. A tidal wave of memories flooded her mind. She could see Isaac and Peter running to the house from the barn, sometimes laughing and sometimes fighting and screaming. She closed her eyes and felt him come to her.

"Oh, my little Isaac, I didn't tell you I love you, but you know I do. I miss you so much. I need to hold you and feel you in my arms again. I need to hear you fight with your brother. He needs you, you know. Your father needs you and I need you too. I know you're okay; I just wish I could say the same for us."

She closed her eyes and lowered her head. The all too familiar tears began to build in her eyes and her nose started to run. She wiped her nose and rubbed her eyes. "Not today. I just can't do it today." She looked up and out the window again. It was a gorgeous day. Her lilies and roses were in full bloom along the white fence, the evergreen was full, and a variety of birds were visiting the feeders spread throughout the yard. It was the beginning of a beautiful day. Anne closed her eyes again and tried to understand why she felt so exhausted already. She wanted to cry, to sleep, or to just to fall into a heap in the middle of the floor. Instead, she pushed herself away from the window and went to work.

Anne worked part-time as a cashier at Birchwood Market. It was a small grocery store with close knit people who had worked together for years. It got her out of the house, and the few extra dollars she earned were supposed to be the family's fun money. As she got into her car, she almost chuckled at the thought.

"Family fun money. We can go to the movies or dinner, or just do something impulsive and fun." She replayed her argument with Bill in her mind. How long had it been since she'd seen her family laugh and have fun? Seven months, two weeks, and three days.

She had begun working at the market years earlier because she'd wanted to get out of the house and have real conversations with other adults. She and Bill had been younger then. Money had been tight, and the mortgage had been more than they could really afford on a young engineer's salary, but by sacrificing other things, they had gotten by. The little bit of extra money she had earned really had helped. Isaac had entered kindergarten in 1971, and she'd needed to get out of the house and be among other people for twenty hours a week or so.

The people at Birchwood Market were a wonderful lot, as were the majority of people who worked in the area. They were a diverse and creative collection of small businesses, and they had a variety of views on everything except naming a business. It was either named for the family or the town. When Al and Jim Burns had opened Birchwood in 1956, they'd decided it would be easier to sell the store when it was time to retire if they named it after their favorite tree. It was one of the many small stores located in Huntington Center; it had seven short aisles, and a butcher shop. It shared the front of the building with Polski's Pharmacy. Down the hill, below and behind the grocery, were Kuen's

Diner, Huntington Liquor Store, Harris's Hardware Store, and Neil's Barbershop. A little farther down Huntington Street was Huntington Savings and Loan, Billy Nick's gas station, and the Huntington Bakery. There was a real estate office, a post office, a deli, a dentist, a small Italian restaurant, and four churches. Huntington Center had almost everything a person needed.

The Birchwood customers never changed, they just got older, and except for the part-time high school kids, the employees rarely changed either. Mike Jones, the store manager, and Dick Teconasovich, the assistant manager, had started there as one of those part-time high school kids eighteen years earlier. Maggie McDougle, now in her sixties, had worked the register since anyone could remember. Over the past several years, Anne had become part of their family, too.

SHE SAT IN HER CAR and turned the key. It seemed heavy and took extra effort to turn it. The engine started and the car moved out of the driveway. It seemed to drive itself to the store. Her mind was bouncing around and she was thinking about everything except driving. The car followed the road, turning where it was supposed to and stopping where it was supposed to.

She thought about Bill and what he was becoming, what they were becoming. He had not touched her intimately since that day, and she really didn't want him to. He had become a man that lived in her house, not in her heart. She still loved Bill; she loved the memories of the energetic man who could solve any problem, the man who always found time for his boys, Bill the passionate lover who made her feel like the most special and beautiful woman in the world. She wondered what was to become of them. Bill had no passion left in him. He was usually late to work and was now usually late coming home as well. He had become a regular at Doc's and often stopped after work for a round or two…. or three. Anne understood why he was drinking; she understood why he had become the man he now was, and she wondered if he would ever return to her. She wondered if she really wanted him to return to her. Maybe, she thought to herself, she wasn't complaining about him staying out drinking because she was actually happy that he wasn't in her house. It was less time she had to spend dealing with his anger and self-pity.

She thought about Peter and what he was becoming. He was so young, so smart, and now so withdrawn. She would look into his eyes and become frightened by the emptiness that she saw in them. It was a struggle to get him to get out of bed anymore. He was never disrespectful or angry at anyone but himself and, she believed, his father. His future used to be so bright. This time last year he had lit up a room when he walked in and his energy had been absorbed by the people around him. Now... now when he walked into a room, it got colder, quieter, and darker.

She missed her boys. She missed her husband. It was as if the river had taken them all from her.

CHAPTER 7

WHAT'S UP, LITTLE MAN?

First Pete heard the branches breaking, and then he heard the voices.

"You're a moron. Could you be any goofier if you tried?"

"Screw you, asshole!" came the defiant reply. Pete sat up as the voices came closer. There was no doubt that they were coming to his fishing hole. He heard more swearing and arguing as the footsteps got closer. He debated whether or not he should reel in his line, but in the end, decided to stay where he was and see what would happen next. He looked into the brush again and saw branches moving and then shapes weaving through the game trail.

After a moment, he saw people emerging from the undergrowth. The first person he saw was a kid he recognized as Jimmy Nevers. He knew of their family; everyone in Huntington knew of their family. They had been living on Mohegan Road for nearly a hundred years. Their house was the smallest in the area and had, by far, the most people—nine kids—in it. Jimmy was one of the younger ones; he was sixteen years old, had a van, an attitude, a reputation, and was as cocky as hell. A moment later, the second kid emerged. He was a short kid with a New York accent: David Mandis. He was a little prick. His family had money and he made sure everyone knew it. He liked to party, and since it was daddy's money, he didn't mind buying.

The next one out of the woods was as tall as a tree and skinny as twig. Wally Pintowski came through the brush and stood straight up. At fifteen, he was already over six feet-three inches tall and still growing. He weighed about one hundred and forty pounds, had Coke bottle glasses, braces, and was wearing homemade polyester pants that were more than an inch too short for his long legs. He had made it into the clearing and was starting to walk towards them when he stopped short and twisted around. His fishing line had come loose from his pole and was now caught in the bushes. He started yanking and pulling on it in an attempt to break it free, and while doing so, he unleashed a tirade of cursing, the likes of which Pete had never heard before. After several minutes of yanking, pulling, and cursing, his line came free.

"About fucking time!" he angrily yelled at the bushes and then he turned to continue towards Pete and the others. In the small muddy barrier that surrounded the secret rock were green, leafy marginal woodferns that stood a couple of feet tall and small green skunk cabbage plants. In his anger, Wally decided to take out his wrath on one of the small cabbages. He kicked it as if it were a football with his enormous boot and it immediately exploded. When the spores that carried the dank skunk-like stench that gave the plants their name wafted through the air, Pete cringed and wanted to cover his nose until the pungent aroma cleared away, but he never moved.

"Oh, you asshole," Jimmy yelled at Wally. "Why do you have to do stuff like that?"

"Because I like doing it, that's why. So, fuck off," he yelled toward Jimmy.

Pete watched, unnoticed, as Wally approached, destroying everything in his path with his giant size thirteen boots. Wally slung his pole over his shoulder and smiled a goofy and defiant grin at Jimmy as he walked past him with a blueberry branch that had surrendered to the onslaught dangling from the end of his line. He had come through the brush with so much crashing, thrashing, and stomping that Pete knew there was no chance of catching any fish in this hole for a couple of hours. He started to get up and leave, but decided he really had nowhere to go, so he got comfortable and watched the show.

"Dude, what the hell is the matter with you?" Jimmy again yelled at Wally. Wally got an indignant look on his face, looked at Jimmy, raised his right hand, and gave him a one finger salute.

"Screw you, Asshole."

"Can you be any noisier? You sound like an army of gorillas. Jesus Christ, you're a moron. There aren't any fish within a mile from here now," Jimmy ranted. He looked like he was going to come unglued. They made their way onto the rock and Jimmy was the first to notice Pete sitting with his line in the water.

"What's up, little man?" Jimmy asked rhetorically as he walked past Pete and looked into the water.

Wally trudged onto the rock and continued his diatribe. "Fuck you, asshole." This appeared to be Wally's standard response to Jimmy, and Pete began to wonder if they were going to start fighting right in front of him.

Jimmy turned from the water and looked back at Wally with a disgusted look on his face. "Is that the only thing you can say? I don't think you can say two sentences without dropping the F bomb."

"Fuck off and die, you fucking dick. There, how's that, asshole?"

"You're such a dick, Wally. Just break it out." Jimmy shook his head and looked back into the water running past the rock they stood on.

"Oh yeah, that's right, go ahead, bust my balls and then tell me to break it out. You are the king of all dicks, do you know that?" Wally looked pissed, but started reaching into his pocket.

Jimmy looked at Wally and laughed. "Yup, I'm king dick. Now shut up and break it out."

Pete had no clue what they were going to "break out," but his interest was piqued and he wanted to see what they were talking about.

"You burn, little man?" These were the first words Pete had heard David say.

"Burn? Burn what?" Pete asked in a confused tone.

"I guess that answers that. Dope. Do you smoke dope?" David looked at him like he was from another planet and shook his head.

Pete got nervous and looked around, waiting for the police to burst out of the woods at any second. He looked at the three large high school kids he now shared the rock with. "These guys are nuts," he thought to himself. He was debating what to do next as panic began to set in. "This is bad. Oh crap. Oh crap," were the thoughts racing through his mind. He had never been around drugs, or people that used them. Pete looked over his shoulder and saw Jimmy walk over to him and look down at him.

"Now listen, little man, I don't care if you don't smoke dope, but you can't be a nark. That's something that we can't have around here. Do you understand?"

Pete had never heard the term nark before, but he knew what was meant by it. Pete looked Jimmy in the eye and said, "Listen man, I have enough problems of my own, and I ain't no rat."

"That's good enough for me." Jimmy seemed happy with the answer; he clapped his hands and then rubbed them together. He smiled and turned back toward the water and then he looked over at Wally. "What are you waiting for, you dumb polack? Fire that mother up."

Pete looked at Wally, who already had what he concluded to be a joint in his mouth. Wally had a proud smile on his face as he lit it and took a long drag. Suddenly, his eyes bulged, his face turned bright red and became covered with a pained expression; and then he started to cough profusely. His body started convulsing so hard that his glasses twisted on his face and almost came flying off. His eyes were streaming with tears, and once the spit started flying out of his mouth, his giant lips began to glow bright red and glisten from the massive amounts of saliva he was emitting. He looked like he was about to die, or at least go into an epileptic seizure. While he was bent over, looking like he was about to fall onto the ground from coughing, he reached out to hand the joint to Jimmy. Jimmy took it from him and looked at it and then back at Wally. He had a look of absolute disgust on his face.

"You nasty, greedy, son of a bitch. Look what you did to this thing.

That's what you get for being greedy. I hope you puke your guts out." He held up the joint for David and Pete to examine. Pete had no idea what was wrong with Wally or the joint he was looking at. David shook his head and spoke up, "Oh, my God, it looks like it fell in the river."

Wally had regained his composure enough to look at David and say, "It's a stream, you fucking New York idiot." It was obvious that, for some reason, Wally would take abuse from Jimmy, but he wasn't having any of it from David.

Jimmy looked at the joint again and then at Wally. "Do something with this thing. Take it home for your little brother or throw it in the garbage. I don't care, but roll me another one, and this time, give it to me before you light it."

"Fuck you. You roll another one. There isn't anything wrong with that thing. Give it to me, asshole."

Jimmy flicked the joint at Wally, who picked it up and put it in his mouth. With exaggerated movements for emphasis, he rolled it all over his mouth and tongue, getting it soaked with his saliva.

"Mmm, now that's just the way I like it, asshole," he said to Jimmy.

"Just roll a joint and stop being a dick," Jimmy retorted.

Pete looked over at David, who was smiling and seemed to be enjoying the show.

"Are these two going to duke it out right here or what?" Pete had never seen anything like these two before.

David looked at him and smiled. "Probably; they do almost every day. Those two will probably be doing this same thing in this same hick town when they're fifty. They're just fucked up hicks, so what do you expect?"

Somehow, both Jimmy and Wally heard what David said in the middle of their fighting and arguing. Silence came quickly to the once noisy rock. Only this wasn't a good silence. Jimmy turned from Wally and glared at David.

"Fuck you, you little New York asshole. I'll kick your ass all the way back to the Bronx where you came from." Jimmy had a nasty tone in his voice now; he was serious.

"I'm from Brooklyn," David replied weakly.

"That's what you tell people, but I don't think so. I think you really come from the Bronx. What do you think?" Jimmy had stepped over to where David and Pete sat and glared down at David.

David looked up at Jimmy and started to say something, but thought better of it and just looked down and away. He then turned and glared at Pete. If David couldn't intimidate Jimmy or Wally, he knew he could scare Pete, and he did. Pete wasn't going to say, or do anything. This situation was getting out of control fast, and the only thing Pete was thinking about was going home, but he decided against making any sudden movements. David looked away from Pete and back up at Jimmy. He was angry, but knew he didn't want to take it any farther. David enjoyed watching and encouraged Jimmy to beat the hell out of Wally almost daily, but he himself wanted no part of Jimmy, or even Wally, for that matter.

The moment had passed. The world was put back in order. David knew where he stood and decided against making dumb hick jokes to or about Jimmy Nevers ever again. Jimmy looked over at Wally, who was finishing rolling another joint. "Hurry up, dick; I want to get high sometime today."

"Here. Now fuck off." Wally reached over and handed Jimmy the joint. Jimmy turned to the stream again and lit it. He now seemed content for the moment. Wally took his wet joint and re-lit it. He then reached down for his fishing pole and announced that he and his joint were going to cross the rocks to the other side and walk upstream and fish for awhile.

As he started to climb down the moss covered rocks toward the babbling brook, Jimmy came over and handed the joint to David. "Ten bucks says that dumb bastard is swimming before he gets to the other side."

"I heard that, you asshole!" came the reply from the edge of the stream.

David took a drag from the joint, offered it to Pete, who raised his hand to wave it off and said no thanks, and then got to his feet and walked to the edge of the rock near Jimmy to see what would happen next. There were several flat rocks protruding from the stream that made a staggered path to the other side, but they were covered with wet moss and algae. The rocks were very slippery and, in places, too far apart to step from one rock to the next, so Wally had to jump and then land with both feet on the next rock. Landing on these rocks with both feet and not slipping into the cold stream required a little bit of agility and balance, two things God had never given to Wally. He took a large step and made it to the first rock with no problem. With his confidence growing, he then took a longer step to the second rock. He slipped a little and one boot splashed into the water. He flailed his arms in the air in an attempt to regain his balance while Jimmy started howling.

"Oh, hell yeah, he's going in!" Jimmy said, and his laughter echoed throughout the woods.

Wally regained his balance, steadied himself, raised his right hand, and gave Jimmy another one finger salute. "Fuck you!" he responded.

His confidence restored, he bravely jumped to the next rock. His left foot landed on the edge of the rock and slid off the moss like it was ice. His feet came out from under him and his legs went in the air, while both hands flew up and over his head. His fishing pole went one way and his joint the other. Wally seemed to float three feet in the air before he came crashing down and into the water. The stream was only a couple of feet deep, but Wally, somehow missing the large rocks, landed on his back, and was submerged. When he broke the surface, his glasses were gone and he had a dazed and confused look on his face as he looked around, trying to figure out what had gone wrong.

Jimmy and David were bent over laughing. Pete smiled to himself, not sure if he should laugh too, but he knew it was one of the funniest things he had ever seen.

"Oh shit, my glasses, I can't find my glasses! Damnit, I can't see without my glasses! Come on you guys, you've got to help me find them." Wally had a look of sheer panic on his face. Jimmy and David were now kneeling down and laughing so hard they were holding their sides. "Fuck you guys. Those are hundred dollar glasses. My old man is going to kill me! Come on; help me find them." Wally scrambled about searching the stream bed on his hands and knees and looked like he was going to cry.

"Hey, dick-weed, did you have that reefer in your pocket when you went swimming?" Jimmy yelled to Wally.

Wally stopped in his tracks. He looked back at Jimmy with a look of total dismay.

"Screw the reefer, you asshole. Those glasses were expensive and I can't see a thing without them. I am so fucking dead!" Wally twisted about, looking around and stomping all over the stream in panic as he kept searching for his glasses. Finally, after a few moments of searching, he saw a glimmer of something at the bottom of the stream. He reached into the water and pulled his glasses, unharmed, from the bottom. He raised them above his head in triumph. "Fuck you both! I found these mother fuckers and I get to live for another day!" Wally proclaimed proudly.

"Hey dick-weed, where's your fishing pole?" Jimmy yelled with a smile on his face as he took another drag from his joint.

"Oh, shit." The triumph was gone and the panic returned, but after searching for a while longer, Wally found his pole a few feet away, lying in the water next to a large rock. He started to feel relieved that he might get out of this mess with only wet clothes when he reached down and picked up the pole and saw the broken handle. His heart sunk to his stomach. It was his dad's pole that he had swiped that morning. He had just broken his dad's new pole, and now his dad was going to break him.

"I am dead…. I am so fucking dead!" The first part was said quietly, but the second part of his profane realization was said loudly and with panic.

He turned and looked at his friends on the rock looking at him. They wanted to laugh, but even Jimmy couldn't laugh now. Jimmy knew what was waiting for Wally when he got home, and it was going to hurt. Wally dropped his head and made his way back to the others. When he trudged up the bank, he was dripping wet and his shoes squished with each step. Jimmy watched him pathetically climb up the bank and started shaking his head.

"I'm going home to change," Wally said with resignation.

"I told you not to take your old man's pole. I would have grabbed my little brother's and let you use his," Jimmy said to Wally, almost feeling sorry for him. Jimmy allowed the compassion to linger for a moment, and then he looked at Wally and gave his next command.

"Leave the dope here."

Wally reached into his pocket to check his illicit treasure. A big smile came across his face when he realized that the baggie had kept the water out of his pot.

"It's still good," Wally proclaimed.

"Excellent. Now leave it here while you go change," Jimmy ordered.

"Fuck you. I'll be right back."

"No, you won't," Jimmy said matter-of-factly. He was fairly confident that he wouldn't see Wally for at least a week.

Wally looked at his bag and then the fishing pole. He hesitated for a moment and then tossed it to Jimmy. He had pondered the various possibilities that fate would be serving upon him when he got home. The possibilities ranged from the very improbable chance of him being able to sneak into the house and put the pole back and escape unnoticed, to the more realistic possibility of him being caught, interrogated, imprisoned, and then sentenced to death.

"Don't smoke it all. I might want some later." Wally was a shell of the defiant kid who had stomped through the trail moments before, and accepted the fact that he would probably never see that bag again.

"Don't worry; I'll keep it nice and safe," Jimmy said with a smile on his face.

"Yea, sure you will. I'll never see that bag again," Wally said with resigned conviction.

"Hey, as much as I enjoy your company, I'm out of here too," said David. "Come on; why don't you give us a ride, Jimmy?" He knew there was no chance of a ride, but he had to try. He knew that Jimmy had come to fish and he was going to fish. Wally didn't even wait for an answer. He turned and began the long trek back to the road and to his house. David waited a moment, then quickly followed behind Wally and disappeared into the brush.

"Well, I guess it's just you and me, little man," Jimmy said to Pete.

Pete was shocked that Jimmy was wasting his time talking to him. Jimmy liked fishing and he liked people who liked to fish. He got his pole ready and looked over at Pete.

"There's no sense in going downstream. Goofball scared the fish all the way to the Four Corners. If we go upstream for a ways, we might be able pull one or two out of the brook." He looked over at the kid he had met only moments before.

"Do you know how to walk through the woods and fish properly?"

"I don't know what you mean by properly, but I do okay when I fish here," Pete answered cautiously.

"Properly means you sneak up on the brook, you're silent, patient, and you pay attention to shadows. If you cast a shadow on the water, the fish are spooked, and you're pissing in the wind. Do you understand? I want to catch fish. You can come with me, but don't make noise like that goofball."

Pete was excited by the invitation and was ready to go. "I know what you mean. Don't worry about me," he eagerly said.

"By the way, what's your name, little man?" Jimmy asked as he started down the slope that Wally had gone down earlier.

"Pete. Pete Taylor," he replied as he started to follow Jimmy down to the brook.

"Well, Pete Taylor, let's go catch some fish."

CHAPTER 8

WORK SUCKS

B ill pushed away his plate containing half his chips and most of his hot dog. He grabbed his glass and quickly finished his third Jack and Ginger. He had given up the beer some time earlier and was now a whiskey man. It was time to head back to work, and even though he wanted another drink, he decided to leave.

"What's my tab, Donnie?" Bill asked.

"Nine bucks," was the reply. Donnie Brunswick looked over at his only customer and flung a white towel over his shoulder. He headed over toward Bill and scooped up the plate, glass, and the ten dollars left on the bar in one smooth motion. Donnie Brunswick was the owner, operator, and daytime bartender of this small dive. He was about fifty five years old, short, balding, and had a large round belly that made him look like he had eaten a basketball. He was a good bartender who understood when a customer wanted conversation and when they wanted to be left alone. Bill had become a regular over the last few months and always wanted to be left alone. Donnie knew to give him a dog and chips, washed down with two or three Jack and Gingers in the afternoon and several strong ones for the ride home after work. Donnie took pride in knowing what his customers liked to drink, without knowing or caring why they drank.

Bill walked toward the heavy doors and pushed. The bright light of the afternoon sun burned his eyes and forced him to squint and pause until his eyes adjusted. After a moment, he collected himself and walked to his jeep and proceeded back to work.

A few moments later, he pulled into the parking lot and got out of his car. He started to walk towards the entry door and then stopped and looked at the plant he was about to re-enter. It was an old single story brick building, dark and weather worn. It had stood on the banks of the Housatonic River for over fifty years and it looked like it. The old asphalt parking lot was marred with potholes; the air was heavy with the smell of oil and chemicals. The noise of passing traffic was pounding his ears. He hated this place. He looked at his feet, shook his head, and continued walking in.

The employee entrance was a small weather worn white door on the side of the building that led to a reception area that was about eight feet wide and twelve feet long. The walls were lined with paneling that looked like it had been installed during WWII. The floor directly in front of the door was a four foot by four foot patch of grey tile covered with an old floor mat that allowed people to stomp the snow off their feet during winter. Dirty, gray commercial carpet covered the rest of the floor with a worn narrow trail that led from the entry door to the shop door. On the wall adjacent to the door was a large opening, and behind that was the receptionist and office staff. The receptionist, Mary, stood sentry and protected the plant from those who should not enter. She signed in and out all employees and redirected customers to the front entrance.

Bill raised his hand and gave a slight wave of acknowledgment. "Hi, Mary, I'm back in paradise." He continued toward the door that led to the bowels of Johnson Metal Works.

"Bill, Jack wants to see you in his office," Mary informed him.

Mary Patterson had been with the company since a few years after Bill Sr. had started there. She had lost her husband during WWII and raised two children alone. She had never held hands with any man except her husband. They had been high school sweethearts and married shortly thereafter. The Great Depression had still been rampant in

America and starting a family had been difficult. In March of 1941, the enactment of the Lend Lease Act gave the President almost unlimited authority to sell, lease, or lend the allied powers in Europe the military equipment they needed to keep fighting the Nazis. In order to get the equipment needed to Great Britain, the government had stepped up orders to American factories for this hardware, and this increased demand had allowed Johnson's to expand production and hire more people.

After three years of marriage and the birth of two children, Harold Patterson had been one of those people. This job had looked like it would finally bring stability to their family. The small Patterson family had been looking forward to Christmas when, on December 7, 1941, everything had changed. Her husband Harold, like so many others, enlisted on December 8th. He left shortly thereafter and, except for a brief weekend furlough before shipping out, Mary had never seen him alive again.

Mary was old, strong, and without humor. Alcohol had never touched her lips, and she viewed it's consumption as something near cavorting with Satan himself. She was near retirement age, and had never worked anywhere else in her life and would probably work at Johnson's until the day she died. She was dedicated to, and protective of, the company that had been her life's work. She looked at Bill and knew he had been drinking. She was filled with disdain for what, in her mind, he had allowed himself to become: a coward.

"All right, let him know I'll be there in a few minutes," Bill replied to the sneering old hag.

"He told me to tell you to go directly to his office upon your return," Mary ordered.

"I hate this place and all the assholes in it," Bill thought to himself as he opened the door and proceeded to Jack Fitzpatrick's office.

Jack was the Production Supervisor. He took what the engineers put on paper and converted it into something to be loaded on trucks and shipped out. He was also responsible for reviewing all production cost analyses. He'd started working at Johnson's sweeping floors and taking out the trash after school. He'd worked his way to lathe operator and then had become one of the best machinists in the area. He was now closing in on sixty and was in charge of and responsible for everything that went out the door.

Bill approached his office door. He felt like a little kid being sent to the principal's office. He hesitantly knocked on the door.

"Bill, come in here," roared Jack from behind his desk, and he immediately started talking to Bill without looking up. When Bill walked into this office for the umpteenth time this year, his mind, which was still floating on the Jack Daniels river, wandered around the room. He looked around at this grand palatial expanse. The office was about the size of a large closet. It had old paneled walls decorated with a shop calendar and a few family photos. Bill had never paid much attention to the photos before. He was surprised to realize that Jack's wife was a surprisingly attractive woman, and his daughter was also quite pretty. They had bright smiles and matching beautiful blue eyes. His eyes glanced at Jack. The disturbing image of Jack, naked and in the process of making that child, came into his mind. His lunch quickly bubbled in his stomach and a cold chill went down his spine. The thought was flushed from his mind with a shiver and he forced himself to return to his mindless observations. The floor was industrial gray tile, the same tile as the entry, he concluded. A small metal commercial desk took up most of the office. There was one chair on each side of the desk. The desk itself was adorned with a telephone, an overflowing ashtray, and his half empty coffee cup. There were various scattered papers covering it, and a few of them were coffee stained. Along one wall was a bookcase filled with technical books and suppliers catalogs. The office was poorly lit and had no windows. This was not a luxury executive office. It was a closet with paneling. His eyes returned to the coffee cup. "Coffee at two o'clock in the afternoon," Bill thought to himself. "Oh, now that's disgusting. The only coffee I would drink at this time of day would be Irish coffee. I wonder if it is Irish coffee; a little scotch or whiskey in there would be nice. Oh, hell yeah, I'm gonna be a coffee drinker too," he pleasantly thought to himself.

Jack finally realized that Bill was not paying attention to a word he was saying. He angrily rose to his feet and slammed his hands on the desk. Jack Fitzpatrick was a bear of a man, nearly six feet tall and well over two hundred and forty pounds. His white hair was cut in a short crew cut. His face was accented with deep wrinkles, and his hands resembled large, fat meat hooks from the many years of handling steel. When Jack jumped up from behind his desk, Bill returned to reality and looked into his brown eyes.

Bill was instantly surprised and quickly looked at the girl with the blue eyes in the picture again and then back toward Jack. His eyes were brown, and they were fiery and bright with emotion.

"Bill, what the hell are you thinking? Are you even listening to a word I've said? Where the fuck is your brain? This hoist you re-designed is ridiculous. Look at all this bracing; look at these gussets. I can't build this thing like this."

"What are you talking about, Jack? That design is bullet proof," Bill argued.

"Yeah, it's bullet proof all right. You overdesigned it again. You have three eighths steel gussets when you only need five-sixteenths. You've got four gussets when we only need three. What the fuck do you think we put these stops in here for? Bill, what the hell are you thinking? There is no load here...ever."

"If they spin the hoist around past seventy five degrees, the fourth gusset..." Bill started to defend his design, but Jack quickly broke in angrily.

"If they spin the hoist past sixty degrees, they have to remove the stops and then they're not using the fucking thing the way it was designed to be used! You can't redesign the damn thing after we have a contract. The limited stress fatigue and failure was in the front gusset. Make the front gusset three-eighths and the two others five-sixteenths, and get rid of this fucking gusset here. We have to make a thousand of these damn things. Go do your math. I'll guarantee it is well within the safety factor... for the designed work load." Jack thrust Bill's designs into his chest. Bill meekly took the papers and sheepishly retreated to his office.

CHAPTER 9

TIME FOR DINNER

Anne pulled into her driveway after work. She parked the car, shut off the motor, took a deep breath, and got out. She then turned toward the house and stopped for a moment to look at her front door. It was a normal, inviting white front door with an arched eyebrow window that let in just enough light to warm the entry way. It opened to a beautiful two-story white farm house. She and Bill had spent many weekends working on it and spending all the money they could afford renovating and beautifying the home.

There was a short concrete walkway that led from the driveway to the front door. The walkway was lined on each side with flower beds filled with crocuses, red and yellow tulips, and climbing red roses on white trellises. The walkway ended at two concrete steps that led to a small landing and her front door. The sun was shining on the flowers; there were a few honey bees flying about collecting nectar and spreading pollen. She looked at the bird feeders hanging from the large maple tree on the other side of the driveway. A blue jay was enjoying a free meal. She admitted to herself that is was a beautiful home, and an incredible summer day. She stood there momentarily, and wished she didn't have to open the door and go inside, but she did. Pete and Bill would be home soon, so, with great effort, she drew some strength from deep within herself, changed her clothes, and started some laundry and dinner.

As she began to prepare the nights meal, her thoughts drifted to the days when Bill came home promptly after work and the four of them would sit down for an enjoyable dinner at six. The sounds of laughter and conversation had been a vital part of their nightly ritual. It was the time of day when they had all stopped what they were doing and had given thanks for their many blessings. They'd spent the time around the table learning what each other was doing or trying to do. Dinner used to be a central part of the Taylor family day, but those days were gone. As she placed some food on the counter, she realized that it was now more common for Bill to call and say he was working late than for him to come home and eat with them. She knew he was lying, but didn't want to argue, and eating dinner, silently, with Pete was becoming a common event. Their meals together were quiet, but at least they were somewhat pleasant.

Too often, when Bill did come home and eat with them, he would be in a foul mood and would use dinner as the time to criticize everything and everyone around him. She always prepared enough for the three of them, but Bill had not eaten with her and Pete for what seemed like weeks, so she spitefully decided to prepare dinner for two.

BILL LOOKED AT HIS WATCH. Four thirty. Crap, he had time to get everything done. That meant a walk back to Jack's office and listening to the old bastard telling him he had been right again. Jack took special pride in proving engineers wrong. He was a brilliant man, but had barely finished high school. The one thing he knew and understood was steel and he made sure everyone knew it. The guys on the floor loved him; the guys in the offices hated him. Mr. Johnson respected him, and that's all he cared about.

Bill grabbed the papers off his desk and began the long walk to the gallows. A moment later he felt like he had reached Jack's office way too soon. "Jack, here's the revisions." Bill said. His voice and his eyes betrayed how tired the man was. Jack was finishing writing a supply list and didn't even look up before he started giving Bill a hard time.

"Well, was I wrong? When you redid your calculations, did you calculate how much money we saved by building the damn things right…. a thousand times?" Jack looked up at Bill and was about to really dig in when he finally saw the tired and beaten man in front of him. "Shut the door, Bill. Sit down for a minute. What the hell time is it?"

Bill looked at his watch. "Ten after five."

"Want a cup of coffee?" Jack asked gently.

"No, no, I don't drink coffee this time of day, Jack. I'd never sleep at night."

"Maybe you're drinking the wrong coffee," Jack replied. He grabbed his thermos and re-filled his cup three quarters of the way and then reached down to his bottom drawer. He produced a bottle of bourbon and finished filling his cup. He looked at Bill as he finished pouring.

"Never a drop before five… and I never wait until five fifteen either. I understand you more than you think, Bill. We have similar problems, just in opposite directions. One was taken from you and one was given to me…" Jack took a long pull off his coffee. "I almost pissed my life away too." Jack hesitated and thought for a moment before continuing. "Bill, we all have stories, and we all face adversity, pain, and suffering in this life. I don't know why, and I don't pretend to understand it. I'm no rocket scientist, but I try to learn about the people around me. I try to discover what they've been through, and what makes them survive. I try to draw strength from their courage and perseverance, and then I try to carry on, one day at a time. You know, at one time, you were one of the best engineers in the area; now you're average to mediocre at best. At the rate you're going, in another two or three years, you ain't gonna be worth dog shit on a sidewalk…"

"I really don't need this, Jack. You have no clue what you're talking about. My work is done, the day is done, and I'm going home."

"Who the fuck do you think you're kidding? You won't go home until you've sat in the bar by yourself for a couple of hours. You'll wait until you think that everyone at your house is getting ready to go to bed before you think it's safe to go home. A couple of quick good nights, the wife and kids leave you alone, and then you drink by yourself until about eleven. Sometimes you make it to the bed; sometimes you just sleep in your chair. So, how far off am I, Bill? I'm not far off at all, am I?"

"Jack, you have a beautiful family to go home to. You've never lost a child. Your daughter is beautiful… and alive!" Bill started to argue. Jack was trying to be nice; it was something he was unaccustomed to, but he was trying, and when Bill started to argue with him instead of listening, it pissed him off.

"I saw your face this afternoon when you were looking at the picture." Jack turned and looked at the picture of his wife and daughter. "She is a beautiful girl...it's just too bad Uncle Don's mule kicked me so fucking hard in '48. Yeah, when your wife tells you she's pregnant and it ain't yours… now that will make a man drink." He looked right at Bill and made sure Bill was looking at him. "I never, ever drank at work; not one time. I would start drinking at five sharp, just like today, but back then I wouldn't stop until I fell down. Now when the thermos is empty, I know I'm done and I go home and go to sleep. Personally, Bill, I don't give a damn about you. If you want to kill yourself, just do it, but I do care about what goes on in my shop. You're making a fool of yourself and the people who work here. If you ever come into my office shit-faced again, I am likely to kick your ass right out the front door. Are we clear?"

Bill looked at Jack. "Yeah, Jack, we're clear. Is there anything else I can do for you?" Bill said meekly. He was furious, but he wasn't going to stand up to Jack, especially when he was right and they both knew it.

"No, go home and get you're fucking head back in the game, Bill."

"Screw you," Bill thought to himself as he left. He left the plant in his jeep and drove straight to Doc's, but for some reason he didn't stop. He drove past and started thinking to himself, "To Hell with it, I'm tired, I'm hungry, and I hate the whole damn world. I'll sit down and eat dinner tonight like a normal person and then lie on the couch and watch TV until I fall asleep. *Kojak* should be on tonight. Maybe Anne will cook something decent and I'll eat in front of the TV. If I play my cards right, I won't have to say five words to her all night. That would be nice, wouldn't it? I deserve something nice for a change. I've been getting shit on for too long." He and his thoughts remained mired in self-pity the entire drive home.

CHAPTER 10

CHICKEN SHIT TOMATOES

Anne heard a vehicle pull into the driveway and she immediately looked at her watch. Not quite five, too early for Bill. She walked to the window and saw Pete getting out of an old white van. She looked at the driver and recognized him as one of the Nevers boys. Mrs. Nevers came into the store every week. Anne liked her; she always had a smile on her face and something nice to say to the people she greeted.

"Nine kids to feed breakfast, lunch, and dinner. Oh, my God," she thought to herself as she looked at her stove and saw two little pans with a few pieces of broccoli and a couple of potatoes boiling. In the oven was two small stuffed pork chops. "How can they do that every day?" Anne shook her head in amazement at what Mr. and Mrs. Nevers went through every day.

She looked out the window again and watched as Pete talked for a moment with the driver. She couldn't make out the words, but she knew she heard laughter. Pete then reached into the van and pulled out two fish on string. With his fishing pole in one hand and his trout in the other, he pushed the van door shut with his backside and made his way excitedly to the front door as the van backed out of the driveway.

She opened the door just as he made it to the top step. She looked at his face; he was beaming and smiling from ear to ear as he proudly held up his catch for her inspection.

Anne was in shock and almost overcome with emotion. It had been so long since she had seen him happy and smiling.

"Nice catch, Peter, but don't think you're bringing those fish in my house to clean. I'll go get you a knife and you take them out by the barn and clean them. Add those and a couple more to the ones in the freezer and we're going to have a feast." She paused for a moment. "You look like you had a good day. I haven't seen you like this in while. It's kind of nice," she said with a smile on her face and a rare warm feeling in her heart.

"Yeah, you know what? I guess I did have a good day. I met these crazy guys from high school. That was Jimmy Nevers who dropped me off. One of them, Wally, slipped on the rocks and landed on his butt in the brook, lost his glasses and his fishing pole, and then Jimmy and the other guy- I think his name was Dave- started giving him a hard time. It was pretty funny to watch." He looked at his Mom and smiled.

Anne went into the kitchen, and when she returned a moment later, she handed him the knife to clean his fish. He took the knife and bounced to the barn. She leaned against the door jamb and watched him go. A warm feeling of hope filled her body and her eyes began to water. She laughed at herself and her silly reaction to a boy cleaning fish and returned to the kitchen and pulled the pork chops out of the oven. She then grabbed two plates, two glasses, two forks, and two knives and started setting the table for dinner.

A few minutes later, Pete came into the house with the knife and the two trout cleaned and ready to go in the freezer.

"Put them by the sink and go wash up. I'll throw them in the freezer," Anne told her son as she finished setting the table.

"All right, Mom. Wow, dinner smells good and I'm hungry, so I hope you made a lot," Pete said as he walked by the stove and inspected his mom's handiwork. She smiled without turning around and kept on working. Anne wrapped the fish and put them in the freezer, and then started putting food on their plates. "Good thing the pork chops are pretty big," she thought to herself as she realized she may not have made enough broccoli and potatoes. Anne was a talented cook who liked her family and herself to have a fresh hot meal. There were two things she hated: leftovers and throwing out food. She tried very hard to cook just the right amount of food to fill everyone's belly without having to put a bunch of food in the refrigerator that was probably going to be thrown out in a week anyways.

Pete came back into the kitchen a few minutes later. He was washed up, wearing new clothes, and had combed his hair. Anne looked at her boy as they sat down to eat. It felt so good to see him happy. It was obvious that he'd had fun, and was full of energy for the first time in a long time. She welled up while she was silently watching him load his plate with food. It was such a relief to see him smiling and enjoying himself. She felt like they'd finally had a breakthrough.

"So, where did you catch those fish, Pete"? Anne asked between bites.

"I went to Wilson's. After Wally fell into the water, he and the other guy left. Jimmy took me upstream and showed me a few nice spots I've never been to. He caught three nice ones and I got those two," Pete explained as he took another bite.

"You know I don't like you walking past those cows by yourself. What if you got hurt......?"

She heard the car door shut and stopped in the middle of her sentence. She looked at the food on the table and realized there was not enough cooked. She was supposed to have gone shopping after work, but just hadn't felt like it. The warmth she had been feeling was quickly replaced by the all too familiar dread of what was about to come. Pete was suddenly silent and expressionless. He looked at the remnants of food on the table and knew what was coming as well.

The door opened and they heard his footsteps as he entered the house.

"That smells good," they heard him say before entering the kitchen. Pete and Anne looked at each other. Sadness and worry filled their eyes and emptiness grew in their hearts.

Bill entered the kitchen with his suit jacket folded neatly over his left forearm. Pete and Anne's eyes were simultaneously drawn to the bottle of whiskey in his hand.

"You started without me. That's not nice," Bill said with a smile as he set his bottle on the counter. He turned and put his jacket over the back of his chair and looked at the table. He then looked at the stove and then at Anne. "Where in hell is my dinner?" The smile was gone. He was standing behind his chair with his hands still on the jacket he had just placed there. He was now glaring at his wife.

"I didn't think you were going to eat with us tonight. You usually don't anymore," Anne replied, trying to defend herself.

"What the hell are you talking about? Here I am. Where's my food? I'm the one that pays the damn bills in this house. I'm the one who puts food in the damned refrigerator. The only thing, and I mean the *only* thing, I want from you is my dinner on the table when I get home. It doesn't matter what time I get here, but when I do, I want my dinner," Bill said with venom on his tongue.

"I know you can't be home for dinner on time because you're always working late, but most people make more money when they work more hours, and most people don't come home stinking like booze and cigarettes when they work late. Here, take my plate." Anne lifted her plate of food and angrily reached over and put it in front of Bill.

"Now you want to give me table scraps. I'm not eating this shit," Bill turned around, reached into the cabinet, and pulled out a glass. He proceeded to make himself a very strong drink. Pete sat silently and watched his parents. His stomach was twisted in knots, and even though he'd had only had a couple of bites of his dinner and nothing since breakfast, he couldn't eat. He looked longingly at his mom and she at him.

"Sit down, Bill, I'll cook you something to eat. It'll only take a few minutes," Anne said to her husband, trying to defuse the situation.

"Oh, don't you bother yourself. I wouldn't want to make you go out of your way for me," Bill said with contempt in his voice. He took a long drink and looked at his wife. She was a good woman and he knew it.

How long was it going to take for her to understand that she needed to move on and find someone better? He hated what he had become and he wanted them both out of his life so he could just lie down and die alone. He took another drink and emptied the glass, then mixed another.

"Bill, it will only take a few minutes," Anne pleaded.

"I've got my God damned dinner right here," and he held up the glass.

"Will you please sit down and be quiet while I make something for you to eat? And maybe you can start acting like a grown man for a change." Pete cringed when he heard her say those last words.

"A grown man…. Fuck you." He slammed his glass on the table. Pete had never heard his father use those words and neither had Anne. "Who in hell do you think you are to tell me to act like a grown man? You sit here all day screwing around. Oh yeah, don't let me forget, you work so hard when you're hanging out at the store for a couple of hours a day and call that work."

Pete suddenly pushed his plate across the table. He looked at both of his parents with tears in his eyes and, without saying a word, ran out the door.

"Peter, get back in here," Bill yelled. Anne looked at her husband and shook her head with contempt. Bill looked at her and started yelling at her again.

"Look at the hell you cause when you can't do something as simple as cooking dinner for your family," Bill chastised his wife, confident that it was her actions that had caused tonight's fracas.

Anne was amazed when she heard him say that. "I'm not even going to dignify that. Go get your son, Bill; he needs you," Anne said as she got up and started to clear the table…and cry.

Bill watched his wife walk around with tears in her eyes. The events of one year had aged her ten. Her skin was pale, she had lost too much weight, and she no longer cared that her hair was not quite perfect. He took another long drink. "He'll be fine; he's not going anywhere. Just leave him alone. Where the hell can he go anyways? We live in the middle of nowhere. Now, why don't you just leave me the hell alone while I go to watch T.V.?" Bill polished off his drink, refilled his glass, then walked into the living room, where he turned on the T.V. and sat in his chair. When he was settled in the other room, Anne sat in her chair and covered her face with both hands and wept uncontrollably. She was falling apart, and she knew it.

Pete started down Mohegan Road, wiping tears and cursing his father as he went. He walked for a while and then looked back toward his house, sniffled hard, and continued walking. He reached the Lucian and Cline houses a few minutes later. They were large white farm houses that were over a hundred years old and sat imposingly atop the hill on each side of the road. They were surrounded by three foot-tall stone walls that had been built when the nation was new. He looked down the road as he walked. This stretch of Mohegan Road was a small country road, lined on each side by large pine trees that stood guard in front of more stone walls. Behind these walls were the Nevers' fields on the right and Lucian's on the left. The Cline's house had once belonged to Grandma Nevers' parents. When they passed, Grandma and Grandpa Nevers sold the house, but kept most of the land. On the other end of the fields, about a quarter mile down the road on each side, was the Nevers houses: grandparents on the left, Jimmy and company on the right. Each house was surrounded by white post and rail fences.

Pete thought about turning around and returning home, but decided to continue walking. He finally reached the big white farm house that belonged to Jimmy Nevers' grandparents. It had a narrow driveway that was on the left side of the two story house. It had a covered front porch that extended across the front of the house with azaleas in front of the porch. The small front yard was dominated by two enormous maple trees. As Pete walked in front of the house, he observed a two foot by two foot sign promoting Jimmy Carter and Walter Mondale in the upcoming election. A vegetable stand, filled with vegetables grown in the large gardens on the other side of the house, was prominently displayed in the center of the front yard. Pete looked up at the house again and saw a fat old man wearing a green John Deere ball cap sitting on a rocking chair on the front porch.

"Hey," Pete heard the old man's voice. Not sure if he was talking to him, Pete waved and continued walking.

"Hey!" Now Pete knew he was talking to him.

"Yes, sir, hello," Pete said to the old man as he stopped and turned toward the porch.

"Didn't I see you walking up the road with a couple of fish the other day?"

"Yes, sir, I caught two more today with Jimmy," Pete replied.

"Get a tomato," the old man yelled from the porch. Pete hesitated for a moment, not sure what to do. "What am I going to do with a tomato?" he thought to himself.

"Best tomatoes you'll ever taste. Chicken shit is what makes 'em so sweet."

Now Pete was really excited to grab one. Chicken shit. What does chicken shit have to do with tomatoes? Pete thought for sure the old man was crazy, but being the polite kid he was, he picked one up, said thanks, and tried to walk off with the tomato in his hand.

"Eat it. Go ahead, take a bite. It's not like anything you'll get in any store. The ones in the store are plastic tomatoes and you might as well eat the plastic they come in. Go ahead, bite that tomato." He leaned forward in his chair and put his hands on the wall in front of the porch and watched. Pete looked at the old man and kept thinking about eating chicken shit. He just knew it was a going to taste just like chicken shit smelled. He raised the tomato to his nose and took a whiff. It didn't smell like chicken shit, and it actually was a beautiful big red tomato. His face cringed as he put it in his mouth and took a bite, not knowing what to expect. The tomato erupted in his mouth. It was delicious; it was almost as good as eating an orange. Pete had no idea a tomato was supposed to taste this good. The old man saw the look on his face and smiled.

"I told you. It's the chicken shit. You go catch some more fish tomorrow and stop on your way home for another tomato." The old man sat back in his chair with a satisfied smile and resumed rocking. Pete said thank you and continued down the road, eating the best tomato he had ever tasted. For a few moments, he forgot about his life and just enjoyed an old man's chicken shit tomato.

As he strolled past Jimmy Nevers house, he was surprised by how small the red Cape-Cod really was. It was about half the size of his house and he only had three people living in it. They had ten or eleven people inside; he couldn't imagine the chaos that must have occurred within those walls. There were two cars and two vans parked in the driveway, and along one side of the driveway were two apple and two pear trees in a perfect row. In front of the house was a beautiful flower garden and a perfectly manicured front lawn. There were maple trees in the front yard, but they were nowhere near the size of Grandpa Nevers' trees; but Jimmy's yard had something Grandpa didn't: the white fence in front of his house was lined with large forsythia bushes that were covered with bright yellow flowers interlaced with sweet smelling purple lilacs. A large barn and chicken coop were in the back, and a big garden was flourishing on the side of the house. Pete noticed a couple of dogs laying in the yard that were lazily watching him walk past, and then when he had walked a few feet further, and was directly in front of the center of the house, his eyes were drawn to a large four foot by four foot sign that brought a smile to his face: Gerald Ford and Bob Dole in '76.

CHAPTER 11

AN AWAKENING

Pete continued down the road for a while, mindlessly eating his tomato. When he crossed Nevers stream as it went under Mohegan Road, he looked ahead and saw some kids throwing Frisbees at Four Corners.

Four Corners was the location where Booth Hill Road intersected with Mohegan Road. Wilson's stream ran through a large tunnel under the road and later joined the Nevers stream before disappearing into the Water Company's property and continued combining with other streams until they ran into and formed the Farmill Reservoir. People were often fishing in the tunnel and stream during the day, and in the evenings it was a popular hangout for teenagers.

Pete peered down the road, and was able to see three people laughing and moving around in the distance. He decided to cautiously approach and see if he could recognize any of them. As he got closer and could see them clearer, he recognized the kids. It was two boys, David Mandis and Al Donato, and a girl, Joanie Klein, from the bus.

"Hey, Pete, what are you doing?" Al yelled with a smile and a wave as he approached. Pete waved back and felt welcomed into the group. Al was an all-around good athlete and a proud, dark-skinned Italian.

He was short and stocky, with a big 'fro that made his head look too big for his body. He idolized Franco Harris and Rocky Balboa. Al took a sideways step toward Pete, reached across his belly, and threw the Frisbee to him. Pete watched as the Frisbee left Al's hand and rose into the air level and true. It peaked at about fifteen feet and then started its decent a few feet to the right of where Pete was standing. Pete started to move to his right to get in the line with its flight when he heard Al yell to him. "Don't move, it will come right to you." It did. It soared gracefully, slowed, tilted to the left, and gently floated into his hand. Pete was amazed at how far the Frisbee had flown and how gently it had come to him. He closed his fingers around it and caught it with ease.

Pete had gotten another chance to forget his life for a while and he took it. He had never thrown a Frisbee before, but he didn't want to go home, so he decided to make the most of this opportunity for mindless enjoyment. Al made throwing the Frisbee look so easy that Pete knew he was going to throw it just as well. He imitated what he had seen Al do; he pulled the Frisbee back against his belly, twisted, stepped into it, and let it go. He had confidence in his athletic skills and was ready to impress all those present with his natural ability. The Frisbee came out of his hands like a bullet. It went about ten feet, turned sideways, and crashed onto the road. It then began to roll like an out-of-control tire, traveling about twenty five-feet, turning violently and rolling into the bushes. Laughter filled the air. Pete remained motionless and stared at his effort for a moment and felt like an idiot. He quickly came out of his stupor and shook his head at his own stupidity, and then ran into the woods to retrieve the Frisbee. After a little rummaging through the brush, he found it and re-emerged. He thought about trying another long throw to Al, but wisely decided to throw it to David, who was standing closer to him. This time, his short throw was much better and David was able to catch it without trouble. The three of them formed a triangle and tossed it around while Joanie sat on the wall and made wisecracks. Pete soon got the hang of it and began having fun. David and Al were doing tricks as they played, such as tapping the frisbee in the air as many times as possible before catching it, or catching it behind the back, or between the legs. Pete was already embarrassed once, and didn't want to make a fool of himself in front of Joanie-who continued her relentless banter and critique of everything the boys did-so he kept it simple and didn't try anything as fancy as the other two were doing.

After a while, the three of them took a break from playing and joined Joanie at the knee-wall. They sat around and made casual small talk for a few minutes, and while they were talking, David looked up Mohegan Road as a maroon van approached.

"Check it out. Here comes Phil in his new van. That thing is so sweet. It's nicer than the blue van, and that one won second place in the Stratford Van Show," he said. Phil Pintowski was a local legend and a giant of a man. He stood at 6'7" and was a self-made millionaire. He'd started hanging drywall at the age of sixteen, and by nineteen he'd had his own company. He worked all day, every day, harder than any man around. When he stocked a house, he carried two buckets of drywall mud in each hand because he made money putting mud on the wall, not walking back and forth to the truck. He'd started building small houses, and soon thereafter sold the drywall business and was now building million-dollar homes.

"Oh, hell yeah. That is a love machine on wheels," Al concurred.

The van approached the stop sign in front of the kids and came to a stop. It was a brand new custom van, dark maroon with a hand painted mural of a mostly naked goddess sitting on a rock in front of a waterfall and reaching one finger toward the stars. The van had a visor over the windshield and a front spoiler hanging low in the front. The windows were tinted so darkly that they couldn't be seen through. It was a classic street machine.

The driver's window began to lower and the kids wondered what Phil would want with them. When they saw the driver, they were shocked. Wally Pintowski, the son of Phil Pintowski, was behind the wheel.

"Oh, my God, what the hell are you doing with Phil's van? Are you nuts?" Al asked while laughing at the audacity, and stupidity, that Wally was showing. Wally stuck his head out the window and had a goofy grin from ear to ear.

"If I do it, I get a whoopin'.….. I do it!" Wally said in his best Bugs Bunny voice. "Listen, there is a killer kegger at Renz's pits and I'm not going to miss it. Any of you guys want to jump in? We're going in style!" Wally stuck his head back in the van, looked straight up the road, and started to roll up the window in a fruitless attempt to look like James Dean.

The four of them looked at each other questioningly. Joanie spoke first.

"Hell yeah, you can count me in," she said and started to run across the road toward the van. Joanie was a short girl with a hard body and a strong will. She raced go-karts, worked on cars, and took shit from nobody. She kept her hair short and her jeans tight. The three boys looked at each other. David laughed at Joanie's enthusiasm, but politely declined the opportunity to challenge death at this time. Al and Pete looked at each other, and, with a smile, Al declined as well. He thought Wally was kind of crazy, and felt unsafe around him when they were on bicycles, so there was no way he was getting into a stolen van with Wally behind the wheel.

Wally tried too hard to live up to the reputation of his father. He always had to swear more, drink more, and push the envelope more than anyone around him. "Well, are you coming or what?" He yelled out the window.

Pete looked at the boys walking away, turned and looked up Mohegan Road toward his house, and then at the van and Wally, with Joanie bouncing in the front seat.

"Oh, what the heck, yeah, I'm coming." Pete said. He ran across the road, slid open the van door, and jumped inside. The van was already filled with a purple haze and the strong odor of dope. He slid the door shut and sat in a large leather seat while looking around the van as it started to move. The van was carpeted in a plush maroon that matched the outside paint. There were four push button leather chairs, a bar and mini fridge to the side, and a leather bench seat in the back that folded into a bed. He looked to the front and saw a drop down visor with an AM/FM cassette player, graphic equalizer, and CB radio. Deep Purple's "Smoke on the Water" was blasting out of the radio, and when he looked forward again, he saw Wally pass a joint to Joanie. She took a small drag from it and turned back toward Pete and smiled.

"We didn't know if you were cool or not when you came walking down the road, so I put this out when you came walking up. You never know who the rats are." She laughed at her own joke and reached back to hand the joint to Pete.

"No, he don't smoke," Wally said and reached for the joint. Joanie started to give it to Wally when Pete leaned forward and grabbed it first. He was angry at his father, at God, and everything that he was supposed to believe in.

"I do now." With that, he held the joint to his lips and imitated what he had watched the others do. He sucked long and hard on the joint and for the first time his lungs filled with smoke. He pulled the joint away from his lips and passed it back to Joanie. He sat back in his seat as his lungs started to expand even more. The smoke felt like it was growing in his lungs. His eyes got bigger. His lips clenched tight, and then he exploded. He started coughing and spewing spit all over the van. Joanie was beside herself laughing. She was slapping her knee and rocking back and forth in her seat.

"What are you doing? Don't puke all over my old man's van! Give me that joint before you drop it and burn the carpet. Fucking rookies, what the hell are you thinking?" Wally was on a tirade. He was paying more attention to the joint than to the road, and the van was swerving all over the place. Luckily, in this farming area there weren't many cars competing for the limited space available on the small road.

He grabbed the joint from Pete. "Give me that thing. Let me show you how to do it, you fucking rookie."

Wally took a big hit and passed it to Joanie. Pete had regained control of his body and was now feeling the effects from the combination of lack of oxygen from coughing and the pot that had just entered his virgin system. He looked at Wally and saw the same expression on his face that he had seen earlier that day. Only this time Wally wasn't sitting on a rock by a stream; he was driving a stolen show van full of underage kids while smoking pot.

Wally exploded. The van swerved and went off the right shoulder of the road. Wally yanked it back on the road as he coated the windshield with his spewing saliva. He never tried to slow down while he kept coughing and swerving as he made his way down the road. Joanie and Pete bounced back and forth as Wally fought valiantly to regain control of both the van and his coughing at the same time.

Pete was soon convinced that David and Al had made the right call and that he was going to die five minutes after doing something bad for the first time. Joanie grabbed the joint from Wally and took a hit while flying around the front of the van, mindlessly loving the ride. Wally eventually got himself and the van under control.

"Now that's how you do it, Mother Fucker. Yeah, that was goood!" Wally said.

He had a gloriously triumphant grin on his face as he sang loudly with the radio and waited for the next hit. Joanie passed the joint to Pete again. He hesitated for a moment, then said, "What the hell," and took it. This time he was gentle and emulated Joanie, not Wally. He felt it expand in his lungs, but this time he had not taken as big a hit and was able to keep himself under control.

When he was done, he reached forward and passed the small joint to Wally. The van was dark, and Wally was driving while looking backwards and swerving all over the road again. His fingers were big and the roach small. They dropped it onto the new carpet and Wally saw his life flash before his eyes. He almost jumped out of the driver's seat to get it before it hit the carpet. The van swerved erratically, sending bodies flying once more, but before Wally could say anything else, Pete retrieved the roach before any noticeable damage was done to the carpet.

"Fuck me, oh my God. I'll get killed for sure if I put a mark on this van. Don't pass the joint to me, you fucking idiot, pass it to Joanie. Fuck man, throw that fucking thing out the window and light another one."

In that mode, they continued up the road. Pete began to think about what had happened earlier in the day, and couldn't help but ask Wally how he could have broken his father's fishing pole in the afternoon and then stolen his van that night.

"He doesn't know about it yet. Nobody was home when I got there, so I stashed it behind his other shit. He's gone fishing once in the last ten years, he probably won't notice it for a couple of years, and by then he'll figure it got broken in the garage. Him and Mom went out and won't be back until late."

When Wally finished explaining what had happened, he cranked the stereo up as loud as it would go and started partying again. They turned onto Moose Hill Road and then onto Route 111, reaching Renz's pit a few minutes later. Renz's was an immense and abandoned dirt pit. The Renz family owned a large construction company and hundreds of acres of land. They had started pulling dirt out of the pits in the fifties. All the dirt that was allowed to be removed had been removed years before, and the pits had now become a popular place for dirt bikes and keg parties.

Wally carefully turned down the dirt road. He drove slowly, but the road was full of ruts from the dirt bikes and large pot holes where puddles had formed. Pete and Joanie were being bounced around once more, but loved the ride. Wally was getting nervous, but he continued undaunted.

"Are you nuts? I thought you didn't want to screw up your old man's van. Why don't we park here and we'll walk the rest of the way?" Joanie asked.

"Screw that. It's a twenty minute walk from here. If you want, I'll stop and you can get out and walk, but I'm driving," Wally answered. Pete sat in the back, stoned and silent. He was shaking his head at Wally because, even in his polluted state, he knew that this was a bad idea. They rounded a corner and saw pick-ups and cars parked on both sides of the dirt road. People were climbing a large, steep hill on foot. Wally brought the van to a stop at the bottom of the hill. He, Pete, and Joanie looked at the immense hill before them. The top of the hill had to be over sixty feet above them and the trail there was steep and rutted. On top of the hill stood a solitary giant oak tree, and beneath it were a few

4x4's blasting southern rock to throngs of people. This was a huge party. Wally looked at the parked vehicles and looked at the hill again. He turned and looked at Pete and Joanie.

"I'm not walking up that fuckin' hill. Hold on, 'cause here we go," Wally proclaimed.

"Wally, it's not that long of a walk," Joanie pleaded. "There's 4X4's parked down here for a reason. We made it this far without hurting the van. Come on, don't be stupid. Let's walk up the hill like everyone else."

"I'm not everyone else, and walking up the hill isn't the problem. I'm thinking of how in the hell I'm going to walk down the hill later tonight," Wally said with a devilish grin.

"If you can't walk down the hill, numb nuts, how are you going to drive down?" she asked.

"I'm going to point the front of the van down the hill and give it gas. Just like now."

With that, he floored it. The tires spun wildly, spewing dirt and gravel behind it. Eventually the van started to gain speed, and people began jumping out of the way. They hit a bump and bounced so high that all three of them hit their heads on the van roof. The van fishtailed in the loose sand and started slowing down, but Wally kept at it, giving it gas and wrestling the steering wheel. By now, most people had stopped what they were doing and had started watching this show van climb a hill that most 4x4's wouldn't touch. The three of them continued to be tossed about, but by now Joanie and Pete had grown accustomed to the experience. As they neared the top of the hill, the embankment was so steep that the occupants began to feel like astronauts on the launch pad. The rear wheels were spinning like mad and the van was barely moving. They could hear the sand and rocks being kicked up by the tires hitting the bottom of the van.

Pete wasn't sure if they were going to flip over end to end or just roll over sideways and down the hill. He just knew that, once again, he was about to die. He began saying confession and then repeating Hail Mary's to himself, solemnly convinced that he was about to be reunited with his brother. Suddenly, the front of the van tilted down and the rear wheels gained traction. They were propelled onto the plateau and quickly came to a stop.

Applause, whistles, and laughter filled the air. They parked the van and emerged to the delight of the crowd. Guys and girls with beer glasses in their hands converged on the van and began looking for damage. None was found.

"You're a Fucking Moron." The voice was loud and decisive. Jimmy Nevers was at the party. "Why the fuck would you bring your old man's van up here, and what the hell are you doing with his van anyways? He's going to kill you, and you deserve it. You're an asshole. Do you know that?" Jimmy raised his hands and shook his head as he started to walk away. "I don't know you, and I have nothing to do with any of this shit,"

"Fuck you, you pussy. There isn't a mark on it. I know what the hell I'm doing. Phil and Mom went out and they won't be home before two thirty or three. As long as I'm home by one, the carriage won't turn into a pumpkin, so give me a fucking beer and leave me the fuck alone," Wally proclaimed defiantly.

Jimmy looked like he wanted to hit Wally, but he didn't; instead, he noticed Pete standing next to Wally and turned his righteous wrath on him.

"What the hell are you doing here with this asshole? Are you going to become dip shit too?" Jimmy was disgusted and walked away shaking his head before Pete could answer. Pete stood still for a moment wondering what he had gotten himself into. Wally never hesitated. Once Jimmy walked away, he made a beeline to the kegs and started pouring. Pete and Joanie followed him. Everyone around the keg was talking about the feat they had just witnessed; some thought it was cool and some thought it was stupid. Wally didn't care as long as he was the center of their conversations. He'd done what the others were too scared to do and he'd come out unscathed. He had created a spectacle and given everyone something to talk about-him-and he loved every minute of it.

The three of them got separated in the crowd for a minute and Pete looked around for Wally. It was easy to spot him; he was at least six inches taller than anyone else and was smiling from ear to ear. People were patting him on the back, passing him joints, and giving him beers. He was in Wally Pintowski heaven.

While Pete was waiting in line for a beer, he continued to look over the scene around him. He hadn't known that there was this many beautiful girls in the valley, let alone at this one party. The music was loud and everyone seemed to be having a great time. As he continued to scan, he looked at the van and shuddered. The side door was open and people were climbing in. The two front seats were taken, and Pete could see them passing a joint back and forth. There had to be four or five people in the back and more trying to force their way in.

"Hey, Wally, look at your van," Pete yelled. Wally didn't hear him. Joanie looked at Pete and shook her head.

"Hey numb nuts, they're fucking up your old man's van," Joanie screamed so loud that it caused Pete to flinch and grab his ears. Wally heard her and turned toward the van. When he saw what was happening, panic gripped him.

"Hey, get the fuck out of the van," he yelled at the top of his lungs. People started laughing. A couple of people who had been about to climb in stopped, but the ones inside were staying put. Wally threw down his beer, pushed his way through the crowd, and ran toward the van. He got there and started yelling at people to get out of the van. A few people in the back complied, but the two guys in the front just laughed and continued passing their joint back and forth.

"Get out of the fucking van! What the fuck are you doing?" Wally pleaded.

"Hey dude, this ain't your van. I know your monkey ass don't own it. You borrowed it from someone, so now I'm borrowing it from you. What's the problem?" said the brute sitting behind the steering wheel. He was looking at Wally and laughing menacingly. Wally looked at the two guys in his father's van. The one in the driver's seat was about eighteen, drunk, and looked tough. The other guy was smaller and skinnier and appeared to be just following his buddy's lead. Wally figured he probably wouldn't fight unless he had to, but the guy in the driver's seat was an asshole. Wally was nervous and unsure of what to do, but he knew he had to defend the van.

"Come on. Party's over. Now get out of the van!" It was Jimmy Nevers. He had walked over and opened the driver's door while the brute was looking at Wally.

"Who the fuck are you, you little prick? Get the hell away from here and mind your own business before you get your ass kicked," the brute said to Jimmy.

"I'm right here, asshole. Now get out of the van before I get you out," Jimmy said in a slow, calm, and controlled voice. A crowd had gathered and was watching the events unfold. Jimmy stood about five feet, nine inches and was about one hundred and sixty pounds soaking wet. The brute in the van looked around. He was Alex Brewer, an eighteen-year-old high school graduate who had been a three-year starter on the Masuk High football team, and now he was being called out by a sixteen-year-old farm boy in front of all these people. There was no backing down. He got out of the van and looked at Jimmy and laughed. Alex stood over six feet and weighed well over two hundred pounds. He took a hit off his joint and threw it on the ground, then glared at Jimmy.

"You little fuck, I'm going to kick the sh..." Before he could finish the sentence, Jimmy had hit him three times. Alex felt the punches, but never saw them. He saw white flashes and his knees buckled. He staggered back against the van and Jimmy jumped on him. Jimmy punched him in the face several more times and felt Alex begin to wilt as the fight started to leave him. Alex tried unsuccessfully to cover up, but Jimmy continued the onslaught and punched him again and again. Alex staggered sideways in a vain attempt to escape, but Jimmy pounced on him like a lion taking down a wildebeest. Jimmy put him in a head-lock with his left arm and bulldogged him to the ground. With his left arm around Alex's neck, Jimmy used his right hand to pummel his face some more. Alex's face was now bright red, with blood pouring from his nose and mouth. When Alex wilted some more, Jimmy spun his legs around and climbed on his back. He put his right knee between Alex's shoulder blades and brought his right arm under his chin, locking it in place with his left hand behind his head. With his two arms locked together, he synched a choke hold around Alex's neck and pulled back. Within seconds, there was no resistance and Alex was unconscious.

"Don't kill him! Stop it! Stop it and let him go!" A girl had come out of the crowd and started yelling hysterically at Jimmy. She jumped on his back and started slapping him repeatedly. Jimmy released Alex and got up. Alex's head fell into the dirt, motionless. His girlfriend lifted his head from the dirt and started reviving him. She cradled Alex on her lap, sobbing, and went back and forth from nursing her boyfriend to cursing Jimmy. Alex soon regained a state of semi-consciousness, and, with the help of three of his friends, got to his feet and quietly walked down the hill.

"Now get the fuck out of the van and stay away from it," Jimmy roared. Those crowded around the van quickly complied. Jimmy was filled with rage at being put in a position that had forced him to do something like that. He'd started to walk towards the beer when Wally approached him.

"Thanks man, but I had it under control. You didn't have to do that for me," Wally said.

Jimmy looked at him with an incredulous look on his face, and said, "What the fuck are you talking about? I didn't do anything for you, asshole. I did it for your old man. He worked his ass off for that van and I'm not going to let those assholes screw it up for him. It's bad enough he has to deal with you." Jimmy was poking his finger in Wally's chest and almost spitting while he yelled. His face was bright red and he looked like he was ready to do the same thing to Wally that he had just done to Alex. Wally saw the look on his face and the anger in his eyes and stepped away, knowing Jimmy was not in the mood to talk, and also knowing that Jimmy had saved his ass, again. Jimmy walked toward the kegs while Wally and everyone else, except Pam Hope, gave him some space for a few minutes, lest they be next.

"Biz Buz, Biz Buz." A tall skinny kid who looked to be about eighteen with bright red hair, glasses, and freckles, had climbed on a tail gate and began yelling in order to get the attention of the crowd. "Biz Buz," the crowd cheered back. Wally, Pete, and Joanie looked at each other, smiled, and made their way toward the crowd. A circle had formed around one of the four kegs, and the ring leader of the group rose to speak again.

"All right, listen! Shut up and listen!" he yelled. "Six, the sums, multiples, and any number with a six in it is biz. Seven, its sums, multiples, and any number with a seven is buz. Are we all clear? If you screw up, you drink." He paused for a moment, then added, "Even if you don't screw up, drink anyways. Are you ready?" The crowd enthusiastically responded in the affirmative.

"One," he started, and it continued around the circle. 'Two, three, four, five." It was Wally's turn. "Six," he proclaimed, and looked at Joanie who was next. When he and the crowd realized what he had done, a chant rose from the group: "Drink, Drink, Drink." Wally smiled and complied, sucking his glass dry and reaching for another. "One" he yelled loudly. "Two, three," they continued around the circle. Wally made it past the first round, but not the second. He drank again. Pete soon realized that math wasn't Wally's strong suit, but damn, he could drink a lot of beer.

With all the excitement of the fight and everything else that had happened, Pete had not had a chance to get a beer yet. A friendly fellow drinker saw him empty-handed, and with a good-natured hello, the self-appointed beer tender remedied the problem and gave him a beer. Pete, having never drank beer before, took the plastic cup, and said thanks. His new friend raised his glass in a toast and touched glasses with Pete, then chugged his beer. Pete felt compelled to do the same, so he raised his glass and started drinking. He didn't like the taste, but he kept drinking anyways. He finished the glass and immediately felt the ground move under his feet. His new friend cheered him on for his accomplishment and took his glass and refilled it. He handed the refilled cup to Pete, smiled, tipped his glass, and moved on. He soon found someone else with an empty glass and repeated the process. Pete looked around at all the people gathered. The party was huge. There were already well over a hundred people, and more were climbing the hill. He counted four kegs of beer and saw a garbage can with people gathered around it. They were dipping their glasses in and drinking what looked like Kool-Aid. He looked at Joanie, who was standing next to him, and asked her what they were drinking.

"Bug juice. You've never drank bug juice before? Oh, come on; you've got to try it. It's much better than beer." With that, she grabbed Pete by the arm and led him to the garbage can. They both emptied the last of the beer in their glasses and dipped in. Pete took a drink. Joanie was right; this was much better than the beer. He drank some more and smiled. In a moment, he finished his glass and scooped up some more.

"Hey, you might want to go easy with that. It's going to be a long night," Joanie warned him.

"This is good. What is it?" Pete asked after taking another large sip.

"It's bug juice: Kool-Aid, grain alcohol, vodka, rum, and just about any other clear alcohol they can find. That stuff will knock your socks off, so be careful or we'll have to carry you home."

"I'm okay, don't worry about me," Pete said as he confidently took another drink. He smiled at Joanie and started bobbing his head to sound of Lynyrd Skynyrd's "Sweet Home Alabama" that was blasting from the truck's stereo. He looked up at the stars and was amazed at how many there were. The night was fantastic. Someone bumped him on the elbow and handed him a joint. He took it, and like an old pro, took a hit and passed it to Joanie.

Pete enjoyed himself for the next hour or so and drank a few more glasses of the bug juice, but before too long his vision began going out of focus and standing was becoming a challenge because the ground seemed to be moving beneath his feet. He soon realized that he desperately needed to pee and looked for a convenient place to go. Not too far away from the crowd he saw a large rock that was almost as tall as him and several times wider that glimmered in the shadows with the reflection of the fire and Pete decided that it was the perfect place to relieve himself. He told his body to go, but it took a moment for the message to get to his legs, and when it got there, they seemed to have gotten different messages because they went in different directions. He staggered for two or three steps and almost fell down, but was able to momentarily regain enough control to stop and regroup. He stared at the elusive rock in the distance and then realized that for the first time in his life, he was drunk.

He looked around, hoping that no one had noticed his aborted attempt to walk. He felt embarrassed for losing control of himself, so he took a deep breath, stood up straight, and decided to focus on the rock. He stared at it, aimed, and started walking. The rock kept jumping from side to side, but Pete was determined to catch that rock, no matter how much it moved. After several more steps, he reached out and embraced it. He put his arms around it and felt its coolness against his skin; it felt good.

"You thought you were going to get away from me, didn't you, but you didn't. I got you, you big fucking rock, and now I'm going to piss all over you. What do you think of that, Mister Rock?"

With that, Pete stumbled back and clumsily fought with his fly until he got it open. Suddenly the urge to pee became overwhelming; he started doing a little dance of desperation as he fumbled around inside his pants. He was doing a nervous jig by the time he was able to finally grasp it and start removing it from the confines of his jeans. He felt a strange warmth run down his leg and was sure he hadn't gotten it out in time, but he kept fighting.

He finally freed his shriveled soldier and relaxed as he relieved himself. He began feeling mischievous while standing there and decided to write his name on the rock. He was happily writing when he burped, and then a moment later burped again, and this time it left a nasty taste in his mouth. Suddenly, his knees wobbled, a cold sweat broke out on his forehead, and then his stomach convulsed, and with the force of a fire hose, it erupted. He sprayed the side of the rock with bug juice, beer, and everything else in his stomach. He fell to his knees with his dick still hanging out of pants and kept puking until he felt like his toenails were going to come out next. When the convulsions finally stopped for a brief moment, he tried to get to his feet, but started dry heaving immediately. His stomach muscles convulsed with so much force that he grabbed his stomach, arched his back and was down again instantly, and this time he wasn't getting up.

It was a couple of hours later when he felt someone shaking his shoulder. He could hear the voices, but was unable to respond. He rolled over on his back. His fly was still open and he was still hanging out of his pants, and pointing straight up. He had to pee again, and he decided, in his logical state of mind, that since he was still hanging out, it was a good time to go.

WHEN HE ROLLED OVER, JOANIE saw his member sticking out and jumped back, but what happened next, she was completely unprepared for. Pete started peeing straight up in the air.

"Oh, my God!" she shrieked.

"Look, he's a fucking fountain," Wally proclaimed, laughing hysterically. People standing nearby turned to look and then started clapping and cheering him on. Pete was barely conscious, and when he finally realized what he was doing, he clumsily rolled on to his side to finish.

"Help him up, Wally," Joanie ordered.

"What, are you nuts? He's covered in piss and puke." Wally paused and was hit with an epiphany. "Oh shit, he can't go in the van. Oh, hell no, we've got to leave him here. Someone else can take him home." Joanie looked at Wally and glared.

"Help me get him in the van, Wally," she said as she bent down to help him up.

"Shit, I just met this little bastard today, and I'd rather leave him here, but just for you, little Princess Pain-in-the-Ass, I'll help, but I'm not putting his dick in his pants, and he ain't getting in the van until he does," Wally proclaimed.

"I can do it." It was the first words Pete had spoken. He, once again, fumbled around with his dick and zipper unsuccessfully while sitting in the dirt. When he realized that he couldn't do it sitting, he feebly asked for help getting up. Wally reluctantly grabbed his arm and yanked him to his feet. Once he was standing, and with all the concentration he could muster, Pete put his dick back in his pants. He didn't bother with his zipper. Wally grabbed him under one shoulder and Joanie the other, and together they moved Pete to the van, opened the side door and poured him in.

"You better not puke in my old man's van," Wally commanded.

"Don't worry about me, I'm tip top." And with that Pete embraced the soft carpet on the van's floor, and pleasantly passed out again.

Wally started the van and drove to the top of the hill and looked down. He could see the distant lights from the cars and trucks at the bottom of the hill. Wally realized that they were far away and a great deal below them. He couldn't see the hill he was about to drive down because his headlights were pointing over the trees on the other side of the pit. Niagara Falls and the Grand Canyon were the things that came to his mind. He was fifteen, drunk, and the hill was steep. He looked at Joanie; she, too, was very drunk, but she put on her seatbelt as she looked at what they were about to do. Wally looked down the hill again. He had royally screwed up and he knew it. He gritted his teeth, turned the radio up as loud as it would go, and then started over the cliff. He felt weightless for a moment and then clenched his butt cheeks as his front tires went over the edge. His headlights quickly pointed down and exposed the hill they were going over.

"Oh shit, oh shit," Wally yelled as they started down. He hit the brakes a little too hard and the wheels locked up and the van started to slide sideways. The momentum inside the van felt like they were about to start rolling over. He released the brakes and turned the steering wheel into the slide and the van started to straighten out, but it was picking up speed rapidly. They hit deep ruts in the path and started bouncing all over the van. Wally hit the brakes again and the whole process of the wheels locking up and the van sliding sideways was repeated.

Joanie was holding on to anything she could get her hands on. She was staring straight ahead with a look of sheer terror on her face. She was convinced that they were all about to die because Wally had no clue how to drive and that the van was about to roll over any second, but she loved the intensity of a race and wasn't going to say a word that might break Wally's concentration.

Wally, on the other hand, continuously yelled profanities at the top of his lungs while wrestling the steering wheel and fighting the laws of gravity with everything he had. Pete was bouncing around the back of the van like a sack of potatoes, but he never woke up. They hit a deep rut and Wally and Joanie both bounced so high that they hit their heads on the roof again. Then, all of a sudden, the van was level. They had made it to the bottom and were still alive. Wally locked up the brakes and brought the van to a stop. He turned down the music and jubilantly yelled in triumphant relief.

The crowd at the bottom of the hill was hooting and hollering; they were clapping and cheering for Wally again and he loved it. He slammed his hands on the steering wheel and looked over at Joanie.

"Yeah, we are alive, Mother Fucker."

Pete was semi-conscious after the thrashing he took, and once he felt the van come to a stop and heard Wally's yelling, he lifted his head and briefly looked around, then dropped his head on the carpet again and went back to sleep.

"He's still alive," Wally said with a laugh, then opened the door and exited the van to join the people who had gathered around the van with their flashlights, actively checking for damage. None was found, not a scratch.

"Oh yeah, don't doubt me, mother fuckers, don't ever doubt me!" Wally yelled. He raised his long arms in victory and enthusiastically received high fives from several of the guys around the van, and then climbed back in, pushed *Alice Cooper's Welcome to my Nightmare* into the tape deck, and slowly and carefully started up the dirt road. They progressed steadily along the path for several minutes until they came over a rise and could see cars traveling on Route 111 just ahead of them. Wally looked at Joanie and smiled. "Oh yeah, home free baby; we made it, and asshole Jimmy thinks I'm going to fuck up The Old Man's van. Don't doubt me. *Don't Ever Doubt Me Mother Fucker!"*

There was a loud and sickening bang in the front of the van. A rock hit the front spoiler, causing a jolt in the van, and then it noisily bounced on the underside of the van as they passed over it. Wally's face wilted like a balloon with all the air going out of it. He locked up the brakes, causing Joanie to fly forward and almost lip lock the windshield. Pete slid forward on the floor, lifted his head, and looked around for a moment, then passed out again.

"Give me the fucking flashlight," Wally demanded. Fear began to grip him because he knew what he was going to find when he stepped out of the van.

"What flashlight? What are you talking about?" Joanie was looking around frantically. She felt bad for Wally. He was screwed and they both knew it.

"It's in your fucking door pocket. Fuck, fuck, fuck!" Wally was screaming and slamming his hands on the steering wheel and he became almost instantly sober. Joanie found the light and handed it to him. He got out of the van and went to the front and shined the flashlight on the spoiler. Joanie sat in the passenger seat and watched through the windshield as Wally's face turned red and his large bottom lip came out and began to quiver. He looked like he was about to cry behind his glasses. He threw his hands in the air and started walking aimlessly in circles. He looked up at the stars and Joanie figured he was talking to God. She didn't think He was going to help Wally this time.

"How? How the hell do we go up and down that hill, drive all over the place, and twenty feet from the fucking road this happens? Fuck, fuck, fuck!" He started kicking dirt and throwing rocks into the darkness. He walked to the side of the road with his hands on his head, pulling at his hair, while looking aimlessly into the night. Joanie watched as he lowered his head and wiped something out of his eye. He looked up again, shook his head one more time, and returned to the van. He walked to the front of the van and flashed the light on the broken spoiler just to confirm that it really wasn't a nightmare. The rock had almost broken it in two. He climbed into the van and looked at Joanie.

"Where does this asshole live?" he asked her while staring blankly out the windshield.

"How the hell do I know? Somewhere on Mohegan near Hearthstone I think. He gets on the bus before me, so I don't know where he lives," Joanie answered.

"Oh fucking great, we don't even know where that passed out asshole lives." Wally was really upset now. "Fuck it; we're dropping him off at Four Corners. The walk will do him good."

"You can't just drop him off like this," Joanie protested.

"Oh, I can't? You just sit your happy ass there and watch me." Wally slammed his foot on the gas and peeled out, sending dirt and rocks flying. Joanie could hear the rocks hitting the van in the back wheel well. They got to the end of the dirt road and Wally slammed his foot on the brake pedal in frustration and locked up the brakes again. When he saw no cars coming, he slammed his foot on the gas pedal and peeled out of the dirt and onto the main road with tires screeching. Joanie was once again holding on for dear life. Wally was driving like a mad man. "This is scarier than going down the hill," she thought to herself. She became convinced that one way or another Wally was going to kill them all before the night was over.

"Quit driving like an asshole. You're going to get us killed," she demanded.

He once again slammed on the brakes and sent everyone flying forward. When the van had come to a complete stop in the middle of the road, he looked over at Joanie.

"If you don't like the way I'm driving, then get out now and walk home. I don't give a shit what you do, but I don't want to hear any bullshit about the way I'm driving. Got it?" He glared at her.

"Just drive the van like a normal person and quit being an asshole before you make things worse than they already are," she answered.

"How the hell can it get worse? I am so screwed. I'm dead. I am a fucking dead man!" Wally proclaimed. He felt the glare in his eyes from the reflection of the headlights in his mirrors. They were coming fast.

"Fuck, fuck me!" Wally slammed the gas pedal down and they started moving. He was gaining speed, but not fast enough. They heard a horn start blaring from behind, and watched in the mirror as a truck came up fast. Joanie turned in her seat and was watching in horror as the headlights came at them. She was convinced they were about to be rear ended hard and gripped her seat as tightly as she could. Suddenly, and at the last moment before impact, the lights swerved around them. Wally looked at the truck as it was going by. He couldn't see the other driver because of the darkness, but as he was going by, the driver of the other truck turned on his interior lights to make sure Wally could see him. He was a big, bearded man, his face in a rage, and his mouth moving rapidly, no doubt cursing up a storm, and he was insistently giving Wally the finger for almost killing them all.

Wally sheepishly looked away from him, let him pass, and then stared straight ahead and drove the rest of the way home in silence.

When they reached Four Corners, Wally pulled off the side of the road to wake up Pete. He walked around and opened the side doors.

"Hey, wake up, asshole. Where the hell do you live? Come on, wake up, or I'm dumping you right here," Wally said to the almost dead body in the back of the van. The body began to stir. It lifted his head and looked around.

"Where are we?" Pete asked.

"Four Corners. Are you getting out here or what?" Wally demanded.

"No.... no. Can you give me a ride to Hearthstone? I'll walk from there," Pete asked. He crawled up from the floor and sat in the seat trying very hard to wake up and not start vomiting again. Wally shut the door angrily, got back in the van, and drove up the road a mile or so to Hearthstone Drive. He looked back at Pete when they had come to a stop.

"All right, here's your stop. Get the fuck out," Wally said.

"Are you sure you'll be all right?" Joanie asked Pete, clearly worried about him.

"Yeah, yeah, I'm fine. Thanks for the ride, it was fun," Pete said without enthusiasm as he climbed out of the van and shut the door. He stood up straight and breathed in the cool night air as Wally took off like a bat out of hell. The cool air felt good on his face. He watched the taillights of the van fade into the distance, and then staggered around for a moment to get his bearings. He felt a cool breeze between his legs, and when he looked down, he saw his zipper wide open and his pants all wet. Memories of what had happened came into his mind as he played with his zipper. He was embarrassed by what he had done, but his mind was so pickled that he couldn't concentrate long enough to worry about it. He finally got his zipper up, pointed himself in the right direction, and staggered home.

He got to his driveway and looked at the house; there were still a couple of lights on. He prayed that they weren't up anymore, but figured that they were and he knew he was going to be in trouble. He turned the knob and opened the door, and for the first time in his life, he was glad they didn't have a dog. He then stepped inside and closed the door as quietly as possible and waited for a moment to see if either of his parents were going to come running towards him. Nothing happened. So far, so good, he decided, and then he began gingerly walking through the kitchen and toward the door that led to the stairs and to his bedroom.

Curiosity got the best of him and he couldn't resist looking into the living room, where he saw his mom fast asleep in her chair. His father wasn't there, so Pete assumed he was in bed. Relieved that he was safe for the moment, he started climbing the stairs. He navigated the first couple of steps, but then his left foot missed the fourth step and he lost his balance and almost fell back down the stairs, but at the last moment he was able to grab the handrail and catch himself. He decided that it was safer to quietly crawl up the stairs, so he dropped to his hands and knees and slowly worked his way up. When he got to his bedroom door, he pulled himself to his feet, began stumbling across the room and was going to fall on his bed and sleep with his clothes on when he saw himself in the mirror. He looked like hell; his hair was disheveled, his shirt was discolored from beer, bug-juice, and vomit, and his pants had a long dark blue wet spot running down the inside of his legs were he had covered himself in urine. He decided that it must have been a good night, so he clumsily undressed himself and passed out on the bed.

CHAPTER 12

THERE'S GOT TO BE A MORNING AFTER

"Peter Taylor, get out of that bed right now!" Anne yelled up the stairs. She looked at Bill, who was sitting at the kitchen table drinking his Saturday morning coffee. "What time did he get home last night?" she demanded.

"How in Hell do I know? I went to bed. You were the one who insisted on sitting up all night. How much trouble can the boy get into living in Farm Land USA? He can't drive anywhere and neither can his friends. He's fine. Just leave him alone," Bill said.

Anne's glare was cold, and if she could have, she would have hit him with a frying pan. She then turned toward the stairwell and vented her rage. "Peter Taylor, you get down here right now or I'm coming up to get you!"

Pete rolled over and slowly opened his eyes. He immediately felt an intense pain on the side of his head, and his stomach felt like it was full of tree bark. He rolled over into the fetal position and wanted to cry.

"Peter Taylor, I'm coming up there in two minutes." Anne was livid. Peter had never stayed out late and her imagination was running wild about all the trouble he could have gotten into. She looked at her husband, who was shaking his head.

"Why can't you just leave him alone and let him sleep for a while?" Bill asked.

"He has work to do and I want him down here now, that's why!" Anne yelled at her husband. The longer she waited for her son to appear, the more her fury began to overtake her. She normally had pale skin and a controlled demeanor, but she was so furious at the two of them that her mouth was puckered, her skin flushed, and she was shaking.

When Pete finally sat up in his bed, he heard them fighting downstairs and knew they were fighting about him. He tried to focus his eyes and his mind. He raised his eyes and looked at his *Steve Austin* poster on the wall in an attempt to focus his eyes. He wanted his hero to help him, but he knew that that wasn't going to happen. He then looked at his bedspread, and there he saw *Steve Austin* staring up at him, and at that moment felt like anything but the *Six Million Dollar Man.* The room was moving and he could only stop it by grabbing his head with both hands and resting his elbows upon his knees. He looked at his clothes on the floor and realized that it hurt when he moved his eyes, and he knew that it was going to hurt even more when he responded to his mother, but he also knew that he couldn't allow her to come into his room.

"Mom, I'll be down in a minute. I'm going to the bathroom." Pete cringed in pain as he yelled as loudly as he could, which wasn't very loud. He hoped his response would buy him a little more time. He put his feet on the floor and immediately wanted to vomit. Once again, he lowered his head in his hands and began talking to God. He begged forgiveness and promised that if He would please stop the pain and let him live through this, he would never drink alcohol again. He began thinking that death was a more pleasant option than continuing life in his current condition.

He eventually fought his way to his feet, and as he stood stark naked and looked at the disaster that were his clothes, he decided that he needed to stash them before she walked in, but when he bent down to pick up his clothes, the stench of vomit and pee made him gag and take a step back. He walked over to his closet, opened the door, kicked them inside, and closed the door quickly. He stumbled into the bathroom, turned on the water, and prayed that a quick shower would cure him.

———

ANNE SAT DOWN AND SCOWLED at her husband. He replied by shaking his head and getting up and walking outside without saying a word. Anne heard the shower start upstairs and felt some relief that Peter was up and moving. She raised her cup to her lips to drink her coffee and realized how agitated she was when she noticed how much her hands were shaking. She set the cup down, sat back in her chair, took a deep breath, and asked God for strength.

———

BILL WENT OUTSIDE TO THE barn and sat down on an old round metal seat in front of his workbench, staring into space. The small red barn was built in the 1930's, the walls and roof were solid and didn't leak. It had painted siding on the outside, but on the inside the walls were bare and made of exposed vertical beams. Bill had attached plywood to the walls behind the bench to hang various small hand tools, and along the wall he had stacked his yard tools. The floors were made of worn and uneven planks that were laid for function, not aesthetics.

Bill loved his barn, but at the moment he wanted to run away from it and everything else that contributed to the never-ending pain that kept ripping him apart. He thought about what had happened last night with his wife and son, and wondered how he could love them so much and yet feel so horrible every time he looked at them. They were a constant reminder of how horribly he had failed them, how he had failed everyone. His eyes began to water and his vision momentarily blurred, but he soon shook his head and chuckled at his own weakness. He felt like he was less than a man, but for some reason he still thought he should act like a father whether he wanted to or not, so he purged the thoughts from his mind and returned to the task at hand.

Bill looked around his bench for his valve stem tool and quickly found it. He then got up and removed all the valve stems from the tires on the riding lawn mower and put them in his pocket and watched in amusement as the tires quickly deflated and turned into pancakes on the bottom. He walked back to the bench with a satisfied smile on his face and put his valve stem tool away, and then took the last sip of coffee from his cup and started back into the house for more. When he emerged from the shaded coolness of the barn and into the bright sunshine he stopped and looked at his yard; it was rather large, there was almost two hilly acres of lush green grass that was in desperate need of mowing. When he turned his gaze upward to the sun midway in the bright blue sky, he knew it was going to be a hot one, and he was glad that he wasn't going to have to mow it.

PETE GOT OUT OF THE shower and felt cleaner, but not any better. He dried off and put on some clean clothes and then, very reluctantly, started descending the stairs. He stopped at the last step and closed his eyes; he knew what awaited him when he got into the kitchen. The door at the bottom of the stairwell was uncharacteristically open, and after pausing for a moment to ponder the implications, he reluctantly proceeded toward certain death.

Anne looked at him as he entered the kitchen. He looked like day-old road kill and everyone knew it.

"Where did you go last night, and what time did you come home? Don't you ever, ever do that to me again! Do you understand me? Well, where did you go and what did you do?" she demanded.

Pete's brain was not working very fast, but he knew the truth was not an option.

"Mom, I walked down to Four Corners and saw some guys from school. We played Frisbee till after dark, and then we went over to a guy's house and watched T.V.," he lied.

Anne looked at him and knew he was lying. She felt bad for her son and what he was going through, but she was not going to allow him to start staying out late and ruining his life without a fight.

"What guys, and who's house did you go to? What did you watch?" She fired off the questions rapidly and the anger expressed in her piercing glare seemed to burn into the core of her son's soul. He fearfully looked away from her and began staring at her shoes, only occasionally would he dare to glance at her face, but while he did, he desperately tried avoiding her eyes, as if she was Medusa herself.

"Look at me," she commanded as the door opened and Bill walked in.

"Pete, get out there and start cutting the grass. I have to go into town and get some parts for my tiller. If you finish with that before I get back, you can start weeding the garden and then you can do your mother's flowers. Are we clear?" Bill asked as he walked over to the coffee pot and refilled his cup.

"I'm talking to him right now, Bill. How dare you come in here and interrupt me like that?" She looked at him with disdain and was furious.

Bill ignored her and then turned and looked at Pete. "Come on, move your ass. I don't have all day: let's go."

Normally, Pete would hate to cut the grass, but this time he was glad his dad was making him do it. He felt relieved and rescued. He looked at his mom helplessly and shrugged his shoulders and, with great relief, followed his dad out the door.

When they were outside, Bill stopped and looked at his son. He was basically a good kid who had done something stupid. Bill knew full well what Pete had done last night. There was no hiding the hangover that was killing the boy. He knew his son was a young man who was dealing with problems he should never have to. Bill also knew that boys would be boys, and Pete was now thirteen, and teenagers had been getting drunk on Friday nights for many generations; but he also knew the old rules that if you were going to play, you had to pay. He told Pete to get working on the lawn before it got too hot, and could see that Pete was actually looking forward to sitting on the tractor for a couple of hours and being left alone.

"Don't worry, I'll get it done," Pete told his father and started to walk toward the barn. Bill watched his son walk off and then called to him.

"Hey, Pete, I discovered four flat tires on the tractor this morning. I think some kids were out drinking last night and must have snuck into the barn and flattened the tires, so I guess you'll have to use the push mower. Make sure it's done when I get back." With that, Bill got into his car and started driving to town.

PETE FELT LIKE HE HAD been kicked in the stomach. He looked at the size of their yard and was now absolutely convinced, without even the slightest doubt, that he would die before the day was over. He slowly pulled the lawnmower out of the barn, and when he bent over to check the gas and oil he felt like his head would explode. With that done, and with great effort, he pulled the cord and started the motor.

After an hour of pushing the lawnmower, the noise and vibration of the mower combined with the heat made death seem like an inviting respite from his suffering, but he also now knew that he wasn't lucky enough to die, and would have to finish the lawn and the other work in extreme pain.

Anne watched him from the window, half of her wanting to go outside and rescue him, and the other half knowing his suffering was a well-deserved punishment. She had gone into his room shortly after he'd started mowing and was overcome by the stench of his clothes. She immediately knew he had gone out and gotten drunk and vomited all over himself. She was mad, disappointed, confused, and understanding. She knew he was bearing a huge cross, and her and Bill's behavior was not helping their son.

Bill came back an hour later, mixed a drink, and spent the rest of the day in his shop, working on nothing. He came in the house occasionally to mix another drink, but never said a word to his wife, and when she tried to talk with him, he ignored her and walked out the door.

Pete didn't leave the yard very much the rest of summer vacation. He didn't see Wally again, and had only seen Al and Joanie as they went by on their bikes a couple of times. Joanie stopped one day when Pete was working in the front yard. She told him that she had seen Wally's little brother and he'd told he what had happened to Wally after the party.

One of his father's workers, who'd bought Phil's blue van from him, was over at the house the next morning and they'd been comparing dings and dents. When Phil's worker had seen the spoiler, he'd started giving Phil a hard time about him driving like an idiot. Phil had been shocked when he'd seen the spoiler, but he'd immediately known who was to blame. Wally had been yelled at, threatened, and grounded, but surprisingly, not beat up. Like Pete, he would probably not leave his house until the first day of school. Joanie told him that her parents had been asleep when she'd gotten home, so she'd gotten off scot free. She hung around and talked about nothing for a while longer, but left soon thereafter.

Pete spent the rest of his summer vacation working around the yard. His parents always seemed to have something for him to do, but he was pleasantly surprised that the incident was never brought up again.

CHAPTER 13

9TH GRADE

The change would do him good. That was the consensus. Peter didn't care one way or the other. He didn't care about much anymore. The only thing he really did care about was his mom. He saw his parents constantly fighting, and figured that she had been hurt enough and had cried enough for one lifetime. He promised himself that he wouldn't cause her any more pain. He convinced himself that he would do his best in high school to make things better.

Shelton is a fairly small city by population, but it is one of the largest cities in Connecticut by land mass. Kids came to Shelton High School from many backgrounds: farmers from White Hills, city kids from downtown, and wealthy suburbanites and blue-collar kids from Huntington. The high school was a fairly new three-story brick building and was built not far from the old high school, which now served as the intermediate school that Pete had attended the year before. The buildings were less than a mile apart, but they were worlds apart as far as what happened within their walls. The intermediate school was occupied by children who were, for the most part, still innocent, but the high school was occupied by almost two thousand hormone-ravaged high school boys and girls with too much time and money on their hands. The students had their own parking lot that was packed with everything from smoke-filled old party vans to hot rod Chevelles. For those unfortunate students who had to ride the bus, they were dropped off in the morning and picked up in the afternoon at a gathering place referred to as "down front." "Down front" was a popular place, complete with a candy store and soda machine.

There were many other things available "down front" for teenagers to spend their money on as well. It was a virtual open-air drug market, with everything from pot to acid and cocaine. The kids would gather and hang out, smoking cigarettes and pot openly until the first bell rang at 7:50. This first bell provided a warning for the kids to stop what they were doing and get to class before the last bell at eight o'clock.

Pete was overwhelmed by the mass of people when he got off the bus for the first time. He walked past all the kids hanging out and getting reacquainted with each other, climbed the stairs to the second floor, followed the map to his homeroom, found a seat in the back, and sat quietly, waiting for his first day in high school to begin. As the classroom began to fill with students, he looked at them and realized that he didn't know many of them. There were a few kids that he recognized from middle school, but none that he considered friends, and as he sat looking at them, he soon realized that he didn't have any friends.

Pete's first day was made up of orientation, getting books, and finding his way around the giant building and endless hallways. He had biology on the third floor, and shop in the basement right after that, and was only allotted ten minutes to get from one class to another. The hallways and stairways were packed with people in a hurry, and since he was a lowly freshman who was usually lost and constantly looking at his map, he spent a great deal of his time in the hallways getting shoved out of the way as the juniors and seniors made their way to their classes.

On Pete's second day of school, he sat in Mr. Janks' general science class, staring straight ahead and pretending to pay attention. Mr. Janks was sixty-four years old, five feet nine, and weighed no more than a hundred and thirty pounds. He wore old clothes, old shoes, and old glasses. He drank Irish coffee, suffered from a severe case of dandruff, and looked like he took a bath every Saturday night whether he needed it or not. This was Mr. Janks' last year as a teacher before retirement and he already had one foot out the door; he knew it and so did the kids in his class.

Mr. Jenks was nothing if not consistent. He promptly started every class with attendance, reviewed the previous night's homework with minimal discussion, and told everyone what chapter he was going over that day and what the homework assignment was for that night. He then turned around and started writing on the board and talking. From that point on, he would almost never turn around until the bell rang at the end of class. As long as kids didn't kill each other and weren't too obvious about what they were doing, he couldn't care less what they did.

Shortly after Mr. Jenks turned around and started writing, Pete felt a bump on his arm. It was Wally Pintowski. Wally and some friends had gotten distracted the day before and had missed the first day of school. This was Wally's second try at ninth grade, although he had no intention of really trying. He would soon turn sixteen and would finally be able to officially quit school and start working legally. Until that time, he was a party machine.

"Want to do a bong?" he whispered.

"What, are you nuts?" Pete stammered in response. He was shocked, but when he looked around he realized that several kids were looking at him and getting ready to indulge with Wally. In the front row he saw two or three kids who were actually taking notes and paying attention, but the majority of the kids were quietly talking or daydreaming.

"Dude, he ain't gonna turn around. Just keep a low profile, lift up your book, and drop your head, like this," Wally said in a hushed voice.

He then reached into the inside pocket of his denim jacket and produced a miniature silver bong about four inches tall with a cap over the top and water already in it; he scrunched down in his seat, looked around, lifted his book to hide his face, and lit the bong.

After a moment, Wally exhaled. "Make sure you hold it in till no smoke comes out. If you show some respect for where you are, you won't get busted." He reloaded the bong and handed it and a lighter to Pete.

Pete nervously looked around. It seemed that everyone knew what was going on and nobody cared. Pete ducked his head behind his book and lit the bong. He handed it back to Wally when he was done and held in the smoke as long as he could. Wally continued doing bongs and handing them out to anyone in the class who wanted one. From that moment on, Pete knew he was going to like his four years at Shelton "*High*" School.

It was in shop class where he met Ray Hanson. The two boys had begun a friendship that would last for four years. Pete and Ray were decent enough kids; they were both semi-intelligent and fairly honest. They both liked Lynyrd Skynyrd, Eric Clapton, Jimi Hendrix, and loved to get high. Ray's bus arrived first and he would wait for Pete to arrive. Once together, they would quickly walk over to the green on nice days or into one of the stairwells on cold or rainy days to smoke a joint and hang out for a few minutes before going to class. It was 1976 and the aroma of marijuana was everywhere.

The boys didn't get into much trouble, but every now and then trouble seemed to find them. The paper ball incident had occurred in the beginning of the year while Ray and Pete had been in shop class. They hadn't known each when the incident occurred. Mr. Samfantelli, "Sammy Safety," was their instructor. The poor man tried, too hard, to stringently follow all the rules, and he constantly harped on the kids to follow the rules too. He wanted to keep them from doing something careless and hurting themselves or someone near them, and his reward for caring had been constant tormenting by the boys in this school for the past fifteen years, and this new year was quickly shaping up to be no different. He tried to keep discipline and teach the boys, and he really did love his job because every now and then he found a student who wanted to learn what he had to teach. He was a fairly tall man with thick glasses and greasy black hair. He wore what looked like the same white shirt, high-water black pants, black shoes, and white socks every day, and he always had his pocket protector in place.

It was during the second week of school that the paper balls had started flying as Mr. Samfantelli was writing formulas on the chalk board. He'd seen one out of the corner of his eye and turned around quickly in a vain attempt to catch the culprit, but by the time he'd turned around, all the boys were dutifully writing formulas in their notebooks and had absolutely no idea how the ten or twelve paper balls had gotten on the floor. He'd been angry and frustrated, but eventually turned around and resumed writing more formulas.

Doug Brock --a short, thick, and mean kid who thought everyone loved him and his antics, but most just didn't want to get beat up by him-- stood up and threw a paper ball that hit Sammy in the back of the head. Mr. Samfantelli spun around quickly and this time he was seething, but, once again, everyone was busy working and completely oblivious to what had happened. He'd begun a very loud tirade about the lack of respect being shown by the group of animals seated before him and the importance of the information he'd been trying to teach them. About a minute into the tirade, Doug had chimed in to defend him.

"Why can't you animals show some respect? You're wasting valuable class time with this juvenile behavior. Don't you understand that this is important information that we'll use for the rest of our lives and that I, for one, am here to learn it?" He'd turned towards Mr. Samfantelli. "I'm sorry for the interruption. Please continue, sir."

Nobody had laughed out loud, but it had been clear that some of the boys struggled harder than others to hold it in. Mr. Samfantelli had been taken aback and had looked at Doug quizzically, not quite sure if he was serious or the ring leader. He'd resumed his lecture for a moment more, and then had turned around and resumed writing. The boys had been relentless and paper balls started flying immediately. Mr. Samfantelli was losing control and the class was rapidly descending into chaos.

When the paper balls had started flying, Pete had been reluctant to get involved in the mayhem, but once he had, he'd quickly found himself enjoying the game. Pete rose from his seat to throw a paper ball at Doug, but this time Sammy had spun around quickly and caught Pete in full stride as he was releasing the ball.

"Taylor, get out of my class and go to the principal's office, now!" he bellowed. Pete had known he was busted and had accepted his fate. He had gathered his things and was getting ready to leave when Ray stood up in his seat.

"I was doing it too, Mr. Samfantelli, so I guess I should go too," Ray had said. Mr. Samfantelli was confused for a moment. He'd been convinced that he had seen it all, but this was finally something new and unexpected.

"Good, get out and go with him," he'd said pointing at the door. Ray gathered his things and joined Pete on the way out the door.

"That was fun. Do you want to go out back and smoke a joint before we go see Twitch?" Ray had asked Pete. "Oh, and by the way, I'm Ray."

"I'm Pete, and hell yeah, I'd love to burn one," Pete had happily agreed.

They'd taken a quick detour down a side hallway to a pair of doors that opened to the back of the school. They'd opened the heavy steel doors just wide enough to stick their heads out and look for teachers or administrators on the prowl. The area behind the shop class was a loading area for the school operations. It had several large dumpsters, a loading dock, and a parking lot for the cafeteria and janitorial workers. Ray had looked in all directions and couldn't see any adults, so he'd slipped out the door with Pete right behind him, and the two boys found a quiet corner behind a dumpster and got high.

They'd gotten acquainted as they'd smoked their joint and Ray had filled him in on his story. He had moved to Shelton from Tampa, Florida right before school started. He had been in the area for only a couple of weeks and didn't know many people yet. He hadn't been sure if he was going to like Shelton or not because there wasn't much to do, but at least there was plenty of pot available. He'd told Pete that his dad had landed a good job at Raybestos, an automotive brake manufacturer, so he had to make the best of it until he got out of school or graduated, whichever came first. Pete had liked Ray immediately and the feeling seemed to be mutual.

When they'd finished their joint, they'd snuck back inside and made their way to the office. Pete hadn't really known Ray very well yet and hadn't been sure how he would act in front of Mr. Kransky, the principle better known as "Twitch." He hadn't been sure what he was going to say either, but he'd figured that boys throwing paper balls was a minor infraction and he wouldn't get into too much trouble.

They'd checked in with Mrs. Walker, and after she had written their names down on her pad, she had pointed to several chairs that were lined up against the wall outside of Twitch's office and told them to sit quietly and wait for their turn. Twitch was a little man with a bad toupee. He tried to be forceful and present an air of authority, but when he got mad, he started yelling and his hair piece would come loose and his eyebrows would start jumping up and down and he would start blinking uncontrollably, hence the nickname. He had been a teacher and, over the years, had worked his way up to house master. He was a nice enough man and tried hard to be an authority figure, but he instilled fear in very few of his students. He'd had a female student in his office when the boys arrived, and two more boys had come in to see him by the time he was done with Pete and Ray.

When Twitch had come out of his office and dismissed the girl, he'd called Pete and Ray into his office at the same time, which surprised them. They had expected to be called in separately so that they could be caught with inconsistencies in their stories, but Twitch had had kids in his office all morning and was getting tired, so he brought them in together. The boys had looked at each other and smiled at their luck as they walked into the office. Pete had begun thinking that it might have been a good idea to have gone over their story while they were out getting stoned, but they hadn't.

Before Twitch had had a chance to close the door behind them, Ray started in.

"Mr. Kransky, you've got to see this classroom. Kids were going nuts in there and he just turned around and picked us out of the crowd. We didn't have anything to do with those idiots throwing stuff. Pete got hit in the side of the head and was getting ready to start yelling at the kid who hit him and Mr. Samfantelli just went off. Here, look at our notebooks, you can see where we were taking notes. He lost control of his class and then blamed it on us." Ray continued, "This isn't fair. You've got to talk to that man. It's not our fault he can't control his classroom."

Ray had never stopped talking, and Pete had decided he was watching a master at work.

Mr. Kransky relented. He waved his hands to stop Ray in mid-sentence, "All right, all right, listen boys; I have a lot of work to do. I'll give you a pass to go to the library and join study hall for the rest of the period, and I'll talk to Mr. Samfantelli this afternoon to get this mess straightened out. I'll call on you boys tomorrow if I need to." He'd started writing the library passes when Ray interrupted him.

"Now, we're not going to be counted as absent or anything, right? I don't want it to show up that we missed class when it wasn't our fault," he said.

Pete had looked at him in stunned amazement and wondered if he wasn't pushing the envelope just a little too far.

"No, you're right. Give this note to Mrs. Walker on the way out and she will take care of the attendance issue when it comes to her desk in the morning," Mr. Kransky had said as he'd written a third note.

Pete had looked at Ray and Twitch and had begun thinking he was in the twilight zone. On the way out, Ray had stopped and very politely handed Mrs. Walker the note.

"I'm sorry to bother you, but I was told to give this note to you," Ray had said as he'd given it to her.

He'd watched intently as she'd jotted the information down in one of her books. Ray had watched everything she'd written and smiled when he'd known the incident was erased from anyone's memory.

"Thank you very much, Mrs. Walker, and have a good day. We're off to the library now," Ray had said to her in his best *Eddie Haskell* tone.

The boys had waved innocently as they'd left the office.

"That's cool. It never happened," Ray had said. Pete had looked at him confused.

"What do you mean? We bought a day. Mr. Kransky is going to talk to Sammy this afternoon and tomorrow we'll be screwed," Pete had said.

"Don't you pay attention, my friend? Mr. Kransky never wrote himself a note to talk to Mr. Samfantelli, and even if he did, he'd probably ignore it. But since he didn't, and since the only thing he did write were our free passes to go wherever we want and the note to Mrs. Walker instructing her to override Mr. Samfantelli's attendance report in the morning, I'm betting that by tomorrow it will be forgotten. All the school records will show that we were in class, so don't worry about it. Come on, let's go down front and get a candy bar and smoke a bowl," Ray had said.

"Don't we have to go to the library? If we're caught walking around the halls and we aren't on our way to the library, we'll get in trouble," Pete had said. Ray had laughed again at his innocence and looked at Pete.

"Look at your pass. It doesn't say what room you came from; it only says where you're going. So that means that no matter where we are, we're on our way to the library. Now let's go get high," Ray had said. Pete happily followed his new friend, and for the next half hour they had walked the halls, smoked a couple of bowls in the stairwell, and had eaten two candy bars each.

Ray had been right. The next day, it was as if the incident had never happened.

PETE AND RAY WERE STANDING down-front a week later, enjoying a free moment during lunch, when Wally and Jimmy Nevers walked up and joined them.

"What's up Fountain? I haven't seen you since you were pissing and puking all over yourself at the keg party. Did we get in trouble?" Jimmy chided Pete.

"Yeah, I paid for that one. The next morning my father let all the air out of the tractor tires and made me use the push mower to cut the grass. I almost puked about twenty times," Pete conceded.

"That's good. You deserved it. Your old man should have kicked the shit out of you, but at least he made you suffer. What's the matter with you? Do you have a death wish or something? How stupid do you have to be to get in a stolen van with this stupid son-of-a-bitch behind the wheel?" Jimmy chastised Pete while Ray looked on and began to have new admiration for his heroic friend.

"Hey, fuck you," Wally jumped in. "I took that van places that nobody else would even think of and I didn't get a scratch on it….well, except for that one little ding on the spoiler, but we were almost out, and we would have been fine if some asshole hadn't spun their tires and kicked up that rock."

"IF is the biggest word in the dictionary," Jimmy shot back.

The bell rang and lunch was over. Pete and Ray started to leave when Wally addressed them.

"Which one of you two are holding?"

Pete and Ray looked at each other. They both had pot in their pockets, but neither was sure if they should admit it.

Wally immediately saw the look in their eyes and looked over to Jimmy. "Did you see that? They're both holding. Come on, sell me a joint, or come with us and blow off your next class. We're going up to his van to do bongs and listen to this new *Queen* tape I bought last night. It's got this bad ass new tune 'We will Rock You', it's fucking awesome."

"Hey asshole, don't tell them to skip class, they don't need to be a dumbass like you. What's your next class?" Jimmy took charge.

"Gym," they both responded.

"Oh, fuck that. Wally's right. You can either to sell us a joint or two or come with us. Gym ain't worth a shit."

Pete and Ray looked at each other, and it only took a second for them to come to the same conclusion. "Bongs," they said in unison.

The decision was made and the four of them began walking to

the parking lot to hide in Jimmy's van for the next hour. They walked stealthily, staying close to the walls so that no teacher who happened to look out the window could see them, and when they got to the edge of the building, they ran to the first line of cars in the parking lot, about twenty feet away. When they reached the cars, they crouched down and looked through the car glass for teachers in the area, and when none were seen, they made a dash for Jimmy's van. It was an old white 1966 Chevy van that was parked in the middle of the parking lot, another fifty feet away. The van stood out in the student parking lot because most of the cars were shiny muscle cars, pick-up trucks, or new sports cars. Jimmy's van was unique; he had painted the body of the van white with a roller, and painted the bumpers and grill with black spray paint.

They reached the van quickly. Jimmy and Wally jumped in the front and Pete and Ray climbed in the back. Ray was surprised when he climbed in and saw a bed in the back, paneling on the walls and giant speakers right behind the front seats. Wally picked up a cassette and pushed it in the tape player, while Jimmy told the boys to start de-seeding their pot. Suddenly the speakers came to life. Boom Boom Clap, Boom Boom Clap, Boom Boom Clap; Wally turned up the volume until the van was almost shaking and then he started singing with Freddie Mercury: *"Blood on your face, Big disgrace, kicking your can all over the place, We Will, We Will Rock You."*

Jimmy reached over and turned the music down and glared at Wally. "You're a fucking idiot. Why don't you just fly a fucking banner that says: Here we are, come and bust us."

Pete had become accustomed to their constant fighting and just watched them carry on with an amused look on his face. Ray didn't know what to think, so he asked for the bong and began loading.

By Christmas, Ray and Pete were fast friends and had added another to the group, Frankie Angelino. Frankie was a good looking Italian boy that sat next to them in history class. Ray and Pete had seen him smoking a joint with two girls before class one day, and had decided that they should get to know him and the girls, so they walked up to them, pulled out a joint of their own, and started passing it around. They had made small talk about an upcoming concert at the Pinecrest Country Club, but the girls had a class at the other end of the school and had left before they had finished the second joint. The three boys couldn't look away from their Levi's as they watched them walk off. They finished the joint, and a minute later walked into history class with bloodshot eyes. They discovered that Frankie liked the same music and, most importantly, he liked to smoke pot as much as the other two did, so the three of them got together at every opportunity, and, by the end of the year, were always together.

CHAPTER 14

SUMMER OF ENLIGHTENMENT

Freshman year went by fast. Before they knew it, the snow was gone and spring was rapidly changing into summer. Pete, Frankie, and Ray cut it close, but they were going to pass and become sophomores the following year. Wally, on the other hand, attended school infrequently, and since he would turn sixteen over the summer, he had no intention of returning the following year. He had a full time job lined up with his father in construction and was just biding his time until his birthday. There were many kids that felt the same way, and had the same plan as he did. They were in a hurry to start a lifetime of hard work.

A cynical view that nothing mattered had overtaken a great number of students in the school. Many of them felt that there were only a few teachers that really cared about them; they were the ones who were feared and respected because they would fail a student and punish them when they were wrong, but they were also the ones that took the time to help them succeed. They cared about what they taught and who they taught. But these students also knew that some of the teachers were incompetent, drank on the job, did as many drugs as them, and had affairs semi-openly. There were also parents, very popular with the kids, who allowed their teenage kids be promiscuous, smoke pot, and drink openly. There was a loss of pride and respect for anything, and an acceptance of mediocrity and doing just enough to get by that was infecting many people.

Pete and the boys became friends with a wide variety of people, from kids who would never think about handing in a paper late and to whom a test score in the high eighties was an earth-shattering disaster, to kids who did a variety of drugs daily and were unfazed by a forty on a test. Pete liked to hang out with Wally, but their priorities were in different places. Pete, Ray, and Frankie liked to party, but they also intended to graduate from high school-- probably not with honors, but graduate none-the-less-- so they wisely kept their distance from the students who they knew had no intention of graduating. It was fairly easy to tell by their attitude which students intended to graduate and go to college, which ones were moving onto blue collar jobs, and which ones were going to graduate to a career of making license plates or worse. Wally, and most of the kids he hung around with, went to school to meet friends and find out where the best party was, but these blue collar kids had an honor code that they held to and would never cheat anyone or steal anything; they knew that they would spend the rest of their lives working, and felt that this was their time to have fun. Others, whom the three boys kept their distance from, were known to be liars, cheats, and unnecessarily violent.

The boys sat in the shade of a large maple tree on a manicured area of grass in front of the school, called the green, in late June, smoking pot and enjoying the last days of school before summer vacation and the time they would spend apart. They lived in different parts of town and knew they wouldn't see each other until September, so they talked about what they would be doing over the summer, which amounted to little more than fishing and cutting the grass, but Ray had them excited about sophomore year because he would get his license before Christmas and had promised to drive them to school every day thereafter. They looked forward to never setting foot on a school bus again, and basked in the knowledge that they had made it through the year, and that in just a few short months, they would no longer be lowly freshman. Life was moving forward for Pete; he was allowing himself to be cautiously optimistic, and finally felt like he had friends again.

School ended and summer vacation began. Pete was depressed because he didn't have his friends to laugh with, nor did he have enough money to buy pot, so he returned to fishing regularly and it helped to pass the time and keep his mind occupied. A little more than a week into his vacation, Pete was mindlessly walking past the Nevers place with fishing pole in hand when he heard a deep voice call out.

"Hey." Pete looked and saw Grandpa Nevers.

He was a big man that looked close to eighty. His hair was white and his belly large. He wore his trademark flannel shirt, and on this day he had chosen a red ball cap. Pete looked at the man sitting in his rocking chair and thought to himself that if he would grow a beard, he would be the perfect Santa Clause.

"Yes, sir. How are doing today, Mr. Nevers?" Pete asked as he approached the old man.

"I'm fine, young man. I've been watching you walk back and forth to go fishing for a couple of years now. That's a sign of good character. A boy should go fishing as often as possible." He paused for a moment, and looked Pete up and down before continuing. "Well, do you want to make a few dollars? I need to get the garden ready, and my grandsons are getting too old to help me with it."

"Sure. I'd love to help. What do you want me to do, and when do you want me to start?" Pete asked without hesitation. He was excited about a chance to make some money, and began what would become a life-long habit of quickly accepting everything that he considered an opportunity without giving it much thought.

"You go ahead and go fishing today. But be sure to stop by on your way home to show me the fish, and then you can come by at about eight tomorrow morning and we'll get started."

"Yes sir, I'll be here in the morning," Pete replied happily. "Oh, and I'll make sure to stop by with my fish on the way home too."

He left the old man and continued on his way. He was excited about finally making some money of his own and had a little extra spring in his step as he walked down the road. When he approached Four Corners, he saw Jimmy's van parked in the shade of the inlet and decided to tell him about working for his grandfather. Pete was really hoping they would be smoking something good and would be in the mood to share some of it with him, and working for his grandfather was as good an excuse as any to start a conversation. When he got to the inlet and was about twenty-five feet from the van, he heard Jimmy arguing with Wally. When he got a little closer to the van, he began to smell the sweet fragrance that he desired.

"You're an idiot. I told you to be careful digging the damn holes, but you can't listen to anybody; you just have to do it your way. You are such a moron!" Jimmy yelled.

"Fuck you! How the hell was I supposed to know there was a water line there? What the fuck, I'm digging a hole for a post. Who the fuck puts a water line in the middle of nowhere?" Wally fought back.

Pete walked up to the window and, cautiously, announced his presence. "Hey, guys, how's it going?" he said in a friendly tone, hoping to calm them down for a minute.

They stopped arguing and looked at Pete. Jimmy had the joint in his hand, and it was obvious that the two of them had spent their morning working. Their clothes were wet with sweat and they were covered with mud and dirt from head to toe. Jimmy took a hit off the joint and passed it to Pete.

"What's up, little man? I see you're going fishing. Good for you. Go fishing as often as you can, for as long as you can, and don't tell anyone about those spots I showed you. Hell, even this galoot doesn't know about some of those holes," Jimmy said.

"Oh, fuck you. I know every damn hole in that stream. There ain't nothing you can show me, asshole," Wally yelled defiantly from the other side.

Jimmy and Pete smiled at each other, and Pete began to think about what David had said about them constantly fighting with each other the first time he'd met them. Pete finally knew what David was talking about. These two were inseparable and would probably be arguing like this when they were fifty.

"I'm going to work for your grandfather tomorrow," Pete volunteered.

"Really? Good for you," Jimmy replied and then looked directly at Pete and spoke slowly and clearly. "You better take good care of him and work your ass off. That's my Gramps, and if you do anything to piss him off, I will hunt you down and personally kick your ass. You understand?"

Pete stood and looked at Jimmy with fear in his eyes. He had seen what Jimmy could do when he was pissed, and this was his grandfather. Pete didn't know whether he should laugh or panic. He didn't know if Jimmy was really serious, or just giving him a hard time, so he stood there and remained silent, and waited for Jimmy to start laughing, but he didn't; he slowly took a hit off the joint, and looked at Pete menacingly.

"Oh, and I am very serious," Jimmy said as he stared at Pete and took another hit from the joint.

"And I'll come and kick your ass too. He's like my grandfather too, so you'd better not fuck up," Wally yelled from the other side.

Wally truly liked old Grandpa Nevers and would defend him to the end of the earth. Grandpa Nevers treated Wally with respect and was always honest with him. Pete was still unsure if these two were serious about kicking his ass, but he knew that no matter what happened, he didn't want to find out, so he was going to take care of the old man.

"Listen, we have to get back to work before his old man has a cow. Some moron-I won't mention names-broke a water line this morning, so not only do we have to finish building a deck today, but we have to be plumbers and fix the water line too." Jimmy handed Pete the joint. "Here, take the rest of this and have fun fishing, and make sure you take care of my grandfather."

Jimmy had started the van and was ready to leave when Wally yelled from the other side of the van.

"What the fuck? You gave him my joint!" Wally protested. He was pissed at Jimmy's generosity with his pot.

Jimmy looked at Wally with a disgusted look on his face. "Can't you stop dropping the "F" bomb with every other word? You've got plenty of reefer, and besides, that's punishment for being a moron, and making me do extra work for free. The kid's going fishing. Let him enjoy a hooter while he's in the woods."

Pete stood and listened to them argue as the van backed up. Pete was amazed; they never stopped fighting with each other, and yet they were always together. Pete thought about Jimmy and his mud and sweat and decided he finally understood the expression "work hard and play hard." Jimmy epitomized its meaning. He also concluded that Jimmy and Wally really were serious and would come and beat the crap out of him if he screwed up. When they were gone, he continued on his way to Wilson's stream, happily buzzed and with a half a joint for later. He caught three nice trout that afternoon and proudly showed them to Mr. Nevers on the way home, as promised.

The next morning, Pete knocked on Mr. Nevers' door at 7:55. He was greeted by a little old lady who didn't look like she weighed more than ninety pounds. He was surprised at the contrast in the two old people. She invited him into the kitchen and told him to sit down.

"Have you had anything to eat?" she asked.

"Yes, ma'am, I had a little something before I got here," he replied.

"You've got to put gas in the tank if you're going to drive the car," came a bellow from the other room.

Grandpa Nevers came into the kitchen and sat down at the table. He had just finished getting dressed and was ready to eat.

"Give the boy something to eat. It's going to be a long day and he has a lot of work to do," he said to his wife, who dutifully put some bacon and eggs on the stove for the two men. "Give him a glass of milk too; he needs something to drink while he waits for breakfast."

Grandma Nevers took care of them, and Pete sat quietly and dutifully as he ate his second breakfast of the day.

"I'll pay you $2.00 an hour and pay you at the end of every day. How does that sound?" the old man asked.

Pete quickly did the math in his head. He could make $16.00 a day and a bag cost $10.00. He happily agreed to take the job. When they finished eating, Grandma cleared the table and they proceeded outside.

"We're going to plant some string beans, corn, make some tea, and then plant some tomatoes today. I've already plowed the garden and tilled the rows, so the next thing you have to do is pick the stones and get the beds ready," the old man said.

Pete followed him as they went into the first of a series of barns, garages, and shops that were scattered around the old farm to gather seeds, tools, and plants. Their supplies gathered, they finally made their way to the garden and the old man pointed to the area where he wanted him to start picking the stones.

"Now, I want you to start over here and pick the stones from each row. Toss them into a pile at the end of the rows, and we'll come by with the tractor and pick them up later. I wish I could grow vegetables as good as I can grow rocks and weeds," he said as he walked over to an old red metal chair and sat in the shade to watch the boy work.

Pete was happy to be working. His belly was full, the sun was out, and he was making money. Grandpa Nevers sat in the shade and kept telling him stories about his family and his life as Pete worked. He never seemed to stop talking, and Pete never grew tired of listening to his tales. A couple of hours later, Pete's back hurt and the sun was burning down on him, but he was making good progress and had almost finished picking the rocks from the area he was told to clean.

"Do you know who the best rock picker I ever saw was?" the old man asked.

"No sir, I sure don't." Pete was confident the old man wasn't going to say it was him.

"My granddaughter Melanie was the best rock picker ever. Yes sir, she would come out here and pick rocks until every last one of them was gone. She never stopped and never complained until it was done right," he said with pride in his voice.

The answer caught Pete off guard. The man had several grandsons; he knew Jimmy and had heard stories about the others, so Pete had just assumed it would be one of them. It surprised him that the best rock picker was a girl. Pete now wondered how he was going to live that one down. He had just been told that he'd been outworked by a girl. Pete redoubled his efforts and, after a while, the old man saw the boy sweating in the sun and turning red in the face and knew he must be getting thirsty.

"Do you want some of the best water you'll ever drink?"

"Yes, sir; I'd love some."

"Go over to the well and drop the bucket down. You won't be disappointed." He turned and pointed to an old well near the house. The well was protected by an old round rock wall which stood about four feet tall, and on top of which the white framed well house sat. It had a metal roof that shielded it from the rain and supported a crank with a rope and a bucket that was lowered down for water. "There's a cup for you to use next to the bucket. Just make sure you put everything back the way you found it when you're done."

Pete walked over to the well and lowered the bucket. He was surprised at how deep the well was, but when he cranked the water up and filled the old tin cup, he was rewarded with the most refreshingly cold water he had ever tasted. When he'd had his fill, he diligently put everything back in place and walked back to the old man.

"All right, how was that? Do you feel better now?"

"Yes, sir, and you were right; that's the best water I've ever tasted." Pete wasn't lying. The cup had given the water a tinny flavor, but it had been cold, clean, and refreshing.

"Mark my words, I will never lie to you, son. Now take that five gallon bucket and go to that big red barn over there. Next to the fence you'll see a pile covered with plastic. Go ahead and pull back the plastic and fill your bucket, and then bring it back here. We're gonna make some tea," the old man said with a happy grin.

He knew that Pete had never been around chicken manure before and was looking forward to his reaction to it; he loved watching the kids the first time they got into it. He had lived in this house and farmed these fields for over sixty years, and over the course of that time, he'd raised his two children and had helped raise all nine of his grandchildren from across the street, making every one of them, girls and boys, get their hands in chicken shit. There were valuable lessons to be learned from this experience, and he was looking forward to teaching Pete. He watched Pete turn the corner and disappear behind a small tool shed on his way to the barn, and then he looked up at the little cotton ball clouds floating in the sky and said, "Thank you." He felt inspired, rewarded, and blessed that he was going to have the opportunity to teach another young man for a while. He got out of his chair and walked to a shaded spot where he could watch the show that was about to unfold.

Pete walked around the corner of the old tool shed, and a couple of hundred feet in front of him was the barn. He looked near the end of the barn, and saw where the old wooden fence, once used as a pasture for race horses, met the barn, and a few feet from there, he saw the plastic covering a pile of something. He thought he knew what it was, but he was praying that he was wrong. He set his shovel and bucket down and gingerly grabbed a corner of the plastic and lifted. Immediately, his nose was assaulted by ammonia. He dropped the plastic and took a step back and started walking in circles. He wanted to run away, but when he took a few steps back, he caught a glimpse of the old man standing in the shade of an apple tree and staring at the clouds with a very content look on his face and then he thought of what Jimmy had said to him.

"Oh, damn it! How did I get myself into this shit?" He thought about the faux pas and almost made himself laugh. He didn't want to do it, but he decided that it was better than Jimmy beating him up, so he returned to the pile and lifted the plastic off the chicken shit. He took a step back, hoping the fumes would die down. They never did, and eventually he gave up and started digging and filling his bucket. He was very tentative and made sure that none of it got on his body or the handle of the bucket. After carefully filling the bucket, he pulled the plastic back over the pile, picked up his shovel and the bucket of manure, and returned to the old man.

"Good job. Now, you see that barrel of water over there? Get a couple of big handfuls of the shit and put it into the water."

Pete wanted to faint. He moved the bucket over to the barrel and tried getting some of the manure out with the shovel.

"I told you to grab a couple of handfuls and put them in the barrel. It won't hurt you!"

Pete looked at the old man and didn't believe him. He had never done anything this disgusting in his life and he didn't want to start now, but again Jimmy's threat came to mind and he hesitantly started to reach into the bucket. The stench hit his nose and he wanted to vomit, but he reached into the bucket and pulled out a small handful and put it in the barrel.

"No, no, no. Damn it. Reach your hands in there and grab a big handful, it won't hurt you. Now listen to me, son, there are two kinds of shit you can get yourself into. This kind of shit you can wash off, but the stench from the other kind will make you smell for the rest of your life. Do you understand what I'm telling you?"

"I don't know. Yeah, I suppose. Oh my God, this is nasty!" Pete turned his face while he put his hands back into the soupy mess, grabbed another handful of manure, and put it in the barrel. He continued until the bucket was empty, and then wondered why the old man wouldn't just let him dump the bucket into the barrel. He was convinced that this was the kind that would smell forever.

"Good. Now, go get another bucket and then I want you to dig holes in the rows about ten inches deep and a foot apart while I stir our concoction. When the holes are ready I want you to put a handful of shit in the bottom of the hole, then I want you to mix some shit with dirt for the next layer, and then I want a couple of inches of clean dirt on top of that. When you're done, I want each hole to be about three to four inches deep. Then we'll be ready to plant some tomatoes. The acid from the shit will make those tomatoes grow like you've never seen before. You know, plants are a lot like people: if you throw them in the shit without a proper foundation, it'll burn the roots, and kill the plant. But, if you take a little extra time to protect them for a while, remain patient, and let the roots take hold before you expect too much from them, they'll grow stronger, and in the end, will bear the sweetest fruit you can imagine. It's important to be patient, and understand that it takes time to grow strong roots. Whenever you try and rush things, you end up killing the roots, and then the whole plant dies."

Pete listened to the old man talking in parables and started working. He was very diligent in making each hole just the right size and depth. He had gotten the hang of it and soon it became like second nature. He looked over and saw the old man stirring his barrel of tea, and Pete started thinking about the words Grandpa Nevers was telling him. He had an epiphany and realized what Grandpa was talking about when he'd told him about the shit smell that follows you forever, and what it took to grow strong roots. He began thinking about the road he was on and the choices he was making, just like the old man had planned. Pete watched the old man working in the shade and decided that he was glad to have the opportunity to spend time with him.

At lunch, they went inside and Grandma Nevers fed them. She insisted he eat a big sandwich, and when he finished that, she put a bowl of fruit, a piece of homemade cake, and a fresh glass of milk in front of him. He was grateful and ate everything she gave him. When their bellies were full, they went back to the fields and continued their work. At the end of the day, almost half of the garden was planted and Pete was proud of his work. They had planted the corn and bean seeds and several rows of small tomato plants that Pete had watered with the special tea. Grandpa Nevers inspected what they had accomplished and was satisfied that the boy was trying.

"Come on. Let's go sit in the shop for a minute and I'll get your money. You did all right for your first day. By the end of summer you might actually know how to work."

Pete knew a back-handed compliment when he heard one, but the old man seemed happy and sounded like he wanted him to come back for the rest of the summer. Pete excitedly followed him to his shop, looking forward to having some money in his pocket. They went into a shop that Pete had not entered yet. When they walked in, Pete looked around and was surprised to see lathes and saws and many other wood working tools. To one side, there were two unfinished rocking chairs, and several bird feeders hung from the ceiling. The old man reached into his pocket and pulled out some money and set it on the bench next to him, then sat down.

"Sit down for a spell and cool off. You don't have to be in a hurry; the girls will wait."

Pete wanted to leave and take a long hot shower, but he was resigned to the fact that Grandpa Nevers had the money and he was going to sit for a while before he was going to get paid.

"Well, when you go to bed tonight, I think He will be proud of you and that's what's important," the old man said to Pete.

Pete was confused. "He, who? My father?"

"No...., well, yes, but not the father you're thinking of. I'm going to give you two pieces of advice before I give you this money and let you go gallivant. First piece of advice: save half the money you earn for a rainy day and have fun with the other half. The second piece of advice: When you have to make a decision, always ask yourself if God will be proud of your decision. Life goes in strange and unexpected directions, and so, you should plan your life like you're going to live to be a hundred and live your life like you're going to meet God in five minutes, because you just might."

Pete's felt a sudden stabbing pain in his chest, his heart sank, and sweat beaded on his forehead. His mind raced right to his little brother when he heard those words. It was clear that the old man had no idea what had happened, but it was also clear that the advice the old man had given him was true. He wanted to start crying and tell him what had happened, but instead, he kept his composure and listened intently to the wisdom of the old man with the chicken shit tomatoes.

Pete ended up working for Mr. Nevers for the entire summer and then some. Some days he worked hard, and others he sat in the shop listening to words of wisdom, stories of life during the Depression, and he also learned how to do some wood work. He came to the conclusion that his real job was to keep the old man company, and by the end of the first summer, Pete was beginning to feel like he had another grandfather. They had long conversations about everything, but what the old man seemed to love to talk about most was politics and religion. He wasn't blatant about the religious talk, and sometimes Pete wouldn't understand the parables he was told until he was lying in bed at night and then, out of nowhere, the meaning of what he had been told during the day would finally become clear.

One day towards the end of that first summer, they were sitting and chatting as usual. Pete was beginning to feel loved and always felt comfortable speaking his mind to Grandpa Nevers.

"You told me you have two kids, but you don't talk much about your daughter and her kids. Do you get to see them much?" he asked.

The old man hesitated for a minute before speaking. "Well, my daughter and her family live in Washington state, so we don't see them much. I've seen her kids a few times and they're good kids, but I don't really know them that well. I wish I had the chance to spend some time with them, teach them a few things and watch them grow, but we all have choices to make. I've been blessed and enjoyed watching my son's kids grow up and I guess that's all I can ask for."

There was a sadness in the man's eyes that Pete had never seen before and never wanted to see again. In all the time they spent together, Pete never asked about her again and Mr. Nevers never brought her up. As Pete continued to work for Grandpa Nevers, he grew to love the old man. He was the one person that made Pete feel important. Pete made it a habit to stop by, even when he wasn't working, and sit on the front porch with him for a while whenever he could. Pete had found someone that he respected, whose approval was important to him, and he didn't want to disappoint the old man. But life at home was horrible. A great void was growing between him and his parents. His father was rarely home, and when he was, he was drunk, or drinking. His mom never seemed to smile anymore, and was withdrawing from life. She, too, had started drinking. She spent most of her time drinking wine, watching television, or crying. During the summer, when Pete spent most of his time with Grandpa Nevers, he rarely smoked pot, and never touched alcohol, but when he got back to school, he went back to smoking regularly and drinking occasionally.

Sophomore year went by fast. His relationship with his parents had deteriorated to the point that they only saw each other a few minutes a day and rarely spoke. Lunch money was left on the kitchen table, and he scooped it up as he walked out the door. Pete was free to come and go as he pleased. He was convinced that his parents had no interest in his school, his grades, or him for that matter. The less they saw of each other, the better they all felt.

Ray got his license in December and started driving them to school every day after that. The new freedom that they were beginning to experience also allowed them to go to concerts at the Pinecrest Country Club, The Waterbury Palace, New Haven Coliseum, and The Hartford Civic Center. They were becoming regulars to the concert scene, and attended one or two shows a month. The three of them partied their way through the year, and passed tenth grade with solid C's. By the end of the school year, Pete was ready for a break from the partying and was looking forward to seeing Grandpa Nevers every day. He told Ray and Frankie about his summer job and made the excuse that the old man always kept him busy, and because of that, he probably wouldn't see them much over the summer.

Pete turned sixteen on July 3, 1980. His parents barely mentioned it to him. His mom gave him a twenty dollar bill, and told him to go and have fun with his friends. His father said congratulations, and went back to watching television. He didn't expect much from them, but in the back of his mind, and deep in his heart, he wanted to feel loved and acknowledged by his parents. When they showed him neither, he wanted to be alone and sulk, but Ray and Frankie came to the house unannounced and took him out for a birthday celebration.

Ray had gotten a case of beer and Frankie had gotten a bag of pot and a new bong. They found a dirt road near Pete's house and decided to drive into the woods and party there. As they bounced down the dark and narrow fire road, they saw the reflection of taillights in the distance and knew they were in the right place. When they found a place to park between the trees, Ray shut off the motor, cut the headlights, passed out the beer, and inserted *Pink Floyd's The Wall* into the tape deck while Frankie de-seeded pot and loaded bongs. The three of them sat together, drank beer, smoked pot, and laughed until late into the night. Pete tried to downplay the fact that his sixteenth birthday was important to him, but it was, and he was happy that his friends had not forgotten him, even if his parents had.

A couple of weeks into his second summer of working for Mr. Nevers, near the end of a hard day's work in the hot sun, Pete and Grandpa Nevers were sitting in the shade while Pete enjoyed a cup of cold water from the well. They were now very close and Pete loved the old man very much. Pete had found the only person he felt comfortable confiding in. They were talking about Grandpa Nevers' childhood when the old man changed the subject and asked Pete about his family. Pete quickly brushed off talk about his parents, but he told the old man about Isaac, about the fun they'd had together, and about his death. He lowered his defenses for just a moment, and opened his soul to the old man. While he spoke, his eyes reddened, his voice cracked, and he occasionally wiped some mysterious dust from his eyes. He looked longingly into the old man's eyes and asked one question: "Why?"

The old man saw the pain and suffering in the boy and pondered for a moment before trying to give him the best answer and advice he could think of. "Well, Pete, I can't tell you why. I do that know life is hard, and I think our faith is constantly tested, and to be perfectly honest with you, I don't know or understand why; but I do know what has helped me and what has helped a lot of other people get through some really tough times. One day when you need to, read Psalms chapter thirty-four, verse four. If you do what it says, then you'll understand." he said.

"Well, can you tell me what is says?" Pete asked, hoping the old man would give him knowledge without effort, but as usual, that was not the way of Grandpa Nevers.

"No, that's for you to do when the time is right. You'll read it when you're supposed to, and I have a feeling that you'll understand and do what you need to do."

Pete was disappointed, but not surprised. He was getting used to how the old man worked. They sat together a while longer before Pete excused himself and made his way home. When Pete went into his house, he wanted to look it up, mostly out of curiosity, but he couldn't easily find a Bible in his parents' house and was soon distracted and gave up looking.

CHAPTER 15

MORE PAIN, MORE LOSS

Anne felt horrible about forgetting Pete's birthday. She'd been so caught up in her own misery that she had forgotten him. She felt like she didn't know what she was doing anymore. She'd recently seen a doctor about her sense of hopelessness and her constant crying, and after she'd told him about her feelings, the tragic loss of Isaac, and the constant fighting with Bill, he gave her a prescription of Valium. It helped for a while, but not enough, and she soon decided that she still needed her wine too. Bill had stopped staying out late, and had been coming home right after work, though she now wished he wouldn't because he started drinking as soon as he walked in the door, and then found something to complain about until he fell asleep.

Pete wanted to stay as far away from them as possible, but he was saving money to buy a car, and didn't want to go out and spend all his money hanging out with his friends, so he spent many nights lying in his bed, listening to them fight. He hated being at home, but he was trying to listen to the advice and wisdom given to him by Grandpa Nevers about saving money. He'd thought about it, and realized how much money he had spent on pot and concert tickets, and didn't want to waste all the money he'd made working this summer the same way he'd wasted the money he'd made the summer before. Since he had recently turned sixteen, he could get a driver's license, but a driver's license without a car was useless. He was determined to save the money he needed for an old car himself, because he was never going to ask anything of his parents if he could help it.

It was late afternoon on a hot August day when Jimmy Nevers pulled into his Grandfather's yard for a visit. Pete was coming out of the barn after putting away some tools when he saw Jimmy talking with his grandfather. Grandpa Nevers was sitting in his red chair under the apple tree and Jimmy was kneeling down by his side. They both had smiles on their faces as they talked, and Pete felt a stab of jealousy because he could tell that they really loved each other and he wanted the old man for himself. They smiled at him as he approached and Pete knew they were talking about him.

"Well, Gramps, how's the little man working out?" Jimmy asked his grandfather while looking at Pete.

"Oh, I suppose he's doing okay. Pretty soon he'll be an expert with chicken shit tea!" the old man said as he laughed fondly.

"Do you think he knows how to drive?"

Pete was happy that they seemed to view him with affection now, and was keenly interested in knowing why Jimmy had asked about his driving abilities.

"I think we'll be safe with him on the road, and if he does anything stupid we'll put his pecker on the chopping block and that'll fix things." This was not the first time that Grandpa Nevers had threatened to put his pecker on the chopping block. As a matter of fact, every time Pete made a mistake, or looked a little hung over, the old man threatened to put his pecker on the chopping block. It seemed to Pete that the old man was convinced that that was the cure for all troubled teenage boys.

Jimmy looked Pete up and down before letting him in on the conversation. "I'm buying a new truck for work and have to sell the van. I was talking with Gramps over here, and he tells me you've been working hard for him, and that you turned sixteen last month. I figure you've earned the right of first refusal if you want it. So, do you want to buy my van?"

Pete was excited beyond belief. He looked at the old white van in the distance-it screamed of independence to him- and then looked back at Jimmy, "Yeah, I want to buy it, but how much do you want for it?"

Pete didn't really want to discuss money in front of Grandpa Nevers because, although he was now trying, he hadn't done what the old man had advised him last year. Grandpa Nevers had repeatedly instructed Pete to save half of all the money he earned and enjoy the other half. The sudden realization of why that was good advice came crashing down on Pete because, had he followed the instruction of the old man, he would have saved more than enough money to buy the van; now he wasn't sure.

"I've got a few hundred saved for a car, but I still have to buy insurance and get it registered, so I don't know if I have enough yet," Pete said.

"Well, if you're sure you want it, I think we can make something work. It's pretty tired, but it runs good, and I've had a lot of fun with it," Jimmy said.

"Too much fun, if you ask me," retorted his Grandfather.

They all laughed, and talked for a few more minutes before Jimmy told Pete to hurry up and finish putting the tools away so that he could take him for a ride and they could talk price. Pete had a little extra spring in his step and hurriedly finished his work. When he was done and had settled up with Grandpa Nevers, the two of them went for a ride. The van was an old 1968 Chevy, with a straight six, and a three on the tree. The motor sat in between the two front seats and was covered with carpet that made it a perfect third seat. There was paneling on the walls and ceilings, shag carpet on the floor, and the famous bed in the back. It had an AM/FM cassette stereo with two big house speakers in the back that actually sounded pretty good.

"Do you want to drive?" Jimmy asked Pete.

"I don't have my license yet. I was waiting until I had enough money to buy a car before I bothered getting it, and I've only been sixteen for a little over a month. When are you getting rid of it, and how much do you want for it?" Pete was hopeful that he could buy the van, and he kept looking all around the inside of the van, thinking about all the parties that had been in the van and how many parties he was going to have in it.

"How much do you *really* have?"

"I only have $350.00, but I have a couple of weeks of full time work for your grandfather left before school starts, and then he'll keep me busy on weekends for a few more weeks. If I get this van, I can get a job."

"I'll tell you what: you've taken good care of my grandfather, and that means a lot to me. He likes you, and that means a lot to me too. The van is worth $500.00. Give me $300.00 and you can have it, but that means you keep working for him during the summer until you graduate. You're a junior this year, right? So that means one more summer. If you can promise me you'll work for him and take care of him next summer, the van is yours."

Pete was bouncing in his seat. He had a vehicle, and would be driving himself to school and to concerts. "Okay. I've got the money at home. We can get it anytime you want," Pete said to close the deal. He was excited, and his mind was racing. He didn't have a license, and he had never driven a standard before, but as he watched Jimmy drive, he was convinced that he could learn quickly.

Jimmy knew that Pete was watching him and that he was nervous. He turned down a new side road. It was built for a new subdivision that was under construction, and was wide and smooth, with no houses and no traffic. "Do you know how to drive?" Jimmy asked.

"Umm… well, I never have, but I think, I mean, I know I can do it," Pete stuttered in response.

Jimmy stopped the van at the bottom of a small hill, put it in neutral, pulled the parking brake, got out of the van, and started walking around. He arrived at the passenger door and opened it. "Come on; let's find out if you can drive."

Pete hesitated, but only momentarily, and then got out and

practically ran around the van and climbed into the driver's seat. He sat behind the wheel and looked around. It was a different view than the one on the passenger side. He put his hands on the steering wheel and rotated it as if he was driving; the steering wheel moved freely for almost a half a rotation before it met resistance and started to actually move the wheels. He put his left foot over the clutch and his right foot on the gas pedal. He bounced up and down on the seat for a second and then looked at Jimmy.

"Should I go? Are you sure?"

"I'd like to see you move one of these days. I've got places to go and people to see. First gear is up and back, second is down and up, and third gear is down and back. Reverse is up and to the top. Let's go. All you need to do is ease the clutch up, and as you feel it engage, just give it a little gas."

Pete pushed in the clutch, moved the shifter into first gear, and then gave it too much gas as he popped the clutch. The motor screamed, jumped forward, and stalled.

"What the hell are you doing?" Jimmy yelled. "First of all, let off the emergency brake; it works better that way. Then *ease* off the clutch as you give it gas. Don't do that shit again. Jesus Christ!"

Pete was now extremely nervous. He started the motor, let off the emergency brake, and started rolling backwards.

"What are you doing? Put it in gear. We want to go forward, and if you don't hurry up, we're going to end up in traffic. Come on," Jimmy yelled with urgency in his voice.

Pete was now scared and wondering if he could really do it. He gave it gas again, popped the clutch, and the van lurched forward. Their heads snapped back, the van bucked, but they were moving forward. The motor was screaming, and Jimmy was ready to explode before Pete finally shifted into second gear. The van bucked some more, but they were making progress.

It took a while, but Pete started to get the hang of it. After twenty more minutes of driving on the empty roads, he was feeling confident and shifting gears fairly smoothly. He was caught off-guard, and brought back to reality, when Jimmy told him to drive to his house. Pete was shocked and filled with apprehension because he wasn't sure if he could do it without crashing. He tried to convince Jimmy that it was a bad idea, but Jimmy wasn't hearing anything else, so Pete relented and soon his butt cheeks were clenched tight, and his knuckles were white from squeezing the steering wheel. They proceeded slowly down the road and eventually made their way to Pete's house without catastrophe. When Pete turned the wheel and pulled into his driveway, he was sitting high in the seat, and was very proud of himself. As soon as he got in front of the house, he shut off the motor and pulled the emergency brake.

"All right, listen, I'll hold the van for you for a couple of weeks. Show me a driver's license and $300.00 and it's yours," Jimmy said as they sat in the driveway.

"Let me run in the house, and I'll get you the money now. I'll get my learner's permit tomorrow, and then as soon as I can, I'll take the test," Pete said excitedly. Jimmy knew how excited Pete was and decided to wait in the driveway for the money. Pete hurriedly ran into the house, got his money, and bought the van, all without a word to his parents. He was worried about how they would react, but in this situation he decided that it was better to ask for forgiveness rather than permission.

He gave Jimmy the money and wanted to jump in the air as he watched Jimmy pull out of the driveway. He went into the house; both parents were home and in the kitchen. He tried to be nonchalant about buying the van, and informed them about it as he was leaning into the refrigerator while pretending to be looking for food.

"What did you say?" his mother asked as he was in the fridge. He slowly closed the door and looked at them.

"I bought Jimmy's van. It was a great deal, I'm sixteen, and I bought it with the money I earned working in the sun for Old Grandpa Nevers." He was defensive and ready for a fight, but he wasn't ready for his parent's response.

"Good for you. You earned and saved the money. I'm proud of you, but don't you need a license to drive?" his father asked. Pete almost fell over.

"Yeah, I was hoping I could get a ride to Motor Vehicles for a learner's permit. Jimmy will help me practice, and I'm sure I'll pass the test. If I could just get a ride to get the permit, and one more to take my test, I won't bother you anymore," he asked hopefully.

"I'll take you tomorrow. I have the day off," his mother said.

Pete wanted to faint. He said thanks and excitedly ran to his room before they had a chance to change their minds. His mother shocked him even more the next day by keeping her word, and taking him to Motor Vehicles when he got off work, and then again a month later when Pete got his license. Jimmy, as promised, delivered the van that very evening, and before September was done Pete was driving.

He was instantly popular in school. He had the party van, and once the word got out that he was continuing the policy that Jimmy had started years ago- that as long as people paid the fee of leaving him some pot, he would let kids skip class in his van- he rarely had to buy any pot and was often given free concert tickets for driving a van load of kids to shows. The van was old, and it was beat up, but it was one of the best party machines in the school.

IT WAS A COOL OCTOBER afternoon during Pete's junior year of high school when he saw the ambulance pulling out of Grandpa Nevers' driveway. He was driving down the road as the ambulance sped out of the driveway and towards him with its sirens blaring and its lights flashing. Pete slowed his van and immediately felt a knot in his throat as he drove towards it. When the ambulance was no more than fifty feet in front of him, the lights went off, the siren stopped, and the ambulance slowed to a safe speed. Pete watched the ambulance pass him and continued down the road with an ominous sense of doom enveloping him. When he got close enough to see Mr. and Mrs. Nevers- Jimmy's parents- clearly, they were standing on the side of the road clinging to each other with tears streaming down their faces. He drove past them slowly, but could not stop. Pete knew what had happened. He was gone. Pete didn't need to be told that it was Grandpa Nevers, and not Grandma Nevers, he felt the pain when that special place in his heart was torn out. He knew; and so he drove his van down a secluded dirt road near Four Corners and cried alone for hours.

The services took place a week later. Pete drove by himself and when he arrived he was surprised to see how large the turnout was, and was even more surprised to see how many young people were at the old man's funeral. The large crowd was made up of people of all ages and it was instantly evident to Pete that he was not the only young man that the old man had helped and influenced. Pete took a moment to observe the people that were at the wake as he walked into the funeral home, and when he thought of how Grandpa Nevers had helped him, his eyes began to water and he felt a lump grow in his throat.

He knew what Mr. Nevers looked like, and when he spotted him, he walked over and gave his condolences. Pete was ashamed of himself and embarrassed because the man standing in front of him was a rock, and even though Pete could see the pain he was in from the loss of his father, he didn't flinch. Pete couldn't help but shake, shutter, and fight to hold back tears as he shook his hand. When Mr. Nevers released his hand and nodded at him, he stepped to the side and was in front of Mrs. Nevers; she pulled him close and gave him a big hug. He instantly felt loved and protected. She released him and smiled at him.

"Thank you for helping him; he really loved having you over. You gave him another couple of years of happiness that he may not have had otherwise." She saw how much the loss was affecting Pete, and how much he was trying to hold back the tears. "It's okay to be sad, but don't be sad for him. He's gone home, and is happy now. Be sad because you've lost someone that has meant so much to you."

The words were comforting to him because he knew that Grandpa Nevers had lived a long life, and if any man was going to Heaven, it was that old man; but Pete really missed him, and needed him. He thanked her for the words, and then moved to the woman that was standing off to the side. He decided she was Grandpa Nevers' long lost daughter. She stood straight, strong, and emotionless. Pete shook her hand, glanced at her, and moved on to Grandma Nevers. She sat surrounded by her grandchildren, staring into space. She acknowledged him, but didn't really recognize him.

Pete said hello to a few other people, and then took a seat in the back of the room next to Wally. Wally was a mess. He was clearly very drunk and very heartbroken. He was unashamed of the tears that flew freely from his eyes, and immediately gave Pete a big wet hug as he was getting ready to sit down. Pete talked to Wally for a few minutes about the times they'd gotten to spend with the old man; they both loved him and missed him. After a few minutes, Pete started looking at the people in the room again. He noticed that the daughter was without her husband or her children. But alongside Mr. and Mrs. Nevers were all nine of their children, plus several spouses and their children. He saw how Jimmy and a sister taking care of Grandma Nevers. Jimmy was acting strong, but his lips were pursed, his eyes were red, and tears silently ran down his face. They left the funeral home after the services and proceeded to the cemetery where the old man was laid to rest.

Pete was lost for a while after that. The death of Grandpa Nevers affected him more than anyone thought it would. He was angry again, and decided to get drunk as often as possible. His pain was so intense that he lost sight of what the old man had tried to teach him and instead vowed to himself that he would never allow himself to get close to anyone ever again. He brooded constantly and dwelled on the tragedies heaped upon his short life and convinced himself that whenever he loved someone, they died, so he concluded that all the people around him were just passing through, and then he decided that that was all he was going to do; just keep passing through. He made sure he passed his classes, and found a job to pay for his partying, gas, and insurance, but he wasn't willing to do much more than that.

CHAPTER 16

WHERE ARE THINGS GOING?

Bill sat at his desk and watched silently as Charlie Bidwell cleaned out his desk across the hall. Charlie came over and said his good-byes to Allen and Bill and then left Johnson's forever. There were now only two engineers left, Bill and Allen Hale. Bill often wondered why he was still employed when so many others, who were much better engineers than he, had been let go. He had kept his word to Jack and quit drinking on the job, and his work was still slow, but it was once again acceptable. He chalked up his employment status to the fact that he was almost born and raised in this building. His father had worked for Mr. Johnson's father and Bill had started working there right after college. This was the only real job he'd ever had.

The production crew had been reduced to Jack and a small skeleton crew finishing out existing orders and doing the small projects that occasionally came in. It wouldn't be long now and everyone knew it. They all kept looking for the one big reason for the collapse of the manufacturing industry in the area, but it wasn't one big thing, it was many small things. Wages were high, pensions had to be paid into, taxes kept going higher, the buildings were older, and more and more people were saving money by buying imported products that came from countries with significantly lower standards of living and costs of doing business.

Bill returned to his office and started working on the project on his desk. After a few minutes of staring at plans and doing calculations, his mind began to wander and he pondered his life.

"Has it really been five years since Zak died?" He added up the time in his head. Pete had been in eighth grade at the time of the accident and now he was about to graduate high school. Yeah, it really had been five years already.

He was worried about his son. He knew Pete was a smart kid and he wasn't a trouble maker, but he also knew that he had taken the death of Mr. Nevers badly and was drinking, and probably drinking a lot. He might also be doing other things, but Bill didn't want to think about that. He tried to reason with himself that his son was doing okay and would bounce back and get his life in order. He reasoned that he was just a kid who had been through a lot and needed to rebel for a while.

Bill tried to think of the last time he and Pete had talked for more than a few brief sentences, but couldn't remember even one time since Isaac's death. Pete left early for school and then went to work at Marsden's Linen afterwards until six or seven. He then came home, ate, showered, and went out with his friends. He was almost never at home because he always had something to do or somewhere to go. He was never a lazy kid. Bill was proud of the fact that Pete had earned the money for his van and was usually home at a decent hour. He was going to graduate high school in the spring, unlike many of his friends. Bill suddenly realized that he hadn't looked at a report card or talked to Pete about school since Isaac had died. He wondered how he could have been so neglectful.

His mind drifted from Pete to Anne. "Oh, my beautiful wife, why have you stayed with me these last years?" He shook his head, and for the first time in a long time began to realize and appreciate what Anne had sacrificed for their family. Her son had died too, and Bill had done nothing except wallow in self-pity and push her away to the point that they hardly ever spoke anymore. He lived his life and she lived hers. If they spoke at all, it was usually to complain about, or find fault with, something the other had done. It had been years since he had kissed his wife, let alone made love to her, and yet she was still there.

He acknowledged to himself that he had driven her to the point where she had gotten a prescription of Valium and was now abusing it and drinking too much wine. Most nights she was reduced to silently sitting in front of the TV in an emotionless haze. She did all that was required of her, but nothing more. He'd done this to her and he knew it.

ANNE OPENED THE MEDICINE CABINET and put two pills in her hand; one did nothing to help her anymore. Through a mutual agreement with the store, she was reduced to working two mornings a week, and this was another day off that would keep her trapped in her hell hole all day. She swallowed the pills and walked into the kitchen. It wasn't even ten o'clock and she desperately wanted a glass of wine, but poured a cup of coffee instead.

It was close to eleven when she finished cleaning the house and poured herself a well-deserved glass of wine. She stood at the window and looked at the snow on the ground outside and felt trapped. Hers was a large house, but the walls seemed to close in on her. She saw Isaac everywhere she looked, and imagined what he would look like and act like had he been allowed to live. He was all around her, but she couldn't put her arms around him and tell him that she loved him, and that tormented her. Pete was often on her mind, but she didn't know what to do about him. He was a good kid, but he was doing bad things, and she knew it. She refused to confront him because he was all she had left, and she didn't want to do anything that might drive him away from her as well. She thought about Bill and wondered if she loved him anymore; she thought not, because she didn't even love herself.

She wondered how he felt, knowing that he'd designed the system that had killed their son, but then decided it couldn't hurt him anymore than he'd hurt her. She wanted to get in the car and drive, but she had nowhere to go and nothing to do. She ate another pill, drank another glass of wine, and turned on *General Hospital* to see what would happen to Luke and Laura. She sat motionless while watching television until it was time to get up and start dinner. At four-thirty, she poured some spaghetti sauce in a pan and turned the stove on. She put the water on to boil and looked at the clock again. He would be home in less than an hour; she went back to the medicine cabinet, took two more pills, and washed them down with another glass of wine.

They ate in different rooms and spent the night in separated silence. Bill watched television in the den and she watched hers in the living room. Pete briefly came into the house, ate a plate of pasta, and was quickly gone, with only a brief acknowledgement of his parents' existence. He had lost all respect for either of them, and wanted as little interaction with them as possible. Then, like most nights, Anne slept on the couch and Bill slept alone in his bed.

CHAPTER 17

HIS LITTLE BROTHER

Pete had another miserable night. He woke before four a.m. covered with sweat. It was the same dream with the same ending. Isaac was sinking to the bottom of the river again. His pleading eyes were fixed on Peter's and his arms were stretched and reaching for his brother and guardian to save him; but once again, Isaac sank into the darkness and Peter turned and swam to the light. Pete sat straight up in his bed and caught his breath, and then he wiped the sweat from his brow and the tears from his eyes. He stared at the walls for several minutes, wishing he could trade places with Isaac, wishing he had just swam a little deeper and tried a little harder. He was ashamed to be alive.

Several hours later, Pete, Frankie, and Ray sat around a table in the back corner of the "senior lounge," skipping class and doing one hitters behind their books while the monitor was gone. The cafeteria doubled as the senior lounge during class periods and was supposed to be reserved for a senior study hall, but some underclassmen always snuck in, or at least tried to.

Mr. Banister was the monitor on duty. He was a history teacher and a former college wrestler who had the respect of the students as a good teacher and a fair man. He hated "guard duty," as he called it, and was in and out of the cafeteria all the time. When he stepped out of the doors on one side of the room, some underclassmen slipped in on the other side and quickly went to the back of the room, keeping their heads down and their books open to give the appearance of doing actual school work. Pete, Ray, and Frankie sat at a table in the back and were amused by their stealth.

"Hey, did you hear about little Volsovik? He nailed Jimmy Salvatori in the back of the head with a snow ball in the parking lot this morning. Volsovik was throwing the snow ball at one of his buddies and the kid ducked and it hit Jimmy right in the head while he was talking to Annie Goodman. By the time Jimmy turned around, Volsovik was already running. Jimmy was seriously pissed, and I think he still is," Frankie said.

"Volsovik is a little punk. He's got no respect for anyone. Fuck him; I hope he gets his ass kicked. Look at the size of that big ginnie. I wonder what it would feel like to have him clean your clock? I'll bet it would hurt like hell," Pete observed.

The three boys looked a few tables over to the three seniors gathered around a table. Jimmy Salvatori was one of them. He was about six feet tall, had thick black hair, a chiseled face, and body too. He wore tight blue jeans and a black leather jacket. He was one of the toughest guys in the school, but he wasn't an asshole. He was smart and treated people with respect as long as they didn't mess with him or his family. A sophomore hitting him in the back of the head with a snow ball, on purpose or by accident, while he was talking to his girlfriend, and then running away was not a good plan and would have to have consequences.

"The only thing that might save Volsovik is the fact that he's only a sophomore. Jimmy might mess with him and bounce him off a wall or two, but he probably won't actually hurt him," Ray said.

"Who gives a shit? Just load me a bong," Pete said. He was tired and miserable and didn't want to be in school.

"Jesus, what the hell's the matter with you today? You wake up on the wrong side of the bed or what? Here, maybe this'll mellow you out." Ray handed Pete the small silver, pocket-sized bong.

Pete looked around to make sure the coast was clear and then put his head down behind his book and indulged. A few minutes later, the cafeteria doors opened and in stepped Billy Volsovik and two of his friends. It was like a wounded pigeon walking in front of a hungry hawk. Pete looked a couple of tables away from Jimmy and saw Billy's older brother Roger, also a senior and about the same size as Jimmy, sitting with his friends. Pete sat up in his chair, his interest now piqued; he wanted to see what was going to happen.

"Hey you little shit, come here," Jimmy yelled.

"Fuck you," Billy responded and kept walking across the cafeteria. The room was now silent and all eyes were on the impending confrontation. Nobody could believe that Billy could be so stupid. Jimmy looked at his friends with shock on his face. They just shrugged their shoulders and shook their heads. In a flash, Jimmy was across the room and had Billy by the front of the shirt, lifting his feet off the ground.

"I ought to kick the shit out of you right now, you little fuck." Jimmy tossed him into a table and started to walk towards Billy. His intentions were to scare him into showing a little respect, but Billy had other plans. He cursed at Jimmy again and brought his foot up; it landed right between Jimmy's legs. Jimmy cringed, but didn't go down. His face became flush and he was now seriously fighting. Instead of just bouncing him around, he punched Billy hard in the face. Billy's nose was instantly shattered and blood quickly covered his face. Billy fell to the floor, but got up again and charged Jimmy. Jimmy side-stepped him and hit him again and again, but Billy Volsovik would not yield nor cower. The fight quickly became an ugly mismatch that was no longer fun to watch.

Pete looked at Roger, who just stood with his friends and watched his little brother getting beaten like a dog, doing nothing. Pete was enraged, and for some unknown reason, jumped out of his chair, leapt across the tops of three tables, and kicked Jimmy in the side of the head, sending him staggering into a table. Pete quickly jumped on top of Jimmy before he had a chance to get up and tried to bear hug him. Pete was crazy, but not dumb, and he didn't want to let Jimmy get his deadly arms free.

He'd never punched Jimmy, and the kick had knocked him off balance more than actually hurt him, but Jimmy was pissed.

"What's going on in here?" Pete had never been so happy to hear a teacher's voice in his life. Suddenly, he felt Mr. Banister's powerful arms around him, pulling him off of Jimmy. The two boys were separated and just looked at each other and never said a word. Billy was off to the side of the action now, and saw that all of Mr. Banister's attention was on Pete and Jimmy. He covered his busted and bleeding face and he and his friends quickly snuck out of the cafeteria. Mr. Banister stood between Jimmy and Pete with his arms outstretched and his hands on both boys' chests.

"Mr. Taylor, what are you doing? Shouldn't you be in class somewhere?"

"We were just wrestling around and it got a little out of hand," Pete replied calmly.

Mr. Banister looked at the two boys. There was no blood and nobody seemed to be hurt. He saw that things were calming down and knew that everyone was going to deny that there was even a real fight.

"Are we done here? I don't want any more problems." Mr. Banister looked at the two boys again, and they both mumbled that there was no problem and that they were done. Pete turned and had started to walk back to his table when Roger Volsovik touched his shoulder.

"Hey, man, thanks for helping my little brother," he said.

Pete turned and looked at him. Disgust and hatred filled him to his core. Without any thought, he punched Roger in the face and, within a span of mere minutes, both Volsovik brothers had broken noses. Pete was suddenly overcome with a blinding rage and started pounding Roger while screaming at him with spit flying from his mouth.

"It was your little brother, you fucking asshole." Pete was out of his mind and hit him again and again. "What the fuck is the matter with you? It was your little brother, not mine."

Once again, Pete felt Mr. Banister's arms around him, and this time, Mr. Banister wasn't letting go. As he pulled Pete off of Roger, Pete threw a kick that landed square on Roger's mouth. Mr. Banister yanked him away, grabbed him by the arm, and took him right to the principal's office. They tried to get Pete to explain to them what had happened, but neither Pete nor anyone else was talking. Pete was suspended for a week.

"WHAT WERE YOU THINKING? YOU'RE supposed to graduate in a few months; it's not like you have stellar grades; and don't you realize that if you keep this up, you might put that in jeopardy? You don't need to get in fights at school. Peter, if somebody is giving you a hard time, just ignore them and walk away. Fighting is not the way to prove you're a man." Anne was suddenly trying hard to be a mom, but Pete wasn't really listening. He remained respectful of his mother, but it had been a long time since she had acted like a mother. He knew why he'd done what he'd done, and he also knew that he'd do it again.

Anne continued lecturing him for the next several minutes. It was early in the afternoon, and Bill was still at work. Anne had decided not to call him-she would deal with him later- but she had been shocked into waking up from her perpetual haze when the call came from the school. She wanted to find out what was going through her son's mind, but she was talking at him, not to him. Finally Pete had had enough.

"He sat there and watched his little brother get his ass kicked. His little brother was a bloody mess and the kid did nothing to help him. I wasn't going to sit there and watch it, so I put an end to it. Are you done now?" Without waiting for a reply, he got up and went to his room, shut the door, and lay on his bed.

At 2:30 he came downstairs and saw his mother sitting at the kitchen table staring out the window. "I'm going to work, all right?"

"Yeah, it's all right. Go ahead." She hesitated and seemed uninterested for a moment, but as he was going out the door, she finally called out to him, "Peter…. Peter, come here."

Pete was halfway out the door when he heard her call him. Half of him wanted to pretend that he hadn't heard her, but he dropped his head and obediently walked back into the kitchen. "Yes?"

"I'm so sorry. I want you to know that I really do love you."

"Yeah, I know mom, but I have to get to work." He felt bad about the flippant way he'd responded to her and was ashamed as he walked out the door. He didn't want to hurt her feelings, but he was tired and short tempered. He felt a tinge of remorse as he momentarily sat in his van, but he didn't go back inside and talk to her; instead, he started the motor and went to work.

Anne told Bill what had happened when he returned home from work. He was momentarily stunned, but when she told him why it had happened, Bill understood and never mentioned it to Pete. The week of suspension went by quickly, and things soon returned to what passed as normal in the Taylor household.

CHAPTER 18

DRIFTING

"**W**ell, were you able to cop?" Pete asked Ray excitedly.
"You know it, man. This is going to be a great show and
one hell of a party. I got enough 'shrooms for all of us.
I talked to Frankie a while ago and he has the killer from manila, Billy
has the tickets, and you, my friend, have the ride. Let's stop and pick up
some 151 Rum on the way and then we're off to the races," Ray said.

"Excellent, and I have a little surprise for you. Have you ever done
crystal meth? My buddy gave me some and I also copped a little opium
to smoke with Frankie's weed. The crystal burns like hell when you snort
it, but it's cheap and we'll stay up and party until the sun comes up.
Unfortunately, this is the last of it because the guy who supplies it got killed
in a car accident the other day." Pete said with a little grin on his face.

He'd been looking forward to this concert for some time. There was
only a few weeks of school left until they graduated and he felt good
about the night ahead.

Ray had a puzzled look on his face and then looked at Pete. "Are
you sure you want to go real fast when you're eating 'shrooms?" Ray
asked. "Isn't that what we're trying to get away from? It is the Grateful
Dead after all."

Pete thought about it for a moment. "All right, that's true. Listen; what we'll do is snort the crystal right after work. I don't have enough for everyone anyways. This way, by the time we get to the show, we won't be too wired, but we won't pass out either. We'll go home after work, grab a shower and something to eat, and then I'll come by and pick everyone up. We're not going to eat the shrooms until we're ready to go in the coliseum, and by then enough of the meth should be worked out of our system that there shouldn't be any problems," Pete said.

Ray liked his reasoning and agreed. They sat in the Marsden's Linen parking lot on Howe Avenue and lit a joint while enjoying some music for a few minutes before work. Pete and the boys worked at Marsden's Linen Services five days a week from three until six. Their job entailed sorting nasty restaurant smocks, napkins, and tablecloths and preparing them to be washed. Ray had started working at Marsden's shortly after getting his license; he had recruited Frankie shortly thereafter, and then after Grandpa Nevers had died, Pete had joined them.

It was a disgusting job that paid minimum wage, but everyone got along, got stoned, and got paid. There were many times that they'd "pump," or empty a duffel bag onto the sorting table and the food encrusted linens inside the bag would be infested with maggots that would spill out onto the table and start crawling everywhere. The boys had become veterans of the never ending war against the maggots, and just brushed them aside and kept working, but a new employee's first encounter with the maggots was guaranteed to be fun to watch. The stench of the rotted food combined with the crawling creatures would often curl their stomachs, and more than one went into the bathroom and puked before they walked out the door and quit. After a while, like everything else, the ones that stayed became accustomed to the smell and accepted it as a normal part of life and work. At least they got paid every Friday and they could get as stoned as they wanted, crank tunes, joke around, and generally make a nasty job fun.

Several times per week, while going through the pockets of the uniforms, the guys would find money or checks. When they found a paycheck, they were diligent about handing it in to the office and getting it back to its rightful owner. Besides, they couldn't cash them anyways. Cash, on the other hand, was untraceable, and it would be impossible to find the owner even if they tried, so they never tried. The four sorters would average about forty dollars extra per week, and several times found over two hundred dollars.

Ray grabbed another duffel bag and threw it on the table. It was moist and heavy, which was never a good sign. He untied the looped strings that closed the top and doubled as a handle and then pulled open the bag and pumped out the contents. The stench was putrid. Maggots covered the table and started crawling all over. In addition to the standard tablecloths and napkins, the boys were treated to what had been a seafood delight a week before. It was now a pile of rotted sauces, maggot-infested lobster claws, stuffing, and other delicacies.

Everyone took a step back from the table when the bag was emptied. Even the experienced sorters were grossed out by what lay on the table before them. They paced in circles near the table and stared at the mess. The cringing look on all their faces was the same; they knew it was disgusting, but they had to get it done, so they reluctantly returned to the table and got to work. First, they grabbed the old food and threw it into the garbage can next to the table. Next, they grabbed the crusty linens and separated them, throwing them into their respective carts. When enough linen was removed from the table, Pete got a broom and brushed most of the maggots off.

Everyone knew that the money was always in the smocks. It was common for the boys to almost fight while rummaging through the linens to find the smocks. The standing rule was that if you touched it, you separated it. That meant that each person was obligated to put the napkins and tablecloths in their respective carts while hunting for smocks. Frankie and Ray had been there the longest and had a standing fifty-fifty sharing agreement.

The fourth sorter was Bobby O'Callaghan. Pete wanted no part of dealing with Bobby, because while he was angry, he considered Bobby unstable. He was a thin and wiry little red-headed and hot-tempered Irish kid. He ate too much speed, talked too much shit, and was an all-around asshole, but he did get good drugs and he did have money. He was an only child whose parents had bought him a new Firebird when he'd turned sixteen. They paid for his gas, insurance, and any other expense he came up with. The boys joked that they probably bought him special lotion to play with himself. Why he worked in a place like this nobody knew. Pete believed it was because Bobby was learning to play the guitar and he had a worship issue with Stewey Marsden.

Stewey Marsden ran the company now and was on the other side of forty years old, over-weight, and one of the best guitar players around. His beard and giant belly made him look like *Mountain*, and he was rumored to have toured with him. Ray told Pete that he had traveled the world touring with different bands for years; he had made a lot of money and had promptly spent it all on women and drugs. Pete doubted he had been as big as the others thought, but after watching him play one Friday after work, there was no doubt that he could perform with the best musicians in the world and not be embarrassed. Stewey had given up drugs, gotten married, and then gotten fat, but he was happy the way his life had turned out and was proud to be running his family's linen service.

Stewey was now a father and a business owner and he took them both very seriously. He'd quit playing gigs and was dedicated to running the business. This was the place his grandfather had built, and now that his father was getting ready to retire, he was committed to making them both proud. He respected the hard work that others had put into the business and he wasn't going to let it slip into mediocrity on his watch. While he was fun and tolerated the loud music and the dumb things that the boys would sometimes do, he didn't tolerate disrespect, laziness, or sloppy work. He knew the job was nasty, he had done the same job while in high school, but he also understood the importance of doing it right and keeping the work areas as clean as possible. He knew that if he allowed one tablecloth or napkin to be left on the floor, he would have shit everywhere in no time.

He could relate to the boys working in his shop. If they got their work done and kept the place clean, he would leave them alone. He knew they got stoned in the back, but as long as they kept moving, took turns, and kept the smell down, he figured they were happy employees, and besides, they had maggots and rotted food all over them. If they wanted to get stoned, they probably needed to.

While Pete, Ray, and Frankie were sorting some linen, Bobby pushed a full cart around back to the washers and loaded a machine. He then lit and smoked a joint behind the washer. He'd offered to share it with the other guys, but they'd wanted no part of his stupidity. Doing one hitters off a pipe and keeping the smoke to a minimum was one thing, but lighting a joint in a place of business was another. It showed a complete lack of respect.

They did stupid and crazy things, but they kept out of trouble by understanding and respecting people and situations. The three boys kept working, and to their amazement, and against their advice, not only did Bobby light the joint and take a couple of tokes off of it, but he sat there and smoked the whole thing by himself. The smell was overwhelming.

As the boys were sorting linen and occasionally looking at Bobby, an old Italian guy came in off the street to talk to Stewey. He stood near the loading dock and waved to Stewey, whom he saw in the office. He was dressed in a white shirt with black vest and pants, and the boys recognized him as a local restaurant owner who was probably here to do business. A moment later, Stewey came out of his office and the two of them started talking about fifteen feet away from where the boys were working.

Stewey kept glaring at the boys from over his shoulder. They put their heads down, shut up, and kept working. After a few minutes, the old man started waving his hands and looking at the boys too. He said something to Stewey and the two of them went into the office and talked for about ten or fifteen minutes. The guys could see them in the office looking out the window at them. When the old man left, Stewey came out and looked like he was going to kill the first person he could get his hands on. Frankie, Ray, and Pete started shaking their heads and pointed to the washers. They liked to get stoned, but all of them had told Bobby not to be stupid. There were other ways to accomplish the same objective. Bobby was a person who felt like he just had to push the envelope.

Stewey stormed past the other guys and went straight to Bobby. He grabbed him by the shirt and body-slammed him against the large commercial washer. "What the hell are you thinking, you stupid little bastard?" Stewey slammed him again. "I ought to kick your ass and throw you right the hell out of here!"

The boys thought Bobby was going to get his ass kicked, and they all wanted to watch it happen. Stewey lifted Bobby right off the ground, slammed him against the washer a few more times, and yelled and slobbered all over him, but he never actually hit him. The three boys were very disappointed.

Big-mouth Bobby looked like he was about to piss his pants. His face was white, his lips were quivering, and he wanted to cry. Stewey finally let go of Bobby and threw him to the ground in a heap, then stormed back to his office. He never said a word to the other guys. He just walked right past them, but when he got to his office door, he turned around and yelled at them to get back to work, then slammed the door behind him as he went in. No one ever lit a joint in that place again.

Pete, Ray, and Frankie looked at each other. Nobody said a word, but they all had little smiles on their faces and wanted to burst out laughing. They looked over at Bobby, who was slowly getting up. He looked at them and threw up his arm and yelled a defiant, "Fuck you all." Bobby got to his feet, brushed himself off, and then went into the back to put another load of linens in a machine. He wanted to get to the back of the shop where no one could see him and he couldn't see them. Pete watched him go hide behind the big machine and then looked at the others. They all busted out laughing. They all knew that it was things like that that made working at Marsden's Linen a great job. Pete looked at his comrades and was convinced that this was going to be a good day.

The rest of the day was mostly uneventful. Ray found a twenty and

Pete a ten. Bobby and Frankie found nothing. Pete knew exactly what he was doing with his ten bucks.

"Bobby, pick me up a quarter from your buddy," he said.

"Fuck you, asshole," was the response that came back to him.

"What are you pissed at me for? I told you not to light a joint in here. One hitters are one thing, but you've got to be crazy to do that shit. But I have to tell you: the look on your face was priceless, dude," Pete said laughing.

"Fuck you, asshole." It was the only thing Bobby wanted to say.

"Okay, fuck me, but are you gonna pick me up a bag for the show or what?"

"Yeah, yeah, yeah. Give me the ten bucks and pick me up by 7:30 so we can get decent parking. We'll party in the parking lot before the show." Bobby had started to return to his normal charming self.

Pete was the designated driver. That didn't mean he was going to stay sober; it just meant he had to buy the gas. When they finished work, he dropped off Frankie and then he and Ray pulled down a road under construction near Ray's house. They parked the van at the end of a cul-de-sac. The road was completed and the lots divided, but no houses were under construction yet. Pete reached into the pouch on the front of the engine cover and pulled out a small mirror. He reached back in and pulled out a small razor blade and small plastic pouch that was made from tearing off the corner of a baggie, and then melting the end with a lighter. He emptied the contents into a small pile of little white rocks on the mirror and then chopped it into four white lines with his razor blade.

He smiled at Ray and gave an evil laugh as he reached into his pocket and pulled out a dollar bill. He rolled the bill into a tight little tube and snorted the crystal meth like a vacuum cleaner. It was worse than he expected. It felt like a branding iron was in his nose. His face contorted and he slapped the steering wheel as the meth burned.

He passed the dollar and the mirror to Ray. Ray hesitated and looked at Pete like he was crazy, but he put the bill up to his nose and snorted his line. His face contorted and a shiver ran down his spine, but instead of passing the mirror back, he switched nostrils and snorted the other line before passing the bill and mirror back to Pete. Pete quickly finished his second line and, after the burn faded, he felt his energy level start to rise.

He turned the music up loud and lit a joint with a big smile on his face. He passed it to Ray and watched his friend take a long drag from it. Pete's mind was racing; it always bounced around, but now he was in hyper drive. For a brief moment, he decided to be philosophical and think about life. He turned down the music and questioned his friend.

"What are you gonna do next year, Ray? Where the fuck are we going?" Ray was caught off guard.

"I don't know what you're doing or where you're going, but I know what I'm doing," Ray confidently pronounced. "My old man has a buddy that hooked me up with a job at Harrell's after we graduate. I'll get into their apprenticeship program, and in a few years I'll be a Master Machinist. It can't say 'Made in the U.S.A.' without machinists, baby. You've always known I wanted to be a machinist, didn't you? It's a steady job, pays well, and good machinists will always be in demand. I can't do the whole college scene. I'm probably going to get an apartment downtown right after I start working there, and then it's off to real life." Ray took a hit off the joint and passed it back to Pete before continuing. "I told you that Mick Branson has a place on Howe Avenue right above the dry cleaners next to the Pizza Palace. Well, he's rooming with Jerry Atwater, but that crazy bastard joined the Marine Corps and is leaving at the end of June. He told me I could move in and take Jerry's room and I'm seriously thinking about it, but he's such a dick that I'm not sure I can live with him. Anyways, I'm going to be a waste case until we graduate, and then it's time to get serious." He looked at Pete and then asked him something he had never asked in the four years they had known each other. "So, what are you going to do?"

Pete looked away from Ray and out the windshield of the van. His mind was racing from the meth. He thought about all the seniors he knew. Everyone, it seemed, had a plan, everyone but him. Most of the guys he knew were getting into construction; some joined the military, a few others were trying to get factory jobs around town, and some were moving on to college. Pete didn't have a clue what he was going to do. He never thought he'd live this long, and often wished he hadn't. He had a flash vision of Isaac's hand reaching up in the cold water and he shivered. With his luck he would end up living to be a hundred. That was something that scared the hell out of him, and his fear embarrassed him. He took the joint from Ray, took a long drag from it, put the van in gear, and started moving.

Pete looked over at Ray and, with a fatalistic smile on his face, said, "I haven't got a clue what I'm gonna do, or where I'm gonna go. How's that for a life plan?"

Ray and Pete laughed together and drove the short distance to Ray's house, blasting music and feeling revved up and ready to go. They were soon at Ray's house, and as he climbed out, Pete told him not to waste time with his parents and to be ready to go in an hour. Ray had a big smile on his face and waved Pete off.

"Don't worry about me. I'm psyched for this show. This is going to be a night of mayhem that we will remember for the rest of our lives." He shut the door and walked into his house.

Pete drove away, and when he was safely down the road, he turned the music down and threw the joint out the window. He drove slowly through the winding hills and small roads thinking about the life that was coming at him quickly. He needed a plan and he knew it. He was smarter than most of the people around him and he knew that too, and yet he was just barely going to graduate. He didn't have the grades or money to get into college, he didn't consider himself warrior material, and loathed the thought of spending his life in a factory.

Pete was lost, but he was semi-confident that he would find his way in the end. He picked up speed and turned up the music again, and, as teenagers can do, he forced himself to be in a good mood again and started blasting his radio and singing with the music for the rest of the ride home.

As he got closer to his house, his mood began to change again.

While he drove down a winding section of Mohegan Road that was little more than a paved goat path full of pot holes, his stomach churned. When the road leveled off as he passed Far Mill Road, about a half mile from his house, he reached over and turned down the stereo again. He hated to go home. A moment later he pulled in his driveway and shut off his motor. He closed his eyes and squeezed the steering wheel.

"God, I don't want to go in there," he thought to himself. It was the same thought he had every time he came home.

Maybe he could get in and out without even being noticed, he thought to himself. He took a deep breath, shook his head, and started in. When he walked in the front door, Anne was at the table. She had a glass of wine and a book in her hand. "Cool," he thought to himself. "She's probably more stoned than I am." When they looked at each other, she knew that he had been smoking pot and he knew she had taken an extra pill or two. He felt bad for her, but he wanted to get up the stairs, in the shower, and back out the door before his father even noticed he was home.

"Where's Dad?" he asked his mother as he was walking past her.

She looked up at him with glazed eyes and spoke slowly and quietly. "He's in the den."

She then returned to the book she was staring at. Pete ran up the stairs, pulled off his clothes, and jumped in the shower. He was combing his hair as he ran downstairs and out the door without another word to either of them.

CHAPTER 19

REBIRTH

Bill sat hunched over his desk. He had a great design for a custom lift that a company in North Carolina needed. He was told their price point, based on a Japanese competitor's preliminary bid. He stared at the plans and ran the numbers over and over. He had cut out everything he possibly could and he was still thousands of dollars over budget. He didn't understand how they could build this in Japan and ship it all the way overseas cheaper than they could build it here and ship it down the highway.

As he was working, Allen Hale came into his office. They talked about the project and Allen concurred that their overhead and wages were too high to be competitive anymore. It was another job that was going overseas.

"You know that we're not going to be here much longer, don't you Bill?" Allen asked.

Bill looked at him, resigned to the fact that he was right and manufacturing was coming to an end in Shelton. They were one of the last operations standing, and soon, they, too, would be a distant memory.

"What are you going to do with yourself when we finally do close?" Bill asked Allen.

"Well, Sandy and I talked about it. The kids are grown and have moved on. Our house is too big and quiet for just the two of us now, so we've put the house on the market and plan to move to Naples, Florida this summer. I figure I can pick up some consulting work here and there and basically just fart around. Hell, I'm going to be sixty in a couple of months. I might as well retire a little early and get my golf game in shape. How about you; what are your plans? You're still young enough to start over. Doesn't your boy graduate this year?" he asked.

Bill had never thought about it. What was he going to do? He and Anne had no plans for the future, and very little savings. They had been so mired in their pit of despair that they never discussed what was going to happen when the plant shut down.

"I don't know, Al; my dad worked here all his life and I just figured I would do the same. It never dawned on me that I would outlive this place. Shit, well, we'll be fine. I can find work and Pete does graduate soon, so he'll probably want to move out as soon as possible. Who knows; maybe we'll see you down in Florida." Allen saw the look of despair on Bill's face as he spoke.

"Oh, I didn't mean to ruin your day, Bill. I wonder how the old man is holding up. I haven't seen him all week. He's been out trying everything he can to keep us going, but it's inevitable; everything is turning Japanese." Allen looked up at the clock. "Oh hell, with all the fun we've been having today, I just noticed it's almost six o'clock. Why don't you wind it down and go home to your wife? You've got a great wife, you know. Sandy sees her at Birchwood every week. She just adores Anne. She says that no matter how bad her day has been, she can count on Anne to have a smile and say something to brighten her day. Sandra said she doesn't think Anne ever has a bad day." Allen got up and started to leave. "You should buy her some flowers."

Bill sat in his chair, stunned at what Allen had said about his wife. He had not seen that version of his wife in years. When Allen left and he was alone, Bill wept.

CHAPTER 20

A GOOD TIME GONE BAD

Pete picked up his buddies and they were on the Merritt Parkway heading north to New Haven. It was shaping up to be a great night. They had plenty of drugs, a bottle of 151 Rum, and great seats for the show. Pete looked at his buddies and smiled. He was having fun and so were they. They were all eighteen and a month away from graduating high school. It just wasn't going to get any better than this.

"Tush" came on the radio and Pete turned it up loud. Frankie passed around a three foot bong that he'd brought for the show. Ray lit joint after joint, and Bobby had his bottle of rum that he passed around. They were not allowed to bring the bottles into the Coliseum, so Bobby had brought a wine sac that he'd filled with very potent rum and coke. By the time they arrived at the coliseum and parked the van, they were already very drunk and stoned.

"Time for some mushrooms, boys," Pete said.

He and Ray climbed into the back of the van to join the others. Once situated, Ray opened a bag of brown dried mushrooms and emptied them on an album cover that Pete kept in the van to de-seed pot and he split them into four piles. He laid the album on the floor in the middle of them. Ray and Frankie ate theirs immediately. Pete finished his bong and handed it to Bobby. Bobby loaded a hit and decided to smoke it before eating his mushrooms. As he was doing his bong, Pete put mushrooms in his mouth for the first time, and as he tried to swallow them, he instantly felt his stomach contract and convulse. They tasted as bad as they looked. When he was finally able to swallow them, he had to make an effort to keep them down. His stomach was doing somersaults as he reached over and grabbed the wine sac. He lifted it in the air and squeezed a large quantity of the powerful rum concoction into his mouth.

The wine sac was filled with 151 Rum that had a little coke in it for coloring. He gagged as he tried to force it into his stomach; his stomach refused to accept the combination of mushrooms and rum, and Pete ended up looking like Linda Blair as he spewed rum and mushrooms all over Bobby.

"What the fuck!" Bobby screamed as he pulled the vomit covered bong away from his mouth and jumped back with a look of total disgust on his face. He set the bong down, pulled his mushroom-and-rum covered shirt away from his skin, and looked down in horror. Frankie and Ray were rolling on the ground laughing.

"Oh shit, you mother fucker! What the hell! Look at this shit…I'm going to stink like puke. You're buying me a new shirt, asshole," Bobby demanded. Pete looked at him and laughed.

"Get over it, dickhead; it ain't that bad, and you can buy your own shirt if you want one," Pete answered. He felt much better now that his stomach was empty. Bobby looked at his shirt and glared at Pete. He was the only one not laughing.

"No, fuck you. You puked this shit all over me, and look at that…. you spit all over my mushrooms too! I'm not eating those. You're a fucking asshole and I want a new shirt!" Bobby demanded again.

Pete looked at him and got serious. "I am not buying you a shirt. If you want one, go get one yourself. Now relax, wipe off the bong, and do another one; it'll make you feel better." Pete tolerated Bobby, but he didn't like him.

"Hey, if you're not going to eat those mushrooms, I will," Ray offered.

Bobby was drinking heavily and he was getting livid. He dismissively told Ray to help himself and Ray didn't hesitate. He pushed aside the couple of pieces that had vomit on them, offered some to Pete, who declined, and then divided the remaining pile between himself and Frankie. They ate them with enthusiasm.

Pete and Bobby were staring at each other, and now both were pissed off. The night was going downhill fast. Bobby finally spoke up and broke the silence.

"Well, you know what? Fuck you guys. I'm out of here."

Bobby opened the side door and started walking towards the show shedding his fouled shirt and draping the wine sac around his neck. The mushrooms were kicking in and Frankie and Ray were laughing uncontrollably as they watched him walk away. Pete had not kept much down, but the small amount that was getting into his system was lightening his mood.

Ray couldn't control himself. "Come on back when you can cheer us up, dickhead," he yelled to Bobby as he walked away. Bobby didn't even turn around; he just raised his middle finger as he kept walking. Pete, Ray, and Frankie started laughing uncontrollably again. Pete reached over and closed the door to the van and told Ray to load the bong.

"Where the hell is he going?" Ray asked as he wiped the bong clean.

"Who cares? He has his ticket and we have ours. We'll see him inside," Pete said as he took the bong from Ray.

When they got to their seats, Bobby was nowhere to be found. Pete looked around the coliseum, trying to spot him as it was filling. Ray and Frankie were no help. They were enjoying their mushrooms and laughing at everything they saw around them. It was a very mixed crowd. Cowboy boots and whiskey were everywhere, as were people dancing with tie-dyed shirts and orange hair, and still others were dressed in leather and looked like they belonged to motorcycle gangs. Pete had already seen two fights in the stands and the concert hadn't even started yet.

The warm up band came on stage and played their set, and when the lights came on Pete looked around again. Still no Bobby. Pete told the boys he had to piss and made his way to the bathrooms. When he'd finished, he walked around the concourse looking for him. After a few minutes, he saw something out of the corner of his eye that caught his attention.

About twenty five feet from him, he saw two large guys, both over six feet tall with long black hair and leather jackets, who had another guy in a corner and were poking him in the chest angrily. Pete looked again and realized that the single guy was Bobby. A cold sweat came over him as he debated what to do. It was his "friend" over there and it was two against one. Pete had no doubt that Bobby had been running his mouth again and had probably started the problem, as he usually did. Pete looked again and knew Bobby hadn't seen him. Bobby was concentrating on the two men in front of him; he was scared and so was Pete.

Pete looked around, hoping that someone would notice what was going on and rescue Bobby, but there was nobody helping. He took a step towards them, but the butterflies in his stomach grew into dragons, and he hesitated. When he looked at them again, it looked like things had calmed down. The big guys had their hands at their sides, and Bobby was waving his hands and talking steadily. He appeared to be explaining the misunderstanding and it looked like he was going to talk his way out of the situation and walk away again. Pete was satisfied that Bobby was okay, so he turned and walked back to his seat without looking back.

After the second band finished their set, all three boys went to the bathroom. When they got out the doors from the arena to the concourse, they saw a crowd gathered around some doors. Outside the doors were police cars with lights flashing and an ambulance with its doors open. Pete immediately felt weak in the knees. "It couldn't be him," he tried to reassure himself.

"Somebody must have gotten their ass kicked bad. Let's go check it out," Frankie said, morbidly excited. Pete didn't want to go near the area. Emotions washed over him that he hadn't felt in a long time. He was no longer stoned or drunk. His stomach convulsed and he vomited all over the concourse.

"Oh, sick. Mother Fucker," Ray yelled. They were at a rock concert in 1981 and a person vomiting in the concourse was nothing new to anyone. Pete felt weak and excused himself to the bathroom to continue his vomiting. Ray and Frankie watched him go into the bathroom and then went to see the guy on the stretcher.

It was several minutes before Pete regained enough strength to leave the stall. When he walked out of the bathroom, he saw Frankie and Ray talking to the police. They were white as ghosts and had a look on their faces that Pete had never wanted to see again. He already knew what had happened. He felt it. As he walked towards his friends, he felt as if he were in a different world. When he reached them, they turned and looked at him. He saw the emptiness on their faces.

"Bobby's dead," Ray said. "He got stabbed and stuffed in a closet to die. What the fuck? There's ten thousand people here and nobody saw anything. Can you believe that shit?" Ray had tears in his eyes.

Frankie couldn't say anything. The cop asked Pete if he had seen anything. Pete lied and said no.

The boys drove home in stunned silence.

CHAPTER 21

TIME TO CHANGE

Bobby was buried on a beautiful spring day. Pete, like everyone else, hated funerals. He reluctantly rode to the funeral with Frankie and Ray, and sat silently in the backseat. Ray had borrowed his dad's car for the service; they had agreed that the Cadillac was more suited for a funeral than Ray's VW Bug, or Pete's raggedy party van. There wasn't much talking on the ride, just the occasional, "Fuck, I can't believe he's dead," that Frankie seemed to keep muttering every few minutes. They were devastated and shocked by Bobby's death, but until today they had been able to deal with it by avoiding any reminders of him and storing the incident in secret little compartments in their minds. Today, they could no longer hide and were forced to face the world, so they drank beer, shared a bottle of whiskey, and smoked a couple of joints on the way to the services. When they arrived at the funeral home and pulled into the parking lot, they were stunned to find it full of people and cars. It instantly became clear that attendance was not limited to family and friends; it seemed like the whole valley had come out to say goodbye. They eventually found a parking space, and decided to employ some eye drops in a vain attempt to look somewhat presentable when they walked in.

The boys momentarily sat in the car and stared out the windows. They were in awe at how many people were in attendance. Shelton was a small town, and a teenager's violent death was shocking to the community. As they looked out the windows, they spotted cameramen from the local newspaper and television station. All three of them had an immediate and magnified sense of dread, but Pete was overcome not just with dread but with panic and he tried to convince the other two to leave, arguing that they would never be missed. He had experienced this collective grief before, and right now he didn't want to face Bobby's parents or talk to any reporters. He had never talked about Isaac or what had happened on the river with his best friends, and they never thought about it. When Pete stopped talking Ray and Frankie looked at him with a combination of shock and disgust. Frankie told Pete to shut up and grow a pair as he and Ray opened their doors and got out of the car. Pete took one last look out the window, swallowed the lump in his throat and reluctantly got out. The three of them gathered at the back of the car and inspected each other for defects in their appearances, and after finding none, they hurried inside. They strategically weaved between cars to avoid the reporters mining the parking lot for an interesting quip.

When they opened the heavy doors and walked into the old, dark paneled funeral home it was instantly apparent to Pete that the emotions being expressed at this funeral were quite different from those at Grandpa Nevers'. He was old, and his death was expected; Bobby was young, and this was completely unexpected, and senseless. Grandpa Nevers' mourners were sad; these people were in shock and filled with anger. As they entered the parlor, their eyes were drawn to the casket at the front of the room. It was a beautiful mahogany casket with shiny brass trim. Half of the lid was open to allow family and friends to look at him one last time. Surrounding Bobby's casket were numerous pictures and flowers and several people were silently looking at the pictures that reminisced Bobby's existence. The pictures reflected the short journey of his life, from sweet little Bobby on his tricycle all the way to his junior prom. The pictures showed a happy boy, full of sunshine, always smiling and having fun.

They stood just inside the doors, momentarily glancing around the room at the people in attendance; they saw several kids that they knew from school, many of whom were crying for a person they'd never known. Pete caught a glimpse of Andy Kennedy. Their eyes met, they nodded at each other, and then they looked away. They quickly spotted Bobby's parents; they were standing beside the casket shaking hands with people as they finished their viewing. Bobby's mom was a mess-she cried openly and loudly-and his father wasn't doing much better. They were in their late forties, but now looked closer to sixty. They looked feeble as they alternated between hugging, shaking hands, and wiping tears. They were clearly struggling to deal with the shocking loss of their only child.

The boys decided to get in line and pay their respects, but when they started to move towards the casket their eyes met those of the parents, and they instantly felt unwelcome. Frankie shrugged off their contemptuous glares and continued to lead the way. Pete and Ray, standing behind him, glanced at each other, and the expression on their faces confirmed that neither was sure if it was a good idea, but they followed anyways.

When they reached the casket, they saw their friend dressed in a perfect black suit and laying in a bed of white silk. His hands were crossed on his chest and in his hands were a crucifix and rosary. His eyes were closed, but he didn't look peaceful; he looked pissed. Frankie and Ray couldn't help but well up and start to cry. They thought that they'd been the last people to see him alive, and they'd been insulting him as he'd walked off to his death. Pete was almost overcome and wanted to scream out and tell everyone that it was his fault that Bobby was laying there. More than anything, he wanted to be dead.

They continued the procession and a moment later stepped aside and looked at a few pictures through blurry eyes before finally standing before Bobby's parents. Frankie somberly extended his hand to Bobby's father, who looked at the hand, and then at Frankie as if he was a leper. Their eyes met, and Frankie could feel the cold daggers piercing his soul. He withdrew his hand, and turned towards Bobby's mother, who had stopped crying and was now staring at the boys. Her cold eyes went from boy to boy, and it was apparent that she regarded them as the spawns of Satan himself.

Frankie mournfully looked at Bobby's mom and quietly said, "I'm sorry, we never meant for any of this to happen."

"What you meant to happen doesn't mean a whole lot to me. The only thing that matters is what did happen, and now my son is in that box, while you three are living it up," she hissed a low and hate-filled voice.

They hadn't known what to expect when they'd arrived, but they hadn't prepared for this. Pete and Ray were still standing behind Frankie and understood that it was time to leave. Frankie lowered his head, turned, and walked out the door, with Pete and Ray following close behind.

When they got back into the car, they sat in silence for a moment, and then Frankie slammed his hands on the dashboard and angrily proclaimed, "Fuck them, he was an asshole anyways. Sweet little Bobby, my ass! He was a self-centered, egotistical asshole that was always running his mouth. Everyone knew that sooner or later somebody was going to kill him; it just happened sooner than we all thought." He sat staring out the windshield for a moment with tears in his eyes, and then he turned to Pete in the backseat, "Give me that bottle and light a joint. Let's go to Indian Wells and get fucked up."

Ray started the car, and that's exactly what they did. When they completed the short drive to the park, the three of them hiked to the top of the falls in their black funeral suits and spent the rest of the day getting drunk and venting their anger at the humiliation they had endured while trying to be respectful. Eventually they ran out of whiskey, and late in the afternoon, Ray took them home.

Pete didn't do any work for the rest of the school year and only went to school a couple of times. He was allowed to graduate because of sympathy over the tragic events that had unfolded, but he didn't bother attending the actual event; he got his diploma in the mail. He rarely saw Ray or Frankie after the funeral. He quit his job and didn't take their calls. Pete was back in a daze. He was silent and brooding again, but now he was drinking alone, and heavily.

ANNE DIDN'T KNOW WHAT TO do about her son. He had been forced to endure so much pain and loss in such a short life. She tried to comfort and encourage him; but she too, was lost and her empty words gave him no inspiration. Eventually she surrendered to the stone wall that had become her son's persona and decided to give him space and time to deal with it in his own way.

Bill had finally started to emerge from the fog that had enveloped his mind for years. He was now scared for his son, but he was unsure of what to do, so he did nothing.

PETE WAS LYING IN BED late one evening in early July, unable to sleep, when he decided to go to a bar and get really drunk.

While he sat alone at the bar, drinking shot after shot, an old man who lived down the road was also unable to sleep, but for very different reasons.

"You want to go out, boy? Hell, I can't sleep anyway," the old man said to his dog. Mr. Johnson got the leash off the hook and attached it to his German Sheppard, Zeus. Together, they walked into the night air. This was becoming all too common; he was reduced to sleeping a couple hours at a time and hadn't had a full night's sleep in many months. He was a proud and portly man on the wrong side of sixty with white hair and a large nose. He had been a widower for several years and had gotten used to Zeus being his only companion.

It had taken decades after he'd come home from the Pacific for the dreams to subside, and now that he'd come to the inescapable conclusion that the company his grandfather had started would end with him, the dreams had returned.

He'd tried everything he could think of to keep the business going, but it just wasn't working. Johnson's Metal Works would close for the last time next Friday. He'd worked very hard to find jobs for the people he'd had to let go. He'd been successful for many, but not everyone, and that haunted him.

He always thought that there was something more he could have done, something he should have done. These thoughts were the same ones that had haunted his sleep years before. He kept seeing the pleading faces of the young men dying in the sand and mud on those islands. He'd always felt he should have done more to keep them safe.

As he ambled along the bank of the Housatonic River with Zeus, he noticed a disturbance a few feet ahead of him. There was a fight. Two young men were going at it pretty hard. He was not averse to men fighting and considered it a very normal part of a man's life. He'd been in many brawls when he was young, but he also knew that he had a duty to make sure no one was seriously hurt.

As he drew closer, he could hear their voices and was able to clearly see the events unfolding before him. The larger of the two was punching the other repeatedly. When the smaller man collapsed in a heap, he stopped punching, waved his hand over his fallen opponent, and tried to walk away, but the other man staggered to his feet and attacked him again by jumping on his back. The larger man threw him off and defended himself again by sidestepping his charging opponent and hitting the other one a couple more times. It was a complete mismatch, but the smaller man was clearly the antagonist. He was screaming threats and insults while spitting blood through his battered face. Then he charged again, but he made no attempt to block the punches or to even hit back. Mr. Johnson shuttered at what he was witnessing and hurried his pace.

When he got closer, he recognized the smaller one as Bill Taylor's son. Mr. Johnson's heart burst because knew more about this family's tragedy than he ever let on. When he got close enough, he could see Pete's face; it was a bloody mess. He was staggering around his opponent and Mr. Johnson wasn't sure if it was from the beating or the drunkenness, but he knew he had to stop this now.

"What the hell are you doing? Knock it off or I let the dog loose," Mr. Johnson yelled at the two. Zeus felt the apprehension and heard the tone in his master's voice and became agitated and started barking feverishly.

"Good, get this crazy bastard to stop. He's fucking nuts!" the larger man yelled.

As he finished saying that, Pete lunged at him again. This time, when the larger man stepped to the side, he hit him with a hard right hand that sent Pete crashing to the ground.

"Stay there, you asshole, and leave me the fuck alone," the larger man yelled. Mr. Johnson and Zeus hurried over to Pete. Pete tried to get up again, but this time Mr. Johnson hit him with his cane and Zeus gave a low growl as he looked menacingly at Pete.

"Peter Taylor, you sit your ass down right now!" Mr. Johnson commanded. Pete was stunned to hear his name and obeyed the old man. He succumbed to the whiskey and beating and laid his head down in the dirt and passed out. Mr. Johnson looked at the larger man and apologized for Pete's actions and told him that he would take care of the boy. He explained that he knew the family and that Pete was going through a hard time, but wasn't a terrible kid. The large man calmed down, brushed himself off, and began explaining to Mr. Johnson what had happened.

"We're in the bar and he walks up to me and just pours a drink on me without saying a word, and then walks over to the doors and holds them open and just glares at me. What the hell am I supposed to do? I follow him out. We come out here and it's just the two of us. I try to talk to him, but the little bastard never says a word; he just punches me in the face. So what can I do? I hit him back, but he don't do nothing; he just lets me punch him over and over. Every time I try to walk away, he jumps on me. What the fuck? I ain't never seen nothing like this. It's like he's got a death wish or something." The man was clearly shaken by what had just happened and waved his hands in disgust at Pete and Mr. Johnson as he finally walked away.

Mr. Johnson bent down and lifted Pete's head out of the dirt. He took out his handkerchief and wiped Pete's face. He examined it for serious damage. His face was battered, but there were only a few small cuts over his eyes. Most of the blood came from his nose and split lip. Mr. Johnson reasoned that he was busted up pretty good and might have a broken nose, but he would be all right. He got Pete to his feet and walked him back to his house, where he sat Pete in a chair and got some ice for his face. As Pete started regaining his senses, he took in his surroundings. The kitchen he sat in was small, but very clean. The small white Formica covered table was against the wall, and it only had two chairs. The cabinets and appliances looked old, but well maintained. Pete noticed the toaster on the counter and saw the rounded shape and decided it was older than he was. He wanted to leave, but Mr. Johnson was having none of it.

"What the hell's the matter with you, boy? This isn't the way to live your life. Hell, if you're going to get into a fight with a big galoot like that, at least learn to lead with your left," Mr. Johnson said as he handed Pete a glass of cold water. Pete laughed a little and then cringed from the pain.

"Go ahead and drink it; you'll be amazed." Pete hesitated but complied. He put the glass to his bloody and swollen lips and drank. He could feel the cold water travel down his esophagus and reach his gut, reviving him as it went. He finished the glass, and Mr. Johnson refilled it, sat down at the table, and looked at Pete. He was a mess and not just from the beating he'd just received. Pete knew the old man was sizing him up and he didn't like it.

"Thank you, sir, I appreciate the help, but I need to get going." Pete had started to get up when the old man raised his voice again.

"You sit your ass down, Peter Taylor, until I'm done with you," Mr. Johnson demanded. Pete complied again. This man reminded him so much of Grandpa Nevers that he felt compelled to obey his commands.

"You know, I've never seen such a display of stupidity in all my life. I know you've gotten hit pretty hard by life, there's no doubt about that, but Jesus man, what the hell are you doing? Believe me, I know it's hard, but you'd better learn that life is for the living," the old man started in.

Pete was insulted by the lecture coming from someone he didn't even know, and the anger began welling up inside him. He had never been disrespectful to an old man before, especially one that had gone out of his way to help him, but he knew he wasn't going to sit there and listen to much more.

The old man saw the demeanor change in Pete. "You have no idea who I am, do you?" Mr. Johnson asked Pete.

"No. Should I?" Pete replied.

"I don't know. You're grandfather worked for my father and your father works for me," Mr. Johnson said.

Pete felt a lightning bolt go through him. He glared at the old man through his swollen eyes and sat up in his seat. His pleasant thoughts of Grandpa Nevers were gone and he just knew that this old man was going to stick this in his dad's face first thing Monday morning, and then it was going to come right back to him. He had now embarrassed both his grandfather and his father in one smooth motion. The repercussions of this event were going to haunt him for a while and he knew it. He was already looking forward to the upcoming fight with his dad.

"So, what now? Are you going to call them and shove my stupidity in their faces? Maybe it'll get you a good laugh at the club," Pete said as he set down his glass and started to get up.

"Hell, why didn't you have that much spirit when that galoot was beating the crap out of you?" Mr. Johnson said with a tinge of anger in his voice. He paused for a moment and then continued in a calmer voice, "You know your dad saved my life, and more than once," the old man said to Pete in a far away voice.

Pete pulled the ice off of his face and looked at Mr. Johnson differently.

"Okay, I'll bite. So how did my father save your life?" Pete asked. Mr. Johnson's face was all business again. He looked at Peter and gave a little knowing smile.

"Your father was born on Sunday, September 7, 1941. Do you want to know how I know that?" he asked Pete. Pete looked surprised.

"No. How do you know that? What do you do, keep files on all your employees?"

"No, no, I'm not Hoover or Nixon or anything like that; I have better things to do with my time. But I will tell you why I know that date and why it means so much to me. You see, I shipped out for the beautiful South Pacific on Monday the eighth. I was planning on going out with my buddies for one last romp, but, just when I was about to leave, my father gave me a card and made me go to the hospital to bring it to your grandparents.

Well, when I got to the hospital, your grandfather was a wreck, but he sure was proud of his baby boy. I hated hospitals then, and I still do, so I wanted to get the hell out of there fast, but your grandfather insisted I hold the new baby. Well, to tell you the truth, that was the first time I'd ever held a newborn baby and I was scared to death, but when I held that baby in my arms and looked into his eyes, I felt something I had never felt before. Then I looked at your grandparents, and well, they were just bursting with pride. I shipped out early the next morning and a couple of months later, in late November, I guess, I received a picture of that baby boy and your grandparents. I was touched. I couldn't believe they'd thought of me, and so I kept that picture with me for a long time. When things got tough, I would pull it out and stare at it. It reminded me of why I had to keep fighting and why I could never give up. We had a hell of a time over there, and more than once I wanted to give up and let those Jap bastards just finish me off…. I was tired." Mr. Johnson's voice drifted as he said those last words, and his mind was flooded with images from long ago. He sat silently and stared into space for a moment before Pete broke the silence.

"I'm sorry, Mr. Johnson, I didn't know any of that," Pete said softly. "I didn't mean to screw up your night. I'll just make my way out. Thank you for the water." Pete then got up and put the glass in the sink. He walked past the old man quietly, holding him in a much different light. He reached the screen door and opened it. With his head lowered, he turned for one last look at the old man, and had turned again to leave when he heard the old man's voice.

"What the hell are you going to do?"

"Oh, I'll just walk back to my van; it's not too far," Pete said halfway out the door.

"No, not tonight, son. I mean with your life. Are you just going to keep beating the hell out of yourself until that gets boring? Or maybe you'll just keep going to bars and find some other apes to do it for you?"

"Excuse me?" Pete said to the old man, stunned by what he had just said.

The old man was quiet for a moment and then he looked directly at Pete, who saw kindness and warmth in his eyes. Pete was caught off guard and was unsure of what he was supposed to feel or what he was supposed to do.

"I understand pain and I know about nightmares. God, I hated to sleep for years. I wanted someone to kill me for so long just to end the nightmares. Every time I closed my eyes I saw their faces. Staring at me, begging me to save them, but I couldn't. I could never understand why I was alive and they weren't." His voice was filled with pain and his eyes became vacant as he stared into the glass of water that he twirled between his hands.

Pete stopped when he heard about the dreams. He came back into the house and shut the door. He walked over and sat back down at the table and stared at the old man. They were silent for a moment. Pete suddenly felt drained and his eyes began to water.

"I hate the dreams. I hate closing my eyes and I get so tired. I just can't take it anymore," Pete said in a quivering voice.

He crossed his hands on the table in front of him and put his battered face down as the tears began to flow. He felt an uncontrollable wave of emotion come over him. He often woke in the middle of the night in a cold sweat with his heart racing. He believed that if he told anyone about them he would be acting like a weak child crying over the boogeyman, but it had now gotten to the point where he didn't sleep unless he passed out from drugs or booze. It had been bad before, but since Bobby's death, the nightmares had been horrendous.

"I know, son. Don't worry; just let it go." Mr. Johnson watched the young man begin to weep openly and uncontrollably. He let him continue, knowing that he had years of tension built up that he was finally letting go of. After a moment, he continued.

"Life's hard, son, and it damn sure isn't fair. I don't know all the answers. Hell, I don't know all the questions, but I do know this. If you keep looking back, you can't go forward without crashing. Do you understand what I'm saying? Don't let the past destroy your future. You're alive, and it's up to you to make that mean something." The old man looked at Pete, who lifted his head and wiped his eyes.

"I'm sorry about that. I can't believe I just did that, Mr. Johnson," Pete said as he lifted his head and wiped his nose with his sleeve. He was obviously ashamed at breaking down and crying in front of a man he barely knew.

"The things that haunt us are not always the things we did; it's the things that; in hindsight, we think that we should have or could have done. I know I could have saved more men if I had done things differently, but I didn't and they didn't come home. At dawn on April 9th, 1942, General Edward P. King, surrendered to the Japanese. Now the Japanese have no respect for someone who surrenders. See, the majority of them have a different religion than we do. They believe in reincarnation and that the soul leaves one body when it dies, and enters another forty days later. A brave and honorable man moves higher in status the next time; a coward moves down and is nothing more than a dog. They looked at us like we were seventy five thousand cowardly dogs." He paused and then slowly finished the story. "As they marched us along, anyone who fell was bayoneted; they didn't waste bullets on someone who was already dead. After a couple of days of this, I knew I couldn't stay there. So, I escaped. I know that because of me, they killed other men as punishment… other young boys who wanted to live too. I eventually made my way through the jungle and found allies. When McArthur said, 'I shall return,' I said 'Yeah, and I'll be here waiting for you.' I hooked up with the Chinese resistance, where I found a real friend. He was a little Iowa farm boy that went on to become a General."

Mr. Johnson paused again, and a little smile came across his face. "He was a tough son of a bitch. Anyways, I don't want to bore you with a bunch of old war stories, but what I'm trying to say to you, son, is that just because horrendous things happen and you get to live while others don't, well, it doesn't make you a bad person. What you need to do is find a purpose for your life." The old man took a deep breath, looked through Pete and into his past. Pete could tell that the memories had taken a toll on him and he was worn out. "All right, enough of that. Go home and try to get some sleep. It's okay; I'll speak with you again."

Pete looked at him and knew that he was tired and it was time to go. With a different attitude, Pete rose and left. When he was gone, Mr. Johnson picked up the phone.

CHAPTER 22

THE MEETING

Bill rolled over in his bed because he thought he heard the doorbell ring, but when he looked at the alarm clock, it read seven AM, and it was a Saturday. He chalked it up to a vivid dream and rolled onto his stomach. He puffed his pillow and put his head back down, desperately wanting another hour of sleep. An instant later he heard it again, and this time Anne stirred as well. He angrily got out of bed and mumbled to himself as he put on a pair of pants. He was visibly annoyed that someone was ringing the doorbell at this time of the morning.

He made his way to the front door with his tee shirt hanging out, his eyes half closed, and his hair messed up from his interrupted sleep. When he reached the door, he looked through the small window, and standing at his front door was the owner of Johnson's Metal Works, Benjamin Johnson. The sight of him at his front door hit Bill like a lightning bolt. His eyes were wide and he was instantly awake. He hesitated for a moment to gather himself, and when his head cleared, he knew his career at Johnson's had officially come to an end.

He opened the door and forced a smile on his face as he welcomed his boss into his home. He wanted to be angry at Mr. Johnson, but he knew there was no reason to be. Mr. Johnson had always treated him better than he deserved to be treated.

"Mr. Johnson, please come in. I'm sorry I wasn't awake. We weren't expecting you this morning. I'd offer you a cup of coffee, but we haven't put it on yet. If you have a few minutes, I'll put some on." Bill ushered Mr. Johnson into the kitchen where, to Bill's chagrin, he sat down at the table and accepted the offer.

Mr. Johnson looked at Bill. "Bill, I wish....."

At that moment Anne walked into the kitchen absent-mindedly tying her bathrobe. When she finished her knot and looked up, she noticed their company and momentarily froze in place. She recovered quickly and continued towards the men in her kitchen as if nothing out of the ordinary was occurring and started the morning coffee, but behind her façade, her heart sank because she knew that Bill no longer had a job.

Mr. Johnson, always the gentleman, rose from his chair as she approached the table. Bill looked up at her but remained seated.

"Oh, Mr. Johnson, how nice to see you. Please forgive my appearance, but I haven't had my coffee yet," Anne said. She was caught off guard by this unexpected visit and was quite nervous, but remained stoic as she joined them at the table.

"I do apologize for waking you up so early, but I have some things I need to discuss with Bill, and because it concerns both of you, I thought I would come here and talk to the two of you."

Anne looked at Bill, who sat across from her. They were all trying to put a friendly face on this meeting, but all three were clearly filled with a nervous dread.

"I received a phone call yesterday," Ben lied. "I have an old friend in Niceville, Florida, and he and his son have an engineering firm there. They are in desperate need of a quality engineer, and with the way things are here, I immediately thought of you." Ben stopped speaking and looked at the coffee maker as it burped out a blast of steam and water.

"It looks like the coffee is done, and I could sure use a cup," he said.

Without hesitation, Anne got up and poured three cups. She placed a cup on the table in front of Mr. Johnson and offered him cream and sugar, which he accepted. She then handed Bill his cup and, with hers in hand, she sat down as Ben continued.

"The truth is, we'll close the doors for the last time on Friday. Of course, we will have a severance package for you and all that, but we'll discuss that this week. What I really wanted to do was to talk to you about this opportunity as soon as possible so that the two of you can have the weekend to think about it. I hope you can let me know on Monday so I'll be able to let Art know of your decision and he can take the appropriate actions." Ben took a sip from his coffee and then broached the subject he'd really come to talk about.

"How is Peter doing?" he asked, and then looked at Bill and Anne, knowing the stock answer was about to come.

"He's doing fine," they both said, almost in unison.

Bill continued, "He graduated last month, but still hasn't decided what he wants to do." He was surprised that Ben Johnson even knew his son's name.

"That must be his old van outside," Mr. Johnson said with a little knowing grin. "Oh.... I remember being his age. It was a rough and tumble world back then and I guess it still is today. Listen, if you decide to take this job, how do you think Pete would like Florida?"

"Oh, I don't know. This is where he's always lived-this is where we've all always lived-but, who knows, he might like the change. I don't know," Anne said, nervously looking at her husband.

She was frightened and unprepared for this conversation. She knew things were bad downtown-everyone knew things were bad-but Johnson's had always been there. Her head was spinning and her stomach twisting.

"You know, I saw him last night," Ben interjected. Anne and Bill looked at him with concern and disbelief. They were now scared of what they were about to hear. Their minds naturally went to the worst.

"Was everything all right?" Bill asked. He was trying to act calm, but was clearly shaken.

"Well, to tell you the truth, he had a rough night. I take it you haven't seen him this morning?"

Anne and Bill looked at each other and shook their heads in unison as they responded in the negative.

"I hate to speak out of place and don't want to put my nose where it doesn't belong, but he got in a little tussle with a pretty big man last night. I broke up the fight and brought him to my house to clean him up. He has a few cuts and will be black and blue, but no major damage. Now, he's going to be sore for a while, there's no doubt about that, but he'll be fine."

Bill and Anne were now both embarrassed by and scared for their son. When they first glanced at each other, their expressions were ones of surprise, as if Pete's trouble had come out of the blue; but when their eyes met and they saw each other for the first time in a long time, they were overcome with guilt.

The truth hit them like a hard slap in the face. They had concentrated on themselves and their feelings for so long that they had let their son raise himself. As long as the police hadn't called and he'd graduated high school, they'd told themselves that everything was fine.

"While he was at my house, we talked for a while, and I got the feeling that he hasn't talked to you much about it, but the truth is, he's still having a hard time dealing with the accident. Now please understand me, he has no reason to feel guilty about what happened, but that doesn't matter; he does. Survivor's guilt can eat a person up. Believe me, I know; I had a hard time for years myself." Ben looked at the two of them and tried to give them some sage advice. "You see, when you survive and the others don't, you get to the point where you hate yourself, and if you hate yourself, well, you end up hating everyone and everything else too. You don't feel like you have the right to laugh, or enjoy a beautiful flower. No, he's not a bad person, but sometimes he thinks he is. I think that when terrible things happen to the people that surround you and they don't happen to you, well, you can be overcome with emotions so strong that they fill you with an emptiness that eats you from the inside out. It can be horrible and takes some time and a great deal of love to heal those wounds. Do you understand what I'm trying to say?"

Ben paused and took another sip of his coffee. He looked at Bill and Anne again before solemnly continuing. He knew that all three of them had been battling with the same feelings, and so did they.

"You know, this town is changing… hell, the whole world is changing. Our factories were built at the turn of the century and we're competing with cheap labor and brand new factories all across the world. We blew 'em up, and now we build 'em up; it's a hell of a thing. It's hard to compete with progress. It's not like it was years ago and maybe it's time we change too. I can't tell you what to do, but I would like you to give serious consideration to Art's offer. There's one good thing about getting into the defense industry, it's a pretty stable enterprise because, unfortunately, I just don't think we'll ever run out of enemies. If you decide to do it, we can work out the details and I'll do everything in my power to help work things out."

He took the last sip from his coffee cup and rose to leave.

"I think a new environment might be good for us all," Ben hesitated for a moment and looked out the window at Anne's flower garden. She had red roses climbing on white trellises, red and white tulips with the purple and white pansies, and several other flowers that were brightened by the morning sun and were enchanting, and for a brief moment, Ben let his mind enjoy them.

He returned to the present and looked at his hosts and their home. It was a nice enough home, with dark wood cabinets in the small kitchen and thick green shag carpet in the paneled living room. The house was nice, but the homeowners were a mess and it wasn't because he had woken them up. He thought back to the company Christmas party of just a few years ago. Bill and Anne were then a young, dedicated, and honorable couple raising two wonderful boys. They'd beamed with happiness and had seemed to be on the road to enjoying a storybook life, but now Anne's eyes were tired. The lines on her face showed the strain of these last few years. She looked like she'd aged ten years in the past few and Bill was just going through the motions. They were existing, not living.

"Mrs. Taylor, I would like to thank you for welcoming me into your beautiful home. I only wish it was under better circumstances, but perhaps it will all work out for the best," he said as he reached out and shook her hand in a soft and gentle manner.

He turned and reached out his right hand to Bill. When Bill accepted the offered handshake, Ben Johnson put his left hand over Bill's and looked him in the eye. Bill returned the old man's gaze and was suddenly filled with a strange feeling of comfort, warmth, and security. He felt shielded and protected and knew that the man in front of him was giving him an opportunity to get his life back, and he desperately wanted to live again.

Bill walked Ben to the door and stood watching him as he got in his car and left. He walked back into the kitchen and was drawn to Anne's eyes. She was shaken and scared as she sat at the table, grasping her coffee cup with both hands. She was not feeling all that warm and secure. She felt like her son was about to lose his life, her husband had just lost his job, and she was being asked to leave the town that her grandparents had been born in almost a century before. She reached over to the counter next to the table and grabbed her bottle of Valium. She had started to open it when Bill gently put his hands over hers.

"Not yet, okay? We can do this. Let's talk about what we need to do and we'll decide together. We can make things better and I want to do this with you. I'm tired of living like this. Listen, Honey, let's make a nice breakfast. We'll wake up Pete in a while and sit down and figure this out together," Bill said as he looked earnestly into his wife's eyes.

Anne looked at her husband in disbelief that he would just assume that after all this time he could flip a switch and everything would be forgotten. She yanked her hands away from his and thought about eating a couple of her pills just to spite him, but instead, just put them back on the counter, got up without saying anything, and started breakfast. She wasn't ready to be excited about their life being thrown into upheaval again.

Bill watched her as she pulled the eggs and bacon out of the refrigerator. He was offended by her rebuke and his warm and fuzzy feeling was quickly replaced by one of anger.

"I'm taking the job and moving to Florida. Are you coming with me?"

Bill was shocked that those words had come out of his mouth and wanted to pull them back before he'd finished saying them. He knew Anne's reaction was going to be bad and she didn't disappoint. She slammed the frying pan on the stove after deciding against putting it upside Bill's head.

"You son of a bitch! Who the hell do you think you are? I'm moving to Florida, I'm moving to Florida! After all this time and all we've been through here, you think you're going to just tell me that line of bullshit. You better listen to me, Mister! I have family here, I have a life, and don't you ever say something like that to me again!"

She was livid and Bill knew it was time to retreat. He couldn't understand why he felt more at peace and confident with this decision than he had with anything since the accident. Suddenly, it hit him and he understood: it was ending. The memories that haunted this family would be allowed to fade into their proper place. He would no longer have to live in and look at this house with its haunting memories of Isaac everywhere. He wouldn't have to drive along and over that damn ice-covered river ever again.

He looked at Anne again and knew she was not as confident. He walked over to his wife and gently put his hands on her shoulders and spoke slowly and softly to her. She turned her head and looked at her husband. There was sincerity in his eyes, and she hadn't seen that in a long time.

"Anne, I'm sorry. That came out wrong."

"You bet your sweet ass it did!" She responded, still angry at Bill for his arrogant statement.

She pulled away from him and began to slam pieces of bacon onto the frying pan. Bill stood back and looked at his wife as she worked; he believed that the glassy sheen that was now forming in her eyes revealed that she was scared by the incredible uncertainty that had just been heaped upon their family, and he didn't blame her. She didn't want to leave everything she had always known, and because Bill suddenly felt like there was an opportunity at happiness again, the emotional wall he had built around himself began to crumble, and he actually felt like he understood her, and, for the first time in many years, he tried earnestly to respond like the loving husband he'd been so long ago.

He placed his hands back on her shoulders and gently turned her around. He looked deeply into her eyes, and this time she returned his gaze. She began to feel calmer, and some of the fear began to ebb as he held her at arm's length and spoke softly to her.

"Anne, it's a chance at a new beginning, and we may never have this opportunity again. Let's talk with Pete when he gets up and see how he feels about it." Bill paused and took a breath to gather his thoughts. "I'm sorry for what I said, and I'm sorry about everything that's happened. Can you honestly give it a chance and think about what this could mean for our family?"

Anne continued to look into her husband's eyes.

"Let me cook breakfast, Bill," she said and slowly pulled away from her husband. She was still upset and scared, but calmer. Bill's hands fell to his side and he reluctantly stepped back and gave her the space she needed.

"I'll go shave and get dressed," he said somberly.

As he turned and started walking to the bathroom, Pete came into the kitchen. Bill heard him enter the room and turned to look at his son. His lips were swollen and discolored, his eyes were both black and blue, and there was a nasty little cut above his left eye. Bill thought that he had prepared himself for this, but he was still caught off guard by his son's appearance.

"Holy shit! Did you get in a fight with Joe Frazier?" Bill asked, trying to take Ben's advice and not jump on the boy.

Anne's eyes grew big and she was clearly taken aback by the damage done to her little boy. Even though he was now an eighteen-year-old young man, he was and always would be his momma's baby, and it hurt her to see his face so disfigured.

"Oh, my God. What have you done to yourself?" she gasped.

Pete let a crooked smile painfully come across his face as he tried to convince his mother that it looked worse than it really was.

"I guess I got the wrong guy mad at me," he said lightheartedly, trying to calm and reassure his mother. "But don't worry, Mom, it looks a lot worse than it really is. I'm fine, I swear. I just won't do any modeling for a week or two, that's all!"

"Don't you tell me it's fine when your face looks like that! Sit down and let me look at you. Oh, my God, Peter." Anne sat down and looked at her boy and then at her husband. The reality of their family's situation hit her like a cold hard slap in the face. She was ready for change.

"Peter, Mr. Johnson was here this morning," she said calmly to her son.

Pete closed his eyes and looked away from his parents, clearly upset by the news and convinced that the old man had betrayed him.

"He offered your father a new job in Florida. We want to see how you feel about it, because moving there would be a big change for all of us. I know you've graduated from high school now and you don't have to move with us if you don't want to, but we were really hoping that if we did this, that you would come with us," Anne said to her son.

She was looking at her baby; he was hurt and she had to protect him. She held his hands tenderly as she spoke to him. Pete was astonished and looked at her and then at his father, who was now leaning back against the stove and observing his wife and son.

"Can you give me an hour to pack?" he asked with a painful grin.

"Now Peter, don't you want to give it some time and think about it? This is a really big decision," Anne asked, surprised by Pete's response.

"Mom, what's there to think about? Shelton or a beach in Florida: come on, that's an easy one! So where is this job? Miami? Orlando? Daytona?"

"It's in Niceville," Bill replied.

Pete got a confused look on his battered face.

"Niceville? Where is that?"

"To tell you the truth, I have no idea. Give me a minute, I'll get an atlas and we can find out together. We were caught off guard by the offer this morning and I didn't think to ask where Niceville was. He came over to let us know that they're closing Johnson's for good this week and I'm going to be laid off, but apparently Mr. Johnson has an old war buddy that's in need of an engineer."

"What else did you guys talk about?" Pete asked suspiciously; he knew there had to be a catch.

"Oh, you want to know if he told us about your adventure last night...." Bill said. "Well, he did mention it and he asked how you were. He said that he stumbled upon you last night and that you had gotten into a fight with a big 'galoot.' He told us that he took you back to his house and cleaned you up a bit and talked with you for a few minutes to make sure that you were all right, and then sent you on your way. That's about it. He didn't say anything bad about you, if that's what you want to know." Bill paused for a moment and came over and sat at the table with his wife and son. "He did say that he thought you might still be having a hard time with Isaac's death. I'm sorry for not being there for you, Pete...."

Pete looked away; he was embarrassed by the attention and not sure how he was supposed to feel. He was sure that his father was lying to him about what the old man had said. He imagined what was in their conversation about the screwed up kid who was trying to kill himself by getting his ass kicked. Hell, why else would he want to send them to Florida?

"That's stupid. I'm fine. Don't worry about me," Pete disdainfully replied to them.

His misconceptions of the conversation that had taken place in his absence caused his mood to change drastically. Pete didn't want to talk about his problems with his parents. Hell, he really didn't want to talk to them at all. Suddenly, a knowing smirk came to his face when he realized that this was the longest conversation they had had in a long time.

"I know you're fine, son. I have faith in you," Bill said tentatively, "Let me get that atlas so we can find the super metropolis of Niceville, Florida." Bill then got up and retrieved the atlas from the other room.

When he returned, he opened it to Florida, and the three of them crowded around it and started searching. Pete's mood lightened as they began their quest. They started at Miami, where they hoped it would be near, and then they started moving their fingers north. Palm Beach, Orlando, Tampa on the west coast, Daytona, Jacksonville, but still no Niceville. They then started to move their fingers west….. Tallahassee, Panama City…..

"Oh, my God! Pete exclaimed when he finally found it. "It's this little dot right there between Panama City and Pensacola. Is that really considered Florida?" Pete asked. There was a little let down in his voice, but he continued. "Just let me know when it is time to go and I'll be ready. I need to do a few things to the van, and then I'm more than ready to get out of here."

Pete was disappointed that he wasn't moving to Miami, but he really didn't care where they were moving, as long as it was out of Connecticut. He would have moved to Panama, let alone Panama City. He got up from the table and went back upstairs to his room, and began thinking about what he was taking and what he was leaving behind. As he was looking at his posters, his concert ticket collection, pictures, and the various other things he'd collected over the years, his mind wandered, and he began to reminisce about his time growing up in Connecticut and the people he'd met. He was haunted by tragedy, but he'd had a lot of fun and there'd been a lot of good people that he'd been fortunate to meet and get to know. But it was time for him to move on, so he crumpled up the posters and threw them and the concert tickets in the garbage can. He felt a great relief as he did so; the nightmare was ending.

Bill and Anne looked at each other as they sat alone at the table.

"Work out the details with Mr. Johnson. I'll call the realtor on Monday," Anne said, and returned to cooking breakfast.

Both Bill and Anne were in a state of shock from the events that had just unfurled. They had never even given any thought to leaving their home and now, in just a few minutes time, it seemed that it had been decided that they were moving to the other side of the country.

They felt like they were caught up in a giant whirlwind and that things were spinning out of control, but Bill felt the same way that Pete did; if he could leave this afternoon, he would. And so it was agreed upon: Connecticut offered nothing but pain for this family and it was time to move on.

CHAPTER 23

PREPARING FOR THE TRIP

"Are you sure you want to do this?" Bill asked Anne for the tenth time in two days.

He sat at the kitchen table excitedly sipping his coffee and getting ready to leave for work. This would be her last chance to back out. He knew she wouldn't, but he'd asked again anyways. When he brought the steaming liquid to his lips he realized that he had a smile on his face; pleased with the change he was feeling, he quickly pondered the fact that he had woken up early and sang in the shower for the first time in a long time. He couldn't help himself; he was excited, happy, and ready to leave at that very moment.

Anne set her cup on the table and grasped it with both hands. She glared at her husband and was repulsed by his gloating little smirk and wanted to smack it off his face in the worst way. She was tired of listening to him going on and on about how things were going to be better for them in Florida and then asking her that same stupid question over and over, as if she had any chance of stopping the onslaught of events that they were caught in. She was so filled with anger that she was almost shaking.

"No, Bill, I don't want to do this. I do not want to pack up and leave everything and everyone I've known on a moment's notice, but I do want my son to have a chance at a decent life and I want my husband to have a goddamn job, so I'll do whatever I have to do in order to make that happen." She glared at him for a moment and then got up from the table and walked into the bathroom and slammed the door, effectively ending any chance at further conversation.

Bill was hurt and disappointed by Anne's attitude, but even her tantrum couldn't wipe the smile off his face. He wanted her to be as excited and happy about this opportunity as he was, but she wasn't. He looked out the window and saw the beginning of a new day and became resolute in the fact that after all they had been through, the change would indeed be good for the family. He could deal with Anne's anger for a little while longer. He knew that the important thing was that they were moving to Florida. He got up and refilled his cup for the ride in and left the house upbeat and excited for the first time in many years.

When he got in his car and turned the key to start the motor, the radio came on just like it did every morning. He heard the familiar voice of Bob Edwards on NPR's *Morning Edition,* who had accompanied him to work every morning since 1979. The news had become his driving companion and security blanket over the past several years because whenever he was in doubt, he could count on something happening somewhere to prove that life, all over this wretched planet, was nothing more than a never ending series of miserable events that justified his anger and self-loathing.

The smile momentarily left his face when he heard the Bob describe a house fire in Brooklyn that had killed two children. He quickly reached for the dial and changed the radio station. He fished through the dial, unsure of what he was looking for. He heard old songs and new ones, religious music and heavy metal. He kept searching for some unknown sound and then he heard the Righteous Brothers belt out "Unchained Melody," and that's when he pulled his hand from the radio, sat back in his seat, listened to the music, and let the smile return.

The soulful serenade pulled him back in time and released a warm memory of a much better time. He was almost there again; that quiet dirt road, lying on the hood of his car with Anne and looking at the stars on that cool and clear autumn evening. They were wrapped in a warm blanket and had snuggled together under the pretense of keeping warm, but they had been madly in love and used any excuse they could to hold each other. Bill closed his eyes and for a moment he was able to smell the perfume she had worn and feel her lips when they touched his.

When the song ended he was pulled back to reality and put the car in gear to begin the drive to work, but the smile never left his face again. His coffee tasted better and the air seemed fresher and cleaner than it had in years. He looked around as he drove and noticed that the sun had risen just enough to brighten parts of the trees in glorious morning light, while casting long sleepy shadows on the dew covered fields. The light and color combinations created a picturesque view that pleased him greatly. He felt like a blind man whose sight had been restored and was finally able to see the incredible beauty that had always surrounded him.

ANNE STOOD AT THE WINDOW, relieved to see him put the car in gear and leave. She had stared at him while he sat in his car with that revolting smile still on his face. He looked like a gloating, spoiled brat who had gotten the toy he wanted, and that made her seethe with anger. She thought about Isaac and how moving to Florida would make it impossible for her secret visits to his grave. Her husband wanted to take that away from her and forget all about their son. She understood Pete wanting to leave and felt no animosity towards him, but it just seemed to her that this was another example of her husband being a coward, and it made her despise the very thought of him.

She walked around the house and looked at everything that they had accumulated over the years. Each item she glanced at seemed to bring back the memory of where and when it came into their home. She glanced at a picture hanging on the wall of her kitchen. It had to be close to one hundred years old. It had hung on the wall of her grandmother's kitchen, right next to her favorite chair, forever. Precious memories of the short time they had spent together came flooding into her mind. Anne could almost see her smile and the gleam in her eye as she snuck an extra cookie to Anne without her mother knowing. Then she focused on the picture and thought of the pain she had endured and the people that she had lost. It wasn't fair. The picture she was looking at depicted Christ with his hands outstretched to her. She looked at it and grew angry.

"What have I ever done to you to deserve what you have done to me?"

She looked away from the picture and returned her memories to the storage compartment of her mind and began to focus on the tasks before her. How much time did she have to pack? What could she take with her? What did she have to leave behind, and how would she manage it all? She felt overwhelmed; everything was happening so fast her head was spinning. She paused and looked out the window at the spectacular yard that they were leaving behind and thought of all the hard work it had taken to make it this beautiful. She walked back to the kitchen, took her bottle off the counter, and took three pills.

IT WAS ALMOST AN HOUR later when Pete opened his eyes to begin the day. A vivid dream of he and Isaac at the river had robbed him of several hours of sleep during the night. Isaac was reaching out and calling to his brother and protector, but this time Peter didn't try to save him; he coldly turned and walked off the ice and got in a car with his father and left. Pete looked out the car window as they were driving off and saw Zak pleading and reaching out to him as he slid back into the river.

He lay in bed with his hands behind his head and tears in his eyes. His face still hurt, and was still very ugly, but not as bad as it had been the day before. He stared at the ceiling and was talking to Isaac while he laid there, begging forgiveness for his desire to leave Connecticut.

"I'm not leaving you, Zak, I promise, but I have to get the hell out of here one way or another. I love you, little brother, and I don't know what to do. I want to stay here for you, I really do, but it's pure hell for me. Mom and Dad are all fucked up, Johnson's is going under, and I have no future here; none of us do. If we stay here, we're just going to keep on living like this until we all die a slow and miserable death. I'm not abandoning you, little brother, I promise you I'm not, but I need a life. Please forgive me, Zak, please."

He wiped his eyes with his forearm, sat up and put his feet on the floor. He sat hunched over for a minute rubbing his eyes with the palm of his hands and then took a deep breath to gather his senses and made his way to the bathroom. Pete looked in the mirror and saw his face; like everything else in his life, it was all messed up. He thought of Grandpa Nevers and Bobby stuffed in the closet, and his eyes watered again. He apologized again for failing them both, turned on the hot water, and slowly got into the shower.

He stepped under the spray and let the water cascade over his young and strong body, but he kept the water away from his sensitive face. The water was so hot that it quickly had him looking like a cooked lobster, but it felt cleansing. He soaped himself up with a washcloth and scrubbed his body vigorously and then rinsed off. There was only one part left to do. He hesitated for a moment and then slowly and gently began applying the washcloth to his battered face and rubbed softly. He tried to put his face into the hot spray, but when the water touched his face, the combination of heat and pressure was too much for him and he jumped back in pain. Without thinking, he completely turned off the hot water, turned up the cold, and stepped under the water again. The drastic change in temperature caused him to become short of breath and lightheaded. He held onto the shower walls to steady himself. After a minute, his pores closed and he came back to his senses. When he turned the water off, he felt amazingly refreshed and clean.

BILL PULLED INTO THE WIDE open parking lot and saw only a spattering of cars in what was once a congested parking lot. He was struck by the realization that the dwindling numbers hadn't happened overnight and that he had just been too preoccupied with himself to even notice the number of cars, and people, that had disappeared. Manufacturing was almost extinct along the Housatonic and it wasn't just him leaving; it was a way of life that was leaving the valley.

He parked his car and sat for a moment pondering the fate of all the laid off people and deliberating on how run down Howe Avenue would become in a few years when there weren't any meaningful jobs in the area. Then he looked at the old buildings across the way and the beat up cars parked along the street and came to the conclusion that it couldn't look much worse.

Once Johnson's closed, it would leave only Ferrell's and Sikorsky's as the last two decent sized manufacturers in the area, and of course there was Wiffle Ball in their little building on Bridgeport Avenue. Bill wondered how long those companies would be able to survive. Ferrell's would have a hard time because they were one of those midsized manufacturers; too small to compete with the big international companies, and too big to do small custom projects. Wiffle Ball was sure to be gone soon, but he reasoned Sikorsky's would survive because they were in the defense business and there would always be bad guys in the distance and wars to be waged. It was the inescapable and unfortunate nature of the human race.

He almost allowed himself dwell on things beyond his control for too long and let it ruin his mood, but he was moving to Florida and those problems were no longer his concern. The Valley would survive; these damn Yankees always find a way to survive. He got out of his car and put a smile on his face as he walked into the almost deserted building. When he entered the building, Mary looked at him and informed him that Mr. Johnson was waiting for him. Without an extra word spoken, she returned to her task of directing the other two women in packing files and preparing for the closing.

Bill smiled at the thought of the tough old lady outliving Johnson's. He walked past the floor as Jack and a helper were moving the last lifts that would be built there to the loading docks. On the far end of the oil-stained grey floor, he noticed workers beginning to disconnect and dismantle equipment. He was again amazed at how fast everything was moving. When Mr. Johnson decided it was over, he didn't waste time.

He arrived at Ben's office to find the door open a few inches and him on the phone. He raised his hand to knock, but decided against interrupting the conversation. Without Ben noticing his arrival, he turned his back toward the door and waited in the hall. He couldn't help but overhear the last part of the conversation.

"Yes, that will be fine. I don't think they'll have any problem with that. Send me the paper work and I'll get it signed and send it back to you. Thank you very much for your help. I look forward to hearing from you." Ben hung up the phone and Bill knocked. Ben rose from his desk and ushered him in.

"Sit down, Bill. I would offer you a cup of coffee, but I fear interrupting Mary and her work. She hasn't been in the best of moods recently, as you can imagine, and she is definitely not very happy with my decisions of late," Ben said with an uneasy chuckle as he seated himself behind his desk. He looked like a man in his element behind the large wooden desk. His hair was grey and he was visibly tired, but he had passion and purpose in his eyes. He was full of confidence as he placed both hands on the table, sat up straight, and looked Bill in the eye.

"Now, William Taylor, let's get down to business. First of all, you will find a severance package in your final envelope that I believe you will find to be very satisfactory. If you would like, I can go over the details with you now or we can move on to other business."

"Mr. Johnson, I have absolute faith that your package will be more than fair. I don't need to talk about it unless you want to."

"No, I don't, so let's get on with it, shall we? I am sure that you had quite the interesting weekend, to say the least. I am truly sorry to have brought that business to your home in that way, but I just felt that that conversation shouldn't take place over the phone, and I wanted you to have the weekend to speak with your family about it. I still believe in sitting down and talking face to face with people. Now, on to business; I hope you and Anne had a chance to discuss this opportunity, and, if so, have you made a decision?"

"Yes, sir, we have. We think that this is a good opportunity for us, and I trust that we'll be able to work out the details, so we'd like to give it a try. When would they like me to start?"

"They're ready for you as soon as you can finalize everything here. Now, you'll need to get a security clearance because you'll be working on classified Department of Defense projects. I don't believe you'll have a problem, but it can be a time-consuming pain in the ass, so they'd like to get to work on that as soon as possible. How long will it take you to be ready?" Ben asked.

"Well, when we told Pete about it, he asked for an hour to get ready. I'm ready to go and Anne is very excited as well, but we'll need time to pack and to put the house on the market. If we need to, I'll move down ahead of them and find a place for us to stay until the house sells," Bill began to explain.

"Well, as I said, Art is a good friend and they have a solid firm. I think you will find working with them to be quite rewarding. I had faith that you'd accept the job, so I took the liberty of arranging a house for you; part of your severance package is a moving allowance and a six month lease on the house. It'll be ready for occupancy in about two weeks, and it won't take long to sell your home. You're in a nice area of Huntington," Ben sat back in his chair and smiled, quite proud of himself.

Bill looked at him in disbelief. "Mr. Johnson, that's very generous, but with the times, you don't have to do all that for us. I'm honored, I really am, and quite stunned actually, but I haven't done anything to deserve this."

"Bill, listen to me; you've worked for this company for a long time, and the truth is, as much as I hate to admit it, this place is now worth more shut down than it was while working. We got a very good price for the equipment from an overseas buyer and the city is planning some big downtown redevelopment project. A developer has already made a very fair offer for the property that I have decided to accept, so I'll be fine. Besides, I don't have any children, so what the hell am I going to do with the money anyway?" Ben looked him in the eye and with sincerity in his heart, he continued. "Bill, I feel very blessed to be able to help a good family make it through a difficult time, so don't give it another thought… or you might piss me off, understand? Now that that's settled, let's move on to other business. There's not much left for you to do here except organize and pack your files for storage and remove anything you want to keep from your office. I think you should be able to complete those tasks by Wednesday. On Thursday morning you'll leave Bradley at 7:20 AM, arrive in Pensacola at 2:17, and you'll have a rental car reserved for you that you'll drive to Okaloosa Island. You'll be staying at the Ramada right there on Highway 98; you can't miss it. Friday morning you are scheduled to meet with Art and his son at nine in their office. They'll go over the details of the position with you, and, if you like what you see, you can officially accept their offer. Your flight leaves Saturday morning at 8:20, and you'll be home for dinner on Saturday night."

Bill sat there looking at his boss; he had everything worked out; that was clear. What wasn't clear was why. Bill was more confused than ever. He should have been let go long before some of the other engineers and now all this.

"Mr. Johnson, thank you again. I don't know what to say except that you've been very busy on my behalf, and I am forever grateful, but I don't understand why. I know I've been here for a long time, but so have a lot of other people and my work over the last several years has been anything but stellar," Bill stammered.

He wasn't sure if he was making a huge mistake by questioning the judgment and generosity of his long-time boss. He knew that Mr. Johnson was a fair man and that he'd helped many people relocate while they were downsizing, but he thought about his work over the last few years and began to wonder if he deserved much more than a boot in the ass on his way out the door.

"Do you really want to know why I'm doing this? Well, I'll tell you. It's because I can and I want to. Is there anything else you need to know?" Ben answered with conviction.

He was quite pleased with himself. While he had been very generous with a few of his key long-term employees, the Taylor family had special meaning to him, and finding Pete the other night had filled him with a sense of purpose that he had been searching for, for years. He now had a project and he relished it.

"No, sir, that's good enough for me. Thank you again, Mr. Johnson," Bill said.

He knew he had been dismissed and started to get up.

"It's Ben; there's no one left here to impress. I'll speak with you soon, Bill. Go ahead and get your office cleaned out. If you hold up Mary, she's likely to kill us both."

PETE CAME DOWN THE STAIRS and saw his mother sitting at the table. She appeared calm and peaceful as she sat at the table drinking her coffee, but he never knew which Mom he was going to run into, the loving-caring Mom or the self-absorbed and angry, stoned, and drunk Mom, so he approached her cautiously. He got a box of cereal from the cabinet and milk from the refrigerator and joined his mother at the table.

"How are you doing, Mom?"

"I'm fine, Peter, I'm just a little nervous about everything that's going on right now, that's all. This is a big change for us. I've never even been to Florida and now I'm moving there. It's just happening way too fast. How about you? Are you sure you want to move across the country to a place you've never even seen?"

"Mom, I'm eighteen. The only thing I want to do is leave here. I don't care where I go. I just need something different than this place has to offer right now. But you and Dad, that's different. You guys have been here forever. I mean, you're old and old people hate change!" he said with a smile as he quickly stuffed a spoon of cereal into his mouth.

"Oh, you little shit, I'm not that old! I just never gave a thought to moving until two days ago. Do you really think it'll work out? I'm worried about you, Peter. You stay out too late, your face looks like it got run over by a truck, you don't want to go to college, and you don't have a real job. I want so much for you to be happy."

"Mom, I'm fine; it's just a few bumps in the road, that's all. I don't have a bunch of friends here and the ones I do have are moving. Frankie's joining the Marine Corps and Ray decided to move to Springfield; his brother got him a job up there and they're going to share an apartment. So, it's easy for me to go, and I saw Dad yesterday and I know he's ready to leave too, but you don't look like you like this idea anymore…. Mom, if you don't want to move, just tell him. You don't have to move; he can get a job here." Pete paused for a moment and then looked away from his mom before continuing. "Frankie has been trying to talk me into joining with him. If I sign up in the next couple of weeks, we can go to boot camp together, and I've been giving it a lot of thought," Pete said, trying to gauge her reaction.

"Oh no, I don't want you joining the Marines. You'll go and get yourself killed, especially with this cowboy actor in the White House. No, sir, we'll manage just fine. This job is going to be good for your father and you'll be chasing the girls on those Florida beaches in a few months, so I guess I'm ready, too." Anne forced a smile as she took a sip of coffee, but she was visibly strained by the thought of Peter going into harm's way on the whims of a politician.

She thought about it a moment longer and decided that the idea of Peter in the Marine Corps repulsed her even more than moving to Florida. She wasn't going to take the chance of losing another son. The thought of him carrying a gun and fighting in a war made her physically ill.

Her reaction was pretty much what he'd anticipated, but she had to understand that he wanted out of this town more than anything in the world and he was going to leave one way or the other. He was filled with mixed emotions because he wanted to move and he didn't care where, but he also didn't want her to do something that she would regret. He knew that the only reason she was even considering this move was because he was so screwed up.

"How long do you think it will take to move?" Pete asked.

"Oh honey, these things take time. Even if we do decide to move right now, we have to sell the house and find another place to live down there. I don't know, but I think if we make it there by Thanksgiving, we'll be doing great. I was thinking we might do one more Christmas here and then move after the New Year. What do you think?" she asked.

Pete was crushed by the thought of staying here for five more months and decided that there was no way he was going to be in this town that long; he was signing up this week. He looked at his mother sitting in her chair, and knew that if she got them to stay through the holidays, they would never leave.

"That would be cool, Mom. You can do whatever you like, but I need to do something with myself and we both know it." He put his hands on hers before continuing. "Mom, don't worry about me. I'm a big boy and I'll be fine, so you do what you need to do and really, don't worry about me," he said.

He put his bowl in the sink and turned toward his mother. She sat looking out her window at the birds in the feeder. When she sensed him staring at her, she turned towards him.

"Do you need help with anything today?" he asked, hoping for an answer in the negative.

"No, no…. I'm going to call Nancy from Beachwood. Her sister is a realtor with Sherman's, and I guess we'll set an appointment to find out what the house is worth and how long it'll take to sell." Anne was silently hoping the house would take a year or more to sell.

Pete got the answer he wanted and was quickly out the door, in his van, and down the road.

Anne picked up the phone and called in sick to work and then ate another pill. She called Nancy and got her sister's name and phone number, and then called her and set an appointment for the next morning. She decided she had everything taken care of and her day was already complete, so she took one more pill, sat on the couch, and put on *The Price is Right*.

When she woke up, it was after three o'clock and she was still in her night gown. She wiped the drool from the corner of her mouth and hurried into the shower. She showered, blew dry her hair, got dressed, and started dinner. As dinner was cooking, she walked to the mailbox to see what Buzzy the mailman had left for them. As she was walking back into the house, reviewing the usual assortment of bills and fumbling through them, she dropped an envelope and bent down to pick it up.

As she rose, she lifted her eyes to the home and the sprawling green lawn in front of her. The maple trees were full and rustling in a gentle breeze, the multi-colored flowers were blooming and were covered with bees dancing from petal to petal. This was her home; it was her childrens' home. She was safe and secure here, and it truly was a very beautiful place to live. She didn't want to leave here, not now, not ever. She tried to convince herself that if she and Bill just tried a little harder, then things would be all right again. She resolved right then and there to tell Bill not to take the Florida job. There were plenty of jobs for a skilled and experienced engineer right here in Connecticut. There was no need to move half way across the country just to run away from their problems. That wasn't going to solve anything. Bill was trying to leave Isaac here and forget him; she knew it, and she was not going to let that happen.

BILL RETURNED TO HIS OFFICE after bringing Mary another box of files and stood outside his door looking in. His files were organized and boxed and most of his office packed; he would finish everything before lunch tomorrow. He looked at his watch; it was already five o'clock. That was it then: a couple of hours tomorrow, and this chapter of his life would end and another would begin.

He was as giddy as a school boy. He flipped off the light switch and headed out the door. On the way out, he saw Mary picking up her things and getting ready to leave as well. He was almost to the door when an uncontrollable urge came over him and he turned towards her, bowed, and with a large smile said, "Miss Mary, I hope you have a most wonderful evening, and I look forward to you brightening my day again first thing in the morning."

Mary stared at him like he had finally lost his mind, but when he left the building and she reflected on his antics, she shook her head and let a little smile cross her lips. She knew what Ben Johnson was doing for him and his family and she was happy to see the old Bill Taylor coming back to life. She liked the change in him and sincerely wished him well.

Bill got in his car, and this time the radio was already playing his music. The Drifters were singing "Save the Last Dance for Me," and it was 1960 again; he was graduating college and madly in love with Anne. He rolled down the windows and turned the air conditioner to full power. The ride home went by too fast; he listened to one song after another that reminded him of his youth and the excitement he felt when he was getting ready to start his new life after college, and before he knew it he was pulling into his driveway.

He came to a stop with music emanating from the jeep like a high school kid. As he walked to his front door, he stopped, bent down, picked and smelled a rose. With a smile on his face, he concluded that Shakespeare was right: by any other name a rose would still smell as sweet. He opened the door and was hit with the luscious aroma of Anne's pasta sauce simmering on the stove.

"Anne, are you here? Dinner smells fabulous." He walked to the cabinet and thought about mixing a drink, but decided against it. He moved to the stove and lifted the cover from the sauce and enjoyed the aroma of dinner. Anne greeted him as he came into the kitchen.

"Hello, Bill," she said.

"Oh, Anne, this smells fantastic," he said as he lifted the lid on the sauce and inhaled. He replaced the lid and then turned towards Anne and handed her the rose, "I hope your day went as well as mine. I'm really looking forward to finishing up at Johnson's. I thought I'd be scared, but instead I feel liberated, and I have some great news for you, too."

"Bill, I don't want to move to Florida. There, I said it. I'm sorry, but this is our home; this is where we belong. You can find a job here. Our son is buried here, and I don't want to move some place where I can never see him again."

Anne sat down, watching her husband's reaction to her statement. He was crushed; she could almost visibly see him deflate right in front of her. He looked at his wife, turned, and opened the cabinet.

"What the hell are you talking about? This morning, hell, all weekend, I asked you if you wanted to move and you said yes, over and over. I went to work today and basically accepted the position. They already have plane and hotel reservations for me. I fly down on Thursday. What am I supposed to do, say I changed my mind? I can't do that, Anne."

"Yes, you can. You don't work for Mr. Johnson anymore, remember? He bankrupted his company and fired you. You don't owe him anything. I'm your wife and this is our home," Anne pleaded.

Bill looked at her in a state of shock. His heart was in his stomach; he didn't know if he was supposed to angrily protest or capitulate and give his wife what she wanted. He sat in silence for a while just looking at her. He didn't want to fight with her, but he was moving to Florida with or without her.

"Anne, I have to go down there and talk to them. Maybe I won't fit in or be what they're looking for, but I have to at least go down and look, all right? Did you call a realtor?"

"Yes, I did, but I want to cancel the appointment."

"Don't cancel it. Let's see what the house is worth. Who knows, we might be able to sell this house and buy another in the area if I take another job somewhere around here," Bill offered.

"She is supposed to be here at ten, but I don't want to leave this house."

"Well, Pete, what do you think? Are you ready for the Corps? It's going to be great. I can't wait to go to Japan and to tour the Mediterranean. Can you imagine what all those girls are going to do to us?" Frankie said.

Frankie was excited and confident that he had finally sealed the deal with Pete, and that after this last meeting with the recruiter, Pete was going to join the Corps with him and the two of them would get a chance to see the world together.

"Yeah, I like it. I'm pretty sure I'll do it. I'm going to see what happens at the house tonight, and if it goes the way I think it will, I'll sign tomorrow," Pete said.

Frankie was going to be a Marine because it was his duty to his family and his country; Pete was joining because he was ready to move on, and Frankie and the Marines offered the best ticket out of town that he could think of. After his conversation with his mom that morning, he knew she wasn't going to leave and he didn't really care what his dad did, so he figured tomorrow he would sign up, and in a few weeks he would be in Paris Island.

The boys talked for a while longer about what it was going to be like to be a United States Marine. Frankie came from a family of Marines. His grandfather, father, and uncle had all been in the Corps. He relayed stories that they had had told him about their adventures, and now Frankie was ready for adventures himself. They smoked and talked for a couple of hours and only after Pete promised, for the third time, to call him first thing in the morning did Frankie let him go home.

When Pete entered the kitchen, his parents were sitting at the table. There was an awkward silence in the room and he knew what they had been discussing. He pulled up a chair and sat with them.

"Well, what's the plan today?" he asked.

"When I left the house this morning we were moving to Florida, but now I think your mother has decided she doesn't want to move. How about you? What's new with you?" Bill said in a sarcastic and exasperated tone.

With that said Bill took a long drink from his glass and set in on the table a little too hard. Pete looked at his father and then cast a contemptuous glare at his mother. At first she wouldn't look at him, but after a moment she gave into his piercing stare and lifted her face to meet his eyes. She had a sad and pleading look on her face, her eyes begged him to understand, but Pete felt nothing. He had told her that morning that she should do what she wanted, but he was still surprised when she had actually done it.

"I went to the recruiter today and decided that I'm signing up for the Marine Corps tomorrow," Pete said.

"Good for you. I think the Marines will be good for you. You'll have an opportunity to see the world and if you're smart you'll save money for college while you serve and when you're done with your tour, you can go to school," Bill said. He really didn't like it, but he knew the change would be good for his son, and the bonus was that it would send Anne off the deep end, and as far as he was concerned, she deserved it.

Pete knew that she would back down and indeed she did. He had started to get up and leave when she grabbed his arm.

"Sit down, Peter. Let's talk about this."

"What's there to talk about, Mom? You want to stay and I don't, and I'm not. I'm eighteen; I'm not going to college right now, so I might as well join the military. Like Dad said, after my four years I can go to school, but I've got to start living my life. I'm sorry, Mom, I'm not trying to hurt you, but can you give me one good reason to stay here, except because you want me to?"

She looked to her husband for help, but there was none to be had. She saw the look in both their faces and knew that if she didn't concede they were leaving her, both of them. She took a deep breath, looked out the window, and gave in.

"All right; your father is going to Florida on Thursday to look at the job. If he takes the job, I'll move to Florida on the condition that I never hear about the Marine Corps from you again. Is that a deal?"

"Mom, don't move to Florida just to keep me at home, because no matter what happens now, I'm going to move out one day because I can't keep living with my parents forever."

"Oh, that's for damn sure!" It was the first words Bill had said in a while and it brought a smile to all their faces.

"I'm not doing it just for you, and I know you'll move out soon, but you have no business in the Marines; that's just ridiculous."

Bill and Pete looked at each other and were proud of their joint assault. It was the first thing they had accomplished together in a long time, and they both found pleasure in that fact. Anne wasn't happy, but they figured she would come around.

They sat at the kitchen table and ate a surprisingly pleasant dinner together. It was uneasy for all of them and they kept waiting for someone to say or do something that would ruin everything, but it didn't happen.

CHAPTER 24

THE VISIT

Bill walked out of the airport doors Thursday afternoon and almost stepped right back in after being hit by the instantaneous onslaught of the Florida heat. When he'd left New England early that morning it was in the low 70's, and now he was standing in Pensacola on a hot July afternoon. It was like nothing he had ever felt in New England. The temperature was close to 100 degrees with over 80 % humidity. He looked out and across the parking lot and noticed that a light blue haze hung in the air and that his body was instantly covered with a sheen of sweat.

The humidity was so thick that he could actually see the air he was breathing. He walked to his rental car, and when he opened the door, a blast of even hotter air came rushing out and hit him in the face with a force that made him take a step back. Eventually he gained the courage to climb in, start the car, and turn on the air. While the car cooled down, he began to have second thoughts and wonder if this really was a good idea. He thought about going back into the airport and getting on the next plane to Bradley, but he was committed to the interview at least, so he put the car in gear and started towards Fort Walton Beach.

He left the airport and found Highway 98 and started traveling east. He crossed the Pensacola Bridge, and as he looked at the bay he was impressed by the contrast of scenery from the land he'd left just a few hours ago. The color of the water was a spectacular emerald green with an abundance of small white capped waves with sail boats leisurely bobbing about. He was looking at a big tug boat that was pushing six enormous barges that were lashed together when suddenly something massive caught his eye. As he looked over his shoulder to get a better look, he yanked the wheel and the car swerved radically. He heard a horn blast alongside him that made him jump and brought him back to reality. He regained control of the car, but couldn't resist looking again. It was a giant Navy ship. He wasn't sure what it was, but he thought it was an old battle ship. He was impressed with the power and majesty it commanded in the bay. As he made his way towards Fort Walton Beach with the windows up and the air on he took in the various sites as he passed. He saw small stores, old houses- some beautiful, some not- that made him question how beautiful the area really was, but then he finally crossed the Okaloosa Island Bridge and looked out at the emerald green gulf and saw the amazing sugar white beaches; he decided that he could live here after all.

He pulled into the Ramada, checked in, and was pleasantly surprised to find that his third floor room was clean, large, and beautiful. It had a king sized bed that was meticulously made, the light green carpet was clean, and the walls were decorated with beach inspired art work that set the mood for a Florida vacation. As he continued to scan the room, his eyes were drawn to sliding glass doors that led to a balcony overlooking the gulf. He put his bags down, opened the door, and stepped onto the balcony. He was immediately hit with a surprisingly strong ocean breeze that caught him off guard. His short hair was blowing in the wind as he gazed down at the most incredible beaches he had ever seen. The sand was so white that it looked like snow and the gulf water was crystal clear, but with an amazing tint of emerald green. He reflected on the Connecticut beaches he had grown up with and knew that they looked nothing like this. There were people lying on the beach basking in the sun, while others strolled along the shoreline enjoying the gentle waves breaking on the beach. He was gazing upon a living Florida beach postcard. He had never seen anything like this and he stood on the balcony basking in the beauty for several minutes before he reluctantly went back inside, put his clothes away, changed, and went down to the pool.

At the pool he saw many more beautiful sights, most of whom were scattered about on lounge chairs and wearing small bikinis. The pool was huge and full of life. It was surrounded by a tall and well landscaped wall that made the area an oasis from the world behind it. He watched kids running around the pool, full of laughter while jumping in and out of the water, and then his eyes were drawn to a large artificial waterfall that had people swimming in and out of it. The water fell about fifteen feet from a big man-made rock. He focused his attention, and after looking closer he realized that there was a cave under the rock and behind the waterfall.

As he stood on the pool's edge and watched the people moving about, a pretty young lady in her early twenties, wearing a very small and very bright pink bikini, came and stood next to him as she prepared to enter the pool.

"Excuse me, what's under the waterfall? I see all those people swimming in and out. What do they have in there?" Bill asked the young lady.

She looked at the middle aged man beside her and smiled a knowing little smile.

"Oh, that's where the bar is. You swim under the waterfall and then swim right up to the bar. It's awesome; you have to try it." With that, she waved to Bill, dove in, and swam under the waterfall.

He was ready to join her, but decided to look around some more before he started drinking. He knew that he had an important meeting in the morning and didn't want to have a hangover when he arrived for it. He turned around and left the pool area before he gave into temptation and took a walk on the beach. As he strolled along the shoreline, he found a nice little restaurant where he enjoyed a great seafood platter before returning to the hotel and swimming under the waterfall. He limited himself to two drinks, leisurely swam around for a while, and then went to his room and enjoyed a very pleasant sleep.

In the morning, he walked out onto the balcony as the sun was coming up and took a deep breath of the ocean air. It felt so good that he decided that if Ben's friends didn't hire him, he was still going to move here, even if it meant he had to wait tables. He showered and enjoyed a small breakfast before heading over to Niceville for his interview.

When he left Okaloosa Island and arrived in Niceville, he thought he was in a different state. Instead of palm trees, he saw large oak trees draped in Spanish moss; instead of pure white beaches he saw Boggy Bayou and its flotilla of shrimp boats docked at the fish house. There were fewer nice cars and a lot more old pick-up trucks. He followed the directions and arrived on time without any problems. Bill entered the office and was offered coffee before being ushered into Stan Evans' office. Stan was the son of Art Evans and he greeted Bill warmly at the door before inviting him in. Stan was in his mid-thirties, about five foot nine and a hundred and sixty pounds. He had jet black hair parted on the side and a small black mustache. He offered Bill a seat and when he got behind his desk and turned to face Bill, a few thick strands of hair fell across his forehead.

Bill almost choked on his coffee and had to do a double take because he was struck by the stunning resemblance to Adolf Hitler and was silently waiting for him to start ranting in German, but he didn't. Instead, he started with the standard pleasantries and made small talk until Art, his father, arrived. When Art Evans walked in the door, the mood instantly changed. There was no doubt that "The Man" had entered the room.

"I am going to assume that you're Bill Taylor. I've heard a lot of good things about you. Ol' Ben Johnson is a good friend and a better man. We go back a long way and I completely respect his opinions," Art said as he introduced himself and shook Bill's hand.

Art was an old bulldog. He stood an inch taller than his son and was close to two hundred pounds. His handshake was firm and his eyes bounced with energy. When he finished shaking Bill's hand, he looked at his son behind the desk and bellowed, "Oh, Jesus Christ, Stanley, when the hell are you going to shave that damn thing off your face? I told you that you look like God damned Hitler, and the last thing we need around here is you walking around looking like that son-of-a-bitch." His face was flushed and he shook his head in anger as he addressed his son, but as soon as he turned towards Bill, he was a different person. He was calm and confident. He made direct eye contact with Bill and made sure he had Bill's full attention before he began to speak in a lowered, but direct voice.

"Listen, I don't have time for a lot of bullshit, so let's cut to the chase. I talked with Ben for some time about you and I trust him completely. This is a different world from what you're used to and it's going to take some time to get you up to speed. He told me what he's paying you now, and I won't pay you anywhere near that. I'll pay you thirty percent less to start; we'll help with relocation expenses and train you. If it works out after six months, I'll give you a ten percent raise, and then a year later we'll review the situation again. Stanley here will go over all the details of the job with you. If you accept, and I hope you do, I'll look forward to working with you." He looked at his watch before continuing, "I have a meeting on base that I have to get my ass to, so I'll leave you in little Hitler's capable hands to give you the grand tour." With that said, the old General got up to leave the room. At the door, he turned and looked at his son.

"Damn it, Stanley, shave that thing off your face." He shook his head and left the office for the day.

"He's quite the character, isn't he? Dad doesn't spend a great deal of time in the office. He's mostly retired, but he likes to schmooze around with his old buddies, tell war stories, and bring in projects. He's a one man PR firm and quite the persistent salesman," Stan said.

He then went over a general description of the job with Bill, who would work in target analysis. Stan briefly explained that when they blew things up, Bill's job would be to assess the target response, identify target failure points, and recommend options for achieving the desired kill level as required; basically, he was to analyze and compare what they expected to happen to the building or vehicle and its occupants when they detonated the weapon with what really happened, and then make recommendations to achieve greater kill efficiency. Bill cringed as his occupational tasks were described to him as nonchalantly as if Stan was giving him the Yankee's lineup.

They toured the office and then drove out to the range where Bill got to witness a live fire demonstration. He was impressed with the raw destructive power unleashed before his eyes, and when he watched some of the engineers after the explosion, he was struck by their professionalism and also a little surprised by how much they looked like big kids playing with big firecrackers. After the demonstration was completed, they got back into the car and headed back into town.

During the ride down Highway 20, a long and desolate two lane road with neatly organized rows of planted pine trees lining both sides, Stan explained that Eglin Air Force Base was approximately the size of Rhode Island in land mass and that the pine tree farms they were looking at were actually leased from the Air Force. The base had huge ranges to the north and the Gulf of Mexico to the south, which enabled them to fulfill their primary missions: testing, and research and development.

They progressed from Freeport and continued west through Choctaw Beach where the road seemed to be a few feet from the bay. Waves were crashing onto large pieces of broken concrete that lined the beach for erosion control. When they finally arrived back in Niceville, Stan treated Bill to a wonderful lunch at a small shack that was called The Emerald House. They enjoyed a buffet of home cooked Chinese food, while Stan explained that many of the small restaurants in the area, like the one they were eating at, were owned and operated by retired GI's and their wives. Whether he liked Thai food, Korean, Japanese, or Chinese, it was here, and it was good.

After lunch, Stan showed Bill the house they had reserved for his family. It was a modest brick-faced ranch house in a pleasant neighborhood just off of John Sims Parkway. Bill stood in the front yard and was pleased with the house. It was convenient to shopping and work.

The house and yard were much smaller than the house in Connecticut, which meant less time mowing and cleaning and more time for golf and the beach. He entered the house and found an unassuming three bedroom, two-bath home. The rooms were smaller than he would have preferred, but they were adequate. He continued through the family room and looked out back, where he saw a swimming pool with a screen enclosure. It was a small yard that was enclosed with a privacy fence and lined with flowering vines.

The sun shone into the clear water of the pool, and he was filled with a warm and hopeful feeling that this could be the place to rekindle his marriage. He knew that all they needed was a little romance, some candles, and a lot of fun. He couldn't see his neighbors through the fence and the flowers and he knew they couldn't see him. He smiled to himself and allowed a school boy fantasy into his mind. It was a pleasant thought that caused a warm and unexpected stirring he hadn't felt in years.

Bill loved the area, he wasn't crazy about his job description, but he had enjoyed the time he'd spent with Stan and couldn't see any reason not to accept the job, so he did. He felt a little trepidation and had some second thoughts as he was driving back to the hotel, but by the time he was crossing the Okaloosa Island Bridge and looked out at the gulf, he was confident that he had made the right decision. He went back to his room, changed from a jacket and tie into shorts and a light shirt, and once again stood on the balcony and looked at the world before him, and as he did, all doubt was erased from his mind. He made his way to the pool and enjoyed a few drinks at the waterfall bar before turning in early. In the morning, he returned to Pensacola and caught his plane home. He was confident that divine providence had given him a second chance and he wasn't going to waste it.

PETE PASSED THE JOINT TO Frankie, who took a deep drag. He started coughing and Pete started laughing. They were parked alongside a dirt road, concealed from civilization by the lush deep green foliage that grew along a rippling stream where they had spent the morning fishing. The sun was shimmering off the water as it passed in front of them and the young men were enjoying their last days of youth before officially joining manhood. Frankie was committed to leaving the first week of September for Paris Island and Pete would decide tonight whether his future was in Florida or Paris Island.

"There is no way that this is really the last joint you're going to smoke. You're so full of shit. There are plenty of guys in the military who smoke dope," Pete said to Frankie.

"Dude, those days are ending. I wish they weren't, but they are. I have to pass piss tests before I can even go to Paris Island, and the last thing I'm going to do is screw up and fail a piss test. Could you imagine my old man's reaction if I got kicked out of the Marines before I even got in? Success in the Marine Corps is far more important to me than getting high, so, I'm not going to take any chances and let that happen. I'd have to move to Alaska and go out on a fishing boat or something, and how many ginnies do think are up there?" Frankie took another hit and passed the joint to Pete. "It's time to grow up and get on with the next chapter of life!" he concluded.

"Yeah, I'll know what I'm doing tonight. My mom will go nuts if I join, but I'm getting out of here one way or another. I'll go with them to Florida to make her happy, but if they don't move, I'm signing up Monday morning," Pete said.

"Well, who knows, this time next year you and me might be in Japan getting naked with Geishas. Some people want to climb Mount Everest, or sail around the world, but I think I'll make that my mission in life, getting naked with as many Geishas as humanly possible," Frankie happily exclaimed.

The thought enticed and excited them both, and they raised their hands and joined in a raucous high five. After they finished their joint, they started making their way home. Pete dropped Frankie off with a promise to call later and let him know how dinner went.

It was strange and rare to have the three of them sitting together on a Saturday night enjoying dinner, but they were. Bill told them about the job, his trip, the live fire demonstration, and the town. He forgot to mention the new salary and the almost unbearable heat and humidity.

Pete liked the description of Okaloosa Island. Anne accepted it with very few questions because she had very few options. No matter what else happened, she would do everything in her power to make sure that her only living son was not going to be killed in the Marines, and that was the only thing she cared or thought about.

Bill described the house that was leased for them-Pete liked the pool-and then he told Anne about the help they were to receive with relocation expenses. He suggested that they hire professional movers to assist them and list the house slightly under market value to facilitate a quick sale.

Pete called Frankie and Ray after dinner and gave them the news. Frankie was disappointed that they wouldn't be putting on the dress-blues together, but he was expecting it. Ray was happy for Pete. He was a Florida boy at heart and knew that the move would be good for Pete. The three of them got together on Sunday morning and went to the top of the waterfall at Indian Wells to enjoy one last joint together and say their good-byes.

"Fire that thing up, Ray," Pete said. "And I told you that wasn't going to be your last joint yesterday."

"Yeah, well, what the hell? One more won't hurt anything. So you guys are moving right away, huh?" Frankie asked.

"Yeah, his new company is paying for the move and they already have a house set up for us that's supposed to be ready in a couple of weeks. We might get a chance to get together again before we leave, but this asshole is leaving for Springfield this week and I know how your family is. You probably have cousins coming in from three states to send you off. I heard that you had almost fifty people at graduation."

"Yeah, it's a pain in the ass to be Italian sometimes. It seems like every day somebody else that I don't know comes over and wishes me well and tells me how proud they are of me, and yeah, there were at least fifty people at graduation. They came all the way from Jersey. There were aunts, uncles, and cousins there that I hadn't seen since I was about five. It was a zoo, and you should have been there, asshole," Frankie complained.

"Yeah, well, I didn't feel like dealing with all the bullshit," Pete said sheepishly.

"Hey, Frankie, at least you're loved!" Ray said with pursed lips as he tried to hug and kiss Frankie.

The boys wrestled around, and at one point slipped and almost stumbled off the edge of the cliff. Their butt cheeks clenched as tight as possible and they grabbed and held on to each other until they regained their footing and balance. They laughed for a moment and were relieved to have escaped serious danger. They then silently decided that it was safer to sit and enjoy their surroundings, so they calmly sat on top of the falls and listened to the powerful cascade of water crashing into the wells below and enjoyed each other's company for a couple of hours.

They hiked back to their cars and said their good-byes and left with optimistic good cheer and confidence that they were all on their way to do great things. Frankie promised to visit Pete in Florida after boot-camp. He told him that he would have to spend most of his leave with his parents, but he would fly down for a day or two before shipping out to wherever they sent him. Ray hugged Pete and wished him well, but refrained from making a promise that he knew he would never keep. The boys drove in different cars and in different directions, but they all felt and knew the same thing: this part of their lives was over and they would probably never see each other again.

The house was on the market for less than a month, and by the middle of August 1982, the Taylor family was in Niceville.

CHAPTER 25

FLORIDA

Pete sat on the lanai drinking a glass of orange juice while contemplating what lay ahead of him. He was getting ready to go job hunting, but he didn't know a soul in the area. As he thought about what he faced, there was a part of him that wanted to linger and hide in the house, while another part of him knew that he'd gotten exactly what he'd wanted and now it was time to get off his ass, explore his new surroundings, and find a job.

He got in his van and drove to John Sims Parkway. He had no air conditioning in the van and began having second thoughts about the wisdom of moving to Florida in August because it was only seven thirty in the morning and it was already oppressively hot. He sat at a red light watching traffic flow in both directions and contemplated the direction he should turn. Left or right: which way would fate take him?

He knew that this moment was a great step towards finding his destiny. He was confident in his ability to find employment because he would do anything and didn't care about pay. He knew that he was without a trade or skill and had no college education, so that made him a prime minimum wage candidate.

To his right was O'Brian's IGA, and to his left was the high school and a long road that led to who knows where. Most of the traffic was heading in that direction, so when the light turned green, he took a left and drove down the road looking at the businesses that lined both sides. He decided to drive for a while to scope out his new surroundings and to work his way back toward the house filling out applications.

As he continued down the road he saw the mouth of Boggy Bayou on his left. Sail boats were docked along the east shore, and a little farther up he saw the shrimp boats docked at the fish house. He crossed Turkey Creek, and as he came around a bend in the road, a turn lane expanded the road to his right and he saw a sign that pointed up a hill that led to Fort Walton Beach. Straight ahead was Valparaiso and Eglin Air Force Base. Most of the traffic was going towards Eglin, so he continued straight ahead. After a while he crossed the Tom's Bayou Bridge, and in the distance he saw the entry gate of Eglin Air Force Base. He quickly realized that there was pot in his van and armed guards at the entrance to the base.

Pete had never been to a military base, and the thought of going to federal prison on his first day in Florida made him start to panic and break out in a cold sweat. As soon as the opportunity arose, he did an abrupt U-turn and started driving away from the guards as fast as he could- which wasn't very fast in a worn out 1968 Chevy van. As he shifted from second to third gear, he nervously looked in the rear view mirror, and when he saw that the guards hadn't been scrambled and there were no cars in hot pursuit, he unclenched his butt and relaxed a little.

As he was crossing Tom's Bayou Bridge again, he looked to his right and saw a large barge with a crane on it being moved by two small boats. Next to it he saw what looked like an old fishing boat, which appeared to be on land and being worked on. It was unlike anything he had seen back home.

He took a right on Bayshore drive and decided to start his quest for work there. He followed the small winding road along the bayou to a four-way stop sign. Under the stop sign was a hand-painted sign that said "Duck Crossing." To his right was an old white building that was twisted and misshapen. It looked like it was a hundred years old and ready to fall into the bayou. Next to the building was the shrimp boat he had seen from the bridge.

The boat sat on what looked like two large metal carrier carts on railroad tracks. The railroad tracks started at a little shack near the road and led into the water. In the shack was a huge winch with large steel cables attached to the front cart. There was a huge stack of blocking on the carts that kept the boat from tipping. Standing under the boat was a skinny little man in a bright yellow rainsuit pressure washing the bottom of the boat.

Pete then noticed four large old men standing in the shade of a pecan tree near the boat watching the man in the rainsuit work. He began to have doubts about what he was doing, but with determination to try, he parked the van and walked over to the men. As he nervously approached them, they stopped talking and stared at him as he came closer. They were all big-bellied, weather-beaten, grey haired old men. Two of them wore plastic white boots that went half way to their knees, and the other two wore old work boots that were only tied half way up with their pants sticking half in and half out, but the one thing they all wore was a menacing glare. When he reached them, a huge man with a thick, dirty black beard and suspenders tilted his head down and spat a big gob of chewing tobacco near Pete's foot. Pete immediately felt unwelcome and thought about turning around without saying a word, but instead spoke up nervously.

"I, um, just moved to the area and was wondering if you needed any help?"

The men looked at each other and grinned. The one with the tobacco spat on the ground again. Finally, the biggest of the bunch, the man that ran the boatyard, looked down at Pete and spoke up. He was well over six feet tall and two hundred and fifty pounds with giant paws that were gnarled and showed the abuse of many years of hard work. His face was discolored, weather-beaten, and wrinkled.

"Where you from, boy?" Homer White mumbled in a thick southern drawl through the six teeth that remained in his mouth. He sounded like he had a mouth full of marbles and his words were difficult to understand, but his intentions were very clear. Pete was intimidated by the men and uncertain about how welcome he was going to be in this town.

"Connecticut," Pete answered.

"Another God damned Connecticut Yankee!" he complained to the world. "What the hell is going on up there? Every time I turn around there's another one of you sons of bitches; you're like a bunch of damned cockroaches. If you got anymore friends up there, tell them to stay the hell away, there ain't no more room around here." He turned back to Pete. "Try next door with them other Yankees. You'll probably fit right in with that bunch of crazy bastards."

With that issue resolved, they turned away from Pete and resumed their conversation as if he had disappeared.

"Thanks," he said quietly as he walked back to his van. "What the hell was that?" he thought to himself as he drove next door. The yard was surrounded by an old chain link fence that was overgrown with flowering vines and stood in varying degrees of leaning over in different areas. It had a twisted gate in the front that was open, so he drove in.

As he entered the yard, he saw to the left of the driveway a large pile of old scrap steel and three old boats on blocks. Various pieces of heavy equipment were scattered throughout the yard. He looked towards the bayou and saw the barge slowly moving around in the water with a boat tied to the back, and another smaller boat in the front pushing on the side. It appeared that they were docking the barge with the nose on the bank. There was a man with a thick black beard wearing a flannel shirt with the sleeves cut off standing on the bank of the water. He was wearing large welding gloves and holding what looked like a helmet in one hand and was waving his arms wildly and yelling at the men moving the barge.

Pete shut off his motor and stepped out of his van. He started walking toward the bank and had gotten about twenty feet from his van when he saw a cloud of dust kick up and a small, but solid black and tan dog with a thick chain attached to a concrete block running at

him with his ears pinned back and his teeth menacingly bared. Pete felt
a rush of panic and immediately started running back to his van and
praying that he could outrun the psycho dog.

The man on the bank heard the dog, turned, and yelled at him
to go lay down. The dog immediately stopped charging and returned
to his shade tree as if nothing had happened. Pete was about to start
the van and leave when the man approached him. He was a bear of a
man; he wasn't very tall, but he was thick, hairy, and looked immensely
powerful.

"Sorry about that. He's kind of protective. Can I help you with
something?" He smiled, spoke clearly, and had a full set of clean white
teeth.

"Yeah, I was wondering if you were hiring. I just moved here and
I'm out looking for work."

"Well, can you do anything? Have you ever been around boats?"
he asked.

"Um, not really, no. But I learn fast and I'll work hard." Pete felt
encouraged by the man's questions and thought he might be in luck.

"Can you swim?"

"Yeah, I can swim."

"Well, what I have is hard, nasty work. I pay minimum wage and
the only benefits I offer are lots of exercise, plenty of fresh air, and
sunshine. Do you want to give it a try?"

Pete was caught off guard, and without thinking said, "Sure."

"Well, you might want to change your clothes before you start.
We've got to secure the barge and then I'll meet you behind the beauty
college in an hour. I'll show you what you have to do when we get there.
Do you know where the beauty college is?"

Pete told him no, and the man gave him directions and started to
return to work before turning around and introducing himself.

"Oh, by the way, I'm Joe, Joe Nevers, and that's my brother Jeff
running the *Osage* and Marty in the nose boat. Listen, I've to get back
over there before they destroy the universe. We'll meet you behind the
beauty college in an hour."

Joe then turned toward the men on the boats and started waving his hands again and yelling some more. Pete was excited; he had looked for a job for about twenty minutes and was now gainfully employed. He pulled out of the boatyard feeling like things were finally going his way and then began thinking about the man's name.

"Nevers. Nah, it couldn't be. This is backwater Florida, but the old redneck did say they were Connecticut Yankees." Pete wondered to himself if they could be some of the long lost Nevers boys.

When he reached the stop sign in front of the boat being worked on, he saw the old man who had directed him to Joe Nevers. Pete smiled and waved at the old man, who just glared at him and never moved. Pete pulled his hand in the van and sheepishly drove back to his house.

When he got home, his father was gone and his mom was unpacking. She wore a simple blue dress and an unhappy expression and looked like she hadn't showered in a couple of days. He walked in and told her the good news about his job and then went into his room and changed quickly. He put on a pair of old blue jeans, a tee shirt, and his heavy insulated work boots. He told his mom goodbye and was out the door before she could stop him and ruin his mood.

He reached the beauty college several minutes early and drove behind the building. He didn't see any equipment, but he did see about an acre of broken concrete that must have been piled fifteen feet high in places. The concrete was in large pieces probably averaging four feet around. It looked like a graveyard for broken sidewalks, driveways, and slabs. He found a place in the shade to park and wait for Joe and his crew to arrive. It was already stifling hot and he was regretting wearing the blue jeans and boots before he had even started to work.

While he sat sweating in the shade, he saw a pick-up truck kicking up dust and coming towards him on the dirt road that ran behind the building. In the front was Joe Nevers, and next to him was another man who Pete assumed was his brother Jeff. Sitting in the back of the truck was the other man from the boat yard. After the truck stopped, the men got out and approached Pete as he got up.

"Another victim, eh? I'm Jeff by the way." The man was clean cut with a fairly small and tight frame and appeared to weigh about one hundred and sixty pounds. The other man, larger and stockier, climbed out of the back of the truck carrying two large sledgehammers. He approached Pete with a big smile on his face and offered him one of the hammers, then set the other one down and returned to the truck and removed a large cooler of water. After he set it down under the tree, he came back over to Pete, and reached out his hand.

"Hey there, lad. I'm Marty, and we're about to go to Hell on Earth, son. Are you ready to have some fun?" he asked with a thick British accent.

He was tall with thick, broad shoulders, reddish hair, freckled face, and a big smile. Pete looked at Joe and asked if he was supposed to fill out an application or something.

"Not now. Just don't die out here; I hate the paperwork. Drink plenty of water, and at the end of the day, if you're still alive we'll take care of it."

He and Jeff looked at each other, smiled, got in the truck and drove off. Pete looked at Marty.

"What are we supposed to do?"

"Well, it's actually a quite simple process, you see. We take these bloody hammers to those piles of concrete and make big rocks into little rocks. I'm sure you've seen it done in the movies," he said in a jovial voice. "You start on that pile over there and I'll work over here. Just smash the rocks in front of you into a workable size and toss them into a pile behind you." Marty smiled at Pete and walked over to his pile. "We need to break about forty tons of rock, so let's get to work before the heat gets unbearable."

"Is this a joke? You're not serious, are you?" Pete asked.

"I'm as serious as a bloody heart attack."

Marty smiled again and swung the hammer over his shoulder and down onto the concrete. Pete watched in stunned amazement as small pieces of broken concrete whizzed by his face. He wanted this to be a bad dream, but it wasn't. It became clear why this job was so easy to get, and he began wondering, once again, what he had gotten himself into. He walked to the pile of concrete where he had been told to start and prepared to work like a convict.

The sledgehammer was heavy. He lifted it and looked at the stamp on the bottom: twenty pounds. He looked up at the sky; it was bright blue with towering white and grey clouds on the horizon. The sun was bright and beating down on them mercilessly. It was only ten o'clock and the temperature was already in the nineties. He was covered with sweat and hadn't even started working yet.

"Fuck me," he said aloud and started swinging his hammer.

An hour later, the two men had made decent piles of rocks. Pete's face was bright red and he was covered in sweat and feeling light headed. His boots felt like lead anchors and his pants were so wet and heavy that they looked like he had been swimming in them. Marty looked over at him and decided to have mercy.

"Hey there, Pete, c'mon, let's get some water before you fall over on us."

The words were music to Pete's ears. He dropped his hammer and followed Marty to the shade tree and the cooler of ice water.

"You'd better sit your arse down for a while and drink some of this water. It's gonna be hotter than bloody hellfire today, and if you go and die on me, I'm gonna hafta break that concrete by myself and I want no part of that," Marty said.

He didn't know if Marty was making a joke and whether or not he should laugh or what because he was as difficult to understand as Homer White, but his voice had a rhythm and tone that Pete found enchanting. He took the cup of ice cold water Marty handed him and drank a couple of sips and then poured the rest over his head.

The sensation of the water going down the back of his neck was electrifying and almost painful. He could feel his body temperature dropping rapidly, and it felt so good that he did it with the second cup as well. Pete was exhausted and the day had just begun. The heat and humidity were getting to him, and Marty decided to take a few minutes longer in the break than he normally would have.

"Well, where ya from, Mr. Pete, and what brings ya to our little piece of paradise?"

"Connecticut. I moved down with my parents. We got here on Saturday. My dad came down for a job and they asked me to move down with them. What the hell, I figured. It's Florida, the land of sun, fun, beaches, and pretty girls!"

Pete looked around and saw oak trees instead of giant palms blowing in the breeze. He was surrounded by piles of concrete, not the white sand dunes he was told about, and Marty sure didn't look like any pretty girl.

"Where the hell am I? Are you sure this is Florida?" Pete said in exasperation.

"Pretty sure. That's what I have on my driver's license, but they like to call this part of the state L.A.," Marty said with a smile.

"L.A.? What the hell does this place have in common with Los Angeles?"

"Not Los Angeles lad; Lower Alabama.

Pete laughed as he concurred with the description, even though he had never been to Alabama. "So where are you from? From your accent I was thinking Brooklyn," Pete said with a smile as filled his cup again.

"I come from Kingston-upon-Hull. We just call it Hull. We're on the River Hull right off the North Sea," Marty said.

"How did you get here?" Pete drank another glass of water and wanted to keep the conversation going for as long as he could.

"I bloody well won the lottery, damned immigration lottery. I started in this very spot last year. I love the job, and the insane blokes we work for. They get the damndest jobs I've ever seen, but I suppose that's what makes it fun. We get shit days like this one, but we have some fun too, and always try to drink enough so that we don't bloody care. So, come on then, up and at 'em. Those rocks won't break themselves, will they?"

CHAPTER 26

TIME TO MOVE ON

The laundry was done. The house was unpacked. Now what? Anne sat in her living room, not interested in what was on the T.V. She looked out the window at her yard and thought about working in the flower bed, but it was too hot to work in the yard. The pool looked nice, but it was just too damn hot to go outside for anything. She was lost, lonely, and bored. She walked over to the medicine cabinet and pulled out her bottle of Valium. With only two left, she reluctantly decided to wait and put the bottle away.

She removed her clothes and climbed into the shower. When she finished, she decided to go grocery shopping; at least that would keep her occupied for a couple of hours. While she was drying her hair and putting on some makeup, she came to the conclusion that she needed to get out of the house and get a job. Idleness was not going to be healthy for her and she knew it. She got dressed and got into her car and started to drive. A short time later, she reached the light at the corner of John Sims and Palm Boulevard and pulled into O'Brian's IGA.

The air was so hot that by the time she walked from the car to the store, she was covered with a film of sweat. She was relieved when she entered the store and felt a powerful blast of air conditioning. She took a shopping cart and started down the aisles, getting familiar with the new local grocery store. It was on aisle four that she overheard the manager and head cashier talking.

"Mary called in this morning and quit. Apparently she's moving in with her boyfriend in Fort Walton and doesn't want to drive this far. It would have been nice if she'd have let us know she was thinking about this," the cashier complained.

Anne walked down a couple more aisles deliberating what to do. When she saw the manager on aisle nine, she reached her conclusion and approached him. She introduced herself and explained her situation. Mike, the manager, listened intently, and when she finished, he directed her to the customer service counter and had her to fill out an application. She did, and after a short interview she was hired. When Anne left the store, she was amazed at how quickly it had all transpired. She now had a job and something to do with herself for thirty-two hours a week. She allowed herself to feel good for a little while as she drove home. She reflected on what she had observed while in the store, and liked what she had seen. The store was very clean and had a friendly, small town, feel to it. She had watched the interaction between the store employees and their customers, and they seemed to know and like each other. Anne realized that she had a little smile on her face as she drove, and while she wasn't quite sure how to feel about it, she allowed it to linger.

CHAPTER 27

I AM ALIVE AGAIN

B ill was happy to be going to work at a new job. It was exciting. He wasn't sure about the details of what he was being asked to do, but he didn't really care. He was out of the Valley, he was starting over, and a new life was in front of him. He walked into the office with a spring in his step and a smile on his face and was greeted pleasantly by Mrs. Weatherby.

She was the office manager and ran a tight ship. She was in her early fifties with graying hair and a thin body and face. She dressed in semi-formal office attire and flat black shoes. She carried herself with an air of pride and dignity, but she seemed to be a very pleasant woman with a warm smile. She got Bill a cup of coffee, gave him a short tour, and took him to his new office. It was not palatial, but it was at least forty or fifty years newer than his last one. He moved behind his desk and sat in his chair to get comfortable in his new surroundings. He had a smile on his face as Mrs. Weatherby excused herself for a moment. When she returned, she put a pile of files and reference books on his desk.

"Mr. Evans will be in shortly. Your personal items were shipped here last week and are in those boxes over there. You can start organizing your office and cataloging these reference books. Ellen and I are here to help you with anything you need. If there is nothing else, I'll let you get started and I'll get back to my work," she said warmly with a slight southern accent that Bill found charming.

"No, that's fine. This will keep me occupied for quite a while. Thank you."

With that said, Mrs. Weatherby turned and left. Bill understood that she was a no-nonsense woman who was very efficient with her time, but she had a southern charm that softened her approach and made Bill feel comfortable around her. He was elated with the way things were starting off. He took a sip of his coffee and casually inventoried the items on his desk, and then leaned back in his chair and looked at it. It was of adequate size, sturdy, dark cherry, and matched the bookcase behind his chair and along the wall. Out the window he saw a large oak tree with Spanish moss hanging from its limbs. Bill took a deep breath and wondered if he was dreaming; this was so far from the old windowless factory office that he felt like a new man.

CHAPTER 28

THE DOJO

Pete was adjusting to his new life and surroundings, and things were getting into a comfortable routine. Despite the nasty nature of the work, he liked his job and the people he worked with, and after a month on the job, Joe began to appreciate his reliability and effort and noticed that he was beginning to understand what was going on around him, so he gave him a raise. Pete was happy; he'd been hoping for a larger raise, but he was satisfied that his hard work had been noticed and appreciated.

The joke around the boatyard was that nobody worked harder for less money than the boys at Becton. That was the only thing Pete didn't like about working for Joe, because he was earnestly trying to save some money for a new truck since the old van was finally wearing out. The trip from Connecticut had been too much for it, and it now seemed like every time he got a few extra dollars, the van would break down and he'd be broke again.

"Come on Numb Nuts, I'll drop you off at Firestone," Joe said to Pete.

"Thanks Joe. I'll get the gate on the way out."

"Well, of course you're going to get it. You didn't think I was getting out of my truck, did you?" he jovially asked.

"No, boss, I know my place. I am the gatekeeper!"

Pete closed the gate as Joe drove out. Bonehead followed them to the edge of the property and stood wagging his tail as Pete locked him in for the night. Pete had begun to become attached to the dog, and said goodnight to him by kneeling down and reaching between the gates and patting him on the head and rubbing his ears one last time. He ran up to the truck and jumped in. The truck smelled of diesel, grease, and hydraulic fluid. The seat was full of papers, clothes, and an assortment of parts and pieces to various machines. Even though it was a full-size truck, they had to move stuff around for Pete to fit in.

They had finished work for the day, and since Pete had dropped his van off at lunch to buy two new, used tires, Joe decided to give him a ride to pick it up. The used tires were thirty bucks, mounted and balanced, and with Pete's wages the way they were, it was a deal that he could afford, and the tires would probably last him until the van died for good.

"I hope they're done," Pete said to Joe. He knew it was wishful thinking and they wouldn't be done with the van, because he was probably going to be the last job of the day. So, he would wind up sitting around reading old magazines for quite a while.

"Well, I'd love to stay and chit-chat with you, but I have many miles to go before I rest," Joe said as he pulled the old truck into the parking lot. Sure enough, the van was parked right where they'd left it when they'd dropped it off earlier.

Pete was resigned to accepting his fate. It was part of the deal when you bought used tires from Bobby Ross: he would fit you in when he got the chance. They were busy and Bobby had warned him that that chance might not come until after they'd closed for the day. Pete understood what this meant; his little cash deal was buying the beer for the shop tonight.

"Listen, why don't you go watch those silly guys play around in that bozo next door for a while? That might be entertaining."

"Bozo? What's a bozo?" Pete asked.

"You know, a bozo, where a bunch of funny little guys put on white pajamas and run around doing that Hong Kong phooey stuff," Joe said as he looked at Pete and waited patiently for him to get out of his truck so he could be on his way.

"Yeah, I might do that. Thanks for the ride, Joe. I'll see you in the morning." Pete jumped out of the truck and caught a thermos as it tried to roll out the door with him. He put the thermos back on the seat and closed the door. Joe waved and left in a hurry.

Pete looked at his watch; it was five after five. Bobby didn't close until six; he could be sitting there for an hour. He turned around and looked at what was around him. Across the street was a barbershop; to the left of that was Giff's Sub Shop. He wasn't hungry and didn't need a haircut. He looked to his right, and attached to the garage was the dojo that Joe had spoken about, and next to it was a furniture store. He started walking in that direction with no real purpose except to waste time.

When he reached the door at the dojo, he saw that it was propped open and he walked inside. The door led to a paneled reception area that had a desk on one side and a sitting area on the other. On shelves along the walls of the sitting area were several rows of trophies of various sizes and shapes. Beyond the reception area was the dojo floor, and in there he saw an incredibly graceful black man in a white uniform doing some kind of routine. In his hands was what looked like a boat oar, and as Pete watched him move, he was in awe at how graceful he was and how effortlessly he glided about. He seemed to barely touch the ground as he danced across the floor.

The spins and jumps flowed so much that it seemed like he was doing a type of ballet. He apparently didn't notice Pete or didn't care that he was watching as he continued his routine uninterrupted. He stepped with his right foot forward, spun the oar over his head, and thrust it out in front of him. When he did this, his uniform snapped like a bullwhip; his once flowing and silky body was instantly straight and strong and seemed to be in perfect position. He paused for a moment, and then spun the oar and snapped it into place by his side and returned to a standing position with the oar braced smartly under his right arm.

He stood at perfect attention, paused for a moment, and then bowed to a picture of an old man on the wall in front of him. When he completed his closing ceremony his body relaxed and he turned towards Pete.

He started walking toward Pete with a smile that made him feel welcome and at ease. It was apparent that he had been fully aware of Pete's presence the whole time.

"Hello, welcome to our dojo. I am Mr. Sanders. Can I help you?" He reached out his hand and Pete shook it.

"No, no, I was just walking by and saw the door was open. I just figured I'd come in and look around."

"It's good to notice the doors that have been left open for you. So, if you're interested, I'd be happy to show you around. We have a children's class that starts at five thirty and the adult class starts at six forty five. I teach the children's class today, so I was just doing a little warm up. Have you ever studied before?" he asked.

"No, no I haven't. That dance thing you were doing was very cool. Have you been doing this for a long time?" Pete was in awe of the man and looked at his black belt and saw five red stripes wrapped around the end of it. He instantly knew how stupid he sounded.

Mr. Sanders laughed in a very kind manner. "That was called a kata, and yes, I have been doing this for a long time. I grew up in Brooklyn and my parents got me started when I was about eight years old. So, would you like to walk through and see the dojo? And remember, you're always more than welcome to sit and watch our classes to see if you'd like it."

"Sure." Pete had nothing better to do, so he decided to walk around and get the grand tour. He started to walk in the dojo and almost let his shoes touch the floor when Mr. Sanders stopped him.

"We must always remove our shoes before entering the dojo. We also bow when we enter and when we leave."

Pete didn't like this part; he had been in the water all day in leather sneakers and his shoes and socks were dirty, wet, and nasty. He hesitated for a moment because he knew that when he took off his shoes and socks he was going to make an angry skunk seem tame. He decided that he was committed to the tour and besides, he was just wasting time and would never see this guy again, so he bent down and removed his shoes.

He was not disappointed. His feet were shriveled up white prunes, and the room instantly smelled of rotted foot death. Mr. Sanders raised his eyebrows as the stench burrowed into his nose, but he otherwise remained stoic and didn't say a word.

When they entered the dojo, Mr. Sanders bowed and Pete followed his lead. As they walked across the floor, Mr. Sanders pointed to the mirrors that covered two walls and explained that they were used by students to see themselves while they practiced their technique. He stopped walking and pointed to the pictures on the walls. His face was very serious and respectful.

"The pictures you see along the walls are the Masters of our style and show the lineage of Goju. That is Master Miyagi, Master Shinzo, Master Taguchi, and others. If you decide to study with us, you will learn all about them. There is much more to karate than just learning how to kick and punch. Karate is a great way to improve focus, confidence, balance, and respect."

They continued across the floor, and when they reached the other side, Mr. Sanders stopped, turned, and bowed again; Pete did the same. He then showed Pete the weight room and the locker room. It was small and simple. Pete looked around again and then he looked at Mr. Sanders. He was not the stereotypical killer karate man that Pete had expected; he was a very intelligent, gentle, and welcoming man and Pete began to feel at ease with him.

"How much does it cost?" Pete blurted out.

"Shihan is having a special: ninety-nine dollars for three months, and that includes a gi, or uniform. You should try it; karate is very good for you and I think you'd like it. If you have some time, come by and watch a class or two. I'm sorry, I'd like to talk longer, but the children will be here soon and I have to get ready. I hope to see you soon." Mr. Sanders smiled warmly at Pete, shook his hand again, and bowed to him. Pete bowed in return, and then bowed again on the way out.

He put his socks and shoes back on his feet. They were cold and wet and full of sand. It occurred to him that Mr. Sanders was probably getting rid of him so he could air the place out before the mothers arrived with their kids. He walked out and back over to Bobby's to check on his van. Bobby saw him standing out front and came over, wiping his hands with a rag.

"Hey, Pete. Sorry for taking so long. We've been slammed all afternoon. As soon as Tommy gets done with that oil change, we'll bring in the van and get you on your way. If you want, I can ring you up now and we'll get that out of the way."

Pete followed Bobby to the counter and gave him thirty dollars. Bobby reached under the counter, pulled out an old bill book, and wrote Pete a receipt for two used tires, then put the money in a bag under the counter. Bobby said thanks and then excused himself to go back to mounting a couple of tires. Pete watched the guys work for a while and then walked back outside.

He looked toward the dojo and saw some children dressed in their clean white uniforms being escorted by parents into the dojo and decided to walk over and have a look at what they were doing. He stood outside the building and observed them through the large plate glass window in front of the school.

There were now twelve or thirteen kids, who looked to be between nine and fifteen years old, bouncing around for a few minutes before class began. Some were practicing moves and others were just laughing and playing. Mr. Sanders walked to the front of the room and stood in front of the sword and the gong. He looked towards the back of the class with a stern but calm look on his face. An older boy, about fifteen, who wore a brown belt with three black stripes called the class to attention; the kids immediately stopped what they were doing and ran into position.

The children were standing straight and tall, with eyes fixed on the front of the room. Their hands were at their sides and they stood in four neat rows. Each student knew where to go and who to stand next to. The leader checked the students and made sure they were in place, straightened the belts of some of the smaller children who wore white belts, and when he was satisfied that everything was in order, he took his place in the right corner of the front row.

He bowed to Mr. Sanders and confirmed that they were ready to begin. Mr. Sanders stood at the front of the class and reviewed his students, and as he did this, he made a point to momentarily look eye-to-eye with each student. When his review was complete, his smile returned and he began addressing the children.

"Good afternoon, students. I hope you all had a great day, you're feeling good, and are ready to work hard." When he finished greeting them, they all knelt down.

The older boy said something in Japanese and they all placed their hand on the floor in front of them, bowed deeply to Mr. Sanders, and returned to the kneeling position. Mr. Sanders said something and they bowed again. Pete was enjoying watching them conclude their well rehearsed opening ceremony, so he moved inside to watch and listen.

"I want you to leave all your problems outside. I want you to close your eyes and take deep breaths and relax. When you close your eyes, you see darkness; I want you to see light. Concentrate on that alone; build a bright white room in the darkness."

The whole class bowed their heads and remained still for some time. Pete saw these children who, moments ago, had been bouncing off the walls, remain still, silent, and amazingly relaxed and peaceful. Mr. Sanders raised his head, took a deep breath, and looked at his class with a satisfied little smile on his face. After a minute or two, he called them to attention, gave them a moment to refocus, and then began calisthenics.

While they were stretching and doing jumping jacks and pushups, Pete kept an eye on both the kids and Mr. Sanders. They were working hard, but he was constantly talking to them and keeping a smile on his and the children's faces. Pete couldn't help but enjoy watching him work with the kids. He began to think differently about karate and the "bozo," as Joe had called it.

He watched as this very kind and gentle, but surely very deadly man, worked with these children, and a strange feeling came over him. He thought about his life and where he was and what he was doing. He was young, single, and was doing nothing with his spare time. He was tired of sitting around smoking dope and watching television. He knew he wasn't a kid anymore, but he didn't really feel like a man either. He didn't want to go to college right now, and while he enjoyed his job, he sure didn't want to be doing it when he was fifty. Pete was intrigued by what he was watching and began to wonder what it would be like to be in a karate class.

Bobby stepped out of the garage and yelled to Pete that his van was ready to go. It caught Pete off guard and pulled him back to reality. He walked over to Bobby, who tossed him the keys to his van, and he was on his way.

CHAPTER 29

BARGE LEAK

It had been over a month since Pete had gone to the dojo. He drove by it every day on his way to and from work, and he couldn't control the urge to look at it each time he went by. He had meant to stop in and check it out again for some time, but hadn't found the time or made the effort. It was on his to do list in the back of his mind and he knew he would go back; he just wasn't sure when.

Pete pulled into the gate, parked his van, and got out with coffee for him and a bacon, egg, and cheese biscuit for Bonehead. Joe, Jeff, and Marty's trucks were already there, but he didn't see them, so he walked over to Bonehead, who was lying in the shade, and gave him the biscuit. As he was petting the dog, he heard the unmistakable sound of the pump starting down on the barge, so he left the dog and walked to the middle of the yard and looked around again, and saw the three men standing on the barge looking down a hatch.

The old and rusty barge was leaking again. It was one hundred and ten feet long and thirty feet wide, and this morning it was listing hard to the deep water side. The barge was divided into six separate compartments by bulkheads which were dividing walls of steel. If one compartment started to leak, the water was confined there and the barge would list but it would not sink. When the barge was built, it was painted black inside and out, and in some places, mostly the sides, the paint was still visible.

Pete made his way towards the barge and noticed that they were getting ready to patch it. Pete walked up the gang plank as Marty climbed down the hatch and Jeff finished putting on a dive tank and mask and jumped overboard. Joe stayed on deck and mixed some two part epoxy and applied it to the bottom of a steel plate. He then put a long bolt through the plate and handed it and a wrench to Jeff, who took the items and disappeared under water.

Marty descended the old rusty steel ladder and entered the leaking compartment. Joe looked at Pete and told him to follow Marty into the barge so that he could learn how to patch it. By the time he made it to the bottom of the ladder, his body was already covered with sweat from the intensity of the heat. Marty hated patching the barge and constantly complained about it, and now Pete understood why. He stood on a lower support beam and crouched down, grabbing onto one of the uprights for balance to avoid smashing his head on the upper beams as he surveyed his surroundings.

The support, as well as everything else in the barge's belly, was covered with a slime that had formed from the paint, oil, condensation, and who knows what else over its many years of service. It was just plain nasty grunge that would take a long time to get off his hands. He stood next to Marty as he scanned the compartment, armed with the tools he needed to patch the hole: a flashlight, a wrench, a two-by-four, a nut and washer, and a long thin stick.

It was early in the morning and it was already stifling hot inside the beast. The air was stale and dank and everything around him was wet from the condensation. The deck above him had a layer of water built up from the condensation and droplets were falling into the water below, making their familiar and almost rhythmical dripping sound that echoed in the enclosed structure. Pete had been inside the barge before and the confinement and darkness, along with the heat, always created an eerie feeling that made him unhappy.

Marty saw where the water was shooting into the air. He told Pete to follow him, and they slowly made their way to the hole, where they found it to be about the size of a half dollar. The sound of the bubbling water was amplified by the steel surrounding it to the point that it sounded like a rushing river. They felt like they were in a steel drum, or an oven, as Marty started to work. He ran the stick through the hole and shined the light at the hole and used them as a beacon for Jeff. He took the wrench in his free hand and started to slowly and lightly tap on the barge near the hole. The only thing for him to do now was to wait for Jeff to find him.

JEFF LOVED BEING UNDER THE water. It was cool and refreshing, and as he looked around the barge, he could see a variety of fish poking at the barnacles and oysters growing on it. He watched several small pin fish poking about and then, in the distance, he saw some large sheep head swimming under the barge. He quickly resurfaced and got Joe's attention and asked him to get his spear gun so that he could get a couple for dinner.

He went back under and Joe went to the truck for the spear. Normally, a diver is face down while under water, but that doesn't work when doing repairs under a vessel, so Jeff rolled onto his back as he went under the barge. As he did, the thin layer of cold water that was on his mask ran down onto his face and into his eyes. When it settled into the corner of the mask and out of his eyes, he reopened them and started moving under the barge. He worked his way to the approximate location of the hole, using his hands to keep him off the bottom of the barge.

Jeff liked diving, but there is an absolute absence of light and an other worldly feeling under a large barge in murky water. His weight belt was not quite heavy enough to sink him and the air tanks on his back were like balloons that wanted to lift him to the surface, so he was forced to continually push on the barnacle encrusted bottom of the barge to keep from floating up and against it. He wore thick dive gloves to protect his hands from the sharp edges of the oysters and barnacles because they were like dirty razors and could easily slice any exposed flesh and create a nasty gash. Jeff was always cautious as he worked because he had seen *Jaws* and from that time on, he had never liked swimming in blood filled salt water.

The Florida bayou is a unique ecosystem. The water is brackish and the salinity can vary enough to have both alligators and sharks visiting the same waters. This knowledge and the lack of visibility fed a feeling that was in the back of every diver's mind that something large and hungry could be lurking very close by.

Under the barge it was completely dark, with the only contrast in color coming from the air bubbles that were trapped between the bottom of the barge and the water. Jeff loved to watch the air bubbles dance about on the bottom of the barge as they found their way to the surface. The sound of the pump running and the water crashing into the bayou were faint noises that seemed to be off in the distance. He looked around and followed the sound of tapping that began emanating from the barge, and as he moved toward the sound, he saw a faint light a short distance away. When he got to the light, he grabbed and wiggled the stick that was protruding from the bottom of the barge. Marty understood the signal and pulled the stick back inside and handed the flashlight to Pete. Jeff took his dive knife and cleaned some of the barnacles from the surrounding area, then took the steel plate with the bolt and inserted it through the hole.

Marty saw the bolt come through the hole and took his two-by-four and placed it across two support beams, pulling the bolt through a predrilled hole in the board. He put on the nut and washer and tightened it as much as he could, then inspected the leak. It had worked. He took the flashlight back from Pete, looked around the compartment, and when he saw no other leaks, he happily made his way to the hatch with Pete in tow. When they emerged from the compartment and breathed the air, it felt like they'd stepped into air conditioning.

By the time they finished on the inside of the barge, Jeff had already resurfaced and taken his spear gun back underwater. Now the three of them stood on the deck and waited for him to come up again, and when he finally did, he had a grin from ear to ear and a large sheep head on the end of his spear. He handed it to Joe, who removed the fish and then handed the spear back to Jeff. This process was repeated two more times before Joe said "enough" and decided it was time to get some work done.

When Jeff finished changing into dry clothes, he, Marty, and Pete got into his truck and, after a quick stop to drop off the fish at Jeff's house, they headed to Bluewater Bay to work on a golf course bridge, while Joe went to a meeting about a large job on the Choctawhatchee River.

CHAPTER 30

WHAT AM I MISSING?

A nne was mindlessly working her aisle at the grocery store. She was always pleasant to her co-workers and her customers, but she was afraid that her life had once again become filled with meaningless monotony. The trauma at home had subsided, but now it was as if she was just going through the motions of life and missing out on living it. She finished handing a customer change when the next one stepped in front of her.

"Hello. Paper or plastic?" Anne asked and gave her customary smile while glancing at him and pulling his groceries in front of her.

"Plastic; it's always plastic for me," Ryan replied. He was looking at Anne and decided that she was an attractive woman and that he wanted to get to know her. "Did you know that you are looking lovely today...." he paused and read the name on her tag, "Anne, and that you have a wonderful smile?"

Ryan Pearson was in his late forties, a large man with stunning blue eyes and a bright smile. Anne glanced at him with a quizzical look on her face. She was debating if he was complimenting her or hitting on her. She decided it was the latter.

"Well, thank you. Oh, and by the way, Dr. Norstrom is right next door and he has a wonderful selection of eye glasses. You should check him out," she said sarcastically with a wry smile as she continued checking his items.

"No, my eyes are just fine. You know, I've been shopping here for over ten years and haven't seen you here before. You must be new. So, Anne, Do you know what I love about living here?"

"No, what do you love about living here?" Anne replied nonchalantly as she worked. When she looked up at her charming customer she was caught off-guard because, for the first time she noticed his piercing blue eyes.

"Well, I travel a lot -I just returned yesterday after being out of town on business for a few weeks- and every time I come home, this town changes something for the better." Ryan was trying his best to make her notice him.

"Oh, that was bad, and yes, I just started a little while ago," she replied and allowed herself to chuckle at his lame compliment.

"You must be new to Niceville as well, because I would usually notice someone as pretty as you. Are you an Air Force wife?" Ryan asked hopefully.

He liked military wives because he knew that they were discreet, and usually moved within a year or two, so there was little chance of an affair getting too serious and interfering with his marriage.

"No, we're not military. My husband is an engineer, and yes, we just moved to the area. That will be $123.97, please."

"Here you go, Anne. I think I'm going to have to do more shopping very soon."

Ryan gathered his bags and smiled at Anne as he pushed his cart away. He was intrigued by her, and when Anne saw his smile, she felt a slight tingle within her that she hadn't felt in a long time. She was flattered because he was a very good looking man, and he had been flirting with her... and she liked it. When Ryan was safely gone, she looked at Penny; the shy seventeen-year-old bag girl had a devilish little grin on her face as she looked at Anne. Her next customer stepped up; she was in her mid-thirties and gave Anne a knowing smile and then commented on the fit of Ryan's jeans as he walked out the store. All three women involuntarily turned their heads and enjoyed the moment, and they laughed out loud when Penny shook her head and commented on how bad the two of them were.

The rest of the day went by quickly, and when Anne got into her car and sat there alone, she couldn't help but think about Ryan. He did have nice jeans and a great smile. Anne indulged in a few curiously naughty thoughts about him and felt like a giddy teenager again as she drove home.

She soon pulled into her driveway, and when she saw Bill's car, her fantasy ended. Her spirit came crashing down and the reality of her life weighed heavily on her. She didn't resent him anymore… she just kind of ignored him. He was more of a roommate now than a spouse. He wasn't drinking much anymore, had lost a few pounds, and was actually looking better, but she felt no emotional or sexual attraction to him. He was just a man that lived in the same house and slept on the other side of the bed.

She walked into the house and smelled dinner. Bill had put some spaghetti sauce on the stove and it was cooking slowly. He had placed a pan of water on the stove earlier and, as per their custom, she turned it on when she got home. Anne looked outside and saw him in the pool, swimming his nightly laps. She waved to him and he waved back and continued swimming. She put her purse and keys on the counter and went into her bedroom to get out of her clothes and into the shower.

When the water got as hot as she could stand, she climbed in. The spray of hot water felt cleansing, and as she lathered her body with soap, she realized that it had been some time since she had shaved her legs and under her arms. She was surprised at how much she had let her body hair grow. She giggled to herself about not wanting Ryan to see her hairy arms and legs and started shaving.

When her legs were smooth, she ran her hands up and down them and was proud of her work. She then examined her legs as the water fell on them and was pleased with their shape and tone. She looked between her legs and saw a thick patch of hair and decided to take care of that while she was in the mood. When she was satisfied that she had recaptured her femininity and was rinsing off, she thought about Ryan and kept her hand between her legs and rinsed herself longer than she needed to. She kept thinking about Ryan and a subtle tremor erupted in her body and impulsively, she turned the showerhead from spray to jet. She was soon leaning against the shower wall enjoying the sensations until her chest was crimson and heaving. She couldn't help but let out a small moan as she reached her plateau, and for several moments she just let the water stream on her body as she gathered her senses.

She turned the water from jet to spray again and put her head under the water. As she turned her head from side to side, she thought she saw a shadow move and was startled. She turned the water off and called out to Bill, but got no answer. She got out of the shower and wrapped a towel around her body and looked around the bathroom and then the bedroom. When she was convinced that it was her imagination, she dried off, put on some night clothes, and went to the kitchen.

Bill was wearing dry clothes and was seated at the table. He had put three plates at the table and was loading his plate.

"Well, I guess Pete's going to miss dinner again. Are you hungry? Come on, dig in." Anne looked at him and didn't know what to think or what to do. She was sure he had been watching her, but she didn't know for how long. Suddenly she felt dirty again and not at all hungry.

"No, I'm not hungry right now. You go ahead and eat. I'm going to watch some TV and maybe I'll grab a bite later," she said shortly and then walked away from her husband and into the family room, turned on the TV, and sat on the couch alone.

Bill stopped loading his plate and held a fork full of spaghetti in mid-air as he watched her walk away. He was insulted and his heart fell into his chest. He became angry with himself for getting excited. He had come in from swimming and when he'd gone into the bedroom he couldn't help but see her in the shower. As he'd watched the only love of his life through the distorted glass of the shower, he'd been reminded of how beautiful she was. He'd only watched for a moment, leaving when he'd realized what she'd been doing to give her some privacy, but he had gotten excited. That excitement had come crashing down, and so he finished loading his plate and ate alone, in silence.

Chapter 31

A Taste of Nature

The buzzing sounded faint and distant, but it was growing louder and nearer. It was a persistent noise that was unrelenting in its attack on his ears. He tried to hide from it by rolling over in his bed and pulling his pillow over his head, but it wouldn't go away; its intensity only continued to increase. He finally raised his head and suddenly realized where he was and what time it was: Five AM; the alarm had been going off for half an hour.

He was supposed to meet Jeff and Joe at the boat yard at five thirty. He quickly rolled out of his bed, threw on some clothes, and made his way to work. When he pulled into the gate, Jeff was already moving the *Sue-Bee* into position behind the large barge. He said hello to Bonehead as he walked by and joined Joe on deck as Jeff nosed up to the bit. When Joe saw him walking across the barge, he looked at his watch and then glared at Pete.

"You're late!"

"I'm sorry Joe, I didn't hear the alarm, but I'm only five minutes late."

Joe's eyes grew wide, and he became incensed.

"Late is late. I don't give a rat's ass if it's one minute. If five minutes is no big deal, then why can't you guys ever be five minutes early? I'm sure you're going to write five thirty on your time sheet, but at five thirty Jeff and I were standing here by ourselves. You knew we had to be out of here early, and you knew that if we don't get it done today then nobody gets paid on Friday. Maybe I should care about you guys getting paid as much as you guys worry about showing up on time." Joe grabbed the nose line off the *Sue-Bee* and then attached it to the center bit of the barge. "Get on the boat and get me the cables to tie this thing off."

"I'm sorry, Joe. It won't happen again," Pete said meekly as he was climbing on deck of the *Sue-Bee* and went to work.

They attached the *Sue-Bee* to the big barge, side-tied the small barge to it, and departed from the boatyard by six with forty-five tons of limestone rip-rap to be delivered to Mrs. Anderson in Garniers Bayou. They knew it would take a herculean effort to accomplish what they were attempting, but they needed to complete the job and be back on the bridge job tomorrow in order to make payroll on Friday, so they were making the effort, hoping that if everything went as planned, they would make it back by seven or seven thirty.

The sun was emerging on the horizon as they left Tom's Bayou and entered Boggy Bayou. The air was clean and fresh, and the morning was shaping up to be spectacular. When they passed Shirks Point, Pete was on the bow of the barge with a hot cup of coffee he'd gotten from Jeff and was watching as an osprey left her nest to begin her morning hunt. He was mesmerized as he watched her glide along the coast, searching for a fish swimming near the surface. She flapped her wings a half a dozen times and then glided for a while. She flew with elegance and grace on a light breeze and kept her eyes trained on the water. He watched as she spotted a school of mullet moving across the shallows. She seemed to stop in midair and stuck out her chest, and started flapping her wings rapidly in order to hover over an area. When she decided on her target, she tucked her wings and crashed into the water. She stuck out her talons at the last second and grasped a fish that was almost too big for her to lift out of the water. She flopped in the water for a moment as she struggled to get back aloft, but soon her powerful wings lifted her and the fish into the air where they started back to her nest.

After a time, he lost sight of her and noticed four dolphins that had come alongside them and begun inspecting the vessel. They swam under the boat and the barge, bobbed up and down, and seemed to be having fun with a new toy. He stood mesmerized as they moved through the water like silvery grey torpedoes, twisting and turning as they leaped from the water, took a deep breath, and went under again. Pete moved to the deck of the *Sue-Bee* and kneeled down and put his hand in the water. The dolphins came close and investigated his hand, but they would never let him touch them. He fantasized about jumping in with them, climbing on one of their backs and going for a ride, but had to settle for just watching them dance inches away from him.

Twenty minutes later they made the turn out of Boggy Bayou and into the Choctawhatchee Bay. The dolphins grew bored with the games and disappeared as fast as they had appeared, and once Pete could no longer see them, he returned to the front of the barge and immersed himself in the serene beauty of what had been created for him. These were the experiences and cherished rewards that made Pete love his job, and it was mornings like this that made the hard work and low pay worthwhile.

It was a spectacular autumn morning with a light breeze, low humidity, and a clear sky. As they continued west past marker one, the bay was almost flat and the gentle breeze was at their back. The trip was smooth, pleasant, and without incident.

By mid-morning they approached the Shalimar Bridge and were entering Garniers Bayou. Jeff eased the throttle back and shifted the boat into neutral. The boat channel under the bridge was too narrow for them to remain side-tied, so working rapidly as they free floated in the bayou; they untied the small barge and moved it to the nose of the big one. The barge was thirty feet wide and the channel only about forty five feet wide. Once everything was secured in place they were nearly two hundred feet long from the bow of the little barge to the stern of the *Sue-Bee*. The light breeze that was at their back and so pleasant on the bay was now hitting them broadside and pushing them into the bridge.

Jeff had no desire to make the evening news, so he took an extra moment to feel the wind, study the incoming current, and prepare for what would be a tight fit on the best of occasions. When he was confident that he had done all that he could, he returned to the wheelhouse and ordered Pete to his position on the bow of the barge. The breeze was out of the east and hitting them broadside on their starboard side. Pete stood at the bow and used hand signals to help Jeff stay as close to the starboard piling as possible. Jeff kept the throttle down and eased them into position, but soon realized that he didn't have enough head-speed and the persistent breeze and current were pushing the barge toward the piling on the port side. He was too long to go straight through the channel without smashing into the bridge, so at the last minute he cut the wheel hard and put the boat in full reverse and decided to approach at an angle. Pete began to worry, but Jeff remained calm and allowed the wind to move him down a little and then he turned his nose into the wind.

He put the motors to slow ahead and worked his way to the mouth of the boat lane, and when he was convinced that there was no turning back and that he was in the best position he could get them into, he cut the wheel to kick the stern around and hit the throttle. Black smoke erupted from the stack as the motor screamed and a giant rush of white water burst from the stern as the barge picked up speed. The stern kicked around as the bow entered the boat lane and they went under the narrow bridge with only a few feet to spare on either side and were so close to the piling that Pete wanted to reach out and touch them as they passed.

When he was under the bridge and heard the cars and trucks clicking and clacking as they ran over the expansion joints above him, Pete couldn't resist and yelled out to hear his echo. It put a small childish smile on his face, and when the sunlight hit him as the bow emerged from the bridge, he looked back into the wheelhouse. Jeff was just getting under the bridge, and Pete saw the concentration on his face and just then realized how big the barge was and how small the opening was. It was sinking into Pete's head that this really wasn't a game or a joy ride; what Jeff had just done and how easy he had made it look showed impressive skill.

Once they made it through the bridge- without touching a piling- Jeff relaxed and eased the throttle back. He adjusted his tack to the northwest and made their way up the ever narrowing Chula Vista bayou.

Twenty minutes later, they saw Mrs. Anderson's dock and began to line up for the push in. The path to her seawall was narrow and difficult to negotiate because it had long docks-with big, beautiful, and expensive boats secured to them- on both sides of their work area. While Jeff was positioning for the push in, Pete climbed into the old crane and fired it up. A puff of black smoke out the stack signaled to Jeff that the crane was running. Pete pulled back on the controls to lift the boom to a forty five degree angle, then climbed out and hooked onto a spud. He then climbed back into the crane, lifted it, and swung into position.

Jeff continued to guide the slow moving goliath between the docks, and once he saw that Pete had the spud in position, and he had the barge drifting in the right direction, he put the boat in neutral and ran onto the barge and guided the spud into the well. When they felt the barge lurch from touching the sand under them, Pete released the brake and the spud dropped rapidly into the sand and mud, causing the barge to immediately stop its forward movement, but their forward energy was now transferred and the barge began to pivot. Jeff quickly unhooked the spud and hooked up the second one; when it was secure, he gave Pete the signal and they moved it into position and set it only seconds before the barge collided with the boathouse.

Once everything was secure and they could relax for a moment, Jeff looked at Pete and congratulated him for his improvement and gave him instruction on the next step. "Good job, Pete. You're getting the hang of it. Now, let's get the little barge alongside here and put the bobcat on it, then I'll swing the crane over to the clamshell and you rig it up. All set… well then, let's get some work done." They moved quickly because they knew that they had a lot of rock to move and very little time to do it.

The two men untied the small barge from the bow and brought it portside of the large barge and lashed the two together. Jeff climbed into the crane and, with Pete now rigging, transferred the bobcat to the small barge, and then they attached the clamshell and began transferring rocks. Once about five or six tons were loaded, Jeff climbed out of the crane and jumped into the water with Pete. The two of them pushed the barge about fifty feet to the seawall, and once in position, Jeff climbed into the bobcat and started unloading rocks.

Jeff almost always operated the equipment when they were on the job. Pete was learning and getting better, but he hadn't yet developed enough touch to keep from sliding overboard with the bobcat or the skill he needed with the crane to set equipment down gently or run the clamshell in tight areas. Lifting things was easy: release the brake and pull back on the lever. Setting them down without destroying everything was another matter, and to make matters worse, their crane was a twenty-year-old Northwest forty that a lot of hard hours on it and tended to be herky-jerky. Even experienced operators would sometimes bounce a loader or swing too quickly, and with this equipment it only took a second to cause major damage or end a man's life.

As Jeff unloaded rock, moving rapidly and tossing rocks into the water, the deck of the barge got wet and the skid steer began sliding around as if it were on ice. Pete stood back and watched with apprehension, unsure if Jeff was going off the side, and although the tires often slid right up the edge, he never went over. Pete studied Jeff as he sat in the operator's chair and was amazed at how relaxed he seemed. He moved fast and fluidly, instinctively knowing just how far he could slide before going over the edge. He would raise the bucket and tilt it back and forth in a way that would toss the rocks a few feet and into rough position against the seawall. Jeff was one with the machine and made it look so easy that he might as well have been sitting on the couch watching television.

When they finished unloading the barge, Jeff shut down the bobcat and jumped into the water with Pete. The two of them pushed the small barge out to the large one and reloaded it. They continued the process until all the rocks were off the barge and in front of the seawall. When Jeff had finally unloaded the last bucket, he moved the bobcat in the center of the little barge, shut off the motor, climbed out and walked over to Pete. They looked at their work and agreed that it would take several hours to dress the rocks. Jeff looked at his watch and then looked at the clouds building in the sky and reluctantly conceded that they wouldn't have time to dress them properly and still make it back in time; Pete would have to come back tomorrow and finish dressing them by himself while Jeff and the other guys went back to the golf course bridges.

They pushed the barge out and re-tied it to the bow of the large barge, lifted the bobcat on deck, pulled the spuds and laid them on deck, and were on the way back to Valparaiso slightly behind schedule.

As they pulled away, Pete began his rounds and checked the compartments for leaks. When he got to the second compartment, he lifted the hatch and heard the water pouring in before he even stuck his head in the hole. They had poked a hole in it while the barge bobbed up and down during the unloading process and now the water was over six inches deep and rising rapidly. Pete knew the routine and immediately carried the heavy pump over to the hatch and put the suction hose in and fired it up. He then gathered a precut 2x4 and a small plywood patch and mixed up some two-part epoxy and climbed into the hole. When he climbed down the ladder and reached the bottom, his ears were assaulted by the loud combination of the *Sue-Bee* motor, the pump overhead, and the water pouring in that were echoing in the steel chamber and made it a very loud and very unpleasant place to be. He sloshed through the water and made his way to the geyser, cleaned the area as much as he could, and put the plywood over the hole. The pressure of the water pouring in was pushing the plywood up and away from the hole, so he placed his foot on it while he jammed the 2x4 in place to create a pressure patch from the deck above to the bottom of the barge. When the 2x4 was finally secure in place, he examined the result; it had slowed the leak, but hadn't stopped it. Pete let out a heavy sigh and was resigned to the fact that they would have to dive on it when they got back to the boatyard; it was going to be a long day.

WHEN THEY APPROACHED THE SHALIMAR Bridge, the bayou widened
and the morning's pleasant breeze had become a stiff wind. Jeff saw the
little white caps on the water and knew that he couldn't push straight
through the channel without the wind pushing him into the bridge,
so he eased the throttle back and allowed the wind to push him west
of the channel again. The wind forced him to drift farther from the
channel than he'd have liked, and it obligated him to approach it at a
severe angle.

Pete stood at the bow and kept looking back and forth between the
bridge and Jeff; he was still relatively new to this and wasn't sure what
Jeff was doing as he drifted farther and farther away from the boat lane.
The more they drifted, the more Pete became convinced that he was
lining up wrong. He frantically signaled for Jeff to turn the boat, but Jeff
ignored him and stayed on course. Once Pete become resigned to the
fact that he was being ignored, he stopped signaling and turned around
to wait for the impending impact. The barge was about two hundred
feet from the channel and heading right toward the pilings.

When Jeff felt that he was far enough downwind, he adjusted his
set and turned the nose of the barge into the wind, throttled up, and
began his approach. Pete felt the surge in power and speed and saw the
bridge coming straight at them, and as much as he liked Jeff, he didn't
think there was any way they could make it through without hitting the
bridge. He looked up and saw the cars passing overhead and began to
wonder if he would feel anything when the massive sections of concrete
fell on him. He quietly talked to Isaac and asked if it was time to see
him again. Pete began to move away from the front corner of the barge
when he heard Jeff yell to him.

"How close am I?"

"You're going to hit the bridge!" Pete yelled back with panic
beginning to well up in his voice.

"I didn't ask that. How close am I?" Jeff came back angrily with his
head sticking out the wheelhouse window.

"Thirty feet."

That's all he needed to know; Jeff pulled his head back inside the window and grasped the wheel tightly. He waited a moment more, asked for God's help, and then eased the throttle forward and cut the wheel to bring the stern around. Pete watched nervously as the starboard corner of the barge come within a couple of feet of the piling as they entered the boat lane, and when he turned to his left, he saw that the port side was now getting ready to collide with the piling on the other side. He lost faith and began to move quickly towards the stern because he knew that they were about to have a massive collision that would probably bring the whole bridge down on his head.

Jeff ignored his panic-stricken first mate and focused on the task at hand. Once he saw the starboard corner enter the lane he cut the wheel the rest of the way, hit the throttle hard, and slipped on through.

Once again, Pete could have touched the piling as they went past, but the barge never touched the bridge. Pete watched in amazement as the stern came around, the bow straightened out, and they eased right through. He turned toward Jeff, raised both hands above his head and began bowing to the master with a giant smile on his face.

When the *Sue-Bee* emerged from under the bridge, Jeff relaxed and let an ear to ear smile cross his face and he felt justifiably proud of the feat he had just accomplished. Once they were several hundred yards away from the bridge, he put the boat in neutral and walked onto the barge in order to repeat the process from the morning in reverse and move the small barge to the port side, and prepare for the ride home.

"Oh, ye of little faith, I saw you. You have to believe, Pete, you have to believe… and, I've got to tell you, this ain't my first rodeo; I've been going under this bridge for many years now. Have faith; I'll tell you when it's time to panic. Pushing barges are generally three hours of pure boredom, bracketed by thirty seconds of shear terror," Jeff said playfully as they pulled the barge around. When it was secure, he looked towards the northern sky and was alarmed by what he saw brewing. Giant thunderheads were growing rapidly. "Get everything secure and make sure the pump is fueled up and ready to go," Jeff said as he quickly made his way back to the wheelhouse.

He put the boat in gear and throttled up nervously, and then looked at the sky around him. He saw more clouds building towards the east, but his view, and the wind, were blocked by trees and condos, so he just prayed that it wasn't going to be as bad as he thought and proceeded forward. A few minutes later they passed Snug Harbor and reached the mouth of the bay. Jeff and Pete now had a full view of the sky before them, and immediately felt the full thirty-mile reach of the bay wind on their faces. The storm was growing rapidly, and the sky was being, quickly and ominously, darkened by giant thunderheads.

During the afternoon, the heat from the north and the cool gulf wind combine to generate strong thunderstorms that churn the bay, but as the heat dissipates and the storms pass, the bay will become calm and gentle again. The Choctawhatchee Bay will change from calm to three foot chops in mere minutes, and then it'll return to a calm and peaceful state in the same amount of time.

Jeff stood in the wheelhouse and looked at what awaited them in the bay, and knew that he had a decision to make. In the distance, he saw a dark curtain of rain falling and it was working its way towards them. He momentarily eased the throttle back when he felt the wind pick up and the temperature drop rapidly. It was going to be a strong storm.

He contemplated his options, and when he looked towards the east again, he saw Snug Harbor. It was merely two hundred yards away and they could safely anchor the barge and wait the storm out, but he knew that if he took that option, they would never make it back before dark, and then they would have to dive on the barge at night. If they tied up for the night and pushed back tomorrow, they would have to get the dive gear from Niceville and they still wouldn't be done until late that evening, and then they would have to push back in the morning. If they did that, they would never make it back to Bluewater Bay tomorrow, so they wouldn't get enough work done for them to trigger a draw on the contract until next Friday and nobody would get paid until then. Jeff had a mortgage and children.

Jeff made his decision and then called Pete to the wheel house.

"I want you to move the bobcat under the crane and strap it down with the come-a-longs. Secure the pump to the bit and make sure it's filled with gas. Then put extra lines on the little barge, and get every other line available and ready to grab quickly. Get everything you can off the deck that might get washed overboard, and put the fuel cans and five gallon buckets down below inside the hatch. It's gonna get rough." He then looked away from Pete and back out toward the bay

Pete stood motionless, but followed Jeff's gaze towards the bay. He didn't like what he saw, and it showed in his face. The bay had begun raging, but he tried to reassure himself that the barge was over a hundred feet long and the *Sue-Bee* was damn near forty feet; he was scared, but his confidence in Jeff and his abilities had grown in the last few hours.

"Why the hell are you standing there? Come on, move your ass!" Jeff screamed into the building wind.

The rain was still several hundred yards off the bow, but it was coming at them quickly. Pete shook his head, gathered all the courage he had, and hurried to his tasks. When the nose of the barge cleared the point at Snug Harbor, it, and Pete, were hit with an unimpeded wind that kicked up the dirt and dust from the deck of the barge and created a small sandstorm. The sand pelted him and felt like needles piercing his skin and it forced him to turn his head and shield his eyes with his hands. The storm was now strong, and the growing waves were white-capped and intense. The barge started to shutter as it was pummeled by the waves crashing into its bow. Pete had never experienced anything like this before and was truly scared, but he continued with his duties nonetheless.

He secured the pump and then prepared to move the bobcat and secure it. As he put his foot on the bucket and started climbing over it to get into the operator's seat, a wave jarred the barge and caused his foot to slip off the bucket. As his leg slid over the bucket, his shin scraped across the sharp steel and as he fell to the deck, it savagely removed the top layer of skin. A sharp and searing pain ran through him as blood began to ooze from his leg. He cursed loudly as he writhed about on the deck of the barge clutching his leg. After a minute or so he began taking deep breaths and worked to regain his composure. He sat up and examined the painful wound, and was relieved to find nothing more than a nasty and painful scrape. He slowly rose to his feet and tried again. On his second attempt, he successfully climbed into the machine and started it as larger and more intense waves began causing the bobcat to start bucking and sliding on the deck of the barge.

Pete's heart was pounding in his chest and he squeezed the controls as tightly as possible. He looked over the side of the barge and saw the deep, dark water surrounding him and briefly allowed thoughts of sliding off the side while strapped in the small machine enter his mind. He shivered and quickly pushed those thoughts out of his mind and regained focus on the task at hand. Pete tried to pull the controls back gently in order to carefully move the machine on the slippery deck, but the barge was jarred again by a strong wave, and he ended up yanking them instead, causing the machine to erratically hop backwards. He immediately pushed the handles forward and the machine stopped abruptly. He took a deep breath to regain his composure as the rain started coming down in small drops that were accelerated by the wind and, once again, felt like little needles were stinging his face. He ignored the pain and braced himself better and then slowly pulled the handles back again, and this time he was able to control the machine and tuck it in between the tracks of the crane without incident. He shut off the Bobcat and secured it to the crane with a strong chain.

The storm was upon them and the rain quickly increased in size and intensity. Pete was pummeled with the largest raindrops he had ever seen or felt. The rain was so intense that visibility was reduced to almost nothing. He looked back towards the boat and saw Jeff sticking his head out one side of the wheelhouse and then the other, trying to find his way through the soup.

"Aren't you worried about other boats? I can't see a damn thing!" Pete yelled at the top of his lungs. He was cold, wet, and miserable, and looked like a wet water rat as he stood looking pitifully at Jeff with his shoulders hunched as the cold rain continued to bombard him.

"There isn't anyone dumb enough to be out here except us. Watch for the markers; I want the green marker off my starboard and the red to my port," Jeff yelled back from the wheel house of the *Sue-Bee,* where he was warm, dry, shielded from the weather-except when he occasionally stuck his head out the door to get a different view of what lie ahead for them- and holding on tight.

Jeff looked at Pete and laughed to himself. He liked the new kid, but he looked so pathetic standing there in the rain. He was wearing an old Marshal Tucker Band tee-shirt, raggedy cut-off jeans, and nasty old sneakers with no socks. He had long stringy hair that was hanging almost to his shoulders and desperately needed to be cut. He stood close to six feet tall and looked like he weighed about a hundred and sixty pounds-and he was soaking wet-but he had no muscle definition. He and Joe were working on that. Jeff laughed because he had stood exactly where Pete was now standing, and felt that he knew what was going through Pete's mind….He hated his life.

A bolt of lightning cracked nearby and made them both jump. The muscles in the small of Jeff's back tightened into a knot as he refocused on battling the storm. He was an ex-jarhead, about five foot nine and a hundred and sixty pounds of naturally chiseled flesh, who got a strange rush from the all too real danger they faced. He grimaced when a series of heavy waves then crashed into them, causing the small barge to smash violently into the large one as it rode to the crest of a wave, and then dropped rapidly into the trough, snapping a two inch line like it was a shoestring. The nose of the little barge instantly began pulling away and separating from the large one.

"Get a new line on that fucking barge right now and tie that pump down better before it goes over," Jeff screamed from the wheelhouse window.

Pete looked into the wheelhouse and saw Jeff's intense eyes bulging with fury as he pointed out the window and yelled at the top of his lungs. Pete had never heard Jeff swear before and was taken aback, but it reinforced the gravity of the situation they faced and though he had wanted to, he didn't panic; instead, he came to life and responded to the urgency of the situation and moved at double time.

Pete made his way to the little barge and discovered that it now had four lines attaching it, and two of them were rubbing so hard against the rusted steel of the big barge that they were severely frayed and didn't look like they were going to last much longer. They continuously rubbed on the rusted steel, being pulled taunt, snapped, and stretched as the barge had been tossed about by the waves. Another series of waves hit them and jarred the pump until it was almost ready to go over the side. Pete was in a dilemma and hesitated because he didn't know which problem to solve first.

"Tie down that fucking pump!" Jeff screamed from the distance. The hesitation was expunged and Pete ran to the pump and re-secured it to the bit in no time.

The wind-driven rain continued to sting his face and the sky was now hauntingly dark and produced frequent flashes of lightning and crashes of thunder. Pete allowed doubt to enter his mind and it compounded the fear that had been welling up in his belly. He was scared, but he kept going and didn't surrender to panic - yet.

The waves grew more violent and continued to pound the barge relentlessly; the crane boom began to bounce and sway and the heavy steel shackles and cables clanked loudly into the chaos of the storm as they smashed into the boom. As he watched with trepidation, the crane itself began to slide on the deck. Pete became filled with an overwhelming sense of foreboding, and started to move towards what he thought was shelter from the storm at the stern of the barge.

"Get some lines on that barge! What the hell are you doing? Come on, move!"

With great effort, Pete was able to put his fear in the back of his mind and obey his orders. He responded well, and moved quickly while holding his hands over his face to shield it from the stinging rain. He gathered two ropes and began to re-secure the small barge to the large one as the barges rose and fell on three-foot waves. He was able to attach the lines to the front bits of the big barge and stood on the edge with the two lines in his hand. He knew that he had to time his jump from barge to barge with the waves and had to jump when the small barge was at its crest and only about two foot below the large one.

When he finally gained the courage to jump, he misjudged the timing and landed on the barge on its way down, and his knees hadn't been prepared for it to start rising as quickly as it did. They buckled and he staggered and almost fell overboard, but, thanks to his natural athletic ability, he had been able to gather his balance before that had happened. He was able to hold onto his lines during his jump and now began to pull the barges back together. He braced his foot against a bit and pulled for all he was worth. Slowly, the nose began to respond, and the barges gradually came together. When the little barge bounced off the tire hanging from the side of the big barge, he got ready to attach the line to the bit on the small one. Again, he misjudged how violently the barge was rising and falling, and this time it almost cost him his left hand. He had one turn on the lower bit and had wrapped the rope around his left hand while trying to keep the barges together when suddenly, the small barge dropped quickly on a wave and the line was forcefully drawn to the bit.

Pete screamed in pain and lurched forward as the rope pulled tight around his hand as it was sucked into the bit. His hand closed to within an inch of the bit when the barge rose and the rope went slack. He immediately unwrapped the line from around his hand and waited for the barge to fall to its lowest point and then tied it off. Once the line was secure, he looked at his hand. It was red and it hurt, but it wasn't broken. He attached the other line and jumped back onto the large barge, and made his way back to the boat while holding and rubbing his left hand and thinking about how close he had come to losing it.

The *Sue-Bee* was secured to the barge with steel cable that ran from winches at the stern of the boat to large corner bits on the stern of the barge. The nose was held in place by a line from the nose of the boat to the center bit at the stern of the barge. Short, sharp waves continuously slammed into the stern of the boat and violently snapped the cables tight and then slack with each wave. Pete watched the lines popping and expected one of them to snap at any moment. He stepped from the barge to the boat just as a wave jolted the barge. He staggered again and lost his footing.

His eyes went to where he was about to fall: in between the boat and the barge and to a certain death. The water was foaming and thrashing between the vessels, and suddenly he found himself looking at the hole in the ice. He felt a physical shutter run through him, but again, he was able to expel it from his mind and regained his determination to hold on and not allow himself to fall into that water. He quickly reached for and grabbed hold of the large bit at the bow of the *Sue-Bee,* and pulled himself upright and onto the deck of the boat. The vision and sense of foreboding had shaken him to his core. On the verge of losing his composure and battling to keep his balance on the tossing vessel, he staggered into the wheelhouse and shouted to Jeff.

"Are you sure we can't go back? This is crazy!" There had been unbridled fear in his voice as he spoke, and he had begun to feel overwhelmed by the battle with the bay.

"No, we can't go back! Now get back on that barge and check the chafing under those lines. If you don't put something between the rope and the steel, the lines will cut like butter. Come on, you've got to keep moving!" Jeff screamed back at him with a ferocity and intensity that was reserved for a man in an all-consuming battle with nature.

Pete looked out at the storm and when he left the wheelhouse he felt the rain pummel his face again. "Fuck me, what the hell am I doing here?" he thought to himself, but yet again, he lowered his head, shrugged his shoulders, and made his way back to the nose of the boat and back onto the barge.

As Pete made his way back to his work, Jeff returned to his conversation with God.

"Okay, Big Man, help us out here. We've got to get through this. I've got things to do and kids to take care of, all right? This is fun, but please don't get too carried away, and don't let this one panic and go to crap on me. Give us strength, courage and wisdom…please." Jeff prayed. He didn't talk about his faith much, but he was unflinchingly faithful. He lived by the motto that his grandfather had taught him years before in the fields back home on Mohegan Road: "Action speaks louder than words."

Two hours and a few more broken lines later, the rain ceased, the wind calmed, and the sun was getting low in the sky as Jeff made the turn around marker one into Boggy Bayou. Pete sat on the bow of the barge and finished reflecting on what they had just been through. He was mentally and physically drained. There were now only two lines attaching the barges, and the port cable between the boat and the barge had snapped and had been replaced with a small line that stretched like a rubber band every time they turned the boat.

They were beat up and looking ragged as they passed the markers at Weekley Bayou. Pete was relieved to be so close to home and was looking forward to the end of his long day. He watched as the large shrimp boat *Naomi* passed them on her way out, just beginning her night's work. He saw two of her deckhands, men unknown to Pete, raise their hands and give a respectful and customary wave as they passed. Pete returned the wave, as did Jeff from the wheelhouse. It was shaping up to be a very pleasant evening on Boggy Bayou.

Pete filled the pump with gas and poked his head down the hatch cover and used a flash light to check the leak. It was still leaking and they would have to patch it before they could go home, but it hadn't gotten any worse during the trip. He started the pump again and walked around the barge checking the other compartments, the lines, and equipment, and when he was satisfied that everything was secure, he sat down at the front of the barge and listened to the water as it broke against the bottom of the rake at the bow of the barge.

In the sky above him a half dozen seagulls were leisurely flying about, scanning the top of the water for anything that could be construed as a free meal, and across the bayou a couple of windsurfers with colorful sails were holding tight to their booms and cruising across the water, enjoying the light breeze and small waves. He was surrounded with so much natural beauty that it humbled him. He was exhausted and his muscles ached from abuse, but he loved this part of the job and it made up for everything else. While a gentle sea breeze kissed his face, he reflected on the day and the adventure he had just experienced. It was great!

JOE AND MARTY WERE WAITING for them on the bank when they arrived twenty minutes later. They each had a beer in their hands and reluctantly put them aside when it was time to dock the barge. Pete dropped the gang plank and Marty climbed aboard to help set the spuds while Jeff kept the barge in position. When the barge was secured, Jeff untied the *Sue Bee* and moved her to the dock. Pete re-checked the other compartments on the barge for leaks, while Joe and Marty gathered the dive gear and mixed epoxy. Jeff secured the boat and then changed into his shorts and prepared to get wet again.

As Jeff was walking to the barge and preparing to dive, he saw Pete and said, "Hey, Pete, you want to go under and check it out with me? Joe brought an extra tank and it's a good thing for you to learn." Pete was caught off guard because every time he'd assisted in patching the barge, he'd always been the one inside the hotbox.

"Sure, I'll give it a shot." Pete said quickly and then, once again, wondered what he had gotten himself into. He looked at the water and thought about what it might mean to be under the barge and became increasingly nervous.

"All right, put on the tanks and get your mask."

Marty finished mixing the epoxy and assisted Jeff with his tanks while Joe helped get Pete ready. They were sitting on a large piece of broken concrete at the water's edge. Pete had never put on dive gear, so everything was a new experience. When Joe put the tank on his back, he was surprised by how much it weighed and was now getting anxious and convinced that he had agreed to Jeff's offer too soon. Joe adjusted the belts and snapped the tank into place and then handed him a weight belt. Pete was again surprised by the weight and thought Joe was nuts and wanted him to sink to the bottom.

Joe saw the look in his eye and said with a smile, "What's the matter? Do you want to float around like a cork? You don't have to worry just yet: when I want to sink you, you'll know. Right now I want my barge patched, so put this on."

Pete reluctantly put the heavy belt around his waist and snapped it tight. He felt better when he looked at Jeff and saw him put on a similar weight belt. Pete put on his flippers and as he was getting ready to put it on, Joe stopped him.

"What are you doing? You have to spit in the mask before you put it on."

"What?" Pete had a quizzical look on his face and looked at Jeff for reassurance again.

Jeff seemed to be enjoying the rookie's panic and calmly spit into his mask, rubbed his fingers around in the spit, and then dipped his mask in the water. Pete was grossed out, but mimicked what he had seen.

"It keeps your lens from fogging up. You do want to see the shark before he eats you, don't you?" Joe said while enjoying the moment.

"There aren't any sharks in these waters. This is the bayou, not the ocean. They don't come in here, do they?" Pete asked with wide eyes.

"Son, they've caught bull sharks a hundred and fifty miles up the Mississippi." Pete turned and looked when he heard the voice. Homer had wandered over from the boat works next door with a can of Busch Beer in his hand.

"Hell, my boy caught a six foot black tip off the Shalimar Bridge. Go ahead and bounce off some of those oysters and swim around for a while. You'll make good chum." Homer had a wide toothless grin on his face and was proud of scaring the shit out of the little Yankee boy. Sharks were rare in the bayou, but not unheard of.

"Now Homer, don't go scaring my bait, I mean, diver," Joe said and they all laughed, except Pete. He didn't think they were funny at all.

"Hey, Pete, don't worry. I'll be there with you and I promise I'll let you know if I see a shark that's about to eat you," Jeff said to add to the fun they were all having at Pete's expense.

"Fuck you guys!" Pete was ready to take the gear off, but he forced himself to keep it on and was only going through with this because Jeff was going with him and he couldn't chicken out in front of all these people, especially Homer White. He put the mouthpiece in, pulled the mask over his eyes, and waddled into the water right behind Jeff.

He submerged himself and started breathing underwater for the first time. It took a few minutes for him to adjust to the air being forced into his lungs and consciously had to think about inhaling and exhaling, but he soon got the hang of it and began swimming around. He was surprised at how buoyant he was, even with the weight belt on. The sun was going down and visibility was limited, but when he got close to the barge, he was amazed at how many fish were swimming around picking at the barnacles.

He pushed himself down and looked under the barge. It was completely black. Fear began to take hold of him and he almost leaped out of his skin when Jeff touched his arm. Jeff saw the terror in his face and was amused by it, even though he, too, hated going under the barge at night. Jeff rolled onto his back, kicked his flippers, and waved for Pete to follow him.

Pete watched him disappear into the darkness and reluctantly followed. His heart was pumping hard while he worked his way underneath. The blackness surrounded him and started squeezing him. When he looked up and saw the water pockets moving along the bottom of the barge, his mind went back to the river, back to the ice. He saw something move out of the corner of his eye and almost pissed himself. Breathing was becoming difficult. His entire body was tingling and his chest began pounding.

When he'd been battling the storm, he'd been scared, but he'd been on top of the water. This was different. His mind was now racing and he was suddenly, and inescapably, under the ice again. His eyes darted from side to side, looking for light. He found it behind him and started moving towards it as fast as he could. He struggled to keep his mouthpiece in place as he frantically tried to get out from under the barge. His hands pushed along the bottom until, finally, he felt the corner of the barge and saw the surface only a couple of feet above him. He followed the air bubbles as they rose, and when he broke the surface, he spit out his mouthpiece and was relieved to be alive.

He had surfaced on the waterside of the barge and was out of the eyesight of those on the bank. Joe was talking to Homer, and Marty was inside the barge helping Jeff patch it. He grabbed onto a spud well and took off his mask and relished in breathing good clean, fresh air. He was shaking, felt helpless, and wanted to cry. He clutched the spud well until his heart began to calm and he gathered his senses.

"Never again; no fucking way am I ever going under that barge again. This damn thing can sink to the bottom of the ocean for all I care," Pete said resolutely to himself. He decided that if he was a coward, so be it. He could live with it and he would fight any man to defend his right to be one if that's what he had to do, but he was never going under there again.

He was relieved that, when he came from the side of the barge, he saw Homer walking away and didn't have to listen to him make jokes at his expense. Joe greeted him at the bank with a big and proud smile on his face.

"Well, how was it? It's nice down there, isn't it? We'll have to get you some lessons and get you certified. What do you think?" Joe asked optimistically.

"I think you're nuts. I'm never going under there again; fuck that." Pete was shedding the dive gear as if it were infested. Joe came over to find out what went wrong and to calm him down before he broke something getting the gear off.

"Relax, relax, calm down. It isn't that bad. Don't break anything." Joe grabbed the tank and helped him slide the pack off his back. Once it was off and Pete had shed his flippers he was ready to leave.

"Don't worry, Pete; come on, breathe; calm down. Listen, going under the barge isn't for everyone. It's kind of spooky under there if you're not used to it."

"Joe, they've got this handled. You guys don't need me to patch the barge. I've gotta go. I'll be here in the morning - don't worry about that - but I gotta go." With that, Pete grabbed his stuff, jumped into his van soaking wet, and left the yard. Joe watched him go, not sure if he would ever see him again.

CHAPTER 32

WHO WE ARE IS
WHAT WE CHOOSE

Pete left the boatyard and went to Lincoln Park to be alone. The park was right up the street and around the bend from the boatyard. It was a pleasant family oriented park along Boggy Bayou with picnic areas, swings for the kids, a beach area, and a boat ramp. There were a couple of people swimming and a few more lying on the beach, but nobody was on the dock, so he went there and sat by himself. He was mad at himself for being so scared and allowing panic to overwhelm him the way it had under the barge. He was still shaking and wanted nothing more than to go home, climb into his bed, and never come out. His mind went to the same place it always went when he doubted himself: Isaac.

He hadn't been scared when he'd been under the ice. He'd been trying to save his brother and had just reacted without thinking, but today he'd panicked and ran away, plain and simple. Maybe he really was a coward, and maybe that's why Isaac and Bobby had died. "If I had just swam a little deeper; if I had just gone down and gotten him away from those guys…." He began to get restless and had started thinking about getting really drunk and stoned when he heard the footsteps on the dock. He turned his head and saw an old man he had never seen before walking towards him. Pete wanted to be alone for a while longer and started to get up and leave when he heard the man speak to him.

"Quite the night, huh?"

"Yeah….., yeah, it sure is," Pete replied with a sarcastic chuckle while getting up and looking at his guest.

He was a large man with a weathered and worn face and bright blue eyes. He put his hands on the railing and Pete saw how large they were. Strength and power emanated from him, and Pete was instantly ashamed of his actions.

"It's nice to come here for some peace, isn't it? I like to come down here when I've had a really bad day; been doing it for over thirty years. I think the breeze and the water help me keep things in perspective…. I haven't seen you around here much. Are you new to the area?" he said in a soft baritone voice.

Pete really wasn't in the mood for a long conversation, but felt compelled to answer the man.

"Yeah, we moved down a few months ago. I work for Becton down by the boatyard."

"Yeah, I know the place well. Old Homer is quite the character isn't he? I don't much care for boats anymore, but I do love looking at the water."

Pete had calmed down and was looking at the water with the man, and somehow began to feel safe and protected in his presence. He somehow knew that standing next to him was a real man…a leader of men.

"I spend most of my days on the water now. I guess I like it…. It's a lot different than back home. So how come you like the water, but don't like boats anymore? Is it because they break down too much?" Pete asked.

"No, they sink! Oh, now when I was young, I loved Errol Flynn and wanted to be like him and battle pirates. I was a Kansas farm boy and dreamed of faraway lands and sailing the oceans to discover them. Thanks to the Japs, I got to do that, but I'm scared shitless of going out in boats now."

Pete looked at him and was taken aback by his statement. He didn't look like a man who was afraid of anything.

"What happened?" Pete knew it was bad question and none of his business as soon as he asked it and wished he had kept his mouth shut.

The old man looked at him, debating with himself if this kid would even understand a damn thing he told him. He stared at Pete for a moment, until Pete couldn't help but look back at him and into his eyes. The old man saw something in him and decided that the young man needed to hear his story.

"Have you ever heard of the *Indianapolis?*"

"No sir, I can't say that I have."

"Well, it was a good ship, with a lot of good men on board. I had just gone on duty at midnight. I loved the Navy; I was young and invincible, and I loved the Philippines too. Maybe we should have done something differently, but we didn't. A Jap sub torpedoed us. I was lighting a cigarette when everything went to Hell. She was a powerful ship, but it only took twelve minutes for her to sink to the bottom of the sea," he paused, stared into the evening sky, and remembered. "We had about twelve hundred men aboard. They say nine hundred of us made it into the water; who knows? But four days later, when they found us, there were only three hundred of us left. Sharks ate the rest. They just swam around and under us and ate till they got their fill. Nobody knew who was next; it was just the luck of the draw. The screams in the night were awful. Hell of a way to die." His eyes and his mind were elsewhere as he told the story, and now that he had stopped talking, he was hearing those screams again and again.

Pete didn't know what to say. He saw the pain in the man's face and the glassy sheen that was now covering his eyes as his mind was back in the water.

"I'm sorry."

The old man was snapped back to reality. "Sorry for what? That's war; that's life, and sometimes it just plain sucks, but we play the cards we're dealt and we keep going. That's all we can do. We all have our burdens, son. You know, when you encounter a person, it's usually only for a brief moment in life, just like us here. For some of us, life is long and hard, and for others, it's way too short. You just never know. It's funny how sometimes a man will fight so hard to live for just a minute more, and other times he just looks forward to getting off this rock and ending the misery." He paused for a minute, took a look around, and then looked into Pete's eyes before he uncharacteristically continued sharing his philosophy with the scared boy he had just met.

"You never really know the road another man has had to walk, and you damn sure have no clue where he's going. We can only see where they are at that instant. I was a farm boy; just like my father and his father before him. I thought I was going to be a farmer too. How the hell was I supposed to know that I would end up here? Who knows where you're going to go and what you're going to see in your life. Nah, you can't waste time worrying about what has already happened. What's done is done. We can only learn from it and move on. The only thing you *can* control is what you choose to do with the time you have and how you decide to prepare for life's next battle, because whether you like it or not, it is going to come. I've met all kinds of people in my travels; some choose to run and hide from problems, some bury their heads in the sand and pretend that there's nothing wrong, while others, we prepare for the next fight and pray it never comes. It's up to you to decide what you're going to do and what kind of man you're going to become."

He looked over at Pete and was confident that he had listened; maybe it hadn't been a complete waste of time after all.

"Well, I've taken enough of your time. I'm sure you have places to go and people to see, as do I. Take care of yourself. I enjoyed the visit." With that, the profound old man turned and walked away.

Pete watched him get in his car and as the car pulled out, he noticed that on the front license plate were three stars. Pete thought he knew what they meant, but he wasn't sure. He then turned and looked out over the water again and pondered what he had just heard. His mind was now clear and he knew where he wanted to go, so he got in his van and went there.

CHAPTER 33

SHIHAN

Pete walked in the front door of the dojo and looked around. There were no children this time, and of the thirteen men present, ten appeared to be in their fifties and sixties. There were a few younger men working out with them, Mr. Sanders being one of them. As Pete studied the men, he noticed that they all wore black belts with between one and five stripes of tape wrapped around the end of their belts; except for the giant who stood stoically in the front of the class studying the men as they worked; his belt was red with a white stripe sewn in the center.

The man was as big as a house; he was well over six feet tall and appeared to weigh close to 260 pounds. He appeared to be in his fifties with a shining bald head and large mustache. Pete watched with amazement when he corrected one of the men's techniques on a complicated move. He stopped the class and made them watch him demonstrate the proper movement. He ordered Mr. Sanders and another of the younger students to attack him. They did not hesitate, but he blocked, moved to the side, punched, and kicked each of the men with a swiftness and gracefulness that left Pete dumbfounded. In an instant, both men were defeated and lying flat on their backs.

Pete stood silently in the entry and continued to watch the men work on takedowns and other techniques for several minutes, apparently unnoticed. He observed how easily the old men tossed the younger ones around and how polite and friendly the men were with each other. He knew immediately that this was what he wanted to do and these were the people he wanted to be with.

After a few more minutes, the large man with the red belt bowed to the class and came over and greeted him.

"Welcome to my dojo. I'm Shihan Van Lenten. Can I help you?"

"Yes, sir, I came here a while ago and spoke with Mr. Sanders. He told me how much it costs and everything, but I don't get paid until Friday, so I guess I'll come back then. I didn't mean to disturb your class. I watched a kid's class once and wanted to check out an adult class, but I probably should've just waited until Friday; I'm sorry about taking up your time and disturbing your class. I'll come back Friday night." Pete was intimidated by the sheer size of the man in front of him and desperately wanted to leave.

Shihan studied the wharf rat standing in front of him. After looking deeply into his eyes he decided that the boy was new clay ready to be shaped and formed. "Are you late for something?"

"No, I just don't want to waste your time and should've just waited until I had the money before I came in."

"I don't run this place to make my money; if I did, I would've been out of business a long time ago. If you really want to study, I'll get you a gi and you can pay me when you have the money," he said in a gentle baritone voice.

Pete was surprised when the man went into a closet in his office and came out with a new gi, or uniform, and handed it to him.

"Tuesdays and Thursdays are advanced classes and Mondays, Wednesdays, and Fridays at 6:30 are the adult classes. Saturday mornings, the dojo is open and we have informal workouts."

Pete began to have second thoughts about committing so quickly; making rash decisions hadn't been working out too well for him, and he felt that once he took the gi, there was no backing out.

"What are your qualifications and what will I learn?" Once again, he cringed at himself and wished he hadn't asked the question. He was teaching a class full of black belts and they were studying karate, duh.

"Come here." Shihan didn't seem offended and waved for Pete to follow him. "Those are good questions that you should always ask of any instructor, because to tell you the truth, there are a lot of people teaching things that they should spend more time studying."

He walked behind his desk, sat down, and opened a desk drawer. He reached in and pulled out several magazines and laid them out for Pete to examine.

"This is *The Official Karate Magazine*. This is me on the cover. I think they did a nice article on me and my history." He tossed it to the side and then opened the other magazine and showed Pete a picture of several men standing together and pointed. "That's me as I was getting inducted into the Legion of Honor, Karate's Hall of Fame. With me is Chuck Norris, Bill 'Super Foot' Wallace, and others." He tossed the magazine aside as if they were of no real importance and then pointed to a series of pictures on the wall. "I'm retired from the Marine Corps and spent twelve years in Okinawa. I'm a former top ranked competitor in both the US and Japan, and the only American to ever win a championship in Okinawa in both Kata (forms) and Kumite (sparring). We teach Goju-ryu karate as taught by Master Chojun Miyagi and passed down through Seikichi Toguchi. Have you seen the movie *The Karate Kid*?" Pete shook his head in the affirmative and Shihan continued. "Well, there really was a Master Miyagi, but he didn't live in California and collect old cars. He was the founder of the Goju-Ryu style."

He pointed to a picture on the wall. It showed him getting off an airplane with several students behind him. On the tarmac were several people, all on their knees and bowing.

"This is when I returned to Okinawa a couple of years ago with several of my students. We were greeted by the Governor and his entourage; that's him in the front."

Pete wanted him to stop. It was obvious that he was more than qualified. He felt embarrassed for questioning him, and after a few more pictures and articles, he did stop.

"We will see you on Monday then?"

"Yes, sir, I'll be here," Pete said, and he knew he was telling the truth.

Shihan rose and shook Pete's hand and then returned to class. Pete went out and sat in his van for a few moments, thinking about what had just transpired. He had never done anything like this before and was nervous. He looked at the plastic-wrapped gi again and was confident that he was doing the right thing. He went home feeling excited and renewed.

CHAPTER 34

YOU WORK VERY HARD

When Pete showed up for work as he had promised and saw the guys loading equipment into trucks and getting ready to go to their respective jobs, he expected to be the morning's entertainment and the brunt of several jokes for panicking the way he had, so he sat in his van a little longer than normal, dreading what he knew was coming. After a moment, he took a deep breath and summoned enough courage to get out of the van and face them. He tossed Bonehead a biscuit as he walked passed and joined his coworkers. To his surprise, nobody mentioned the incident, and neither did he. He was apprehensive as he started loading hoses onto Jeff's truck, but relieved because it was shaping up to be just like any other morning; the guys worked while Joe barked out assignments and Bonehead happily ate his biscuit.

After a few minutes, everyone was ready to go to work. Jeff took Marty and three other men to Bluewater Bay, while Giles took a couple more to another job. Joe told Pete he was going to take him to Mrs. Anderson's to dress the rocks that they had placed the day before as soon as he got done talking to Homer. Pete stood and watched everyone pull out of the boatyard elated by the fact that that nobody had said

269

anything to him about the incident. He knew that Joe was the only one who'd really seen what had happened, and then he realized that Joe must not have said anything to anyone. A weight was lifted from his shoulders and he learned something about Joe Nevers and trust that he would never forget.

Joe finished making a deal with Homer to pull the *Sue-Bee* and do her bottom and returned to the boat yard by walking through a small trail through the overgrown brush that separated the two businesses. Pete saw the bearded man emerge from the growth and couldn't help but think of how much he looked like Grizzly Adams. He finished petting Bonehead and walked over to Joe's truck and tried to get in, but once again, there wasn't enough room to sit and Pete had to clear a space; so he quickly shuffled parts, pieces, and papers, and jumped in. When they got out of Valparaiso and started toward Ft. Walton, Joe finally brought up the incident.

"Hey, listen, about yesterday. It can get pretty spooky down there. It's not for everyone. Don't let it get to you and don't worry too much about it. There are lots of other things you can do without diving under the barge. Okay?" His voice was soft, sincere, and comforting.

"Yeah, thanks Joe. I didn't mean to wig out... I don't know what happened. I'll do anything else you want. I like my job; I just don't want to go under there again, okay?" Pete wanted to tell him why he was so frightened... to explain everything to him about what he had experienced on the river, but he looked at Joe and decided that to do so would be whining and making excuses, and Pete wanted no more of either.

"Lots of guys talk about wanting to dive, but they're thinking of TV and Jacque Cousteau and swimming with pretty little fishes on pretty reefs, but we do commercial work and it's not that pretty very often. When I dove in San Francisco Harbor, you couldn't see your hands in front of your face. That was spooky. Now listen, I'm going to drop you off and go to a meeting. I'm bidding a job that'll be coming up next year. It's a big job, about ten thousand tons of rock, and it's going to take a couple of months to finish. It's going to require someone to stay in Caryville on the jobsite. You know, five days up there, home for weekends. I think I have a deal on a nice little fishing cabin right there on the river. If we get it, do you think you'd be interested in staying up there and helping Jeff?"

Pete was pleasantly shocked by Joe's faith in him, and he continued his pattern of making a decision without thinking about it and accepted the offer. This was a sign of confidence that was totally unexpected. If Joe was making this offer for a job that wouldn't start for such a long time, then he was planning on keeping him around. Joe was usually a loud and hard man, but now he was being kind and almost sensitive. This was a side of Joe that he had never seen, nor expected. Pete looked over at Joe, and at that moment he would have done anything Joe asked.

As they drove down the road, Pete began to think about what he had just committed to, but after a moment of silent contemplation, he reasoned that he was young and single and that living in a fishing cabin on the river for a few months would be fun. He didn't ask where Caryville was and didn't really care. He felt like he was becoming part of a team that wanted and needed him.

They arrived at Mrs. Anderson's house a short time later and Joe walked out to the seawall with Pete. It was still early in the morning and the bayou was calm and quiet. The day was just starting and everything was peaceful at the water's edge. The bayou was gently lapping at the new limestone rip-rap in front of the seawall. The rocks that were untouched by water were a light grey and still covered with dust, while the ones in the water were darker and richer in color. The rocks were scattered and uneven along the wall. Pete's job was to move them as needed to make a uniform height and slope, and when he walked down onto the rocks and started moving them, Joe exploded.

"Where are your gloves? I'm tired of buying gloves for you guys! You use them once and then lose them and expect me to buy more. Well, I'm sick of it!" Joe was back to his charming self: yelling at Pete as if he was a moron.

"I forgot them in my van. Don't worry, I'll be fine." Pete felt like an idiot because Joe was right and they had been through this before, several times.

"Well, I don't have any with me and I don't have time to get you some before my meeting, so you're just going to have to suck it up and deal with it until I get back!" Joe was pissed at Pete.

He hated seeing guys tear up their hands unnecessarily, but there was nothing he could do about it now. He showed Pete the high spots and the low ones and told Pete what he wanted to see when he returned, then stormed off to his truck. Pete climbed down into the water and started moving the rocks into place. Some of them were quite large and too heavy for Pete to lift by himself, so he had to clear an area and roll them into place. He was careful and took his time with the big ones because he knew that if they rolled onto his fingers or toes that it would hurt for a long time and there was nobody to help him.

He worked diligently, taking rocks from the high spots and tossing them into the low ones as instructed. A short time later, the sun was higher in the sky and the temperature had risen to the point that Pete decided that he could take off his shirt and turn this job into a workout that would help him get ready for karate. He looked down at his stomach and then at his arms; he was still too thin, and without much muscle tone, but he was fairly athletic, had a good frame, and was now making an effort to improve himself. He was a full six foot tall, had gained almost ten pounds since he started working for Joe, and was now only twenty five pounds shy of his goal of two hundred pounds. He began thinking confidently about his future for the first time in a long time.

Three hours later, his back hurt and his fingers were wrinkled and raw, but the rocks were done, and as he stood back and surveyed his work, he was proud of what he had accomplished and knew that it looked good. The waves were picking up a little and he enjoyed watching the water run up the rocks and gently fall back to the bayou with the wave energy dispersed by the rip-rap. He saw all the crevices and places for small fish and crabs to hide in the rocks and was also proud that he was creating a better habitat for the little sea creatures. He knew that without little fish, there could be no big fish.

He looked at a neighbor's wall that had no rock in front of it and saw how the water smashed into the vertical wall and churned violently in front of it. The seawall had more than a foot of water in front of it and offered no hiding places for small fish to escape predators. Pete knew that he was doing menial labor, but he felt good about his job and found satisfaction in how his work affected the world around him.

He picked up his shirt and put it back on and began to walk towards the road. He was done and Joe hadn't returned. He was unsure of what to do, and was wishing he had brought his van, so he wandered around and found a nice shade tree to sit under and wait for Joe. He was wet and somewhat miserable, but the sun was bright and began to warm him up as he sat and relaxed. He was soon closing his eyes and drifting into a peaceful nap when he heard a voice in the distance.

"Would you like some iced tea?" He heard a woman's voice with a strong Asian accent, but could see no one. "You have been working very hard. Come, sit. The tea is good for you. It is very hot outside."

He looked again as the screen door opened and a small Asian woman appearing to be in her late-fifties waved him over to a table under a magnolia tree. She had a pitcher of tea and two glasses on a tray and once she set it down, she filled the glasses and waved for Pete to sit down.

"I have been looking out the window and I see you work very hard. Thank you. I am a widow now and my sons used to do those things for me. They took care of everything around here, but now they are grown and have families of their own to take care of. I don't want to bother them and they really don't have the time. They are good sons and work very hard." She was friendly and wore a constant smile. "If I ask them, they would do it, but they need to take care of their families now," she continued in broken English.

Pete looked back at the seawall and thought about the rocks he had just finished moving and was trying to figure out how her sons could do that job without heavy equipment and concluded that they wouldn't be able to. She must have seen the look of doubt on his face.

"Did you see all the broken concrete down there when you start? My sons put all those rocks there many years ago. George, my oldest, had a

pickup truck and I worked on base before I retire, so I always watch for
where they fix sidewalks and I would go and tell the men to let my sons
haul away the old concrete. The men were always happy; they don't have
to haul off and I get for free. They bring the concrete here and back the
truck up to the wall and put it out there." She was very proud of herself,
and Pete looked at her and he was proud of her too.

He immediately knew that she was a determined little woman who
got things done. They sat and chatted for a few minutes, and when
Mrs. Anderson had finished properly interrogating him about his life,
his views on things, what he was doing with his spare time (she was
happy to hear that he was going to be studying martial arts), and once
she was satisfied with his answers, she asked Pete if he wanted to do
some work around the yard on weekends. She had a large yard with
many flowering bushes that needed attention and she would pay him
cash. Pete liked the idea of extra money, and agreed to be at her house
on Saturday morning. He loved extra money and had nothing to do on
the weekend anyways.

Joe showed up after they had finished their second glass of tea and
the three of them walked to the seawall and examined his work. They
were all very satisfied with what they saw, so Joe told Pete to wait for
him in the truck while he spoke with Mrs. Anderson and gave her a bill.
The two of them chatted for a few minutes, and to Joe's delight, Mrs.
Anderson immediately wrote him a check and made his day. Joe soon
climbed into the truck and took Pete back to the boatyard, and for the
next day and a half, Pete helped Joe work on equipment.

On Saturday morning, Pete was at Mrs. Anderson's and she was
ready for him. He was surprised to see her standing in front of the open
garage door wearing a white wide brimmed hat and a pair of gloves. She
had their tools already laid out and the trunk of her car was open, and
when he looked inside he saw that it packed with bags of mulch. The
wheelbarrow had containers of flowers in it, along with a shovel, rake,
and hedge trimmers. The lawn mower and weed-eater were gassed and
ready to go.

"Good morning, Peter. Thank you for coming and helping me. We have much work to do. First we do flower beds and shrubs, then we rake and cut grass. Now we make this place look good again," she said confidently.

She looked out over her yard and was ashamed of the mess she had let it become. Pete looked around at the blooming red azaleas and the Spanish moss hanging elegantly from oak limbs and thought the place looked good. She led him to where she wanted to begin and they started working. Together, they planted flowers, mulched several beds, trimmed hedges, and raked leaves. By lunch time, Pete was tired and hungry. Mrs. Anderson had disappeared into the house while he'd raked and he was about to tell her that he was going to get some lunch when she walked out with sandwiches and tea.

"Come, sit, eat," she said and motioned him to the picnic table in the shade. They sat and ate, and after a few minutes Mrs. Anderson started to reminisce.

"When my husband was alive, he did everything for me. This whole yard was beautiful garden. He was a very good man and worked very hard. We were married for twenty three years and he was the only man I ever kissed, except for my father and brother, but that is not the same thing. One Sunday after church he was raking leaves and had heart attack and die right over there in backyard. He was only fifty and never sick, always so strong." She paused and thought about their time together before continuing.

"We met right after the war. I was going to be nun, but I fell in love. I was scared and I spoke with my priest and pray for long time. I did not want to disappoint my parents or God, but my priest convinced me that Jesus would still love me if I got married, and that I could serve God in other ways and he gave us his blessing. My husband was an engineer who help with rebuilding after the war. It was very hard times for all of us. The Japanese were very cruel to us Philippinoes, but they were even worse to American prisoners. During the war, my brother and I would sneak food to prisoners. We were so young and crazy… If we were ever caught, they would kill us, but we figured the Americans had come and they fight for us and many die for us, so we could not just watch them starve to death, and I knew God would protect me; he always has."

She paused for a moment and chased away the horrid memories of what she had had to do in order to distract the guards while her brother snuck the food to the prisoners. In the blink of an eye, she changed the subject and became Mrs. Anderson again and started to talk about what she wanted to get done after lunch. When they finished eating, she cleaned up the table and sent Pete back to work. It was about four when they finished. Mrs. Anderson waved to Pete and led him to the front of the house where they stood and looked at what they had accomplished. Now he understood what she had been talking about in the morning, because the yard was being transformed and it was now coming to life. The colors of the new flowers and mulch brightened the azaleas and the oak limbs were now trimmed evenly. It was truly a beautiful yard.

She handed Pete his pay and said she looked forward to him coming back next month. She explained that she was going on vacation with her daughter and their church. They were going to Medjugorje, Yugoslavia for two weeks.

CHAPTER 35

IS THIS WHAT I
REALLY WANT?

A nne was so happy to see Bill leave that she popped up from her stool and went into the bathroom to start getting ready for work hours before she normally would. Her friend Robin was moving and the girls were going out for a couple of drinks after work to say goodbye. Word had somehow gotten to Ryan and he had followed up by informing Anne that he had been invited to have a drink with them-unless she objected. Anne hadn't objected.

She couldn't stop thinking about his smile while she showered, shaved, and started putting on makeup. Usually her intention was to look presentable and she would have her makeup done in mere minutes, but today she wanted to look perfect. She wasn't getting ready for work; she was preparing for a date.

The day seemed to be moving painstakingly slow. Anne worked her register and was friendly to all her customers, but she couldn't keep focused or resist looking at the door every time it opened to see if Ryan would walk through and come to see her. She hated herself for being so childish and not being able to control her involuntary reaction to the sound of the door sliding, but she also enjoyed the stimulation that she felt.

When it was close to seven and time for her shift to end, she felt bitter disappointment that he hadn't come in. She admonished herself for taking the time to primp and prep for something that she knew probably wouldn't, and definitely shouldn't, happen. Anne felt like she had been stood up and was embarrassed by her emotions and wanted nothing more than to make an excuse and skip the party and sneak out the door unnoticed. Her only desire at this point was to go home and crawl into bed without interacting with another human being, but as she was standing at the time clock punching out, Alice came up from behind her.

"Are you ready to have some fun, Annie?" she asked.

"I'm really tired, but it'll be nice to have a drink with Robin before she leaves," Anne replied.

She had purposefully said "a drink," hoping that Alice would get the hint that she didn't want to stay too long. Alice was having none of it and was ready to have fun.

"Yeah, *suuure*, we'll only have one drink! Listen, Annie: we're both married and tonight we have a legitimate reason to go out with the girls and have some fun. This opportunity doesn't come around too often. Who knows, I might get lucky and be too drunk to drive home tonight, so I might just have to spend the night at Robin's, or somewhere close to there!" Alice said with a wink and hopeful laugh.

Anne was getting nervous because she knew that Alice was on the hunt for fun wherever she could find it. She was fun to work with, and always had a wise-ass joke to keep her co-workers laughing. Every time Anne looked at her she thought of Flo from the TV show *Alice*. She clocked out right after Anne and then the two of them walked a couple of units down in the shopping center to Walt's. Walt's was a small bar in the strip-mall that was a local hangout for the over thirty crowd. It was a cozy little place where several romances had been formed and many divorces finalized over the years.

When Anne walked in behind Alice and saw that she was greeted by half the people in the bar, it was immediately apparent that she was a regular. She and her husband were born, raised, and lived in Crestview.

They were high school sweethearts and married soon after graduation. He was a strong and proud country boy who worked close to his house and rarely made the thirty minute trip south to Niceville unless he had to. He didn't drink often and had never stepped foot in a bar in Niceville, which made Alice feel safe to do whatever she desired.

Over the years she had fooled around with several men in the bar, but she justified her infidelity by convincing herself that the many times her husband had gone fishing or hunting with his buddies for the weekend, bass and bucks weren't the only things that they had gone looking for.

They looked around the small bar and quickly spotted Robin and Marjorie sitting at a table in the corner. They waved to each other and then Alice led Anne to the bar to order drinks.

"Hi, Bobby, you're looking good tonight, Sugar. Can I have four shots of tequila and two margaritas? And be a sweetheart and put it on my tab, will ya, honey." She put on the sweetest accent and brightest smile that she could conjure up for the bartender.

"Oh, I'm not sure about drinking shots of tequila, Alice. I was planning on having one drink and then saying goodnight," Anne protested.

Bobby put the shots on the bar and started mixing the drinks. Alice grabbed the shot-glasses and handed them to Anne, completely ignoring what she had said.

"Be a doll and bring these to the table. I'll be right there with our drinks."

Anne didn't like it, but she complied and brought the shots to the table. When she set them down, Marjorie looked at her like she was crazy, but Robin just smiled. She was excited about spending some time with her friends because she didn't get out much and rarely drank, but tonight she was in the mood for fun and craziness.

"Well, I don't know why she had you bring four of those things over here, because I sure as hell ain't drinking one," Marjorie announced.

Marjorie was a stout woman in her mid-fifties with graying hair and wire-rimmed glasses. She had lost her husband of over thirty years a few years earlier and now lived alone. She was pleasant, sometimes funny, and always strong willed. She enjoyed having a drink once in a while, but never more than a couple. Marjorie had only really gotten drunk once in her life. That was the day she had unexpectedly lost her husband to a car accident. He'd been on his way home from work, just like every other day, when an old man going the other way had had a seizure, crossed the center lane, and crashed head on into him, killing him instantly.

Alice stood at the bar making small talk with a man she had never seen before while she waited for her drinks. Bobby put the drinks in front of her, but before letting go of them, he looked at Alice and reminded her of her tab balance. She looked at him with an innocent pout and put her hands over his.

"Come on, Bobby, don't be mean. You know I'll take care of it like I always do. Robin's leaving tomorrow and we just want to have some fun."

She batted her eyes again and gave him a sweet and presumably innocent smile. It worked and Bobby relented like he always did. He had to give her a hard time, but he liked when Alice was behind on her tab because she made the late payments to him after the bar closed and it was always worth it.

With Bobby taken care of, Alice sauntered over to the table, handed Anne her drink, and made an announcement before sitting down.

"Ladies, we are going to let our hair down and have some fun tonight!"

"You can let your hair down, but mine is just fine where it's at," Marjorie retorted while taking a little sip from her drink. She liked Robin, but only worked with Alice. She didn't like her attitude, nor condone her actions.

"Oh, Margie, you can smile and have some fun. It won't ruin your reputation," Alice said while sitting down.

She pushed the shots in front of everyone and raised hers in a toast to Robin. "To one of the most wonderful people I've ever met. May you enjoy your new home, live a long, happy life, and get everything you want out of it."

She raised her shot to the center of the table and three shot glasses met. Marjorie lifted her drink and tipped it, but was not going to do shots of alcohol for anybody.

"Come on, Marjorie, just one. Robin is leaving," Alice pleaded.

"You are out of your mind. You're all adults and can do whatever the hell you want, but I can enjoy myself without getting drunk and entertaining the first man that puts his hand on my ass. Thank you very much."

Alice looked at her with disdain and thought to herself that the only man that would ever put his hand on her ass was blind and dumb fishermen who wouldn't be able to smell the difference between her and his fish, but she said nothing and just smiled at the others as they drank their shots. Alice ordered more, and before she knew it, Anne had drank them too.

The girls sat around talking and drinking for over an hour. Alice excused herself to go to the bathroom, and on her way back she stopped at the bar to order another drink and talk to her new friend again. When she returned to the table, she didn't sit down. She grabbed her pocket book, gave Robin a quick hug and wished her luck, and then she and her new friend went out the door arm in arm.

"That woman is a piece of work," Marjorie said to the girls. "She's going to end up alone, pushing a shopping cart, and wondering what the hell happened."

"Come on now, Margie, she's not that bad. She just got married too young and is unhappy," Robin chimed in to defend her friend. Robin was in her mid-forties, happily married to her second husband, and could never bring herself to say anything negative about anyone.

"You can say what you want, but if she wants a divorce, she should get one. What she's doing ain't right. It does nothing but make her look like a tramp and her husband a fool. In the end it always brings shame into your life and into your home." Marjorie was almost done with her second drink and was beginning to feel its effects.

"No, life is hard enough, and what I don't understand is why people do things that they know are just going to make it worse," Marjorie continued. "I'm getting old and it just don't ever change. Some people just do what makes them feel good at the moment." She put her hands in the air, a stupid look on her face, and began mocking the 'If it feels good, do it' mentality that drove her nuts. "They live by that 'I have a right to be happy' horseshit and don't ever think about how their actions are going to affect them or their families down the road. When they get old and find themselves alone, broke, and almost homeless, they're the first ones to jump on a soapbox and cry that it wasn't their fault and that life ain't fair. Well, hell no, life ain't fair, but what does that have to do with anything? And as far as it not being their fault, that's the one that just chaps my hide, because it's never their fault; they just have bad luck." Marjorie paused to finish her drink and then looked at her friend and rested her hand on Robin's.

"I'm sorry for carrying on like that. This is your night to say goodbye and I shouldn't run off at the mouth like that. Now you listen to me. You take care of yourself and that husband of yours. You're a wonderful person and I am so glad that I got to know you. Go with God and you will never go alone," she concluded.

Marjorie grabbed her pocket book and stood up to leave just as Ryan walked up to the table.

"Ladies, how nice to see you," Ryan said with a big broad smile.

"Ryan Pearson. What a surprise to see you here. How is your wife?" Marjorie said to him in a sarcastic tone that let everyone know that she approved of him far less than she approved of Alice.

"Mrs. Jones. What a pleasant surprise. This is not the place I would normally expect to see you," he replied.

"Oh, I'm full of surprises. Again, how is Joyce?" She was not going to let him get away without confirming to all present his marriage.

"Joyce is just fine. May I buy you ladies a drink?" he retorted and kept on pouring on the charm.

"No, I was just leaving. The smell of bullshit is starting to foul the air in here. Robin, you have a safe trip, and Anne, I'll see you on Saturday. Whatever you two do, don't order the shark in here. It has a terrible aftertaste." She looked at Ryan and then walked away.

"Do you mind if I sit down? You know, I love that old bird. She calls 'em like she sees 'em. I've known her for over twenty years and I think she's finally warming up to me." Ryan sat down and they all had a laugh.

After a few more minutes and another drink, it was Robin's turn to say her goodbyes and then, with a wink and a smile, left them alone.

"You and Margie go back a long ways, huh?" Anne questioned. She was excited to be with Ryan, but Marjorie's warnings kept going through her mind.

"Oh, yeah; it's a small town. Her husband remodeled our house years ago. He was a nice enough guy and did a damn good job, but she and I never got along."

"How long have you been married?" Anne asked with a tone of condemnation in her voice.

"How long have you been married?" he replied. "Let's get this straight from the beginning: I have a marriage that old Mrs. Hard-ass does not approve of. My wife is Swiss and we have what some people call an open relationship. She actually likes women too. We've been together for a long time and we both travel a lot and it just works for us. Just so that we are clear, I'm not going to fall in love and leave my wife. We're happy, we never had children, and we don't give a damn what people like Mrs. Hardass think."

Anne was taken aback. Part of her was repulsed by this revelation and wanted to get up and run as fast as she could, but something else kept her at the table. When Ryan was convinced that she wasn't leaving, he ordered another round and the conversation moved to her and her life. She quickly got over her initial shock and found him intelligent, charming and easy to speak with. They reminisced about their youth and the music they had listened to growing up. He told her about his time flying planes in the military and his new computer company. She found him intriguing, and when her glass emptied, she ordered another round.

They sat and talked and drank for a couple of hours until Ryan announced that he had to leave. Anne was disappointed; she didn't know what to expect, but she didn't want the night to end.

"I have a very important meeting first thing in the morning, and to tell you the truth, I normally don't go out when I have something scheduled, but I couldn't resist the opportunity to sit down and get to know you, and I'm glad I did. But, I really do have to go. Can I walk you to your car or are you going to stay here?" he asked.

"Oh no, I can't stay here; it's time for me to get home too. I had a real nice time with you and, I guess, I'm glad you didn't resist the temptation. And yes, I would appreciate you walking me to my car," Anne replied.

She stood up and grabbed her purse. She hadn't realized how much she'd drank until she stood up and felt the effects of the alcohol. He placed his hand under her elbow and escorted her from Walt's. When they got to her car, she turned to face him. He was standing very close and she hadn't realized how big he was. She nervously looked into his chest and then at the ground. She wasn't sure how the night was supposed to end. Was he going to kiss her? Should she kiss him back? She hadn't been on a date in a long time and wasn't really sure if she was on one now.

She felt his hand touch her chin and gently lift her face to look at him. He looked into her eyes and she was sure she wanted to be kissed. Ryan put his lips to hers and she closed her eyes. It was a soft and delicate kiss that left her wanting more. He pulled away and opened her car door.

"When can I see you again?" he asked.

She opened her eyes and looked at him. He had a radiant and confident smile and a look of pure lust in his eyes. The first reply that went through her mind was right now. She would have done anything he asked at that moment, but she controlled herself.

"Next Thursday night. I get off work at eight. Can I meet you here at Walt's again?"

"I'll be here and I'll clear my schedule for Friday too. If my meeting goes well tomorrow, and I think it will, I'll end up going out of town until Wednesday night. It must be karma."

He bent down and kissed her again after she was in her car and then gently closed the door and watched her drive off.

CHAPTER 36

FIRST DAY SURPRISES

O ver the course of the weekend Pete had washed his gi and
tried it on several times. As he had stood in front of the
mirror, he had sometimes been embarrassed and thought
that he looked silly wearing the bright white uniform, but on most
occasions he had stood and posed while imagining how he was going
look and feel as the belt gradually changed from white to black. When
Monday morning finally arrived, he woke early and popped out of bed
excited and ready to go. He left the house with a bounce in his step
and arrived early for work, even after stopping for coffee and a biscuit
for Bonehead.

Pete was the first to arrive at the boatyard, and as he walked over to
Bonehead with biscuit in hand, the dog began bouncing up and down
and wagging his tail in exuberant anticipation of his warm breakfast.
Pete knelt down and gave him the biscuit and as the two of them sat
together, he told the dog about his decision to study karate. He told
Bonehead- who seemed to listen intently once the biscuit was devoured-
that he hoped he wasn't making a fool out of himself. He was vigorously
rubbing behind the dog's ears and looking for encouragement as he
explained why he had decided to join the dojo, and after a time Pete

came to the conclusion that it would be best for him to keep his new adventure to himself. After all, Joe called it the bozo, and most of the other guys thought karate people were crazies who wanted to be Bruce Lee.

When everyone arrived at the boatyard, Joe gave out the day's assignments. Pete was ordered to go to the golf course bridge job at Bluewater Bay with Jeff and three other men. He, along with everyone else, dreaded going to the wire grass swamp, because the piling for the bridges were huge and the black flies were everywhere. It was always a long, hard, and muddy day. The final bridge elevation was about three feet above the ground, just above the top of the grass, but because the mud was so deep, they had to use piling that were forty feet long in order to get through the muck and into good sand that would support the bridges.

Pete jumped into the back of the pickup truck along with another crew member, David, and they began their journey to the job. As they rode on John Sims Parkway, Pete began to reflect on the job. He had been there when the barge was moved into position to begin the project. But, he had also helped with the preparations for this project that had begun long before they were actually on site. In order to cross the marsh and build the bridges, Joe and Jeff had designed and built a special barge, about forty feet long and twenty feet wide, for this project. They had put a large winch from a crane on one end and twin thirty feet high gallows on the other. The gallows were used to raise the piling and guide them into place as they were set into the earth and the winch was used to pull the barge across the marsh.

When the barge had been completed and it was time to bring it across the bay, Pete had been flattered to get an invitation to the maiden voyage early one Saturday morning with Joe, Jeff, and Giles. But once they had crossed the bay and arrived on site, Pete had quickly understood why he had been invited. As soon as the barge had been pushed as close to the beach as possible, Joe had told him to jump off the barge and pull a heavy steel cable across the beach and through the marsh and hook it to an old cypress dead head on the other end of the swamp, about three hundred yards away. At first he had thought Joe was joking, but when he had looked at the three of them and saw their devious smiles, he had grudgingly accepted that he was serious and that it had to be done.

Pete had reluctantly stepped off the barge and draped the cable across his chest. They had to two-part the cable for the winch to have the strength to pull the barge across the marsh, so Joe had given him a large block and a long, heavy length of chain to carry as well. Joe had explained that when he reached the dead head, he was to wrap the chain around the stump and attach the block to it, run the cable through the block, and then drag the end of the cable back with him so that it could be shackled to the barge.

Pete had felt the weight of the cable, the block, and the chain, and hadn't been sure if he could do it, but he had started walking anyways. He made his way through the shallow water, over the sand berm, and into the marsh. It was a pristine marsh and there was no path for him to walk through, only a giant stump several hundred yards away for him to walk towards. He began fighting his way through the aptly named wire grass that had been chest height and was continuously poking his skin with every step. Wire grass has been aptly named because it is thick, strong, and straight with sharp needle-like ends that scrape, stick, and pierce the skin.

The grass had been a constant irritation and he had been unable see more than a couple of steps in front of him. He had been worried about the gators and snakes that he knew were plentiful in the marsh. He had had a haunting belief that they were all around him, just watching and waiting for him to stumble and fall so that they could pounce; he had been unable to see them through the grass, but he knew that they saw him, and he had prayed, with every step, that he wouldn't step on anything that was going to bite or eat him. Halfway across the marsh he had begun talking to himself and wondering what the hell he was doing. He was trudging through an infested Florida swamp for five dollars an hour. He had turned to look at the barge, which was now several hundred feet behind him, and had thought about dropping the cable and walking off the job, but he had realized that he had no way to get home and he would have had to walk through the marsh anyways to escape, so he had put his head down and had kept pulling the heavy cable across the marsh.

The farther he had gotten from the barge, the heavier the cable had become, and by the time he had reached the stump, nearly an hour later, his shoulders hurt and he was exhausted. He felt a great relief when he had finally been able to discard the chain and block. He had wanted to take a break, but there was nowhere to sit and he desperately wanted to get it done and over with, so, without stopping, he had wrapped the chain around the stump, attached the block, and fed the cable through. He had taken a deep breath, wrapped the cable over his shoulder again, and started walking back. The cable had become heavy and hard to pull, but he had had a path to follow on the return trip that had kept the wire grass from tormenting him as much as it had the first time through, and he had been able to make it back in half the time.

When word had gotten out about Joe's plan to pull the barge across the swamp, most people doubted that it could be done and the local paper had even sent out a reporter to photograph the event. He and a couple of other spectators had stood on the beach, talking amongst themselves and watching Joe and his crew work. They had entertained themselves by debating whether or not the barge would successfully slide across the swamp, or pull the stump out and get bogged down in the mud and destroy the marsh. So, when Pete had returned to the barge, Jeff and Giles had quickly hooked the cable to it while Joe had fired up the motor and put the winch in gear. Once the cable pulled tight, the barge lurched and then started to slowly move off the beach and across the swamp. The wire grass had laid down as the barge moved over it and had made a perfect mat for them to slide across. The four of them were elated to see everything go according to plan. The photographer had yelled to them from the beach and the four of them had stood on the deck of the barge, mugging for the camera, and enjoying the ride as they gradually moved into position to start construction. The land-barge made the front page. Once the job had gotten underway, Pete had been sent to the job only periodically and was always surprised to see how much progress was being made every time he had returned to it.

WHEN THE MONDAY MORNING RIDE was over and the four of them arrived on site, their first task was to install a new foot valve on the suction hose. The heavy cast iron foot valve was attached to six inch PVC pipe that was 'L' shaped, three feet in both directions, and weighed about fifty pounds. The foot valve was big, bulky, and hard to maneuver.

The water hole was in the middle of the swamp, several hundred feet from the bridge, and was about thirty feet across, twenty feet deep, and full of water moccasins. They used a heavy black suction hose to pull the water to a large industrial pump that supplied the water jet that was lowered into the ground in order to make a hole for the piling.

The moccasins that swam too close to the suction hose would be drawn into it by the sheer power of the pump. The snakes were pulled through the hose, then the pump, and shot out the jet pipe, often thirty feet below the surface, and then they would float to the surface and around the feet of the men wrestling the piling into position. When the first snake floated to the surface the men screamed and jumped out of the way, fearing a snake bite, but they soon realized that after the long journey through the pump and hose, the snakes were very dead by the time they floated up. On some days fifty or more snakes would be drawn through the pump, and until the job ended, there always seemed to be more snakes.

The roots of the grass formed a mat that covered the soupy mud beneath it, and when a person jumped up and down gently, it was possible to see the grass rising and falling as waves visibly moved under the grass. If a person jumped hard, there was a good probability that they would penetrate the mat and continue down until they were able grab the mat and stop themselves from sinking beneath the grass.

Jeff had repeatedly warned the workers of this danger, but David always thought he was exaggerating and being overly cautious. Jeff had yelled at him several times to step off the barge gently, but on this Monday morning, David decided to be a comedian and prove Jeff wrong, so with a big grin, a wink, and a nod to the other men on the barge, he jumped off the deck, put his feet together, and held his arms straight out from his side, but when he hit the grass his smile disappeared instantly because he went through the layer of roots like it wasn't even there. He started screaming and the others started laughing. He sank all the way to his armpits. He screamed and begged for help, but nobody was willing to jump down and rescue him from his own stupidity. They enjoyed his dilemma and left him where he was while they started to work, but after several minutes of non-stop begging for rescue, they had mercy, and stopped laughing long enough for Pete to hook him to the winch and pull him out. Jeff never had to remind anyone about jumping off the barge again.

There were 2 x12 planks laid across the grass for the hose to sit on and for the unlucky person who had to service the hoses and foot valve to walk on, and after they pulled David out of the mud, Pete was chosen to install a new foot valve and replace a ten foot section of hose while the other guys moved piling into position. He hated this part of the job, and took his time walking across the planks with his heavy and awkward cargo for fear of falling into the swamp or the water hole.

When Pete finally reached the water hole, he dropped the foot valve and returned to the barge to get the new section of hose. When he got to the barge, he was greeted by Adam, a retired accountant who had decided he wanted some adventure and came to work for Joe for a few months. Adam was a small and slim man with short grey hair and a thick grey mustache. He was a man of few words, but he thought Pete was taking too much time hooking up the hose and voiced his opinion.

"What the hell is taking so long? You're walking around like you're dying out here. We don't have all day," Adam chastised Pete.

"Listen, I'm not falling into that water hole. You're more than welcome to come out there and show me how to do it if you want to," Pete retorted. He rarely said anything in a defiant tone to Adam out of respect for his age, but he was offended by the comments and let him know. Without another word to anyone, Pete put the hose over his shoulder and started back across the planks.

There was only a few inches of wood on either side of the hose and it made walking difficult, but after a few minutes he was at the water. He carefully started disconnecting the faulty section of hose while keeping an eye out for snakes. He'd finished replacing the section of hose and was beginning to attach the foot valve when he heard a sarcastic voice behind him.

"Jesus Christ, I'm going to be ready for lunch by the time you hook up that hose," Adam said. Pete responded by angrily throwing down the foot valve and hose and stepping out of the way.

"Here you go. Show me how to do it. I want to watch this." Pete stepped out of the way and let Adam take his place.

Adam had to stand right on the end of the plank while wrestling the hose and foot valve. The hose was thick and unbending and the foot valve was awkward and heavy. Adam was standing over the hose and fighting the foot valve that didn't want to attach to the hose when his foot slipped off the plank. He lost his balance and fell into the water hole. Pete was laughing before he hit the water and was amazed at how fast the old man jumped out of it. Adam was soaked from head to toe, but he had only been in the water for a second. When he climbed out and stood on the planks with an embarrassed and disgusted look on his face, he looked at the hose for a moment and then started walking past Pete and towards the barge in complete silence. Pete enjoyed the show, but he was still seething from his comments and couldn't resist the opportunity for some payback.

"You are the man! Come on, it's still not hooked up. Where are you going? I thought you were going to show me how to do it? Hey look, Adam, your hat's floating in the middle of the pond; aren't you gonna jump back in and get it?" Pete said while laughing at his retreating colleague.

When Adam was gone, he resumed his slow and steady battle with the hose, and a few minutes later they were hooked up and ready to go.

They spent the rest of day moving and setting piling for the bridge. Pete was positioned on top of the gallows and guided the tops of the piling into place. He hated being so high in the air and wrestling the monsters. By the end of the day his arms and shoulders ached from pulling, pushing, and twisting the massive piling. He was covered with mud, smelled like a swamp rat, and wanted nothing more than to go home, take a hot shower, and go to bed, but he had other plans. When they left the job he had just enough time to stop home, wash, and get to his first karate class minutes before it was to start.

Pete rushed to the dressing room and changed. When he put on his gi and obi, he felt kind of foolish; neither he nor anyone he knew had done this before. He watched another student tie his belt and tried to mimic what he saw. He did the best he could and timidly walked alone to the dojo floor. He looked for a familiar face but saw none. Neither Mr. Sanders nor Shihan were present. He nervously stood off to the side and watched a few students getting in some last minute stretching before class. Soon a young man in his early twenties with a stocky build, a face that revealed his Asian ancestry, and four red stripes on his black belt approached him with an outstretched hand.

"Welcome; my name in Mr. Park. I'm happy that you've decided to train with us. Has anyone explained to you how we line up? I can see that nobody showed you how to tie your belt," he said with a friendly smile.

Pete explained that it was his first class and that he knew absolutely nothing. Mr. Park reassured him that everyone went through the same emotions when they started. He showed him how to properly tie his belt and how they lined up by rank with the highest rank in the front right and the lowest in the back left. He explained that everyone was addressed by their surname and he was to always introduce himself as Mr. Taylor. After a brief introduction to their rituals, Mr. Park looked at the clock and yelled "shugo" and everyone in the class stopped what they were doing and scurried into their line-up positions. From the back of the class Pete got a chance to look at his fellow students. There were thirteen of them lined up, both male and female. They ranged in age from mid-fifties to about sixteen, the youngest age allowed in the adult class.

In the front row were four black belts: a heavy set man in his fifties, two solid and strong looking young men, and a short and stocky teenage girl. In the second row were three brown belts: a slender girl with dark skin and jet black hair, who appeared to be about sixteen or seventeen, and two teenage boys, one of whom looked exactly like her and the other had short blonde hair and wire rimmed glasses that made him look like John Denver. The fourth person in the row was a slender guy that appeared to be a couple of years younger than Pete. He wore a green belt and had perfectly combed and feathered brown hair that just touched his shoulders. When he turned his face slightly, Pete did a double-take; the poor kids face was red and pitted with one of the worst cases of acne Pete had ever seen. The next row had three orange belts, two younger guys, a man in his mid-forties with greying hair and a little belly hanging over his belt, and a woman with a white belt in her thirties. Pete stood alone in the last row.

Mr. Park yelled "kiotsuke" and everyone snapped straight and tall and put their arms at their sides. He stood in front of the class and reviewed his students while they stood at attention. "Matte," everyone put their hands behind their backs, spread their feet a few inches, and stood at a military style relaxed position.

When the most senior ranking black belt in the front row yelled "seiza," the class knelt down. Everyone sat on their heels with their backs straight and their clenched fists on their thighs. The man said "Shomen Ni Rei" and the class bowed, until their noses touched the floor, to the picture of the elder on the back wall. The man then said "Mokuso".

"I want you to close your eyes and leave all the world's problems outside. Breathe in through your nose and out your mouth. Instead of darkness, I want you to concentrate on light. Build a white room in your mind. Start with a white dot and let it grow; build the walls, ceilings, and floors. It is not easy and will take a long time and a lot of concentration." With that, the class closed their eyes and Pete got his first taste of meditation. There was absolute silence in the room for an excruciatingly long two minutes. Pete was astonished by all the noise that was around him once he was exposed to silence. He heard the hum of the water fountain that was in the other room; he heard the buzz of the florescent lights and cars traveling in the distance. Eventually his mind drifted to the empty darkness that was his mind, and he was unsettled by it. He never saw a white dot, but he did tell Isaac that he loved him.

When Mr. Park loudly said "Mokuso yame," the command to stop meditating, Pete became aware of a strange and peaceful feeling that had overtaken him. It was almost as if he was floating outside his body, and when he opened his eyes he realized that he felt lightheaded. Mr. Park gave the class a moment to gather themselves and then nodded to the black belt. He said "Sensei ni rei," and the class repeated the deep bow they had done earlier, this time directed towards Mr. Park. When everyone sat up, Mr. Park then said, "Sempai ni rei," and he and the class bowed to the senior student. When they finished bowing, he clapped his hands together and said, in English, "Stand up." The class quickly jumped to their feet. "Heiko-dachi, kiotsuke." Everyone stood straight with their feet shoulder width apart and their hands at their sides. "Matte," he said, and they relaxed.

"Good evening, I hope everyone had a great weekend and that you are here with a clear mind and a good attitude and are ready to work. For our new students, don't try to do everything the advanced students do. I want you to push yourself and do as much as you can, but stop and rest when you need to. There is nothing to be ashamed of. I do calisthenics for the black belts who have been training for a long time. If I make the workouts easier and only do enough to make the white belts sweat then our more advanced students will never get the challenge that they need to continue their advancement."

Pete's arms still ached from work, but he thought that he was now a big and strong construction worker that was used to hard work and would be able to handle anything that they threw at him. Mr. Park had the class put their hands on their hips and balance on one foot. He then explained how they should rotate their foot clockwise and then counter-clockwise in order to start loosening up at their ankles. They started at the ankles, and then they did calves, knees, hamstrings, thighs, the waist, and the rest of their bodies until they had loosened every muscle, including the neck. When they started doing splits, Pete felt like his groin muscles were going to snap like rubber bands that had been stretched too far. Then Mr. Parks cheerfully led them into leg raises, sit-ups, crunches, pushups, and more.

Pete began to feel nauseous and wanted to stop, but he refused to give up. In the end, he couldn't do as many pushups, or sit-ups, or leg-raises as the advanced students, but he did keep pushing himself and was soon rewarded for his efforts by advancing from nauseousness to feeling like he was going to pass out.

"Matte. All right, turn and face the back and fix your gi's and obi's." Everyone turned around, fixed their uniforms, composed themselves, and turned back around to face the front. "One minute break for water. Hurry up," Mr. Park relented.

Pete was staggering and barely able to walk to the water fountain. He was gasping for air, his face was bright red, and his hair and gi were soaked with sweat. The students lined up by rank, black belts first and Pete last. When he finally made it to the fountain, he drank like a man out of the desert, and then stuck his head into the fountain and let the stream of cold water shoot onto his head and down his back. He opened his mouth and started drinking another big gulp when Mr. Park called everyone back into line. He then had them practice kicks and punches until Pete thought he was going to pass out again. He was awkward and off balance, but he kept trying. Mr. Parks finally stopped, called out "Matte, kiotsuke" again, and everyone snapped to attention. He had them straighten their gi's again, and then allowed them one more them one more drink of water.

Mr. Park split them into groups and gave instructions on what he wanted them to work on. Pete was not included in any group, and when the others began working on their assignments, Mr. Park called Pete to him.

"Do you know how to throw a punch?" he asked. Pete felt insulted and answered yes. Everyone knows how to throw a punch, he thought to himself.

"Okay, let me see."

Pete raised his hands into fighting position and threw an off balance looping haymaker into the air. Mr. Park raised his eyebrows and brought Pete to a mirror.

"Put your right hand behind your back and hold onto your belt. Your left hand goes into the chamber just below your chest. When you throw a punch, let your arm rub against your gi as it comes out. Do it slow and focus on technique, not speed. I want you to do a few hundred punches in the mirror and I'll be back to check on you in a few minutes."

He left Pete alone for a while and moved around the class helping students with various techniques. Pete watched him walk away and thought his assignment was ridiculous, but did as he was told. A few minutes later he could barely hold his arm up. His shoulder burned and his arm felt like a lead weight extending from his body.

"Okay, let me see how you're doing." Pete was relieved to be getting a break for a moment and was convinced he was doing it exactly as told. He punched for Mr. Park and was surprised to hear his comment.

"All right, Mr. Taylor, we have a lot of work to do. Remember, let your arm rub against your body as you extend the punch and allow your hips to rotate. That is where your power will come from. I want you to switch hands and do the same thing with your right. I'll be back to check on you."

An hour passed and Pete was still in front of the mirror throwing one punch at a time.

"Line up." When Mr. Park said that, everyone stopped what they were doing and returned to their starting positions. Pete was relieved to stop punching. His arms burned so badly that he could barely lift them. Mr. Park made the class get into a heiko datchi stance. Pete mimicked the other students and kept his back straight while he squatted until his hamstrings were parallel to the floor.

"Arms in chamber, count with me. Punches to solar plexus; ichi, ni, san, shi, go, roku, shichi, hachi, kyuu, juu." He counted to ten in Japanese over and over. They did one hundred punches with each arm before Mr. Park mercifully dismissed them for the day. Pete made his way back to the locker room to change and could barely lift his arms. When he attempted to put his tee shirt on, it hurt to lift his arms over his head. He went home, fell on the bed, and didn't move until he woke up the next morning.

WHEN PETE OPENED HIS EYES, every muscle in his body hurt. He didn't want to go to work, but knew he had to. Putting his pants on and getting into his van took effort as his legs hurt so much. He pulled into the Tom Thumb to get a cup of coffee, opened his van door, and then decided that getting out would take too much effort, so he closed it again and went to work. He drove into the boatyard, parked his van, and gingerly walked to the men loading trucks. Joe saw him walking in pain and was concerned that he had hurt himself at work.

"What's the matter with you? Did you hurt yourself or something?"

"Yeah, or something; I joined that dojo and they beat the hell out me. I hurt from head to toe," Pete said. He thought he was going to get sympathy for his pain and encouragement for his attempt at bettering himself.

"I'm not paying you if you're going to walk around like a cripple and can't work. I don't give a rat's ass about any damn bozo. I have work to get done, and if you want to get paid, you better be in pain on your own time, not mine." Joe was in a rage again.

His day had started badly and was getting worse every time he turned around. He'd arrived at the boatyard before everyone else, as usual, and had started to get things ready for his guys. He'd picked up the suction hose for the pump and discovered a now worthless piece of expensive garbage. It had been run over with a loader and then put away as if nothing was wrong with it. That in itself was bad enough, but what had really pissed him off was that nobody had said anything to him about it, and now Pete was going to be worthless all day. Joe turned around and started screaming at the gathered men.

"What's wrong with you people? Do you have any brains at all? How can I fix something if you don't tell me it's broken? You all want to get paid on Friday, but you don't think about where the money comes from to pay you. If we don't get work done, we don't get paid. How hard is that to understand?"

Pete forgot about his pain and picked up his pace without another word and started loading equipment.

Joe barked out assignments and sent the men on their way. He told Giles to push the small barge to a dock job in Shalimar and to take Pete with him. Pete was relieved to not be going back to the bridge and was stunned when Joe told Giles to have him run the boat to gain some experience.

There were no bridges to go under, the weather was clear, and they were pushing the small barge, so Joe decided that it was a good opportunity for him to get some time at the wheel, and besides, Pete was obviously going to be worthless for doing anything else. They secured the equipment on the barge, attached the *Sue-Bee*, and were on their way. Pete was nervous while pulling away, but he knew Giles was there to save him if they got into any real trouble, so he took his time and was relieved to be heading out towards the bay without incident.

Giles was a short man with a little pot belly and a full beard. He spoke with a slur and always had something to say, usually about how much the women loved him. Over the months of working and hanging out with him, Pete had learned that Giles was a surprisingly good athlete. They played basketball together and Giles could shoot; then they played golf and Giles could putt. When they'd first met, Pete had thought Giles was an ignorant redneck, but over time he'd begun to learn not to judge what you don't know. Pete liked working with him because he was usually in a good mood and told stories that made him laugh all day.

They had just left Tom's Bayou when Giles came to the wheel house of the *Sue-Bee* holding an unlit cigarette.

"Hey Pete, do you have a light?"

"No, I sure don't."

"Oh shit. How the hell can I light this damn thing? There's got to be fire on this boat somewhere," he said, clearly becoming concerned about the situation. He climbed past Pete and into the cabin behind the wheelhouse. The cabin consisted of a set of bunk beds, a tiny stainless steel sink, and some old cabinets with speckled white Formica tops. Giles began to go through all the drawers and cabinets trying to find matches. He began mumbling obscenities under his breath as he fumbled around, and as his search became more futile, he began slamming things and the obscenities spewing from his mouth grew louder and louder.

"God damn it. How can you have a boat and not have a pack of matches on board? This is bullshit. I'd rather be out of cigarettes and have fire than to be sitting here with this damned cigarette and no way to light it. What the hell is going on here? This is fucking ridiculous," he complained.

He gruffly made his way past Pete and to the back of the boat where he went down into the engine room. He looked around the shelves and toolboxes for something that would light his cigarette. He knew it was a waste of time, but while he was contemplating his next move, he held his cigarette against the exhaust of the engine for a couple of minutes. As he expected, it wasn't hot enough and nothing happened. He desperately looked around some more and finally saw something he could make work.

He found a roll of wire and cut off a piece about two feet long and scraped an inch of plastic off both ends, then walked over to the batteries. He bent the wire into a semi-circle and attached the wire across the battery terminals. It sparked more than he'd expected and he stumbled backwards. His foot slipped off the walkway and into the oily bilge.

"God damn it!" he yelled on the top of his lungs. He lifted his foot out of the bilge and inspected the slimy black sludge that now covered his shoe. He shook his foot to get some of it off and then returned to the batteries. He was now semi-confident that he wouldn't blow up, so he determinedly returned to the battery and this time he held the wires to the batteries for a few seconds. Sparks flew and the wire almost melted, but it was red hot and it lit his cigarette. He proudly took a couple of drags and made his way out of the engine room and around to the wheelhouse, leaving one wet, black shoe print with every other step.

"Well, it looks like I'm chain smoking until we get back to the boat yard. I ain't lettin' this thing go out, that's for damn sure. I almost blew my ass up down there," he said while standing next to Pete.

"I heard you crashing and cursing down there and I have to admit that I almost fell off this chair laughing. How'd you get it lit?"

"A little wire and a lot of imagination can go a long way, Son. I feel much better now, but you know what we could use right about now? We need a fat hooter to smoke and a big pair of breastages to play with!" He and Pete laughed out loud and Giles happily took another drag off of his cigarette and looked out at the bay. Pete really didn't like his vulgarity, but he had heard and said much worse, so he ignored it and enjoyed the moment. The sky was clear, the bay was calm, and there wasn't a boat in sight. It was another gorgeous morning on the bay.

"There ain't nothing like a nice rack on a hot little blonde honey, is there? You're still too young to understand, but let me tell you what the perfect woman looks like. She's about three feet tall, blonde hair, no teeth, and has a flat head for me to rest my beer on!" He laughed out loud at his own joke and Pete just shook his head, not sure what to think about this perverted little man.

"No, I'm just kidding. The perfect woman is about five feet tall, blonde hair, with a set of 38's and an ass you can bounce a quarter off of! What do you think of that? Is that the perfect woman or what?"

"Or what!" Pete said, "I'm not a blonde guy myself. I like a brunette and a little taller, probably 5'4" or 5'5," with dark skin and smaller, maybe 34's or 36's. She should be smart, funny, love football, and of course have a nice body. What do you think of that?"

"You've really given this some thought, eh? No, that wouldn't be bad either. I just like big tits; no, I love big tits!"

Giles left the wheelhouse shaking his head and dreaming of titties and beer. Pete watched him make his rounds checking the lines on the boat and barge. Giles was on the front of the barge enjoying the sun and the breeze, when Pete noticed a large boat heading their way at high speed. He yelled to Giles and pointed at the boat as it closed the distance between them quickly. Giles walked back to the wheelhouse, watching the boat as he moved and stood with Pete as the boat approached to within fifty feet of them and then idled down. It was a beautiful white Hatteras about forty feet long that slowed quickly and gently came closer to their barge.

Both men's jaws dropped when out of the cabin strode a young woman in her early twenties. She was a brunette with soft, bronze skin, about 5'5," wearing a small orange bikini and a big smile.

"Excuse me; do you guys know where we could buy some shrimp?" she asked. It took a moment for them to return to their senses and acknowledge her, and then a moment more to realize that there was another person on the boat with her. Up top, in the wheel house, was a man who appeared to be in his late forties. Giles and Pete looked at each other again and wondered the same thing at the same time: father or boyfriend? They saw his proud smile and concluded boyfriend. Giles looked at Pete and shook his head; the woman that Pete had just described was now standing in front of them.

"Go into Boggy; right before the oil terminal is the fish market. You can probably side tie to the dock or a boat and they'll hook you up with whatever you need," Giles yelled to her.

They waved and she said thanks as the man at the wheel hit the throttle, causing the girl to stumble a little with the surge of power, and they were off, leaving a white trail of foaming water behind them and large waves emanating from the sides of their powerful boat.

"Did you see that? Holy shit, you should have jumped on that boat and kicked that guy's ass and taken his boat and his woman!" Giles laughed and the two men shook their heads in amazement as the boat disappeared in the distance.

The two of them finished their delivery of the barge in a great mood.

They secured the barge in Shalimar and brought the *Sue-Bee* back to the boat yard without further adventure or incident.

They had an early day and Pete was glad that he could go home and rest his aching body.

CHAPTER 37

DILEMMAS

Bill sat at his desk and stared at his work. The job had lost its luster. He had become an engineer because he'd wanted to build things that made people's lives better and now he found himself in a job where success was predicated on his ability to help design tools to be used in the efficient elimination of human life. He aimlessly shuffled through the papers and files on his desk while becoming ever more consumed with the thought that the rest of his life was going to be spent thinking of better and more effective ways to destroy things and kill people. He desperately wanted a drink.

"Hey, Bill, how's it going?" Bill looked up to see Stan standing in his doorway. The question and look of concern on his face was not about Bill's health or feelings, but the business he and his father had spent decades building.

"Pretty good," he replied without conviction. "I'm just trying to work through some of these calculations. Some of the numbers aren't quite coming out the way we'd hoped. It's kind of frustrating."

"You've looked frazzled the last couple of days, Bill. How about if I buy you lunch? There's a great little place next to O'Brian's. It's the only place in town that has a great shark steak and the service is out of this world. Give me a few minutes to button up and I'll come and get you," Stan said. He tapped the palm of his hand on the doorway and was gone just as fast as he'd appeared. It was immediately clear to Bill that it was not an invitation but a command. He shook his head. "Just more shit being piled on," he thought to himself.

After Stan had left Bill, he walked to the other side of the building to his father's office and closed the door behind him after he'd entered.

"Well, did you talk to him?" Art asked with irritation in his voice.

"Not yet. I'm taking him to Walt's and we'll talk there; it might be a long lunch, so I'm going to have Fran cancel my 3:00. I'll see if I can find the problem and straighten him out. I've reviewed his work and he's actually quite brilliant, but if he can't wrap his mind around these projects, you're going to have to find him something else to do or you'll have to give your buddy his money back and send him on his way."

"It has nothing to do with damn money and you know it. We have a job to do and if he doesn't like his job, well tough shit. God damn it, how do I get myself into these messes? See if you can talk some sense into him. We need him to go to Albuquerque with you next week without him making a damn fool out of us and I want that damned mustache off your face before you go!"

"I'll talk to him and we'll see how things go, and I suppose I'll think about shaving, but I kind of like it, Pop, and you should see some of the looks I get." Stan got up and left with a little smile on his face, confident that his father was sufficiently briefed, and gathered Bill for lunch.

They walked in the front door of Walt's and were greeted by a packed house. Walt's was famous for a quality lunch and strong drinks. It took a couple of minutes for them to get a seat, and as they were sitting down, a shapely waitress was promptly at their table.

"Good afternoon gentlemen, my name is Rita. Can I get you something to drink while you decide what you want?" asked the young waitress in a sweet southern accent. She was average in height, had shoulder length dirty blond hair, a full figure and strong body, and the power of manipulation in her bright blue eyes. When the men responded to her voice and turned their heads towards it, they were chest high and their attention was instinctively drawn to her blouse. It looked to be about two sizes too small with buttons that looked ready to pop at any moment.

"Yeah..." Stan stuttered. "I'll have bourbon and seven. Bill, go ahead and get something good. I know the boss." Bill realized he was probably staring, but he was intrigued by the strength of the thread holding those buttons. Stan's voice brought him back to reality and he knew he had a decision to make. He was proud that he had stopped drinking at lunch and really didn't want to get into the habit again, but he also knew that under the circumstances he should probably comply and he did.

"I'll have the same." She scribbled on her pad and they watched her walk away.

"Good God, man. Didn't I tell you the service was out of this world? If the food is bad, I probably wouldn't even notice or care. I'd bet that she brings in as much money in tips as a damn lawyer does in court." Stan looked at the menu briefly and then returned his attention to Bill. "Have you ever had shark steak? It really is fantastic," Stan continued before Bill could respond. "It's not always on the menu, but when it is, I highly recommend it; and look, there it is. You should give it a try."

"What the hell; when in Rome and all that crap. Thanks for the lunch, Stan. This is a nice little place and you were right, the service is pretty damn amazing. It almost makes you want to be twenty five again, doesn't it?"

"Hell no, that girl was designed to ruin men's lives. Women like that are meant to look at, but never to touch. She's a hell of a lot more dangerous than any shark on that menu, and I'll tell you what, I'll bet that within five years, she marries a forty something year old guy in the middle a mid-life crisis, makes him feel young again, gets him to spend money he doesn't have, pumps out a couple of kids and is retired by the time she's thirty-five. No, sir; run away! Do not walk!"

They laughed together and finished their first drink before the food came, and as soon as Rita was nearby, they summoned her over and ordered another round. They talked about nothing until the food arrived, and once Bill had taken a few bites of the shark, he realized that it was as good as Stan had advertised. Bill was astounded at how succulent and white the meat was and ate it with great enthusiasm. After the meal, some meaningless small talk, and a couple of more drinks, Bill began to relax, and Stan began to get serious.

"So Bill, I'm sensing that there's some conflict in you about your work."

Bill had known it was coming; he just hadn't known when. "Well, I guess I'm not fooling anyone, am I?" Bill shuffled his drink in his hands before continuing. "I just never thought I would spend my life designing things that are going to be used to kill people."

Stan had known what he was going to say before he said it and had tried to prepare himself for it, but it still pissed him off when he heard it. He had advised his father against hiring a stranger with no military experience because it was a huge risk with little chance of success.

"Bill, I don't know how to put this to you in a nice way. I know you've never been in the military or out of the country for that matter, so I can somewhat understand where you're coming from, but understand this…we are in the business of protecting young, American soldiers from real assholes who want to kill them and destroy us. It's the unfortunate nature of the human beast that the man with the biggest stick makes the rules, and I'm proud that my job helps to make sure that America has the biggest fucking stick. I've seen firsthand the horrors of what men will do to each other, and make no mistake about it, this country isn't perfect; because nothing on this planet is. We are imperfect creatures, but this is by far the greatest country in the history of mankind, and if you fuck with it, you should be crushed like a cockroach." Stan took another drink and Bill knew he was getting on a roll. "Bill, if you have a moral issue with what we do, I really don't give a damn. You're a nice enough guy, but this is a hard business and a cruel world. The long and short of it is that we design weapons that eliminate our enemies, and we're damn good at it."

"I know. I like you guys and your father is a true piece of work. I just…I don't know. How should I feel? It's clear from all the people that

I've met since I've been here that you're well respected. I think I just need some time to get used to it or something."

"Well, there isn't any time to get used to it. It must be crystal clear in your mind what we're doing and why we're doing it, and then if you decide to continue, we need you to commit to your job, and we need you to do it with enthusiasm. We want you to go to Albuquerque with me next week. We have to make a presentation, a demonstration, and do some meet and greet. We leave on Wednesday morning and return late Friday night, but there's no sense in continuing this if you're not all in; so tell me what you don't understand and what makes you uncomfortable besides the whole 'I don't want to kill somebody' horseshit, because you can bet your ass that there are a lot of people who would love to kill you right now just because you're an American."

"Why… why do they hate us and want to kill us? Why do we always have to dominate everything? You know that a Russian mom loves her kids just as much as the American mom does, and the Russians think they're just as right as we do, and doing things to provoke them like calling them the 'Evil Empire' only makes it worse," Bill contended.

"You see, Bill, the truth hurts. The Union of Soviet Socialist Republic, just like the National Socialists in Germany, and The Red Chinese, have killed millions upon millions of people. Look at the facts: The greatest mass murderers in world history have all been socialists or communists. Stalin made Hitler look like an amateur when it came to mass murder, and Chairman Mao was even worse than Stalin. The systems they put in place are still running strong. They still put dissenters in prison or mental hospitals. Maybe I'm wrong, maybe Siberia is really just a nice resort community where people enjoy visiting to relax and get their mind right," Stan said sarcastically before taking a sip from his glass and continuing.

"Have you ever noticed that all the communist countries have 'reeducation camps' for people who don't understand that the individual- that means you, your wife, and your son- means nothing? There can be no God, no independent thought, the state is everything, and those in power are the State. People go to prison or are killed just for reading the Bible. They feed the people a line of bullshit about equality and fairness. They tell them that the government is going to clear the streets of guns and gangs and the police will protect them. Then the people are told that the government is going to protect them from greedy corporations and evil businessmen who lie and steal from them. Well, how's that working out for them? Ask the Romanians or the Poles about the Soviets. Just take a look at the difference between West and East Germany, or North and South Korea. When we defeat a country in war, we do our best to set their people free and we use our national treasure to rebuild them. Hell, all the stereos and half the cars on our roads are built in Japan. How did those great National Socialists treat the Greeks or the Poles? The Khmer Rogue were really nice guys, weren't they? Clear your mind of all the bullshit you've heard from weak-kneed sympathizers and open your eyes. Look at the difference between Japan, West Germany, and France, and those that the Soviets 'liberated.' If we hadn't had people like us doing the work we do during WWII, the Axis would have won, and if people like us didn't do the work we do today, who would, or could, stand up to the Russians? Look at a map sometime. Communism is still quietly expanding and it's done over and over with the same pattern. First it starts with protests against economic inequality, littered with promises of social justice and free this and that, then the country goes bankrupt and things devolve into coercion and violence. Soon thereafter the government has no choice but to disarm the citizenry, and then before you can blink, its game over." Stan took another long pull off his drink. He hated reality. He was a kind and considerate man who prayed every night for peace, but was resigned to the fact that evil existed, and he was not going to be the good man who did nothing and allowed evil to prosper. He was a man who was willing to fight with every fiber of his body. Stan was on a roll, and after he took a breath and another drink he continued his sermon.

"People talk about the greed of the evil corporations. Well, take a look at the countries where people don't have the right to join together, work hard, and enjoy the fruits of their labor, because understand this: that's all a corporation is, a group of people *voluntarily* working together for a common goal. Wouldn't it be so much better to live in a country where there is no corporate greed like in Russia, Cuba, North Korea, Romania, or Cambodia? Socialism and communism are two heads of the same snake and they are evil. Plain and simple, the idea is a sweet sounding elixir, and it sounds so logical. It promises all this wonderful equality, but how come wherever it's tried, it fails and within a few years of the promise, people are poverty stricken and enslaved? The problem is never the fault of bad government policy. No, no, it's always the fault of the rich, or big business, or the Jews, or the Church, or the '*war mongering industrial military complex.*' Well, how are the people doing in all those countries where they have eliminated the Jews, and the rich, and the Church? Funny thing is, these bastards get into power complaining about the oppression of the military and the police, but once they secure power, they never eliminate the military or the secret police; they make them stronger. Mark my words, if we're not diligent and careful, the same shit will happen here in America too. The American left always says that it can't happen here; after all, this is America." Stan took another drink, paused, and then looked Bill in the eye before continuing. "Well, here's the thing, America is made up of people from all over the world, and if it can happen all over the world, it can happen here. The left never wants to be measured based on results. Hell no, their intentions are good, they're open minded, and the snake oil they sell sounds so wonderful. Well, mark my words; there is evil in the world and my job is to help those that fight evil be safe and victorious," Stan said in the commanding voice of a preacher. He finished his drink, raised his glass to signal Rita to bring another round, and then stared coldly at Bill, waiting for his reply.

Bill quietly pondered his words for several moments. Stan had just challenged everything he believed in. He'd loved Carter in '76, but not so much by '80. He thought about all the government programs that he supported because they sounded so right and had such good titles, but then he acknowledged the results. He next thought about the world around him and when he was done, he lifted his glass in salute. If Stan was the preacher, he had joined the right congregation.

"I'm in," were the only words Bill said, and instantly a great weight was lifted from his shoulders and he realized that his job was of great importance and his life did have purpose. It was not what he had envisioned or anticipated, but he was now an enthusiastic defender of America and her ideals, and he was proud of what he did for a living, and if that meant designing something that stopped those that wanted to destroy her, then so be it, but he was going to embrace his job and do it with enthusiasm.

The two men sat together, told stories, and drank for hours. It was near five when they decided to order dinner and after seven when an old friend of Stan's walked in the door and joined them at their table.

"Bill, I want you to meet an old buddy of mine. This is Ryan Pearson. He sells computers now that he's old and doesn't fly anymore. Ryan, this is Bill Taylor. He recently joined our firm as a new engineer. By the way, how is your lovely wife doing? I haven't seen her in a while," Stan asked Ryan.

"She's just fine. Hey, can I buy a round and join you? I got done early and I'm supposed to meet someone here in about an hour," Ryan commented as he pulled out a chair and sat down. Stan and Ryan quickly began reminiscing about their days in Vietnam and some of the stupid things they had seen and done. They laughed loudly and often. Bill had made peace with his job, he was making friends, and Niceville was starting to feel like home.

"Have you ever heard of the Red Balloon, Bill?" Stan asked, hoping he hadn't heard the story.

"No, I don't think so, what's the Red Balloon?"

"Well, sometimes when you have the worst job in the world, you have leverage. When I was in Thailand the first time, I was nineteen and scared shitless. My job was to arm the bombs on planes before takeoff. I was paired with what I thought was an old guy at the time; he was twenty-three and his tour was almost up, so he just didn't give a shit. We had to run down the runway and jump into a foxhole while Vietcong were on the other side of a chain link fence taking pot shots at us. Luckily, they couldn't shoot worth a shit, but when a plane came down the runway and got ready for takeoff, we would get a call on the radio telling us to go, and then we would run out and arm the bombs as fast as we could, and then run back to the foxhole and wait for the next one. Remember, we're basically unarmed and they're shooting at us. Well, every day we would be given a code name, and when we showed up one day and were assigned the name Fox Trot Alpha or some shit like that. Well, Benny tells the guy our code name is *Red Balloon*. The guy looked at him and said, 'Your name is Fox Trot Alpha; now get into position.' Benny gives a weak salute, nods, and says nothing. We leave and get into our little fox hole and a moment later we hear the radio 'Fox Trot Alpha, you are clear to go.' Well, I start to get up and Benny grabs my arm and says, 'They're not talking to us. We're Red Balloon.' The plane is sitting there, other planes are lining up, and the radio comes back on and the guy sounds pissed. 'Fox Trot Alpha, You Are Clear To Go!' I look at Benny and say that we'd better go or we might get in trouble. He laughed at me and said, 'What the hell can they do to us? Look around; nobody wants this job, and if they get rid of us then one of them will have to do it.' A moment later, the voice came back on the radio: 'Red Balloon. You are clear to go. Acknowledge.' Benny picked up the radio. 'Red Balloon here, we're ready to go!' It was an epiphany for me and I learned that sometimes when your job sucks you can get away with a lot more than when you have a nice cushy job, because nobody wants to take your place."

ANNE FINISHED CLOCKING OUT AND hurried over to Walt's. She had anxiously waited for this night since she had first felt his kiss. She, once again, had that giddy teenager in lust feeling. It had been a long week that had seemed to drag on painfully slow. Bill had walked around all week moping about something at work. He'd tried talking to her about it, but she really wasn't interested in his problems anymore and had ignored him.

She eagerly pulled open the door of Walt's, took a step in, and before she released the door from her hand, she almost had a heart attack. She froze in her tracks and wanted to turn around and run out the door, but Bill had already seen her. Her mind raced with plausible explanations for her sudden appearance in the bar, but she had none. She was petrified in place as she stared at the table where her husband and his boss were sitting with her soon-to-be-lover. Bill waved her over and she reluctantly released the door and slowly made her way to the table as her mind raced. When she reached the table, it was obvious that Bill was as surprised to see her as she was to see him.

"Stan, Ryan, this is my wife Anne. Have a seat and join us. What would you like to drink?" he asked her.

Anne glanced at Ryan, who was gleefully playing along with the ruse. Bill and Stan had obviously been here for some time and were on their way to being very drunk. Ryan was hiding his Cheshire Cat smile by taking a sip from his glass. Anne was devastated, Bill was oblivious, and Ryan was having fun.

"Um….a margarita please." Anne nervously sat and joined them.

"Anne, it's a pleasure to finally meet you. I'm glad you stopped in. Have you eaten? I'm sure we could rustle something up for you," Stan asked.

"No, thank you. I was going to meet a couple of the girls from work for a quick drink before heading home," Anne lied.

"Well, bring the girls over and we can have a party," Ryan enthusiastically chirped in to Anne's dismay.

"They got off an hour ago. I guess they must have already left," Anne retorted quickly as she pretended to look around the bar.

"That's too bad. I was supposed to meet someone here as well, but it's beginning to look like something more interesting has come up. But hey, that's the way it goes. I learned a long time ago that I have to be flexible and appreciate the moments for what they are. Besides, I'm always glad to get a chance to enjoy the company of an old friend and the opportunity to make some new ones." Ryan raised his glass to the center of the table and continued. "To old friends and new friends. May the memories of our times and adventures together live in our hearts forever."

Glasses clinked together and everyone drank to the toast. Anne wasn't enjoying the situation as much as Ryan seemed to be, and was irritated that he found the situation so amusing, but she smiled and played along. When they finished their drink, Stan placed his hand on Anne's forearm to get her attention.

"Anne, I know this is short notice, but I would like to steal your brilliant husband from you next week for a couple of days. We're working on an important project and need to go to Albuquerque. If we have your permission, we'll leave Wednesday morning and I'll have him back in your loving arms Friday night. Does he have your permission to go?" Stan said to Anne with a charming, albeit slightly snockered, smile on his face.

She was still on edge from the predicament she found herself in. Everything was happening so fast. And had this man just called her husband brilliant? She looked at Bill, who shrugged his shoulders and wore a dumb smile on his face with pride. He was clearly the happiest and most relaxed she had seen him in years. She turned to look at Stan and then Ryan, who just looked at her with a gleam in his eye and a naughty little smile on his face as he again sipped his drink to conceal his amusement.

"Yes…yes, of course. Unless, of course, this is some kind of ruse that you three put together and what you're really planning is a trip to Las Vegas for a couple of days, because then I would say no, unless of course you were taking me with you," she declared. They all had a good laugh together and began an enjoyable evening filled with laughter, innuendo, and secrets.

"Then it's settled. Bill, you're on board; your lovely wife is good to go, and I'm convinced that this is a great opportunity and good things are coming our way."

The four of them sat at the table for a couple more hours. Ryan and Stan swapped war stories and they all had a good time. Bill and Anne had fun and laughed together for the first time in years.

When they finally walked out the door, it was clear that Bill was in no condition to drive, so he agreed to leave his car at the office for the night and climbed in the passenger side of Anne's car.

"I'm glad you came in and joined us tonight," Bill said while gazing at his wife with a drunken smile. "It was very fruituititis…frutuita…it was nice and worked out well. I enjoyed seeing you laugh again."

She stopped what she was doing and looked at her husband and thought about what he had said: it was nice to see her laugh again. Had it been that long since she'd laughed, and what was there to laugh about? But as she thought about it, she had had fun; she was having fun.

"It was good to laugh, and I had fun; maybe we should do it again." She put the car in gear and drove home. They didn't speak again on the ride; both of them were lost in their thoughts about the night and would only occasionally sneak a look at the other. They had been through a lot together and both wondered what lie ahead for them.

When they got home and Anne shut off the car, they looked at each other before getting out.

"I used to know this girl. Damn she was hot, and smart and strong. She used to date this guy. He was kind of a geek, but she liked him anyways. That guy would like to take that girl out on a date."

"Oh, a date, huh? What kind of a date did he have in mind? Girls like that are kind of picky!"

"He was thinking about a nice dinner, a movie, some dancing, and maybe a moonlit walk on the beach to end the evening."

"That sounds nice, but she'll have to think about it." Anne looked at her husband and saw a man that she had not seen in a long time.

CHAPTER 38

MIRACLES DO HAPPEN

Pete sat at the kitchen table wolfing down a bowl of cereal before work. He was in a good mood, but his body hurt from the workout Mr. Sanders had given him the night before and he was running late. The Connecticut Yankee was quickly becoming a Boggy Boy and he liked it. He was really enjoying his job and the people he worked with, even if he hated the pay. Anne sat at the table watching him eat while sipping her coffee. Bill was in the shower getting ready for work. Pete had noticed a slight thawing in the air between his parents since the other night when they had come home together late and drunk. But they, nor he, had brought it up.

"Are you working for that woman this weekend?" Anne asked in an attempt to have a dialogue with her son.

"Mrs. Anderson? Yeah, she always seems to have something for me to do. She's a neat lady," he replied in between spoonfuls of cereal.

"Oh, and what makes her so neat?" Anne was hopeful that she could have a pleasant conversation with him. She was desperately trying to allow herself to be optimistic again. She was beginning to look at her husband as a man again, and now she was trying to reconnect with her son.

Pete paused for a moment and gave some thought to why he liked Mrs. Anderson so much. He had begun to think that she gave him work to do as much for his company as for the work she wanted done. The two of them would sit and talk, sometimes for hours. She told him stories of life in the Philippines during and after the war and about coming to America and how scared she'd been. Pete had gained an immense respect for her generation and the battles they'd fought for his freedom. He was beginning to realize that the freedoms he had taken for granted had been paid for with the blood of real people. Like most kids, he'd read about the events of their day, or saw them in movies, but it was completely different hearing the stories from the people who'd actually lived through the horrors of war.

"She's seen and done a lot. I'd never thought about what it would mean to live in an occupied country during a war before. She talks to me and tells me stories, and I don't know why, but after all she's gone through, she's a happy woman. I don't know why I like her, or why she talks to me, but she just helps me put things in perspective when I'm around her, and I like being around her."

"I'm glad to hear that. So, do you like this karate thing you're doing, and is your job okay?"

Pete was surprised that she wanted to know so much. He wasn't sure what was going on, but at least she was sober when she was asking; he liked that. He finished his cereal, put his bowl in the sink, and for some weird reason, gave his mom a kiss on the cheek as he walked towards the door.

"It's actually going great, Mom. I'm glad we moved here. But if I don't get to the boatyard, I'm going to get screamed at."

He walked back over to her and kissed her on the cheek again, and then hurried out the door. He had kissed her, twice. She felt a warmth within her soul that had been missing in her life for a long time, and when her husband kissed her goodbye a short time later and told her that he loved her, she believed him.

PETE WAS ADAPTING TO, AND enjoying, life for the first time in a long time. The first time he pushed a barge on Choctawhatchee Bay as the sun was rising, and stood behind the wheel of the *Sue-Bee* as the captain with a hot cup of coffee in his hand and the sweet smell of a Backwoods cigar in the air, he was hooked. He was a natural with boats and had earned Joe's trust over time through hard work and by paying diligent attention to the maintenance of the boats and equipment. He began to understand winds and currents and was now trusted to run the boats and push the barges when Jeff or Giles were not available.

He was also proud of his growth and accomplishments in the understanding of karate and was relieved to no longer be in constant pain from Mr. Park's workouts. After a couple of months of hard work, he was more limber, confident, and was now mentally and physically stronger than he had ever been. He had not had a nightmare in a long time and no longer dreaded sleeping. For the first time in many years, Pete was happy to be alive.

Mrs. Anderson had returned from Medjugorje a month earlier, but didn't speak much about the trip except to say that she'd enjoyed the vacation. On Saturday morning she gave Pete a list of things to do and told him that she was going shopping and was going to have the pictures from her trip developed. She told him that she'd return in an hour.

Pete went about his work and was trimming the azaleas in the front yard when she returned. She was driving much faster than normal when she pulled into the driveway and came to a screeching halt. Pete couldn't help but think about "the little old lady from Pasadena." Mrs. Anderson popped out of her car and waved Pete over excitedly.

"You grab the groceries in the back and come in the house. I have something to show you. Hurry, hurry, this is very important," she said as she scurried into the house with her pictures in hand. Pete grabbed the three bags in the backseat and followed as quickly as he could while wondering what the emergency was. He set the bags on the counter and she waved at him to sit at the table with her. This was the first time that he had been invited to sit at her table and she was more excited than he had ever seen her.

"Sit down, Peter. I have something to show you. I told you that when I was young I was going to be a nun. Peter, I love Jesus with all my heart. The only man I have ever kissed was my husband. I missed out on many things because of my faith and my love of my husband and of God, and I know this may sound selfish, but when I went to Medjugorje, I asked God for a sign to let me know that I had not been foolish. I know I should never ask for something like that, but I did. We climbed the mountain and toured the villages and had a wonderful time, but I did not get my miracle. I have been disappointed since I returned. I never lost faith, but I was sad. Today, on my way to go grocery shopping, I dropped off my film at One Hour Photo on the way to O'Brian's and picked them up on the way home. You look at them; tell me what you see." She was as excited as a school girl and he, of course, wanted to make her happy.

"Sure, I would love to see pictures of Yugoslavia. I've heard it's really a beautiful place."

"Yes, it is very beautiful. Now, Peter, understand that I just dropped off this film today. I have not touched it since my return and I am sure the seventeen-year-old girl working at the photo shop could not have played with these photos either." Pete began to wonder just what he was about to see when she laid a photo on the table.

"My daughter took this picture as we were climbing up the mountain. I want you to look at this picture and tell me if you see anything wrong with it." Pete looked at her and then at the photo. He saw Mrs. Anderson, her parish priest, and a couple of other people trudging up a narrow path on a steep hill. There was a statue of Mother Mary, very similar to the one in Grandpa Nevers' yard in Connecticut, but this one was severely tilted over the path. It looked like it was going to fall over at any moment. Pete examined the picture closely, knowing he was supposed to find something, but he didn't know what.

"It looks like a nice picture, but I don't see anything out of the ordinary, except the statue of Mary. I think someone should stand the statue upright and show some respect. Other than that, I just don't see anything."

Mrs. Anderson was beaming now. "Peter, there isn't a statue on that mountain. Now, I want you to look at this photo. I took it myself on the last day of our trip. I was very disappointed that I did not get the miracle that I so desperately wanted, but it was such a nice view and a wonderful morning that I just had to take a picture. I knew I would never be back, so I wanted a picture looking down the valley to remind me of the trip." She placed another picture on the table and Peter almost fell out of his chair. He looked at her and then back at the photo. The clouds above the valley in her photo had formed a giant cross.

"There was no cross in the sky; it was just a pretty morning. Peter, I could not make these photos. I don't know how to do those things and I know that girl could not have done this. She did not have time, she doesn't know me, and believe me, I don't think she was smart enough to do anything like this." She looked at the photo and then at Peter. She had a tear in her eye and he had never seen a more beautiful or happy human being in his life.

She reached over and placed her hand on Pete's forearm and looked deeply into his eyes before she continued. "Peter, I got my miracle. It was not what I expected and it did not come when I expected it, but I got my miracle." She wiped the tear from her eye and patted his hand. "You go clean up the tools and I will see you in two weeks. I have a lot to do." She got up and started putting away the groceries and Pete knew that it was time to go. When he finished cleaning up and was about to leave, she came outside again.

"Peter, you did not take your money. You worked very hard." She came up to him and put her hands out and clasped both hands around his right hand and he felt the familiar touch of cash in his palm. She held his hand for a moment and looked up and into his eyes. "Peter, today I got my miracle. I am so happy. Now go and have fun; I will see you again in two weeks."

CHAPTER 39

A VISIT FROM A FRIEND

"Peter, the phone is for you," Anne called out to her sleeping son. Pete heard her call and reluctantly got up and staggered into the kitchen and took the phone from his mother. As he put the phone to his ear he was convinced he was going to hear Joe's voice calling him into work.

"Hello."

"Hey, Pete, how's it going down there? I bet you didn't expect to hear from me." A bright smile came across Pete's face and he was wide awake as he immediately recognized the voice of his high school buddy Frankie.

"Holy shit, Frank, it's great to hear from you. How are you liking the Marine Corps?"

"I love it. I'm sorry I didn't stop down after boot camp, but things were crazy. I think we had half of Italy in our house the whole time I was home, but hey, I'm shipping out for a Med tour pretty soon and this is my last leave before I'm gone for a year. We'll hit Greece, Italy, France, and we might go over to Lebanon for a little while; but before I do that I want to go to New Orleans and get drunk on Bourbon Street. I went through boot camp with a guy from down there and he told me all about the place. Check this out; when I got back from Paris Island, my dad and my uncles gave me a plane ticket and a weekend pass, most expenses paid, to anywhere in the U.S. I wanted. That shocked the shit out of me. It kind of helps to have an uncle that works for Eastern, but what the hell, I'm flying free. I guess they're pretty happy that I joined the Corps. My dad was at the Frozen Chozen you know, and my uncles were all over Korea too, so I guess it meant a lot to 'em. So anyways, I figured New Orleans was pretty close to you, right? Maybe we can hook up and party for a weekend. How far are you from New Orleans anyways?" Frankie sounded different to Pete. He was stronger and happier.

"I don't know. I think three or four hours. When are you coming down?"

"Next weekend, big boy. I'm going to fly into New Orleans on Friday morning; I land at 11AM, and leave for Lejeune a little after noon on Sunday. Are you in?" Frankie was excited and there was no way Pete was going to miss seeing his friend again.

"Oh, hell yeah, I'm in. Do you have a hotel yet?" Pete said excitedly. He was going to New Orleans for the first time.

"Yeah, everything's taken care of. Just bring beer money. Can you pick me up at the airport?"

"You know it. I'll be there." They continued their energized conversation for a while longer and caught up on each other's recent adventures. Frank gave Pete the gate number and the time to pick him up, and they agreed to see each other at the airport on Friday. When Pete finally hung up the phone, his mother was standing near him. She had never heard him talk on the phone for so long.

"So, what was that all about?" she asked him.

"That was Frankie, from Shelton. He's on leave from the Marine Corps., and wants to meet me in New Orleans next weekend before he ships out on a Med. tour," Pete replied. He was excited to hear from, and was looking forward to seeing his old friend.

"Are you planning on spending the whole weekend there?"

"Yeah. I've got to let Joe know. He wants me to pick him up Friday morning. His flight out is early on Sunday, so I'll be back Sunday afternoon."

"I don't know if I like that, Peter. You be careful while you're in that city, and don't drink too much."

"Mom, I think we'll be able to handle ourselves." Pete was thinking to himself that he was getting in pretty good shape and his karate was improving, and Frankie was a Marine; they'd be fine.

THE WEEK WENT BY FAST. Joe and Jeff were both former Jar Heads and were happy to give Pete the time off to see his friend before he shipped out. Before Pete knew it, he was looking for a parking space at the airport and waiting for Frank's plane to land. He entered the large terminal, and after wandering around lost for a while, he found his way to the proper gate with plenty of time to spare. He got a cup of coffee and a newspaper and settled in front of the large window overlooking the loading area. Twenty minutes later, the plane had yet to arrive. He looked at the board and saw that the flight was delayed for several minutes, and then he looked out the window and saw fire trucks and ambulances gathering outside. He wasn't familiar with airports and procedures, so he looked around and wondered if that was normal protocol. More people began gathering around the window and watching the activities outside. He soon concluded that this was not normal and that something bad must be happening. He looked around to make sure he was in the right place, and unfortunately he was. He began to get nervous while waiting and all kinds of horrible thoughts started racing through his mind. He begged God not to let anything happen to his friend, and he was relieved a few minutes later when he saw the plane land and taxi to the terminal without any problems. He moved toward the unloading area to greet the people exiting the plane. They were very excited and talkative when they emerged from the tunnel and were greeted with big hugs from family and friends at the gate. After about twenty people had gotten off, he saw Frankie coming up the gateway from the plane arm in arm with a pretty blonde who appeared to be several years older and quite a bit drunker than him. They were laughing all the way up the gateway and walking right towards Pete. The girl started waving and smiling at him as if she knew him. Pete sheepishly raised his hand and waved back, quite confused. When they were about two feet in front of him, Pete realized that she was waving to a man who was standing right behind him.

"Hi, honey," she drunkenly giggled. "This is my friend Frankie; he's a Marine. Isn't he cute? Frankie, this is my fiancé, Robert." Both men looked at each other and Frankie just grinned and shrugged his shoulders and handed her off to Robert. He seemed very upset, but didn't say a word. He nodded his head in acknowledgement, and then took her arm and the two of them strode off to presumably live happily ever after.

"What was that all about?" Pete asked.

"They couldn't get the landing gear down. We were circling up there for about twenty minutes. Then the stewardess comes in front of us and gives us the 'put your head between your legs and kiss your ass goodbye' speech, and then she says that we can't smoke and that they won't serve any more alcohol. We're sitting three wide. I've got the window; Stacey, whom you just met, is in the middle, and this guy Matt is on the end. Matt has never been on a plane before and he don't like it. When we hit turbulence, I thought he was going to piss his pants right there. Well, now the stewardess comes and tells him he can't have another cigarette and no more booze; well, it was the funniest thing I ever saw. When she gets done with her little speech, he calmly waves her over, and in a very nice and calm voice says, 'Ma'am, I can understand not smoking and I can deal with that, but you just told me that I am about to crash and die because some asshole didn't check the landing gear, then you tell me I can't have alcohol. I'm being good right now, but if you don't bring me a drink and keep 'em coming, things could get ugly.' The stewardess didn't know what to say. She stood up and walked to the front of the plane and spoke to her supervisor. We could see them talking to each other and then looking back at Matt. Finally she came back and told him he could have a drink. He whipped out a hundred dollar bill, put it on the tray, and ordered a double Jack and Ginger, and then told her to get us whatever we wanted. I think we sucked down four doubles in the last twenty minutes and we ended up laughing our asses off. Old Robert there didn't seem too thrilled to see his fiancé barely able to walk because apparently they haven't seen each other in four months, and now I'll bet she's passed out before they get out of the parking lot. Enough of that though. Damn, it's good to see you again. How do you like it down south?"

"I almost didn't recognize you with no hair. You went from John Travolta to high and tight! You've gained weight too. But yeah, I love it down here. There ain't no money, but it's a cool place to live. Are you hungry? I haven't eaten anything since five this morning."

"Yeah, I'm starving and I'm in New Orleans, so there are two things I have to do before I leave," Frank said.

"Oh yeah, what's that?"

"I want to eat some shrimp Creole and I want to piss in the mighty Mississippi!" he declared proudly.

The two friends high fived each other and then went to find Frank's luggage, their hotel room, and then some food. They found their Hotel at 330 Loyola Avenue and checked into their room on the eighteenth floor. They went in and tossed their bags down. Pete flopped on the bed while Frankie went in the bathroom. He was taking a leak when he yelled out to Pete.

"Hey, do you know the history of this hotel? My Uncle Manny stayed here a few years ago and he says it's haunted."

"You're crazy and he's just fucking with you. Whoever heard of a haunted Howard Johnson's? Get away from me," Pete said confidently, but he sat up a little straighter and started looking around.

Frankie walked into the room and sat on the bed opposite Pete's.

"No, it's true. You've got to understand; this is a crazy fucking city with a lot of that voodoo and hoodoo and all kinds of shit. They've got witches and ghosts and all kinds of weird stuff around here. N'Orleans has history; this building has history and this very floor has history too.

On New Year's Eve in 1972, some crazy mother fucker named Mark Essex went on a rampage and started killing a bunch of people, and on January 7, 1973 it all ended on this very roof. Somewhere on this floor, in this very hallway…it could be right outside our door, he started killing people. He got in the building through the eighteenth floor fire door, the one at the end of this hallway. A couple of maids had propped the door open while they were working and as he ran past them with his rifle, they became scared, but he told them not to worry because he was only there to kill white people. He started his killing soon after that with a doctor. The doctor and his wife were getting ready to check out. Well, asshole confronts the doctor, or the doctor confronted him, we don't know which, but he ends up shooting the doctor in the chest somewhere in the hallway outside that door. When the doc collapsed and fell to the ground, his wife starts freaking out and cradles her dead or dying husband, and then this cold blooded mother fucker walked up to her and put his rifle to the back of her head and shot her as she lay over his body. He set their room on fire and then threw an African flag on the ground next to them. Then he went down to the tenth floor and killed another guy and set more fires. By the time they got him, he had shot nineteen people, ten of them cops. In the end, the cops got him on the roof. When they finally got to his body, he had been shot two hundred times; they said he was so shot up they had to pick him up with a scooper! Yeah, there's a lot of freaky shit that has happened in this city over the years." He paused to make sure Pete was taking it all in and then he continued.

"Uncle Manny said that when he stayed here, he swore he could hear someone running up and down the hallway late at night. He said the footsteps woke him up and pissed him off. After a while he got up to check it out and tell them to knock it off; you know how Uncle Manny is… Well, he said there wasn't anybody there. He swore that the footsteps were right outside his door, but when he opened the door and checked…nobody and nothing. It could be the ghost of Mark Essex, the doctor and his wife; who knows? I guess we'll know tonight if Uncle Manny is right or if he's full of shit, eh? That's why he insisted to my dad that he make us stay on this floor. Those two have a great sense of humor, don't they? Well, let's go get something to eat and check out the city." Frankie slapped his hands on his lap and stood up and walked to the door and held it open for Pete. Pete sat on the bed staring at his friend without moving.

"Fuck you. You are so full of shit. That never happened, and it damn sure never happened here." Pete got up and started walking out the door after deciding that Frankie was messing with him, but he looked over his shoulder continuously as they made their way down the hallway.

"Oh, it happened, and it happened right here. You'll see; the killing part I know is true. The ghosts, well, like I said, we'll find out this weekend, won't we?"

"Screw you; and besides, I ain't afraid of no ghosts!" Pete said, but he wasn't too confident.

They left the hotel, and, after a slight discussion, had decided that it would be safer to leave the van at the hotel and walk around town since they were probably going to be pretty drunk by the time the night was over. Frankie had wanted to drive around and see the sights, but Pete convinced him that the last thing they wanted was to be two young white boys from Connecticut in a Louisiana jail on a Friday night. Pete reminded Frankie that they made movies about things like that. Frankie thought about the two of them locked in the cities jail cell at two or three o'clock in the morning for a moment and reluctantly agreed with Pete's logic and then, with enthusiasm and excitement, they started walking towards adventure.

They walked from Loyola to Canal and then headed down towards the French Quarter and the river. They meandered along and stopped occasionally to look at various shops and stores. Pete loved the change from the small town that was Niceville to a big city. He had been to New York a couple of times to watch Yankee games in the Bronx and was surprised at how much nicer it was to walk down the street in the Big Easy. The sounds and smells of the city were everywhere. The sidewalk was busy, but not crowded, as it was still early in the day. They made it to the end of Canal and decided to walk towards the warehouse district where everyone was getting ready for next year's World's Fair. They finally gave in to their hunger and found a pleasant little restaurant on the water where they could watch the boats moving up and down the river as they ate and drank.

They were looking at the menu and catching up on old times when the waitress came to take their order. She was young and pretty, but understood the art of making her customers feel like the only people in the room and charming them into an extra-large tip.

"Hi boys, my name is Sharon and I'll be you're waitress today. Do you know what you want, or do you need more time?"

"I know what I want. I'll have a Budweiser, a bowl of your spicy gumbo, and an order of shrimp Creole," Frank ordered proudly.

"Are you sure you want to do that Frank? This stuff is pretty spicy, and it might hurt you," Pete cautioned him.

"Screw you; you can be a wimp if you want to, but I'm in 'N'Orleans and I'm going for the gusto."

"You go, boy," Pete said and then looked at Sharon and shook his head. "I'll have a Bud, the shrimp scampi, and a bowl of medium gumbo. You know what? Instead of two beers, why don't you just bring us a pitcher; I think we might need it." When Pete handed Sharon the menu, the two of them shared a knowing smile.

"OK, I'll scrap the two singles and bring out the gumbo and beer in a minute. I'll bring y'all some extra crackers too. You might want them," she warned in a sweet Cajun accent.

The two young men watched her walk away. She knew they were watching and put a little extra sway in her step.

"Welcome to N'Orleans, Pete! We're going to have a blast and get ripped all weekend long!" Frankie said a little extra loudly. Then he looked at his friend that he hadn't seen in a long time, and liked the changes he saw in him. "It's fucking great to be here with you brother. Look at you, you gained weight, cut your hair. Shit, there's finally some meat on them bones. You look better than I've ever seen; I think Florida really agrees with you. Hey, did you hear they finally got the guy who killed Bobby?"

Pete was kicked in the stomach at the sound of that name. He involuntarily shivered and shook his head in the negative as Frankie continued. "Yeah, it was one of those jail house confessions, or bragging to another cellmate kind of thing. The bastard was in for armed robbery and started bragging about how bad he was. The other cellmate wanted out early and made a deal with the cops," Frankie said.

"What did the guy look like, some big ginnie or what?" Pete asked. He hadn't thought about Bobby in a long time and was brought back to the last time he'd seen him alive.

Frankie was taken aback by the ginnie comment, but continued, "No, it was some little meth head. He's a greasy, little blonde haired asshole. He tried to sell Bobby some baby powder or something, and you know Bobby, he called him on it and one thing led to another, and the next thing you know, Bobby is dead and stuffed in a closet."

Their beer and gumbo arrived just as he finished giving Pete the revelation. The waitress gave them their soup and poured their first beers, then reached into her apron and pulled out several packets of crackers and placed them on the table. She looked at Pete and smiled. They both knew how Frankie was going to react and were looking forward to the show. When she left, they returned to their previous conversation about Bobby. Pete was strangely relieved to hear that Bobby hadn't been killed by the men he'd seen, and that he had walked away from them as Pete assumed he would, but he still knew that he should have done more that night. He looked at Frankie and needed reassurance that he had heard him correctly. "Are you sure?"

"Yeah. What the hell do you mean am I sure? It was in the papers; the guy confessed and copped a plea. He's screwed. Of course, he's not as screwed as Bobby, but Bobby just had no respect for anyone or anything. He was an arrogant little prick who was always letting his mouth write checks his body couldn't cash and it was just a matter of time before he pissed off the wrong guy. It was a drug deal gone bad. I feel bad for him, I really do, but hell, he treated everyone like shit and we all knew that eventually he was going to run out of luck." Frank took a long drink from his beer and then looked at his friend and continued. "What the fuck was he doing buying drugs in New Haven from people he didn't know? That's just plain stupid. We had plenty of party supplies, but he was so pissed at us, that he couldn't even come to his seat and watch the show. Oh, what the hell; we're here to have fun. Here's to Bobby; rest in peace, man." He raised his beer to Pete and the two men toasted their departed acquaintance and finished their beers.

Sharon reappeared at their table to check on them, and when she was satisfied everything was okay, she said, "Now you enjoy that gumbo, and if there is anything you need, you just holler."

Once again, they watched her walk away and then smiled at each other. Pete watched as Frankie took his spoon and dug into the gumbo. He quickly ate several spoonfuls, enjoying the genuine New Orleans cuisine and atmosphere. He had his spoon in the bowl getting ready for another mouthful when he paused and then sat up. He was suddenly turning white and a bead of sweat had appeared on his forehead. His hand was shaking as he instinctively grabbed his beer and started chugging it down. When the glass was empty, he looked at the crackers and had an epiphany. He quickly opened the pack and began shoving them into his mouth, followed by more beer. When he regained his composure somewhat, he looked at Pete with an expression of disbelief.

Pete started laughing out loud at his friend. Frankie looked like he had been violated in a perverse way. Pete broke open a couple of packets of crackers, put them in his gumbo and started to eat.

"Oh, my God; it doesn't burn right away. At first it tastes great-it's a little spicy, but it tastes good-and then it gets into your stomach and becomes Mount fucking Vesuvius. Oh my God; I think I'm on fire. Oh, and I can't wait until morning; I'm going to be screaming like a little girl! What the fuck was that? That shit should be illegal; it could kill somebody."

Frankie stuck more crackers in his mouth and washed them down with more beer and pushed the bowl away as if contained a toxic substance. Pete could hardly contain himself, he was laughing so hard his side hurt, and just to make it worse he responded with some extra slurping while eating his gumbo. Even the medium gumbo was spicy,

but Pete wouldn't admit it, because he was having a great time at his
buddy's expense. He was laughing out loud and having more fun than
he had in years.

"Damn, my wimpy gumbo is good. Come on, man up; finish that
bowl. You're a Marine now! You're in N'Orleans. I told you that shit
was dangerous, but you didn't want to listen to me," Pete said with a
big smile on his face as he finished his bowl of gumbo.

When their lunch arrived, the results were the same. Pete ate his and
enjoyed watching his tough guy Marine buddy suffer. Frankie took two
or three bites and almost went into an epileptic seizure. Pete watched
the show and almost pissed his pants laughing. Frankie pushed his plate
away and Pete finished his meal and then made a point to eat extra
bread and crackers in anticipation of a long night and a lot of drinking.
The two men sat and drank a couple of pitchers of beer, catching up on
new events in their young lives. When they finished and paid their tab,
they left an extra large tip for the waitress who'd started their weekend
right.

Pete contemplated the news he had learned about Bobby's demise.
He wasn't sure how he was supposed to feel, he still felt guilty, but he
was, nonetheless, relieved and decided that he shouldn't allow himself
to get into a funk by thinking too much about it because he would ruin
the weekend for Frankie, and so he resolved to have a good weekend
with his best friend who had, after all, traveled a long way to see him
before he shipped out.

They left the restaurant and started to wander around the city.
Neither was surprised to discover that they had walked to Bourbon
Street. They picked up a Hurricane from a stand that looked like it was
nothing more than a large broom closet where they mixed Hurricanes
and the guy sold them over a door that was cut in half like a barn door.
They sipped their drinks and continued their stroll. They turned on
Toulouse and Frankie found a bakery that sold beignets. He bought one
and ate it while they walked, finally putting something in his stomach
that didn't cause him pain. Toulouse turned into Basil and they found
themselves in front of the legendary St. Louis Cemetery #1.

"Last night my Old Man and Uncle Manny sat down at the kitchen table with me. Pop pulls out a bottle of Jack and the three off us proceed to polish it off. They're both Marines and I'm shipping out and all that shit. Anyways, Uncle Manny tells me about this book he's got on all the weird shit you want to see when in New Orleans. He said that this is one of those places. There's this voodoo queen buried here. I think her name was Marie Laveaus or something like that; they say she comes back to life on Saint John's Eve in June and her and her voodoo followers have orgies and all kinds of shit. During the rest of the year, they say you can make a wish or cast a spell by knocking three times to wake the dead, marking three xxx's on her tomb with chalk, knocking three more times, and then leaving an offering. Personally, I think a grave keeper married a woman who owns one of those witch shops and started the 'leave an offering' shit so he could collect some free booty from drunken tourists and give it to his wife to sell to the next drunken tourist who comes along. We should check it out while we're here and then maybe come back tonight and see how many voodoo people are walking around. Who knows, we might even run into a zombie or two," Frankie said as he grabbed Pete by the shoulder and led him into the cemetery. They walked under the old iron cross at the entrance and joined the other people milling around in the land of the dead.

They wandered about with the rest of the tourists for a while and saw the statue of the weeping woman, the tomb of Marie Laveaus, and others. They were struck by how narrow some of the walkways were and how old and decayed some tombs were while others nearby were clean and gleamed in the sun. After a while, they got bored and thirsty and made their way back toward the French Quarter. They sat and drank in several bars as the day turned into night, and while in one they saw The Big Red Rooster play some hot blues guitar. They wandered about and checked out various witch shops and sex shops. As the evening wore on, the streets filled, and by eleven o'clock things were humming along.

The men entered a western clothing store, very drunk by now, and proceeded to check out their wares. They had denim jackets, denim jeans, and all sorts of other things, but what caught their eyes were the cowboy hats. Pete grabbed a hat and put it on Frankie's head and proclaimed him the first ginnie cowboy. Frankie then grabbed a hat and put it on Pete's head and proclaimed him a born again redneck. The men continued to walk around the store and Pete bought a jacket and Frankie a belt.

They left the store and walked past a bar that had music blasting into the street. They paid the five dollar cover and walked in. The first thing they noticed was that it was full of men, and they were all wearing black leather. They looked on the dance floor and saw two men dirty dancing with each other and quickly realized they had entered their first New Orleans gay bar. They looked at each other and were out the door in an instant. When they got back into the street, they looked at the people walking around and wondered if half of New Orleans now knew that they had been in a gay bar. They quickly started walking away like it was a crime scene and went into the first bar they saw that had naked women in it. As they were walking in, Frankie looked at Pete and started laughing out loud.

"Holy shit, you still have that cowboy hat on!" Frankie exclaimed.

Pete felt his head and then looked at Frankie and said, "You still have yours on too. I guess we got free hats because I wouldn't know where to return them even if I wanted to." They laughed together, paid the cover, and went into the bar feeling as though they were on top of the world.

Three beers later, Frankie looked at Pete and said, "All right, come on; one more drink and then I want to go piss in the Mississippi." Frankie put his glass on the table and ordered one more round. When the beer arrived, so did the dancer. She danced in front of Pete first. She bent over and and gyrated in a way that made Pete think "What if...?" She turned around and put her breasts in his face and her hands on the back of his head and pulled his face between her young and firm bosoms. He inhaled and was intoxicated by her perfume; she swayed from side to side, gently slapping his face with her breasts. He believed he knew what he wanted Heaven to be like. She pulled away from him and smiled at him teasingly, turned and pulled her g string away from her hip. Pete put a dollar in and she moved over to Frankie, where she performed the same ritual and made him feel like he was the only man in the bar.

"Damn, I love New Orleans!" Frankie said when she had moved away. They finished their beers and drunkenly made their way to the river.

They found a river walk with an aluminum rail that worked its way along the river.

"Come on, I'm pissing in this river, right here!" Frankie exclaimed when he saw the river and staggered towards it. He started pulling down his zipper while stumbling along, still twenty feet from the river. Pete was not as drunk as Frank and was still aware of the people walking by them, and the thought of going to jail for doing something stupid came rushing into his mind.

"Dude, come on, you can't piss right here. There's too many people; we'll go to jail for indecent exposure or some shit and then Bubba's gonna make you his love slave." Pete grabbed Frank's shoulders and pointed him to a darker, less populated area towards the warehouse district.

"Come on, let's go piss in the mighty Mississippi over there. Nobody will see us and we won't go to jail." Pete started walking into the darkness, hoping Frankie would soon follow.

"Fuck it. It's N'Orleans; nobody gives a shit. We're just a couple of tourists that came to piss in their river." Frankie stood in the middle of the river walk with his zipper down and his hands on his underwear debating if he should pull the trigger when a couple came walking by. He drunkenly looked eye to eye with a woman about his mother's age. She looked at him disapprovingly as she walked past and he relented and decided to follow Pete. They walked a couple of hundred feet and came to an area with several broken lights overhead and no people walking around. Pete started getting nervous when he looked at the buildings on the other side of the road, and wondered if this really was a good place to be. They were old warehouses that at one time had been used for importing and exporting various commodities from fish to sugar and coffee, but now they were mostly dark, abandoned, and empty. He turned and faced the river as a large boat made its way down the river. It was lit up like a Christmas tree with red and green lights on the front and a bright white light high in the air that looked like the star on top. The boat's motor made a soft and smooth rumble as it steadily moved along. Pete reached down, undid his fly, and let it go.

"Is this place good enough for you? Are you far enough away from civilization to hide your little bitty dick?" Frankie asked. He noticed that Pete had already cleared his gun from the holster and was ready to start spraying.

"Whoa, cowboy, holster that gun. You've got to wait for me. It was my idea to piss in the Mississippi and you aint goin' before me. Clamp down on that thing and wait a minute till I'm ready." Frank staggered next to his friend and pulled his dick out. He looked at his partner and saw that he was standing there with dick in hand and ready to go.

"All right, let her rip!" They started pissing away, adjusting their aim to see who could reach the farthest from the bank. They finished at about the same time, and while they were congratulating themselves for their effort and putting their guns back in their holsters, Pete noticed four figures moving towards them from the shadows. Frankie hadn't noticed them yet and was still laughing when Pete brought his attention to the approaching bodies. Frankie pulled on his zipper and then yelled to the shadows.

"What's happening, fellas? Damn, I love New Orleans. This place is fucking great." Frankie was being overly gregarious and seemed oblivious to the danger they were in. Pete was not; he just kept thinking about the New Orleans psycho, Mark Essex, that Frankie had told him about earlier. The men approached and formed a semi-circle around them. They appeared to be in their early twenties and were all black. Pete looked over his shoulder and realized that they had been turned around so that their backs were toward the river. The only thing between them and the river was the railing and it was about waist high. Growing up near New York City, he knew the stories of the bodies floating in the East River, and as he glanced over his shoulders and then at the four men who stood between them and the lights of the city, he figured the New Orleans underworld probably used this river for the same purpose.

"What's happenin'? We didn't catch you with your dicks out, did we?" the one in the center said with a gold toothed grin. He spoke with a heavy accent that was hard to understand and appeared to be the leader of their little entourage.

"Fuckin' eh you did; we came all the way from Connecticut to get drunk on Bourbon Street and piss in this great river, and I am proud to say we have done both. You mother fuckers have a great city here. I love this place," Frank said again.

He was barely able to stand and was still fumbling with his zipper while Pete looked at each of the men standing opposite him. Three of them were stone faced and staring back at him through the hoods of their sweatshirts. They all had their hands in their pockets and Pete wondered if it were knives or guns in their hands. The one talking to Frankie had a big smile. His gold and white teeth shone bright in the dark and he seemed very friendly. Pete looked at him and was stunned by how much this game seemed to resemble a cat playing with a mouse- and they all knew how that game ended.

"Hey, are you a gambling man?" he asked Frankie. He glanced over at Pete with a smile that scared Pete to his soul and then returned his attention to Frank. "Yo man, is you a gambler?"

"I don't know; depends on the bet," Frank said.

"Oh, don't worry, somethin' simple. I just want to get a beer. I tell you what; I'll bet you five dollars that I can tell you how many kids your daddy had. Come on now, that's easy, ain't it?"

Frankie looked over at Pete and put his hand on his shoulder. "What do you think, Pete? Does this guy know how many people are in my family? Oh, what the fuck, we're havin' fun, ain't we?" Frank was all smiles, and before Pete could try to talk him out of the bet, Frankie was back having fun with his new best friend.

"Sure I got five bucks to waste and besides, I'm shipping out on Monday. I'm gonna be stuck on a ship for six fucking months. What the hell am I gonna need money for, right?" he said to his new friend.

"Yeah, right. So, you in the Navy or somethin'?"

"Fuck no! I'm a Marine. I aint no squid! I figured before I left the U.S. of A., I would come down south to see my best friend and get drunk in this city. And, Fuckin' eh, we're doing it!"

"Yeah, well, that's cool, but your daddy didn't have no kids. Your Momma had'em all." He put his hand on Frank's shoulder and then smiled at him. Pete was watching and waiting for the cat to bite down on the mouse any second. Frank looked at him and started laughing and patted his new friend on the shoulder. Pete knew that once Frank pulled the money out of his pocket to pay the man, the best they could hope for was to be robbed of all their money, and the worst case scenario.... Mark Essex.

"Oh… you got me, mother fucker. That was good. You got me." Frank reached into his pocket and pulled out a wad of cash containing several hundred dollars in small bills and began fumbling with the money. All eyes were immediately on Frankie's hands. He found a five dollar bill and handed it to his new friend.

"All right, here you go man. That was good." The man reached out and took the money and quickly stuffed it into his pocket.

"Thanks. You boys have fun and be safe. But listen, you don't want to be walkin' around too much this way. There is some bad people around here. You boys need to head back over towards Canal." He pointed towards the lighted area just a few hundred feet away. "Oh, and hey, I was Army, so, good luck on that ship with all those Navy boys at sea. Don't drop the soap, right!"

The four of them turned and walked away and Pete started to breathe again. Frank was drunk and jovial when he waved good-bye to his new friend.

"Yeah, that was cool, and now I can happily say that I've pissed in the Mississippi and I've been had in the Big Easy. Come on, I'm ready to call it a night. We've got a long walk back to the hotel, so let's get started." Pete listened to Frankie and watched him stumble away in front of him, wondering if he was oblivious to what could have just happened or if it was his Italian street smarts that had let him know they were in no danger. Pete shook his head, happy to be alive, and followed his friend back to the hotel.

They made it back to their room where both of them immediately plopped on their beds. Their feet hurt, the bed was spinning, and they were having a blast. Neither of them said a word for a while, and Pete was debating to himself whether he should bother to take his clothes off or if he should just pass out like he was.

"Hey, did you hear that?" Frankie asked in a hushed voice slightly above a whisper.

"Hear what? I didn't hear nothing," Pete responded.

"Shhh...I think I heard footsteps outside the door. You're the closest; go check it out, man," Frankie said again, feinting fright.

Pete was awake now. He picked up his head and listened intently outside the door, and when he didn't hear anything he knew Frankie was having fun with him. "Fuck you. If you want to see who's out there, you go. As long as they stay out there, I don't give a shit what they do." He was sounding tough, but he was nervous and had started thinking about the ghosts that lived in this city.

Frank started laughing. "I ain't afraid of no ghosts!"

"Yeah, I ain't afraid of no ghosts either," Pete said quietly to himself. His ghosts were quite different than the one outside the hotel room door, and he wondered if he would ever stop being afraid of his ghosts.

Both men started laughing and soon passed out. They spent the rest of the weekend in much the same way, and when Frank made it onto the airplane on Sunday and got in his seat, he was relieved to be able to get some much needed sleep. At that very same moment, Pete was shifting gears and getting on the highway while trying to figure out how he was going to drive four hours in his present condition. Pete pulled into a rest area as soon as he made it into Mississippi, locked his doors, and went to sleep. He woke up several hours later and finished the ride home.

CHAPTER 40

DECISIONS

Bill was using his mind again and immersing himself in his work with enthusiasm. Wednesday morning he left for the trip, and when he kissed Anne good-bye and hugged her, she held him just a little longer and squeezed him just a little tighter than she had to. Bill kissed her again, almost with passion this time, and as he walked out the door and was greeted by the morning sunshine he was feeling encouraged by the emotions he felt and the glint in his wife's eye that their lives were turning in a new direction.

Anne was confused by her feelings as he walked out the door because she usually felt relief when he left; this morning she felt sadness and remorse. She went to work on Wednesday and couldn't understand why she walked around in a perplexing daze. She came home from work to an empty house. Pete was gone; Bill was gone; she had spent many hours alone in the house, but tonight it was empty and silent. She let out a little squeal to hear the echo off the tile floor and looked around. She was lost. She put on her pajamas and climbed into bed much earlier than normal. She laid there and tried to read, but she kept looking at the empty pillow next to her. Finally she closed her book, shut off the light, wept, and then prayed.

Thursday morning she got dressed for work, determined to meet Ryan after work as planned, but instead of committing herself to what she knew would be a disaster, she was going to tell him that she could not go forward with their affair. She was nervous all day and kept looking at the clock. She was convinced it was broken because it rarely seemed to move. When, mercifully, it was finally time to clock out, she walked over to Walt's, and to her surprise, Alice was there. It was apparent that she had been there a while. She greeted Anne warmly and invited her to join her and her new friend for a drink. Anne looked around the bar for Ryan, and not seeing him, she accepted.

"Who are you meeting here, honey?" Alice said with a knowing and devious smile.

"Oh, just a friend," Anne replied, wishing she could escape or that Ryan would walk in and rescue her.

"Yeah, I'm sure it's just a friend! So, is this friend good looking?"

"Oh, I don't know. He's just a friend, so I haven't really given it much thought."

"Oh, I know who it is! It's that stud Ryan from the other night. You go girl; I would ride that bull all night long." She looked at the man she was sitting next to and reassured him. "Don't worry, baby, you're the only bull I'm riding tonight." She then planted a wet kiss on him. Anne was embarrassed by her open display and relieved to see Ryan walk in the door.

"You go, girl, your secret is safe with me!" Alice said as she momentarily broke away from her new lover.

"Well, you're late," Anne said to Ryan.

"I'm sorry, I got hung up and got here as soon as I could. Let's go find a table so that we can sit down." He spotted a table in a quiet corner of the bar and put his arm around her waist to guide her towards it.

"Ryan, there's something I have to tell you."

He saw the trepidation in her face, and the fear in her voice. "Okay, I understand, but can you give me a few minutes first? Let's have a drink and relax for a moment and then we can get serious." He ordered a drink for himself and another for Anne and they made small talk and laughed about the other night until their drinks arrived. Ryan did everything he could to keep the conversation light. He knew she wanted to back out and probably would. He, too, was having second thoughts, because after meeting Bill he'd decided that he was a decent enough guy, but he also knew that this was probably going to be his only chance to be with this woman that intrigued him so much, so he was going to give it everything he had. He controlled the conversation and did his best to keep her smiling until she had finished her second drink.

"Ryan, I need to be serious for a minute and talk to you. I don't think I can go through with this. It just doesn't feel right. I'm still married."

"Well, I'm still married too, and your husband is in New Mexico and my wife is in Europe. At the end of the night we're both going home to empty houses. We're already out and having fun, so let's just enjoy ourselves for a little while. We aren't doing anything bad and we don't have to do anything bad either, that is unless you want to…. So, what do you think? Can we just enjoy each other's company for a while and then we can go home to our empty houses?"

"Well, one more drink, and then I have to go."

"That's the spirit. Let's have another drink and a little fun for a little while." Ryan ordered another round for them. They enjoyed each other's company and one more turned into three more. Ryan was charming and she was bedazzled. The bar was almost empty and the night had turned into early morning when they walked out of the bar. Ryan put his arm around Anne's waist and she enjoyed the feeling of warmth and security. She hesitated, but then put her arm around him as they approached their cars.

"Listen, this is probably going to be the last time I get to be alone with you, and I would really love to talk with you just a little while longer. Can we sit in my car and talk for a couple of minutes before we leave?"

Anne looked into his eyes. She knew the obvious answer should be no, but she couldn't stop herself from agreeing and getting into the open car door. As Ryan walked around the car, she couldn't help but notice how good looking he was. He stood close to six feet tall, and for a man in his mid-forties he seemed to be in great shape. His face was soft and warm with almost no wrinkles, and his short hair was neatly trimmed with only a hint of grey near the temples. She was very nervous, and questioned her judgment as Ryan entered the car and sat beside her.

"Anne, I'm glad I got the chance to get to know you. I just wish it were under different circumstances and we had more time together." He put his hand behind her head and pulled her to him. She did not resist. His kiss started very gently. Anne loved the feeling of his lips on hers and kissed him back. His hand reached her breast and she let out a heavy sigh. She wanted to stop, but she didn't. They became more passionate and their hands began exploring each other's bodies. Their tongues intertwined and danced like they were young again. He put his hand between her legs and she instinctively brought her legs together, but when his hand didn't move she relaxed and let him continue. She didn't know why, but her hand drifted between his legs as well, and she felt the large bulge in his pants that pronounced his excitement. Ryan was getting more excited and his hands roamed over her body as she moaned her approval into her kiss. Ryan broke the kiss and held her tightly as he looked into her eyes.

"Should we go to your place or mine?"

Anne came back to the reality of what was happening. Nervousness had become panic and it began to run through her. She looked at the lust-filled man next to her and reached for the door handle.

"No...no, this can't happen! I am so sorry Ryan, but I have to go and I can't see you anymore. I want you and I want this to happen, but it just can't." She burst out of his car and into hers and was gone from his life forever.

BILL PULLED INTO THE DRIVEWAY at about ten o'clock on Friday night. The meetings had gone well and he'd made a good impression on all present. He'd quickly found out how rare he was: he was the only defense contractor there with no military experience. He'd been the brunt of many good-hearted jokes, but had taken them in stride and had won over people with his knowledge and understanding given how little experience he had. He felt confident until the moment he pulled into the driveway and turned off the key. He knew Pete was in New Orleans for the weekend and they would be alone, but he didn't know what to expect when he went into the house. He wanted to be excited, he wanted to be in love, but he was afraid he was going to be disappointed again. He looked inside and saw no light, so he resolved himself to the fact that she would be on the couch or in bed sleeping.

He opened the door and entered the dark house. There was a light on over the stove that shed enough light to see around the room. She wasn't on the couch, so he turned and started to walk towards the bedroom when a flicker of light on the lanai caught his eye. He noticed it came from a candle, and as he looked he saw that there were several candles burning. He was drawn to the light like a moth, and when he got to the lanai, he saw his wife sitting on a chair. On the table in front of the chair were a pitcher and two glasses. He didn't know what to think. His mind naturally went to worst case scenarios. Was she getting drunk alone? Having an affair? Was there someone else here?

It never occurred to him as he walked out the door that the second glass could be for him. It had been so long since she'd fixed him a drink to sit and enjoy with her…since before Isaac had died. When the door opened and he stepped onto the lanai, she leapt to her feet and looked at him for a moment and then rushed to him and wrapped her arms around him and kissed him passionately. Bill was dumbfounded; he slowly brought his arms around his wife and hugged her while he hoped she would not break his neck as she was squeezing him so tightly. When, finally, she broke the kiss and stepped back, she looked into his eyes.

"William Taylor, I want to be your wife again and I want you to be my husband again too."

"What?…well, yeah…yes, of course, I want that too. What happened? Why all of the sudden do you love me again?" He wanted to be happy, but he was guarded. She had hoped he would just wrap his arms around her and they would make passionate love right there, but it didn't happen. Bill sat her down and then he sat down and poured them a drink from the pitcher of margaritas that Anne had made.

"What happened while I was gone?"

"I got a chance to think about life without you, about being alone or with someone else, and I just don't want that. We have spent a lifetime together. We lost our son together and almost lost the second one too. I don't want to be with anyone but you. We've traveled so far and fought for so long. I want to be happy again. The other night when you said it was good to see me laugh, well, that made me think. I want to laugh, but I want to laugh with you. I want to be happy, but I want to be happy with you. I know it won't be easy, but nothing has been easy in our lives. We loved each other once. I know it and I felt it and I want to feel it again. You are a good man and I want you to be my man." She had tears in her eyes as she spoke.

They didn't make love. They talked until the sun came up. They cried together and they laughed together, and when they had agreed to a plan of what was to come, they went to bed as the sun began to rise and they held each other tightly as they drifted into sleep.

CHAPTER 41

A LOT TO LEARN AND A WAYS TO GROW

A couple of weeks later, Pete had finished changing and was on his way out the door of the dojo when Shihan called him over to his desk. Pete had been working very hard and Shihan was proud of his progress. Pete was usually one of the first Ques to arrive and one of the last to leave. He accepted the pain inflicted on him without complaint and had proven himself to be very teachable over the last several months. Shihan had concluded that he was a good student and a decent young man.

"Mr. Taylor, I know you work construction all week and I was wondering if you ever do any weekend or side work. I've got a friend who just bought a house and needs some help getting it in shape. He asked if I had a student that wanted to make some extra money, so I told him that I'd check. It's some yard work and painting mostly," Shihan asked.

Pete was honored to be addressed by Shihan and surprised that he even knew his name. He greatly admired Shihan and his accomplishments, both as a Marine and as a karate master. Shihan very rarely got involved with teaching the beginner classes and rarely had any direct contact with students under a brown belt. He would usually sit in a chair near his office and watch the class. If he saw something he wanted addressed, he would call Mr. Sanders or Mr. Park to him and explain what he wanted corrected or done. Pete understood how the system worked and was not offended by it. He intended on being a student long enough to get at least a brown and hopefully a black belt, and he knew that once he had proven his commitment, he would be taught by one of the greatest American karate masters. He understood that a freshman in high school does not study under a Nobel Laureate until he has studied for many more years and has proven that he is worthy of the instructor's time and effort.

"Yes, sir, I'd be happy to help. I have to work at an old lady's house on Saturday morning, but I should be done around two o'clock and I can be there after that and on Sunday. I would be there first thing Saturday, but I made a commitment to her and she always gives me work and kind of counts on me to be there, so I really need to take care of that first," Pete said. He was afraid that he would miss an opportunity and was conflicted on what he should do. Mrs. Anderson would get over it, but she was always good to him and he was obligated to her.

"That'll be fine, I'm sure. I'll call him and let him know. I'll give you directions and confirm everything at class on Friday. By the way, you're doing a good job in class, so keep it up."

"Thank you, sir; I am trying," Pete said. Shihan turned and looked at some papers on his desk and Pete knew the conversation was over. He left feeling elated. His hard work had been noticed. Pete got into his van and went home with the music playing a little louder and sounding a lot better than normal.

When he entered the driveway, he noticed that his mom's car was gone. She was probably at work, he reasoned, and when he went inside, he saw his father sitting in front of the television. They gave each other a cursory greeting and chatted for a moment about the latest *Cheers* episode, and then Pete made his way into his room and got ready for a shower.

When he removed his clothes and was walking into the shower, he stopped and stood in front of the mirror and looked at himself. Physically, his body was becoming well defined. He was six feet tall and weighed one hundred and eighty pounds. His muscles did not bulge, but they were pronounced. He practiced a few blocks and punches in front of the mirror and liked what he saw... he stopped and stared at the mirror with that realization. He was finally proud of what he was, and what he was becoming. He sang in the shower and slept well.

Bright and early Saturday morning, Pete was at Mrs. Anderson's house ready to go. She didn't have a lot of work to do, which made Pete happy. She told him to mow the lawn and rake the leaves under the big oak trees. He examined the yard and believed that he could be done before noon if he busted his ass, so without hesitation, he got to it.

He wanted to finish early and get to Bill Hitchcock's house and help him get ready to move in. He was intrigued to meet one of Shihan's friends and hear what he thought of his sensei. Pete pushed the lawnmower at a brisk pace around the hedges, but every now and then he couldn't help but glance at Mrs. Anderson working in her flower garden from time to time. She was quietly singing to herself as she planted some flowers around her patio. She was in another good mood, he thought to himself. It seemed to him that she was always in a good mood lately and Pete was happy for her. She had her miracle and nothing else mattered.

She, too, glanced at him while he worked and was happy to see him putting in so much effort and taking pride in his work. He is a good young man, she thought to herself, and would make a good husband if he got more education. As she continued weeding and planting, she put her mind to work. He was worth her effort, she concluded, so she would try to convince him to go to school and then she would try to help find a good wife for him. She nodded her head to herself, knowing what her new mission was. She believed, now more than ever, in the power of love, and she always liked to play match maker. She continued her thoughts out loud: "Young people should be in love and they should make a family."

She thought about her husband and the passion they had felt when they were young. They'd made love at every opportunity and had continued to have an active and passionate sex life right up until he'd died. "Maybe I killed you," she thought to herself with a sly little smile. He was and would always be the only man she would ever kiss with passion. She was proud of their love and devotion and convinced that she was right all along, and now she had proof. She looked forward to seeing him again when God called her, but until then, she had work to do.

Pete finished before noon and Mrs. Anderson made him sit down and have a glass of lemonade before he left. She wanted to make him a sandwich, but he politely explained that he had another job to go to and couldn't stay for very long. She was disappointed, but glad to hear that he was ambitious and working hard.

She gave him his glass of lemonade, and while he started drinking, she began her pitch. "Peter, I don't hear you speak of a girlfriend. Do you have a special girl?" she asked. Pete was shocked by the question and almost choked on his drink.

"No, no, I don't have anyone right now, Mrs. Anderson. Why, do you know any single girls? I'm looking, but I guess I'm just looking in all the wrong places." Pete laughed uncomfortably. He was flushed and his eyes darted around, but they never came in contact with hers. He didn't know what to say and was looking for an escape from his surrogate grandmother.

"Well, you should go to school-college is very important-and then you find a good girl there. It will make you very happy. You can't find a good wife in a bar or on a dance floor. Those girls only bring you trouble. You should go to college; that's where the smart girls are." She thought that was the best incentive to get any young man to go to school. She looked at him again; he was flustered and blushing. She was embarrassing the boy, and then it dawned on her that Pete had never been with a girl. "Oh, he is going to be good husband….," she thought to herself.

"Let me know if you find a girl for me, okay?" Pete said and quickly finished his drink. He agreed to come back next week to start painting the boathouse for her and escaped as fast as he could. He was driving down the road wondering how badly he had embarrassed himself. He kept replaying the conversation over and over in his head and seeing that knowing little smile on her face. He knew that she had probably guessed that he had never been with a girl; he had just never gotten around to it and had never really wanted to be close to anyone before.

He knew that that was one conversation he never wanted to have again; after all, what would she know about modern relationships anyways? Things today were so different and so much more complicated than they were in the past. Pete thought about how different his generation was from the one before him. He convinced himself that everyone over thirty had remained a virgin until they met their spouse and never had to deal with the things modern kids had to deal with.

CHAPTER 42

GET READY

Joe and Jeff sat in the conference room with Mr. Red Bryant and the other sub-contractors at the John Creel Bridge Repair preconstruction meeting waiting for the Project Manager to enter the room and start the meeting. There were ten men in all sitting around the large conference table making small talk and discussing their roles in the project. Mr. Bryant had won the bid to supply and install seven thousand tons of limestone rip-rap under the bridge on I-10 at Caryville. Mr. Bryant was going to supply the rocks and Joe was going to install them.

The door opened and in came two men carrying eight manila files stuffed with papers. The younger of the two, appearing to be in his mid-forties with a slight build and little paunch belly and thick dark mustache, stood at the head of the table and greeted the men in the room.

"Good morning, gentlemen, my name is Jimmy Alden. I'm the project supervisor for this job, and this is Frank Beakon; he's the project manager. Today we want to go over our schedule, address any issues you may have, and make sure we're all on the same page. If everything goes well, and we want everything to go well, you will have very little interaction with Frank except in picking up money and signing releases. I will be the point man on the job and I plan to be on site most of every day. We will coordinate and schedule all of our activities through my office." He continued explaining the time frame and went over the work of various subs and was happy with their plans and schedules.

He then turned his attention to Mr. Bryant and the rip-rap to be placed at the base of the bridge piling. The rip-rap was designed to repair existing scouring around the piling and to prevent future scouring from occurring.

The Choctawhatchee bottom consisted of mud and clay, and when the bridge had been built, the water around the piling had been about eight feet deep at normal river elevations. Many years of eddies, storms, and erosion had created holes around some of the piling that were now over forty-nine feet deep. The plan was to bring in a couple thousand tons of base rock to fill the holes around the piling and then to cover that with large, class two limestone rip-rap from one side of the river bank to the other.

"Now, Red, once we get done with the demo up top and finish driving the new piling, you're free to start your survey and then we can start placing rock. We understand that the rock is going to be trucked into the Caryville landing and barged down, is that correct?" he asked.

"Yeah, we got the okay to store the rock along the boat ramp and to load and transport it down river from there, so we're all set on our end. Once you give us the go ahead, we'll get the trucks rolling," Red replied.

"Now, when are you going to truck in your compartment barges and start to assemble them at the ramp?" he questioned Red.

Red hesitated for a moment; he looked down at the pencil he was fumbling with in his hands, and then cast a quick glance toward Joe before replying. He knew that what he was about to say would probably send the two men sitting at the head of the table into a panic. He was proposing what most sane men would consider impossible. It was not a new idea; in fact, it had been tried twice before and had ended in disaster both times.

"No, we're not going to do that. Joe here is bringing his barge up the river from the bay," Red replied. He wasn't disappointed when he heard their response.

"What are you talking about? How big is this barge? We should have known this before you submitted your bid. We have a time limit on this project, and I don't think it can be done," Jimmy proclaimed excitedly as he digested what he had just heard. The Choctawhatchee was a primitive meandering river. It had twists and turns every few hundred yards and was cut through the middle of a giant cypress swamp. The river bottom was littered with stumps and was famous for destroying propellers on boats because of how rapidly the water elevation could change. It was a great river for fishing, and in the 1920's had been logged heavily, but it was now considered impossible to move large vessels on.

"Joe, I'll let you handle this," Red said and nodded to Joe.

"The barge I'm going to use is ninety-eight feet long and twenty-eight feet wide. We'll be able to move a hundred to a hundred and thirty tons per trip depending on the river height, one or two loads per day, so we shouldn't have any problem getting done on time, weather permitting," Joe responded. The room was silent. Jimmy and Frank just stared at the two men for a moment and gathered their thoughts. Frank sat up straight and put his hands on the table and stared coldly at Red.

"It can't be done. I don't give a rat's ass about how many tons the barge can move when it gets there, because you can't get up the river from the bay. This is a non-navigable, meandering river. It's hard enough to move a bass boat on that damned river. I'm telling you, it's been tried before and it can't be done. You'd better rethink your plan, because we have a contract and I'm not hanging my ass out to dry because you have a half-assed scheme. If I had known ahead of time that this was your plan, I would never have awarded you this contract." Frank was clearly upset and letting everyone know it.

"If Joe says he can do it, then he can do it. We do have a signed contract and we'll get it done," Red replied calmly and confidently.

Jimmy and Frank looked at each other and were clearly taken aback by this proposal, and both were in silent agreement that they would start getting back up contracts ready.

"Red, I know that you've been in this business a long time, so I'm going to let you try, but if you get behind schedule and we feel that you can't get it done, then we're going to have a different conversation. Are we clear on that point?" Frank asked.

Joe interjected and explained that he had gone down the river from the Highway 90 boat ramp to the bay before he'd submitted his bid. He told them how he had mapped, measured, and sounded the entire river. He told them of some of his experiences pushing barges along the Northwest coast from San Francisco to Alaska, and by the time he was done speaking he had convinced them that he had the experience, and had done his homework, but they were still not convinced that he could get it done. They finished the meeting shortly after that exchange, and when they reached the parking lot, Red stopped Joe and looked him in the eye and said, "Joe, you can do this, can't you? I've laid my ass on the line here and I need to be sure that you can do this."

"Mr. Bryant, it's like I told you before, we bid this job, I took my john boat up that river, and I can do this. I don't care what other people couldn't do. I know what I can do, and I won't let you down." Mr. Bryant looked at him again and reached out his hand for a handshake.

"That's good enough for me, Joe. I'm going to start dropping rocks on site in the next couple of days, so get your equipment ready and let's go to work." Red and Joe vigorously shook hands, got in their separate vehicles, and headed back to work.

Joe and Jeff drove on old Highway 90 out of Chipley on their way to I-10 in silence for several minutes. The road was long and straight and both men pondered the events of the preconstruction meeting. Finally, Jeff turned and looked at his brother with concern on his face and his confidence a little shaken; the meeting hadn't gone at all like he'd anticipated.

"Are you sure we can do this? That guy didn't seem too thrilled about our plan," Jeff stated.

"Listen, I told you I checked out every inch of that river. The *Osage* only draws eight inches; the prop's twenty to twenty-four inches and the barge a foot. We should be able to skim right across the top. The new barge is narrow and we can do it. There are only a couple of turns that concern me, but we'll have the crane on deck and chainsaws, so we'll get through. I'm sure of it. I don't care about them other bozos. They didn't know what they were doing," Joe said, trying to reassure himself. "Now, when we get back to the boat yard, we have to get to work repairing the barge. I ordered the steel and it'll be delivered on Monday. You can get Pete and Elliot to start cleaning the compartments while you start cutting the bad pieces out of the deck tomorrow and then we can cut out and replace the uprights that need done. We should be ready to go up river in about three weeks if everything works out." Joe stared ahead, talking to himself almost as much as talking to Jeff. "That puts us in the middle of April. It's going to take a day to get to the mouth of the river and probably five days on the river to get to Caryville. If we make it up there by the end of the month we'll be fine. I know it. We should start installing the filter weave by Monday the fifth and have that installed by Friday and start moving rocks for real on Saturday. Yeah, that should do it. We have to be done by Labor Day; that gives us a hundred and three days to complete it. I think we can get two loads a day a couple of days a week and we might do well on this one. The job is a piece of cake. I'm sure of it; we'll be fine," Joe said while he silently pondered all the ways it could go wrong.

He was staring out the windshield, but not really looking at the road as he was talking. He was going over every possible scenario in his head. In every one it would be tough and he knew that, but he also knew that they would get it done.

When they returned to the boat yard, several of the guys were there to greet them. Marty had moved on like so many others, but Giles and the two new young helpers from his crew were there, as was Pete and his helper James. They had finished their jobs early and were drinking a few beers while waiting for Joe and Jeff to return from their meeting. Pete had been running jobs and all the equipment and had earned Joe's respect for that.

They pulled the truck to a stop and got out while the guys gathered around them. Giles turned toward his new helper Elliot, a blonde haired kid of about nineteen with "Ozzy" tattooed on the fingers of one hand and "Rush" tattooed on the fingers of his other, and yelled at him.

"Elliot, what the hell's the matter with you? Can't you see that these men are thirsty? Get Joe and Jeffrey a beer, and get one of those nice cold ones off the bottom of the cooler." He then turned toward Joe and Jeff. "Well, when do we start? I'm looking forward to this boat ride. It'll get me out of the house, although I don't know what I am going to do for lovin' when I'm out there. Ain't none of these guys pretty enough for me! I'm tellin' ya, Joe, you ought to think about getting a little hostess to do the cooking and cleaning and servicing of our needs on this trip. You know… none of these guys can cook either," he said with a smile. When Elliot approached, Giles took one of the beers from him and opened it and handed it to Joe. Elliot gave the other to Jeff.

"Here you go, Joe, a nice cold beer. Here's to the Choctawhatchee River." He lifted his beer and tipped it to Joe's.

The new guys watched and laughed at Giles' overt ass kissing. They weren't sure if he was joking or if he was trying to pull off the ultimate brown nose, but it was none of those; it was just Giles being Giles. Joe laughed with him and they drank the beer. Everyone was excited about the adventure of doing the biggest job they had undertaken-everyone except for Joe and Jeff. They were still going over all the things that could go wrong and trying to find something that they had left out or overlooked. After a few minutes, Giles looked at Joe and saw the serious concern on his face.

"Come on, Joe, this is time to celebrate. All the years of hard work are finally going to pay off. You're going to make piles of money. Come on, drink a beer and enjoy yourself," he said.

"I'll celebrate when we're done with the job and the barge is parked right out there," Joe said. He took his beer and walked down to the new barge and tried to figure out exactly how long it was going to take to cut out the sections of deck that needed to be done and rebuild it. Jeff saw Joe and walked down and joined him on deck. They had purchased the barge from a company out of Mobile, who had delivered it earlier in the week. It was old, rusty, and beat up, but it was the perfect size for the river. It was smaller and narrower than their big barge, but it was still large enough to handle the crane and everything else they needed for the job.

"Well, shit, Jeff, now we have to pull this off. I've got enough gas to get you started cutting the deck open tomorrow. I'll go first thing in the morning and get a demo tip for your torch and get another set for me and Pete to use. He can help with the demo; I don't know how good he'll be at gluing it back together, but he should be able to help cut it apart. I'm hoping you guys can have all the deck and supports demoed by Monday. You can teach him how to burn rod on the deck, but I would really prefer you to weld the supports down below," Joe said while Jeff looked at him with a "no shit" kind of look on his face.

"We should be fine, Joe; we'll probably have a little left to cut out on Monday morning, but Jacob's Steel usually doesn't get here until two in the afternoon anyways. I think we can have it back together in two weeks if things go good. Who knows, we might even be up there a little early. We're due a break. We've been getting our asses kicked enough lately." The two men walked the deck of the barge and contemplated what lie ahead of them.

"There's supposed to be some rain at the beginning of the week that might last a few days. I just hope it passes and doesn't screw with us too bad," Joe said. He had looked at the weather in the morning and it didn't look good for the beginning of the week.

"We'll be fine," Jeff said. The two of them looked at each other and sipped their beer, hoping that that was a true statement.

CHAPTER 43

NOTHING IS EASY

The next morning they all arrived at the boatyard around seven. It was an unseasonably cold, grey, and blustery morning in March. The wind was coming from the north and had a bite to it that put everyone in a foul mood. Joe was complaining about everyone moving so slowly. He had a lot of things on his mind and was impatient and short-tempered. Nobody was in the mood to work, but there was a great deal to get done.

Giles and his crew were bitching and moaning and doing everything in their power to waste time and avoid going to their job. They had to set piling for a new dock and they knew that their day was going to be unpleasant at best. The truck that had delivered the piling and lumber couldn't get into the backyard because of low power lines and had dropped the materials in the front yard. They had to carry everything from the front yard to the back and then down a steep embankment and out to the water's edge. Each piling weighed a couple of hundred pounds and usually took two men to carry.

By the time they got all thirty pilings to the water, their shoulders would be sore and rubbed raw, and that was just the beginning of their morning. Once that was completed, they would be standing in cold water about two and a half feet deep with icy waves lapping at their crotches all morning while they were installing the piling.

They would be doing the "marine contractor jig," and from the shoreline it would look like a strange and comical dance: three men standing in water just below their waists, jumping up and down with each wave, trying to keep the frigid water from making contact with their groins. It was hard work on a beautiful day, but on a day like this one, it became an icy hell.

Joe soon tired of their delaying tactics and sent them on their way. After they left, he went over everything again with Jeff. When he felt confident that they were all on the same page, he went to the supply store to get the new torches and bottles. Jeff was given Pete and Elliot to help him begin the work of prepping the barge for the trip. He took them around the barge explaining what he needed done. Their job was to pump all the water out of the barge and then to clean the bottom until it looked like new. He sent Elliot into a dry compartment and told Pete to start pumping one that had water in it and was causing the barge to list a little.

Through many years of service, the barge had accumulated several inches of dirt, debris, and rocks from the holes in the deck and the hatch covers. The copious quantities of limestone dust, mud, rock, and water combined to make the fines congeal into a concrete like substance. Elliot climbed into the hatch with his bucket and shovel while Pete carried the pump to the left front compartment and put the suction hose in the hole. He looked inside and estimated about two feet of water; they would be diving today. While he was priming the pump, he saw Elliot come up from below with a bucket of muck that looked to be about half full. Pete quickly grew agitated and concerned. He looked at the size of the barge and thought that if they worked at that pace, they would never get done.

He pulled the cord to start the motor and a moment later the pump caught its prime and started pumping water into the bayou. He watched the water start to go down inside the compartment and estimated that it would take about thirty minutes to pump all the water out, and when he was confident that everything was secure, he joined Elliot down in the dry compartment with his shovel and a five gallon bucket.

Their job was to scrape every piece of dirt, rock, and rust that they could find in the bottom of the barge to lighten the load. Every inch of draw was important on this trip and Joe wanted the barge to look like new. It was dark, damp, and clammy inside the barge, and they were rarely able to stand up inside the compartment without hitting their head on a deck support beam, but at least they were protected from the wind. Pete and Elliot looked at each other and concurred that their job sucked. They reluctantly began shoveling and Pete was overcome with the desire to show Elliot that he was the lead dog and that he could outwork everyone around him, so he picked up his bucket and relocated to the biggest pile of compacted fines in the area and, in an effort to show his machismo, lifted his shovel high in the air and slammed it into the fines. He barely scratched the pile and his shovel bounced off with absolutely no effect. Elliot, who had had the same experience when he had started digging, laughed when he saw the embarrassment on Pete's face. Pete was disheartened, but he was not going to concede, so he readjusted his approach and moved to an area that had less rock and more exposed steel. He was able to lay his shovel flat on the steel and slide his shovel underneath the fines and break the rock into pieces. He shoveled fast and hard, and had decided that he wanted to move twice as much rock as Elliot, so he filled his bucket until it was overflowing. Elliot, who had seen the scorn on Pete's face when he'd brought up his first bucket, stopped working and turned to watch the show. Pete set down his shovel and bent down to pick up the bucket; but when he lifted, the bucket barely moved.

"Holy shit! This thing is heavy," Pete said to Elliot.

"Yeah. I saw the look on your face when I carried out that last bucket; you thought I was being a pussy, didn't you? Well, guess what... it's heavy as hell, ain't it? I want to see you carry that damn thing up that ladder," Elliot responded, and then muttered under his breath, "Think I'm a pussy, well, screw you, I ain't no pussy, I just ain't dumb." Pete heard Elliot's mutterings and took it as a challenge. He looked at Elliot and then the bucket and finally the ladder.

"How much?" Pete said.

"How much what?"

"How much are you going to bet me that I can't get this bucket up that ladder and onto the deck?"

"Lunch at the Emerald House; I could go for a free Chinese buffet."

"All right, lunch at the Emerald House." Pete smiled and then put the bucket between his legs and grasped the handle with both hands. He swung the bucket forward and let it fall to the ground and then he moved forward and did it again. He leapfrogged his way over to the ladder while Elliot stood and watched in amusement. When the bucket was under the opening, Pete climbed the ladder and went on deck. A moment later Elliot heard the hum of the bobcat motor and felt the barge shift around him as the machine made its way over to the hatch. Elliot saw a rope fall into the hole, followed shortly by Pete making his way down the ladder. He tied the rope to the bucket and looked up the hole and yelled.

"All right, take it up." Pete looked at Elliot with an evil grin as the bucket lifted up and out of the hole.

"Oh, bullshit, that was raw. You didn't say anything about getting Jeff and using the bobcat," Elliot protested, but he knew that he had been had and lunch was on him.

Pete laughed and then climbed up on deck to empty the bucket. He tipped the bucket of sludge into the bobcat bucket. When he saw how little material was in a bucket and looked at the size of the barge, he thought about how long it was taking to move each five gallon bucket and it dawned on him that it was going to take a few days of ass-busting work for the two of them to scrape the bottom of all the compartments.

He walked over to Jeff, who was kneeling down and getting ready to pull the goggles over his eyes and start cutting, and asked him, "Do you know how long it is going to take to clean this out?"

Jeff looked up him with a devilish smile on his face and replied, "You just figured it out, eh? Yeah, you two are going to get real close and buddy, buddy for the next couple of days at least! Unfortunately, it has to get done and someone has to do it, and that someone is you! But look on the bright side; you could be with Giles and the boys enjoying their day at the beach. They're freezing their balls off this morning." With that said, he pulled his goggles over his eyes and finished adjusting his flame.

Pete couldn't help but stare at the flame as Jeff put the torch to the rusted steel. It immediately popped loudly, sending bits of molten rust flying through the air, one of which landed on Pete's arm and burned him. The burn felt like a bee sting and Pete yelped in pain and jumped back, quickly brushing it off and hoping to avoid any more contact with the exploding slag. Jeff looked up and laughed at his discomfort.

"That's what you get for standing around watching other people work instead of doing your own work."

Pete brushed his arm some more in a vain attempt to make the burn stop as he silently walked back to the hatch to continue his work. He climbed down the ladder and watched Elliot work his way towards the opening with a bucket of muck and he began to think that cleaning this barge was a stupid and impossible task. He said nothing to Elliot as he walked past him and over to his bucket. He picked up the shovel and slid it under more of the rocky coating in front of him. Within an hour or so they were miserable, but as much as they hated it, they kept working at a steady pace without much talking and complaining.

At the end of the day, they were covered with a layer of stinking, brown, oily muck, their backs hurt, and their hands were raw, but as they stood on the deck of the barge with Jeff and the cold beer that Joe had brought, they realized that they had actually made good progress. Two compartments were now cleaned and they started to believe that not only was it possible to clean out the barge, but when they looked at the water line on the outside of the barge they could see the end of the barge sitting a couple of inches higher in the water. Joe was right after all. It was going to work, and by the time they had the bottom of the barge cleaned, they would probably gain close to three or four inches of draft.

Pete watched Joe walk up the ramp and over to the three of them carrying a blue cooler that he had taken out of the back of the truck. He set it down in front of them and opened it. It was full of ice and oysters.

"Dig in. These are Apalachicola Oysters. And, do you know that they are considered to be some of the best oysters in the world? And boy, these are good! I couldn't resist trying a couple when I was putting them on ice." Joe handed Pete the oyster knife. "You do know how to open an oyster without impaling yourself, don't you?" he asked Pete.

Pete took the knife from Joe. "Sure, of course," he lied. Pete watched Joe suck the raw oyster out of the shell and was disgusted by it, but Joe was insisting that it was a delicacy and Pete didn't want to seem like a coward, so he reached into the ice and pulled one out and began examining the shell in his hand. It was odd shaped with a rough surface. The thing was just plain ugly; it was dark grey, cold, and wet in his hand. He saw where the lips of the two shells came together and tried to find a place to insert the knife to split them apart. Joe, Jeff, and Elliot watched him try in futility to separate the shells until Joe finally snatched the oyster and knife from him.

"I thought you said you knew what you were doing. If you don't know how to do something, say so. You're going to impale yourself or play with the damn thing so long we'll starve and die before you get it open. Now watch, you goofball. See here, on the back of the shell is the hinge. That's where you insert the knife and twist it like this." Joe did it as he was explaining and then an audible "pop" was heard and it was open. He slid the knife along the top of the shell to cut the oyster free from it and then he repeated the process on the bottom shell.

"Do you want some hot sauce? I have some good habanera sauce from South America that a friend brought back with her and gave to me. It's a set of three sauces. There's the Gecko, which gets a single X and has a pleasant bite. The Iguana gets a double X, and it's kind of dangerous, so you only want to put a drop or two on your oyster, and then there's the Monitor which gets a triple X. I don't know how good it is, because I haven't worked my way up to that one yet. I think it's more of a cooking sauce. A few drops of that in a giant pot of gumbo would be just about right."

"I'll try the Gecko first and give it a shot," Pete said. He knew about hot and spicy food and remembered how much he had enjoyed watching Frankie suffer in New Orleans and didn't want to give them the same show. Joe obliged him and put a drop of the hot sauce on the oyster and handed it him. Pete looked down at what appeared to be a giant grey and cream colored wad of snot in the bottom of the shell. He got a queasy feeling in his belly and then looked at the three men watching him. They all knew it was the first time he had ever looked at a raw oyster and they all had smiles on their faces as they watched him contemplate what he was about to eat.

Pete decided he probably wouldn't die, so he turned it up and emptied the shell into his mouth as he had watched Joe do. His first impulse was to vomit, but he held it in and swallowed. The hot sauce did have a little bite to it and there was a slightly salty tang, but it was good. It was really good, and Pete was hooked and ready for another.

Elliot took the knife from Joe and easily popped open an oyster.

"Joe, can you hand me the Iguana? I love hot sauce; the hotter the better. Hell, give me that Monitor instead; I'll try that." Elliot was standing tall and trying a little too hard to impress his comrades on the barge.

"Well, cool your jets a little there, crazy man, and try this first." Joe handed Elliot the bottle of Iguana sauce and Elliot immediately turned the bottle over and began shaking vigorously. When he had coated the oyster in a layer of red sauce, he quickly emptied the shell into his mouth. Joe looked at him with raised eyebrows as Elliot started to turn pale and his eyes began to water. He swallowed the oyster and stood in silence as his eyes began to widen. The three of them looked at him, wondering if he was going to pass out. Elliot wanted to cry; he knew he had made a fatal error in judgment, but he wasn't going to allow them to torment him forever, so he calmly raised his beer to his lips and sucked on the bottle until it was empty. Jeff, Joe, and Pete started howling with laughter, but Joe stopped laughing long enough to give him credit for sucking it up. Elliot was pale and sweating, but he stood tall, and tried to hand the knife to Jeff.

"Hell no, I don't need the knife. I'm not eating those things. I ate a bad oyster once and that was enough to last a lifetime," Jeff said as he directed Elliot to pass the knife to Joe.

"That's what you get for getting drunk and wandering around Italy eating food from who knows where," Joe said to Jeff and then turned to the other two and continued. "He was one of those dumb young Marines that weren't careful where they ate." Joe popped another oyster open and put a drop of sauce on it before handing the knife to Pete.

"I spent New Years Day 1976 in the hospital in Italy. I thought I was going to die; hell, I wanted to die!" Jeff said. "We were pretty drunk, that much is true, but it was early in the evening and we went to what looked like a nice restaurant. Nobody else got sick; of course, nobody else got the oysters on the half shell either. I will never, ever eat another raw oyster. They're okay grilled or fried, but not raw."

Pete was nervous as he put the next oyster to his lips, but they were so good that he couldn't stop and decided it was worth the risk.

"Okay, boys, I have some good news and some bad news. The good news is that we have lots of oysters and beer. The bad news is that I don't have payroll today. I get my draw when the pilings are set at Quimbies. Those guys wimped out and gave up a little after three. They were a light shade of blue, but they only had five more poles to go. I can't believe they gave up. It's going to be cold again tomorrow, but they said they'd come back and finish in the morning when they thawed out, and Mr. Quimby will write me a check as soon as they're done, but not a moment before. I can give you about fifty bucks each to hold you over, but that's all I've got right now. I'm really sorry guys, but I'll have your check tomorrow or Monday morning; until then, let's eat some oysters and drink some beer." He was embarrassed and disappointed that he was unable to pay them, but he was confident that he would have their money soon.

Pete looked at Elliot and both of them were dejected, but they loved Joe and didn't really have any big plans anyways, so they lied and told him it wasn't a problem; but they did take the fifty bucks for Saturday night. The four of them were resigned to the fact that they might as well drink the beer and eat the oysters and make the best of a crappy situation, so they sat on the barge, told stories, laughed, and ate a bag of oysters until long after dark. At the end of the night, Pete said good-bye to Bonehead, closed the gate, and was thankful for the fact that he had enjoyed a great Friday night on Tom's Bayou.

PETE WENT TO THE DOJO for a couple of hours on Saturday morning. He was nursing a slight hangover, so his energy level and concentration were not at their best, but he worked hard and enjoyed himself. He then spent the rest of the afternoon working around the house and cleaning his van. He ate dinner and had planned on watching television for a while and then going to bed, but he was surprisingly reinvigorated by the shower, and as he stood looking in the mirror while combing his hair and brushing his teeth, a strange feeling came over him. He liked the face, the body, and the smile that was looking back at him. It was a stranger, but a stranger that he wanted to get to know. Feeling good about himself, he decided to put on some decent clothes and go for a ride to the Island and see if he could have some fun. He didn't have much money and didn't plan to be out late, but he wanted to live for a while.

An hour later he was crossing the Okaloosa Island Bridge and when he saw the lights and the traffic, he became excited. He took a left at the bottom of the bridge and found a secluded area to park in a cluster of bars and clubs. He popped in his new *Peter Gabriel 4* cassette and when "Shock The Monkey" started blasting, he lit a joint and enjoyed a few hits before making his way to Hog's Breath Saloon, where he sat at the outside bar, listened to music, and watched the crowd for a while. After a couple of drinks, he walked over to Victor's, a large dance club that had a powerful beat emanating from the building and a lot of girls going in the front door. He paid his cover and made his way to the bar where he ordered a drink and then looked around to see if he knew anyone. Of course he didn't know anyone, because the only people he knew in Florida were his fellow mud-ducks and the people he studied karate with, neither of whom he expected to see in this club.

He wanted to move around, but moving was difficult because people were packed in the bar like sardines. Pete hadn't thought that there were this many young people in Okaloosa County, let alone one bar. He attempted to move around and explore, but by the time he walked twenty feet he had almost spilled his drink on several people, so he decided to stay put and look around. The dance floor was full to capacity with *beautiful* people, none of whom appeared to be over the age of twenty-five, and all were moving to Michael Jackson's "Beat It", which was blasting through the speakers with such force that he could feel the bass pounding on his chest. Disco lights were flashing various colors around the black room and the effect made the dancers appear to move in stop action. He continued to look around and noticed a balcony that seemed less crowded and since he was beginning to feel claustrophobic, he finished his drink, ordered a second, and weaved his way through the crowd and up the stairs. As he stood at the railing looking down, he realized how immense the place was. There had to be several hundred people milling about, none of whom he knew. He stood around a little more and as he was finishing his drink and getting ready to call it a night, he saw a girl that caught his eye. She was standing just off the dance floor with a drink in her hand and moving to the beat of The Eurythmics "Sweet Dreams (Are Made of This)" as she watched the people dance. He had the feeling that he had seen her before, and that was strange, because he had never seen anyone as beautiful as her, and then he realized that she looked exactly like the girl he had met on the water with Giles. He studied her some more and then decided that it was her. She had more clothes on, but it was her. This was too much of a coincidence for him and he decided that he had absolutely nothing to lose, so he quickly made his way down the stairs and towards her. When he got closer, he became nervous and hesitant, but decided to carry on. By the time he got to her, Annie Lennox had been replaced by Duran Duran's "Hungry Like a Wolf", and the music was so loud that he could barely hear himself think. When he came alongside her, he almost had to shout to her.

"Hello. I'm Pete, and I know this sounds stupid, but you look exactly like a girl I once met out on the bay while I was pushing my barge, and you really look like you should be dancing instead of just standing here, so….do you want to dance?" he yelled over the music.

She looked him up and down and then remembered. She smiled in acknowledgement and decided that he cleaned up nicely. The stone washed jeans and shirt made him much more appealing than those nasty cut-off jeans and old T-shirt that she had first seen him in.

"Yeah, sure. Come on, let's dance." She set her drink on the railing and led Pete onto the dance floor. They danced three songs and never took their eyes off of each other. They tried to talk while they danced, but the music was just too loud.

"Do you want to go outside where we can talk without screaming?" Pete finally asked.

He could tell she was sizing him up while she thought about it. "Sure, let's walk over to Hog's Breath. I'll let you buy me a drink."

Pete was shocked by her answer, but didn't hesitate in leading her to the door. When they got outside, there was instant relief from the noise and they enjoyed the fresh night air. Pete was nervous, but excited as well. He had just met this girl, and yet, he felt completely relaxed and open with her, as if they had known each other for years. They made the short walk across the street and decided to sit outside, where Pete had earlier sat alone. When the bartender came over, he recognized Pete and greeted him like an old friend. He took their order, and after looking at the girl next to him and giving Pete an approving glance, he got them their drinks. Pete looked around and saw an abandoned little table in a corner and ushered her there, where they sat and began to get to know each other.

"You know, when I was standing on the balcony and looked down and saw you, I thought it was you, but it was quite a while ago, and I really never thought I would be lucky enough to see you again, and by the way, I told you my name was Pete, but you never did tell me your name." Pete wasn't sure what to say and searched for anything to start a conversation.

"That's sweet. I'm Karen, and I have to admit, you look much better tonight then you did that day. It took me a while to recognize you."

"Was that your boyfriend on the boat with you that day?" Pete knew it was a dumb thing to say before he got it out of his mouth, and figured his night was about to be over.

"No! That was my uncle. I was home visiting for a few days and he took me out on his boat to cruise around and have some fun. I'm almost offended that you think I would date someone twice my age. What kind of a girl do you think I am?"

Pete was now scared. He'd finally met the girl of his dreams and the first thing he did was insult her.

"No….. I didn't mean that. I couldn't see him very well, and to be honest with you, I really wasn't looking at him. He could have been twenty or two hundred and twenty for all I knew. I was just stunned, because I had just described the perfect woman to my buddy and then you showed up, and I have to tell you, you're the person I described," Pete said.

She thought about it, accepted the excuse and liked the compliment, so she forgave him. The two of them sat and talked like old friends for a long time. She told him that she had just earned her degree in mechanical engineering from the University of Florida and was getting ready to start working on base. She was very proud of the fact that she was one of very few women who pursued that field. She was a girl that liked to be challenged and to run against the tide. She'd grown up in Florida, but loved the Oakland Raiders. Her career counselor in high school told her to be an English major, so she became an engineer. She knew Pete was younger than her, but she was strangely intrigued by him.

He told her about his job and his studying of karate and they soon decided to go on a walk along the beach. They started walking east, and before they knew it, they were at a deserted stretch of beach between

Okaloosa Island and Destin that belonged to the Air Force and was covered with dunes. They were holding hands and enjoying the sound of the waves meeting the shoreline when she stopped walking, looked at Pete, and kissed him.

He was taken aback, but enthusiastically returned her kiss. When they broke the kiss, she took his hand and led him into the dunes where they found a quiet spot out of view of anyone else. They sat in the sand holding each other close and looked at the stars. The sky was bright and full, there was a gentle and cool sea breeze blowing, and in the distance gentle waves lapped at the beach. It was a perfect night and they were soon caught up in the moment and began kissing passionately; and before either of them realized what was happening, they were tearing at each other's clothes, and for the first time in his life, Peter Taylor made love to a beautiful woman.

Pete awoke and laid in bed on Sunday and couldn't stop thinking about her. He wanted to call her as soon as he opened his eyes, but he knew he should wait. The day seemed to drag on, and by late in the afternoon he could resist no more and called her. When she answered the phone, it was apparent that she was happy to hear his voice; he was relieved that she even took his call. They talked about nothing for almost an hour and finally set a date for the following weekend. When Pete hung up the phone he was so excited that he jumped in the air and screamed out loud. He went into his room and didn't stop thinking about her the rest of the day.

He was slapped back to reality first thing Monday morning. Jeff had worked through the weekend and was finished cutting the deck by mid-morning. When he was done, there were various sized holes over each compartment and, in all, about 30% of the deck was gone. Monday afternoon it started to rain. It was light, cold, and steady, and it made it impossible to start welding the new steel supports and decking in place, but Pete and Elliot spent most of their time below deck and kept on working in the miserable conditions until they finished cleaning the last compartment Wednesday afternoon. It was still raining, and it kept on raining for twenty days straight.

Pete and Karen spent every moment possible together. She had tried to explain her feelings to her parents, but she was having a hard time explaining them to herself. He wasn't the guy she was looking for; in fact, she wasn't looking for a guy; she was looking for a career. But there was something about him, and since he had come into her life, he'd consumed her thoughts. He was nothing like her preconceived notions of who a construction worker was. He was kind, polite, and intelligent.

He met her parents soon after they started dating, and they seemed to tolerate him, but they were both unhappy that he wasn't in college. They liked him as a person, but they wanted a man who could provide a good life for their daughter and an uneducated construction worker was going to have a hard time providing the life they felt their daughter deserved. They knew that she was absolutely smitten with him, and they didn't understand it. He was younger than her, had no money, and a very uncertain future.

Karen's father was a very successful architect, and her mother an accountant, and both were devoutly religious. She was their only child, and they were a very close and protective family. They were resigned to the fact that Karen was an adult, and they couldn't tell her who she could date – they knew it wouldn't do any good if they tried – so they tolerated the relationship, and decided that if she was going to continue to see him, they would convince Pete to get in school and make something of himself.

CHAPTER 44

CAN WE GET THERE FROM HERE?

"I know it's raining and I don't give a damn, Joe! I'm delivering two thousand tons of rock tomorrow, and if you don't get up there and get going, there's going to be hell to pay for both of us. The penalty for being late is $2,150.00 a day and it won't take many days before a damn big hole gets eaten out of our pockets. Do whatever it takes, Joe, but you've got to get your ass on that river. We're behind schedule already and not only are we not on the damn job, but we don't even have a barge yet," Red said. It was very seldom that Red was ever cross with Joe, but he'd gotten the nickname Red because of the shade of light crimson he turned when he lost his temper. For the first time in ten years of working together he was turning that special shade of red in front of Joe's eyes.

"The weather man says it is going to stop in the next couple of days. I'm ready to go as soon as I can get dry enough to burn some rod for a few days without getting electrocuted." Joe was as frustrated and upset as Red. He was losing money every day it rained and it had now been raining the same cold, steady, light rain for eighteen days in a row.

"Red, as soon as the rain stops we'll start welding, and we'll be under way in about five days. That's all I can tell you. The weather's beyond my control."

"Damn it, Joe, I know it. I'm just frustrated as all hell." Red rose from his chair behind the desk and Joe was relieved to know that the meeting was over. The men shook hands and Joe walked out of the office and into the rain. Having checked all the equipment and secured everything for the day, he went home with his friend Jack Daniels and watched it rain.

Three days later, Joe woke to a sunrise, an actual sunrise, where he could see the sun rising over the trees. The air was clean and crisp and there was an actual orange ball rising in the sky. He put on his clothes and hurried out the door. When he walked out his front door, he was greeted by a soggy world. Water seemed to drip from every leaf and converged on the ground, forming little streams and puddles and making mud everywhere. He slogged through the muck to his truck and made his way to the boatyard. When he opened the gate to enter, he saw little rivers of runoff everywhere. It would take a while to dry out, but they would be welding today. Joe knew how far behind schedule they already were, so he had recently bought another welder and had hired a new man to go with it; he and the rest of Joe's men were supposed to start showing up in a few minutes.

Joe was past nervous; he was scared. He had bet everything on this job. He and his brothers had built this company from nothing. They had come to Niceville with very little money and had moved into their Brother Mike's house; his wife had moved out shortly thereafter. Mike had a steady job, and had supported Joe and Jeff when they'd started the company, and worked with them whenever he had some extra time. They'd started the company with a barge they'd built in Mike's backyard out of scrap steel, scrounged lumber, and barrels they'd bought from the junkyard. Over the years they had scrimped and saved and had purchased the tug boats, barges, and cranes. For the last three weeks they'd been unable to generate any income, but their overhead costs had continued to pile up. They were already three weeks behind schedule, and if they finished three weeks late on the job, the fines would put them out of business.

Pete was the first to pull in the gate, followed closely by Jeff, Elliot, the new guy, and pulling in last was Giles and his crew that he'd had to pick up on the way in. Between the three of them, Giles was the only one to still have a driver's license and a truck. Joe gathered his men and went over what needed to get done. He sent Elliot with Giles' crew and assigned Pete to help Jeff and the new man, who was introduced as Tom Jefferson.

He was a heavy set man with blonde hair and cold blue eyes. He was in his middle thirties, but looked like he was pushing fifty. He was quick to smile but slow to laugh. Pete wanted to like him but something in the back of his mind told him to be careful. The group broke up into two crews, Jeff's and Giles', and they went to their assigned duties. Giles pulled out of the yard with Joe right behind him.

Jeff knew what was at stake when he got his guys together and climbed in the driver's seat of the 1958 Bantam truck crane and began moving it to the bank of the bayou. The crane's paint was faded and peeling and its operator's seat consisted of a piece of plywood laid across a rusting metal frame that was once an operator's chair. Jeff hated the machine; it vibrated, bounced around, and beat the hell out of the operator. If Jeff spent more than a couple of hours operating it, he was sure to have a backache for a couple of days. The crane motor was an industrial six cylinder Continental with a loud and leaking exhaust that was mounted a few feet behind the operator's chair. The gears were old and worn and rattled loudly as the machine was asked to move. Jeff wore large headphones in the hopes that he would be able to hear again after running the machine.

When Jeff had the crane in position, Pete and Tom ran a large pipe through the top of an outrigger and the two of them pulled together to extend the heavy steel outrigger from its sleeve. They then screwed it down onto large heavy pads, lifting and leveling the crane as much as they could. Jeff operated the crane, Pete rigged the steel on the bank, and Tom guided Jeff and unhooked the steel on the deck of the barge.

They had the steel loaded on the barge and were ready to start welding in a few hours. Pete was assigned to cut the steel used for bracing into sizes as needed by Jeff and Tom while they tacked them into place. When the supports that they had planned to replace were all tacked into position, they went back to the beginning and started welding them in place permanently. Joe came back to the yard and helped with the welding. In the evening he walked through the barge with Jeff and Tom and they decided that they should remove and replace a few more supports and some additional decking.

During the time that they had been working on the barge, two brand new Outboard motors had been delivered. Joe pulled Pete away from Jeff and the two of them installed the motors on the *Osage* and prepped the boat for the arduous journey to come. She was an old aluminum Navy boat with a tri hull and flat bottom. It was designed for a diesel motor and direct drive, but all of that had been removed and the holes for the shaft sealed. Without the weight of the motor, the boat itself drew less than four inches. They made a special mounting unit on the back of the boat so that the motors would sit low enough in the water to operate properly. They put new push knees on the front of the boat and installed a hydraulic steering system that had come out of an old shrimp boat but still worked fine.

Pete could sense the nervousness in both Joe and Jeff. They were short-tempered and kept mumbling to themselves regularly. He liked them both very much, and knew things weren't going according to plan, so he made sure that he was the first one at the boatyard in the morning, and didn't leave until it was time for karate class. He wanted them to succeed and was willing to do anything he could to help them. Some of the other employees thought Pete was being a brown-noser because they didn't care what happened to Joe and Jeff as long as they got paid on Friday. Giles understood and cared, and so did Elliot, but the others were just passing through and considered this a very temporary job.

Red came by religiously for his daily visits to be sure that progress was being made. By Thursday afternoon, there was some excitement and anticipation in the air as Jeff and Tom finished the welding on the barge, the *Osage* was put in the water, and they were almost ready to depart.

When they put the boat in the water for a test on Thursday evening, Joe operated it. Pete and the other men walked onto the now completed barge and stood with a celebratory beer in their hands, cheering as they watched Joe make the boat dance in the water. Pete watched as the shallow draft of the flat bottom boat and the twin motors allowed Joe to move the boat around with a grace and beauty that looked like water ballet to him. Joe was always a slow and cautious captain when he moved the boats, but now he was playing and Pete saw the pure joy of a big kid and his new toy on the water. The men stood on the barge and looked at their work and then looked at Joe playing and raised their beers in several triumphant toasts. Pete cheered and laughed and knew that there was nowhere he would rather be at this moment in his life.

On Friday afternoon they loaded a port-a-potty on the barge, mounted a four hundred gallon gas tank for the *Osage's* fuel supply, and then they took the boats and barge to the fish house and fueled up for the trip. By Friday evening they were making final preparations for the trip. Saturday was spent getting personal affairs in order, and on Sunday they loaded the food and supplies for the five day trip. Joe, Jeff, and Mike checked and rechecked everything. Excitement was gone and now nervousness, caused by the reality of what they were about to undertake, began to sink in.

CHAPTER 45

THE CHOCTAWHATCHEE RIVER

I t was still dark when they departed from Tom's Bayou at five AM Monday morning. Joe was at the wheel of the *Sue-Bee,* the *Osage* was side tied, and the little Boston-Whaler, which was used for the nose boat, was tied behind the *Osage.* The *Sue-Bee* drew too much to go up the river, but in the bay she was faster and more fuel efficient than the *Osage,* so she would push the barge to the mouth of the river, and then the *Osage* would take over and push the barge up the river to Caryville. Joe had selected his five man crew for the push up the river, and Pete was excited to be one of them. Giles and Elliot were not part of that crew, but they were riding with them to the river where they would camp with them for the night and then return the *Sue-Bee* to the boatyard in the morning.

The sun was coming up on the horizon when they left Boggy Bayou and entered Choctawhatchee Bay. It was a glorious spring morning. The air was crisp and the bay flat. Everyone, even Joe, was in good spirits. The barge had no leaks, the boats were fueled up and running great, so there wasn't much for the guys to do other than enjoy the day and tell stories. Giles kept them entertained with his never ending tales of female conquest (most of which were deemed purely imaginary). The seven men celebrated and enjoyed the boat ride and the camaraderie. It was a great day to be alive, and Pete was relishing every minute of it.

Pete sat on the large bit on the front of the barge with Leroy Turner, enjoying the day and watching as the Highway 331 bridge came into view. Leroy usually worked on Giles' crew, but Joe wanted to bring him on the voyage up the river. Leroy was a gentle giant, and Joe thought his bulk might come in handy. Leroy stood about 6'1", weighed a little over three hundred pounds, and wore a crew cut. He looked intimidating, but was seldom seen without a smile and an optimistic word of encouragement. His dream in life was to become a professional wrestler, but while Pete had no doubt he could do it, he wasn't sure if Leroy was ambitious enough to make his dream come true. Leroy was a nice guy, and tried hard, but he didn't want to do much more than work eight hours, watch television, and eat. He had played football in high school- lineman- but since then he had stopped exercising but had continued eating.

Pete had worked with Leroy a couple of times in the past and liked him very much, but was amazed at some of things he'd do. A few months earlier Pete, Leroy, and another man had been dressing rocks in front of a seawall when Leroy had called Pete for help with a large rock that he was unable to move. Pete had walked the fifteen feet over to where Leroy was working and struggling with the boulder, and watched him grapple with it for a while, bewildered by what he was witnessing.

"I just can't get this rock. It's stuck in the sand or something," Leroy had said with anguish on his face and frustration in his voice. He reached down into the water again, and pulled with all his might on the rock, but it wouldn't move.

After Pete had watched the show long enough, he matter-of-factly commented to Leroy, "It might be easier to pick up the rock if you weren't standing on it."

Leroy had then looked down at his feet, and then back up at Pete. "Oh," was all he had said. He had then stepped off the rock with a big smile, a goofy little laugh, and reached down and picked up the nearly two hundred pound rock and tossed it onto the base of the wall with ease. Pete had been impressed with his raw strength, but astounded by his brain.

As the barge slowly moved across the bay, Pete was enjoying lightheartedly reminding Leroy of that day. They laughed together as they sat in the sunshine and chatted aimlessly. It was one of the most pleasant days in Pete's young life. The entire crew remained in high spirits, and the weather cooperated as they moved along.

The sun was beginning to lower in the sky when they finally passed under the bridge. When Pete felt Joe turn the boat towards the northeast, he looked across the bay in that direction. He was astounded at the array of waterways emptying into the bay. The shoreline was broken up by four large rivers and many smaller tributaries that converged with the bay in the area they were moving towards. There were no lights or developments of any kind to be seen. Pete contemplated his view, and reasoned that this part of the bay had probably looked just like it stood before him thousands, or millions of years earlier. He kept waiting for a Brontosaurus to stick his head up through the trees and was almost disappointed when none appeared.

He hoped Joe knew where he was going because nobody else on the barge seemed to. As they moved closer to the shoreline, Pete began to clearly make out the swamps and cypress trees. The feeling of entering a land that time forgot returned, and the reality that he was entering a prehistoric world began to set in. As they approached the shoreline, Pete heard and felt the motor back down as Joe eased the throttle back and stuck his head out the window. It was time to go to work.

"Jeffrey, I'm going to try to take it into Duck Lake for the night. I need you to get on the bow and guide me in. We're at low tide now, and the water is still pretty high after all this rain, so I think we can get the *Sue-Bee* in there. If not, we'll anchor her out here and push in with the *Osage*."

Joe idled down the motors and reduced forward speed to a minimum. Jeff ran to the bow of the barge, picked up two long poles, tossed one to Pete, and ordered him to the starboard bow, while he moved to the port. They used their long poles to determine the water depth by sounding the bottom. They pushed their poles into the muck on the bottom and kept yelling out depths, which were relayed to Joe by Giles as they slowly crept along.

"Six feet....six feet....five feet...three and a half. It ain't gonna make it. We'd better drop a spud," Pete yelled out.

While Pete and Jeff were doing the soundings, Giles had climbed into the crane and fired it up. Leroy moved into position to rig the spuds. A small puff of black smoke momentarily appeared from the exhaust in the back of the crane as it came to life. Giles pulled back on the controls and the crane's boom slowly began to rise from the deck. When the crane was in position Leroy moved quickly to rig the spud and then he stood back, pointed his index finger toward the sky, and Giles began lifting the pipe. The cable came taut and he smoothly lifted the spud into position. Elliot stood next to the spud well and guided the long steel pipe into the hole. When it was securely in position, Giles applied the brake and held it at the ready.

Jeff was getting the same results from his sounding pole as Pete. He decisively turned towards the boat and gave Joe the signal to put the boat in reverse. Joe responded quickly, and the motor roared to life. Copious amounts of black smoke rose from the exhaust; a wave of dirty water emerged from beneath the boat, full of sticks, leaves, and black muck stirred up from the bottom by the powerful propeller. When forward momentum was almost completely stopped, Jeff looked towards Giles, pointed his index finger to the ground, and Giles released the brake. The spud quickly and violently dropped through the well and into the ground. Everyone staggered a half a step as the barge came to an abrupt halt. The barge, now pinned in one corner, began to pivot on the spud. Joe turned the wheel to counter the motion, while Giles swung the crane over the other spud and the team repeated the process.

When both spuds were down, and the barge was secure, Joe shut down the *Sue-Bee*. When Giles had secured the crane, he shut off its motor. There was a strange and instantaneous silence that erupted around them. The lack of any kind of noise seemed to almost be overwhelming to the men as they stood on the bow of the barge, looking at the primitive forest before them. Giles couldn't take the silence and quickly broke it.

"All right, I'm ready for a cold beer."

"Now, now, we're not done yet; just hold your horses on that beer, Giles," Joe responded pleasantly as he climbed out of the wheelhouse and onto the deck of the barge to assess the situation. He joined his men gathered at the bow of the barge looking at the entry to the small lake.

"Well, we made it," Elliot said with a big smile on his face and a real feeling of accomplishment as he greeted Joe.

"Don't get too confident or comfortable just yet. We've got a ways to go, and haven't done shit yet. There's still a lot of work to do before we get to relax." He turned to look at his brother. Joe was happy to be nearing the end of the first day, which had, so far, been pleasantly uneventful. "What do you think Jeff? Can we make it in?" Joe wanted to go into the lake because it was protected, calm, and didn't have any currents to mess with.

"I'll tell you, Joe, I don't think so. The barge will make it in, but the *Sue Bee* is going to have a problem. What's the weather supposed to do tonight? Maybe we can just park out here?"

"Screw it. Let's pull the spuds and run up into Bell's Leg; we'll tie up there for the night," Joe decided. Bell's Leg was near the mouth of the river and would be a safe place for them to spend the night.

Everyone returned to their positions, and within an hour they had moved into position and were slowly making their way into Bell's Leg. When Joe was satisfied that they were in a good position, they pulled alongside the river bank, dropped the spuds, and were finally allowed to relax.

The cooler of beer was opened, tiki torches were put out and lit, tents erected, and Pete was assigned grill duty. The men ate a simple meal of burgers and potato salad, washed down with several cold beers, and then enjoyed a night filled with comradery, excitement, and adventure. The more they talked, and the more they drank, the more they became overly confident that the rest of the trip was going to be as easy as this first day, and no matter how he tried, Joe could not curtail their beer-induced optimism.

They woke with the sun, and after a quick breakfast and a few visits to the port-a-potty, they got underway. Giles and Elliot fired up the *Sue Bee*, untied it, and left Joe and his crew to their journey while they piloted her back to Valparaiso. Giles looked out the wheel house as he pulled away, and watched as Joe stood behind the wheel of the *Osage* as the barge pulled away from the bank and they started to make their way up the river.

The Choctawhatchee River was fed by smaller tributary rivers, various springs, and rain starting in southern Alabama and ending here at the Choctawhatchee Bay. It was a primitive and meandering river that was preserved and undeveloped in most places. There were scatterings of houses along the way, but they were mostly along the lower part of the river near Rooks Bluff. Pete, as well as the rest of the crew, felt a sense of adventure take hold of them as the barge slowly made its way upriver.

Pete and Jeff were at the front of the barge as they got underway. A few minutes later, they made their way to Indian Island and turned Northeast where the tributaries joined together to form one river. This section of the river was wide, deep, and fairly straight. Pete began to wonder if Joe and Jeff had been exaggerating about how rough this trip was going to be.

"Pete, you climb down in the whaler and get it started. Just idle alongside us and keep your eyes on Joe in the wheel house. You're going to have to move from side to side quickly depending on the turn of the river. I'll throw you down a line and tie you to us when we need to. It's going to get crazy in a little bit, so be ready and pay attention," Jeff told him.

He stationed Tom and Leroy at each corner of the bow of the barge and then he climbed into the house of the crane. He started the motor and kept it running so that it would be ready when called upon. He then climbed down and checked the chainsaws that were on deck. Satisfied that they were as ready as they could be, he gave Joe a signal that all was ready. Joe took a deep breath, gave the *Osage* a little more throttle, and picked up the pace.

Pete sat in the small boat and cruised alongside the barge as it made its way up the river. When he sat in the whaler, his head was barely a couple of feet off the water and he felt dwarfed by the barge. The nose of the little boat was braced with timbers and wrapped with a tire split from a tractor trailer and it was powered by a camouflage colored, hot rod, military surplus motor that was a little too big for the small boat, and put together it made it quite the sight. When he was close to the barge, all he could see was a big black wall of steel rising six feet out of the water and the tires hanging off the sides for bumpers. He had just enough visibility to look back and see Joe at the wheel and Jeff if he was standing on the edge of the barge.

When they reached Live Creek Cutoff, the river veered to the right and Joe ordered Pete to the starboard side of the barge. Pete was confused by this command, because he thought he should help push the nose to the right, but did as he was told. It didn't take him long to figure out what was about to happen; as they came around the first corner, Pete saw the river turn 180 degrees in what seemed like a few feet.

"Get right up on the bow and take this line," Jeff bellowed. Pete ran to the bow and in his haste almost tripped and fell out of the little boat. He regained his composure and grabbed the line quickly and tied it off on his bow bit. He moved back to the operator's chair a little more cautiously, and as soon as he sat down he saw Joe pointing at him to push. He moved the throttle all the way forward and heard the motor scream and kick out a spray of white water behind him. The river was turning and the barge was going into the bank. Pete began to get worried that he was about to be crushed between the bank and the barge, and he thought about jumping off when his prop started to push mud out the back of the motor. Joe kicked his port motor into reverse and his starboard motor full ahead. Slowly the behemoth began to come about.

They made it around their first turn and the barge began to slowly move up river again and into a small straight stretch. Pete breathed a sigh of relief that was short lived as he heard Joe screaming at him to get to the other side. He untied and gently pulled away from the barge and eased over to the other side. When he came around the front of the barge and saw Joe, he began to panic. Joe was red with anger, and seemed ready to come out and end Pete's existence.

"What the hell are you doing? Move that damn boat, or get the hell out of it. This ain't a damn pleasure cruise. You're gonna get someone killed, or sink my damn barge. Now, move your ass." Joe was frantic, and Pete soon learned why. Before he could get the line tied and back to his seat they were already going into the bank. He stumbled to his chair and hit the throttle before he was secure and had the wheel turned the right way. The back of the boat kicked around facing the stern of the boat. Pete looked up just long enough to see Joe about to explode, but, fortunately for Pete, his concentration was securely on the river before him. Joe kicked the starboard motor into reverse and made it scream with all it had, and then slammed his port motor to full ahead. Pete regained control of the whaler, moved it into proper position, gave it full throttle, and soon felt it pushing the nose around. When it came about, Joe waved for Pete to go back around to the starboard side.

"Don't tie that damn thing on, just get your nose into it and push," Joe screamed.

This time Pete pulled away from the boat and hit the throttle quickly. He moved across the front of the barge and into place with precision and confidence. Pete looked at the narrow river in front of him, and then the enormous barge beside him, and began to think that they were trying to put a camel through the eye of a needle. He began to understand what to do, and continued going back and forth from port to starboard as they made their way up the river, the motors from both boats screaming and churning mud as they went. They soon came around a narrow turn and Pete saw a large willow tree that had grown over the side of the river, and when he saw it, he was sure that he was going in the bushes.

"Shit, I hope there ain't no snakes in that tree," Pete yelled to Tom, who was standing on the corner of the barge.

"Don't worry about the snakes. They'll get out of the way. It's the damn river wasps that you want to watch out for. They're ferocious, and the only thing you can do is get under water to get away from them; of course, if you try to get under water, you're gonna end up getting run over by the barge, so either way, it sucks to be you. Tom said with a sinister little smile.

Pete looked at the tree with a new sense of panic as it rapidly drew closer. He studied the tree and tried to look at every branch, but there were so many thin branches, all of them hanging like strings in the water, that it was hard to tell what was there, and before he knew it he was in the tree, pushing branches out of the way and hoping not to get knocked out of the boat by a limb. His motor was screaming, and he was scared of the things that might live in, and around, the tree, but he was gaining in determination and confidence and began to embrace the challenge and the adventure. The barge came around and he emerged from the tree relieved and scratched, but otherwise unscathed. Before he had time to celebrate, he looked up river and knew that he would have to do it again on the other side a moment later. The river kept getting narrower, and he was constantly being thrust into bushes. This pattern continued throughout the day. It was late in the afternoon when they reached Rook's Bluff.

The river widened and straightened out for a stretch and that's where Joe decided to tie up for the night. The sun was getting ready to go below the tree line, and Joe wanted to be secured before it got too dark. Jeff got in the crane, Leroy and Elliot took their positions, and then they picked a spud off the deck and set it in the front corner. They then tied off the stern and let it float freely with the river. Once the barge was secure, the men started getting out their tents and prepared to settle in for the night. Pete started the grill and was getting ready to put some more hot dogs on it when Jeff walked up behind him.

"Is that all you're going to cook on this trip, hot dogs?"

"Listen, I didn't know I was supposed to be the cook, and I've got to tell you, there ain't much more than hot dogs and scrambled eggs that I know how to cook," Pete replied.

"Who told you that you know how to cook eggs? If those eggs you cooked this morning are the best you can do, then we really are in trouble," Joe chimed in as he walked over and began observing what Pete was doing.

"How did I get elected cook?"

"Well, I don't want to do it, Jeff doesn't have to do it, and, to be perfectly honest with you, I don't want those other goofballs anywhere near my food, so that leaves you," Joe said.

"Well, you guys can enjoy your gourmet meal, but I'm not eating hot dogs tonight," Jeff said. Then he took the gangplank that was lying on deck and slid it onto the river bank, picked up his fishing pole, bounced down the gangplank, and, with confidence and determination, disappeared into the woods.

"You'd better cook some extra dogs just in case, I think he'll be hungry when he gets back from wandering around in that swamp," Tom joked to Pete.

"You don't think he's gonna catch anything?"

"Hell no, he's got a better chance of gettin' eaten by a gator than catchin' anything. Ten bucks says he don't catch *shit*," Tom asserted as he stood behind Pete and acted as overseer and cooking expert while he sipped his cold beer.

Tom had agreed to go on the trip as long as he could bring a cooler of beer. He'd agreed not to start drinking until they were tied up for the night, and so far he'd kept his word. When Jeff dropped the spud, he got a cold beer from the cooler and stood holding it at the ready while he supervised Leroy tying the lines off. He'd popped the top before Leroy could stand up straight from securing the line on the bit, but the barge was tied off before he had started drinking.

"Okay, I'll take that bet. Ten bucks." Pete turned and shook hands with Tom, hopeful that his faith in Jeff would be rewarded.

"All right, ten bucks says *he won't catch shit*," Tom emphasized the last words while shaking Pete's hand. Pete went back to his food prep, while Tom walked over to Joe with a smile on his face.

"Young bucks; its fun when they don't pay attention," Tom

commented quietly to Joe while finishing his beer and preparing to pop open his second.

"Now, Thomas, that's kinda mean, isn't it?" Joe asked.

"I'm just having some fun, and teaching the boy to pay attention to what people say to him."

Pete had just finished cooking the hot dogs when Jeff bounded up the gangplank with two beautiful fish that he held up with pride.

"I told you, I'm not eating hot dogs, and as much as I'd like to let you do it, Pete, you're not cooking my fish; I want them edible." Jeff said with a sly smile as he made his way to the back of the barge where he happily cleaned his fish and anticipated his meal. Pete was excited about winning the bet and turned and grinned at Tom. He was happy, almost gleeful, thinking he had finally gotten one over on him. Pete watched as Tom slowly walked over to him, sipping his beer.

"You got my ten bucks?" Tom asked. Pete looked at him as if he was from another planet.

"What are talking about? He caught not one, but two nice fish, and you said he wouldn't catch......, oh screw you. We were betting on him catching fish and you know it. I'm not giving you ten bucks," Pete protested.

"Now, Pete, a bet is a bet, and any man who doesn't pay his gambling debts around here usually gets taken out into the swamp to play with the gators. And just look around you, we're already in the swamp, so that part's taken care of. I said he wouldn't catch shit. I even said it again while we were shaking hands, and you agreed to the wager again. He didn't catch shit, now did he? So, it looks like you owe me ten dollars." Tom coldly stared at Pete with his piercing blue eyes. Pete looked towards the other men on deck, hoping to find support or to see one of them to start laughing. None did.

"I think it was a mean bet, but like he said, a bet's a bet. That's why I don't gamble unless I know I'm going to win. You've got to pay attention to what you're betting on, and you didn't pay attention. You just assumed what the bet was, and you stopped listening," Joe said.

"Light bills and the phone bills don't mean shit, but you've got to pay gambling debts no matter what," Tom said menacingly as he stared at Pete.

Tom had already finished several beers, and it was bringing out a side of him that Pete hadn't seen and wasn't sure he wanted to see. Elliot and Leroy stood off to the side and were watching the situation unfolding in front of them. Joe and Tom were staring at him, and seemed to be wondering what he was going to do. Pete again looked at Tom; he was getting drunker by the minute.

"Oh, screw you. All right, I'll pay you as soon as we get back. You're an asshole, do you know that?"

"What do you mean, when we get back? Who says you're gonna make it back? Did you make a bet and not have the money to pay it?" Tom asked. He had gotten close to Pete and was beginning to sound threatening.

"Why the hell would I bring money out here? Do you see any stores?" Pete was now getting scared, and had an almost pleading sound to his voice.

"Relax, Pete. I know you're good for it, but if I have to wait too long, there'll be an interest charge." Tom patted Pete on the back and everyone started laughing again.

Pete was no longer scared; he was pissed. Tom soon came up to him with a big smile and patted him on the back. "What's the matter? You can't take a joke? Lighten up and drink a beer. We're just having some fun with you."

Pete calmed down and opened a beer, but he wasn't laughing. After eating, the men sat around the fire barrel and told stories as they drank, and when the stories drifted to high school, Tom got a faraway look in his eyes, and he seemed to mentally drift away as he began to speak.

"I remember in May of '68, me and my buddy Tommy Arnsbar were on top of the world. We were stars on the high school football team; we were doing cheerleaders together and were completely invincible. We signed up the day after graduation. Damn, we were hung over, but we joined together 'cause that's what you did in our families. Uncle Sam calls, you answer. By October we were stompin' around in the jungle...."

Tom was looking at no one as he spoke, but all eyes were on him. "We got this mission; it was a damn good plan. That's what they told us anyways. The Viet Cong had a shipping trail, and we had to shut it down. We were told that they always sent their scouts out ahead, then some infantry, with supplies, artillery, and heavy equipment towards the back. We shipped in a hundred Marines. Our job was to see the scouts come over the hill and hold them up with small arms fire, and then while they were stuck on the hill, air support would come in and take them out. Now, I have to admit, that sounds like a good plan. We all liked it…. but there were two problems. The first was that nobody told the Viet Cong to make sure they sent the scouts first, because those little fuckers came over the hill with everything. We never did see any scouts. There had to be a couple of thousand of those assholes, and they were loaded for bear. Things went to shit real fast, and I remember screaming something to Tommy….. and his head just came off. He was still standing, but he didn't have a fucking head anymore, and for some stupid reason, the only thing I could think of at that moment was, 'How the hell am I gonna tell your mamma that I let you get killed?' Well, we got our asses kicked that day. Those little fuckers were on the move, and they weren't taking prisoners. When the shooting stopped, they went around and bayoneted all the wounded; didn't want to waste bullets. I buried myself under a couple poor bastards who'd bought the farm and hid there for a few hours until it was clear. Now that was a bad fucking day. But, that's life…… What the hell can you do?" he concluded while finishing his beer and staring into the night with watery eyes that glistened in the firelight.

There was silence around the circle for a moment.

"Well, on that note," Jeff interjected, "I'm going to crash in my tent with a full belly of fish, and say thank you to God that I have never had to experience anything like that in my life. I was lucky; I joined in '74 and the worst thing that happened to me, besides the food poisoning on New Year's Eve, was getting drunk in Japan and waking up in someone's house. For some reason, I think it was the sake, I thought I was home, warm in my own bed. I had gotten a taxi and told the driver to take me to Mount Fuji; he drove for a while, stopped the car, and told me to get out. I did, and when I couldn't find Mount Fuji, I guess I wandered into this house and went to sleep on the couch. Next thing I know, there's this old Japanese couple screaming and yelling and hitting me with a broom and all kinds of shit. I guess they were surprised when they came home from a night on the town to find a drunk Marine passed out on their couch. Yeah, that one didn't go over too well; I caught a lot of shit for that. Maybe that's one of the reasons I didn't make Sergeant, but I did learn a valuable lesson: sake can really kick your ass, and the sake they have in Japan is not like the stuff we have here," Jeff said to lighten the mood as he got up and wandered off to his tent. The rest of the men sat and talked for a while longer, but as the fire began to fade, they soon followed Jeff into their tents for the night.

When everyone crashed, Pete lay in his sleeping bag and thought of Issac for the first time in a long time. He knew exactly what Tom was talking about, except he had to face his mother and father every day. He'd let his little brother die, and he'd also killed a big part of his parents that day. Tears silently rolled down his face, and sleep avoided him again.

ON THE THIRD DAY THEY had to break out the chainsaws because they ran into trees that had grown over the river and made it seem very narrow. Elliot and Pete were sent into the river and the trees to attach cables to the limbs as Leroy and Tom cut them and Jeff swung them onto the bank. It was a long hard day, and they made very little progress. It was soon painfully clear that it wasn't going to be a five day pleasure cruise. Joe decided to radio Giles for extra supplies and extra help, so at the appointed time he put Leroy in the Whaler and sent him to pick up Giles and the supplies and bring them back in a few hours. They radioed Joe in the evening and explained that they were lost in the middle of nowhere. It had taken longer than anticipated to get the supplies and there was no way for them to return that night, but they assured him that they would be there by first light.

It was slow going on the fourth day, made slower by the fact that Giles and Leroy didn't return until late in the afternoon. They had gotten lost on the river and by the time they arrived, they had drunk almost a case of beer, and the outboard motor was in the center of the boat. Pete tossed them a line as they paddled up to the barge, and then walked away as Joe approached because he didn't want to be a witness to murder.

Giles explained to Joe how they had hit a submerged dead head while cruising down the river. The motor came off the back of the boat, flipped into the air and landed in Leroy's lap, still running. Leroy had almost lost his family jewels and nearly shit his pants at the same time. Joe was furious, but Elliot and Pete were laughing. Leroy didn't like getting yelled at and he didn't think it was funny either because he'd truly thought he was going to die. Jeff had broken out the tool box when he saw them tie up and he and Tom jumped on the boat and started working without saying a word, and after a couple of hours work, they had the motor back on the boat and were ready for the next day.

ON DAY SIX MIKE NEVERS was bringing more supplies to the crew and was looking for the barge at the Cedar Log Lake Bar and Boat Ramp. He saw a pot-bellied little man with long black hair and a goatee wearing an old ball cap standing at the ramp, holding a beer and looking at the water. Mike walked up to him and asked the strangest question the man had ever heard.

"Hi, I'm Mike Nevers. Have you seen a crane barge go past here?"

The man looked at Mike, and then held up his beer can and looked at it with a most quizzical look on his face. He was sure that this crazy Yankee was doing better drugs than him, and he decided that this might be a fun conversation.

"Howdy, I'm Bill, and I hate to tell ya mister, but you're a long way from the bay. There ain't no crane barges goin' up 'n down this here river. Hell, a man is lucky to get around in a decent sized bass boat in some places. I think you're a bit lost," the man replied with a strong hillbilly accent.

"No, no, they're coming." Mike cut the conversation short and returned to his truck and decided to go look further down river and see if he could find them. Bill watched him drive off and was sure that he had just met the craziest man alive. He went into the bar and told a few of his buddies the story of the crazy Yankee while he ordered another beer. He was leaning against the bar and laughing with the other patrons when he looked out the window and saw a hundred foot barge with a crane on deck being pushed up the river by a strange little boat. At the wheel, he saw a stout man with a big beard yelling at the men scurrying about on deck.

"Well, holy hell. Will ya look at that? He wasn't crazy after all! Sally, hurry up with that beer, and make sure it's a warm one; I can't stand cold beer, 'cause I gotta go."

"Where are you runnin' off to in such a hurry?" the large middle aged woman asked.

"Anybody crazy enough to run that barge up this river is my kinda' people. I've got to find out where there a goin', so I can catch a ride. Waylon, come on, it's time for us to go. We gotta get yer boat and go catch a barge. Sally, why don't you just get me a few extra beers for the road?" Bill said. He soon had his warm beer and his cousin and they were on the road.

It was about six in the evening when Bill and Waylon found the barge tied up near Hog Island. It was getting late, and as they approached they could see the men on deck standing around a fire barrel drinking beer. He recognized one of the men as the crazy Yankee from the boat ramp. Bill turned and ordered Waylon to pull up alongside the vessel.

"Howdy. You're that crazy Yankee from the boat ramp. Well, I guess you ain't so crazy after all. Mind if we come aboard?" Bill asked.

The men on deck looked at the hillbilly climbing on deck before they had a chance to answer, and in their minds they heard banjoes and were wondering who was going to be squealing like a pig. The first one to come on deck was Bill. He was followed shortly by his cousin, who he introduced to the assembled men.

"I'm Joe. How are you doing? Are you from around here?" Joe reached forward and shook his hand. Joe had been on the boat for several days without shaving and had only packed enough clothes for a five day trip. His beard was full, his hair was tussled, and he was looking and smelling rough, which made Bill feel right at home.

"Me? Oh, hell no! I'm from Boonestown, Kentucky. I guess yer the man in charge here, so you must be the feller I need to speak with. Are ya a hirin'?" he asked straightforward.

"Well, I don't know yet. I'm just trying to get to Caryville right now, and I'll figure out where we're at from there. Do you know anything about working on barges?"

"Well, not barges exactly, but I've run just about every other piece of equipment you ever seen. I've worked the coal mines since I was a kid back home in Kentucky. I saw this here barge goin' up river and I figured anyone crazy enough to bring this thing up this river is just the crew I need to be working on," Bill said with a big smile.

It was impossible not to take an immediate liking to him. He and his cousin, who barely spoke, hung out with the men for a while and told stories. Bill had everyone laughing for at least an hour. He reassured the men on deck that they would be off the river and at the boat ramp by the next evening. When he and Waylon were getting ready to head off, he told Joe that he'd stop by in the next day or so, and Joe could let him know about work. The guys all stood by the edge of the barge and watched Bill and Waylon as they headed up river in their small john boat. When they were out of sight, the guys hung around the fire for a few minutes discussing the hillbillies they had just met. They soon gave into their exhaustion and retired to their tents, for, what they hoped, would be the last time. An hour later it started to rain, and didn't stop until midmorning the next day.

The rain came down in sheets, and as the men got ready for their day they conceded that it was too wet to cook, so they packed their stuff away and prepared for another exceedingly unpleasant day. They worked their way back and forth as they moved up the winding river, shivering in the cold rain. There was very little talking on deck, and surely no smiling as the rain pounded them mercilessly. Several hours later they were given a reprieve when the rain stopped, but by then everything and everyone was soaked, short tempered, and hungry.

It was midday when they eased the barge around a wide bend in the river and it began to open up and allow the first rays of sunshine through. They had been under the canopy of the overgrowth for so long that sunshine had barely reached them for days. A five day trip was now on its eighth day, and their cheerful optimism had been replaced with disheartening anguish.

Pete was sulking in the whaler alongside the barge when he saw the sunlight ahead. He couldn't help himself; instinct took over, and like a hungry animal that saw food for the first time in days, he hit the throttle and zoomed away from the barge and into the light. When he was a couple of hundred feet in front of the barge, he came around another bend in the river and it opened up with bright and inviting sunshine. When he got to the bend, it hit him and felt like a warm blanket. He put the boat in neutral and leaned back in the operator seat and basked in the sun's warmth. He heard the barge approaching and Leroy yelling obscenities at him. He sat up in his chair and looked around. He was drifting into a stand of trees, but there in front of him was one of the most beautiful sights he had ever seen: the John Creel I-10 Bridge. Elation filled him, and he raced back to the barge, put his whaler on the starboard corner to prepare for the turn, and with a big smile and incredible sense of relief, he yelled on deck and let them know that the trip was almost over.

A couple of hours later, they tied up the barge and dropped the spuds. While the men were packing their stuff and loading it into the waiting truck that Giles' wife had brought to the ramp, Joe informed them that someone had to spend another night on the barge with the equipment. Giles, Tom, and Jeff were leaving, so that left Leroy, Elliot, and Pete. After drawing straws and some arguing, Leroy and Elliot loaded their stuff in the truck.

Pete felt like he had been kicked in the stomach. He wanted to quit right then and there, but he felt something special towards Joe, and knew that he was right about having someone stay with the equipment. So, he relented, and, as he watched the truck pull away, he felt alone and wanted to cry.

CHAPTER 46

IN LOVE AGAIN

Bill and Anne, having just finished a pleasant dinner at Giuseppe's, strolled hand in hand along the marina, looking at the boats moored there. It was getting late and the restaurant was getting ready to close. There was another couple walking about, but they felt like they were alone in a quaint little wonderland. The stars were bright and the moon and nearby lights shimmered peacefully on the water. The spring air was clean and moved with a gentle breeze. The boats that were secured in their slips rocked gently as small rippling waves lapped at the waterline of the boats, causing a few of the rigging-line clips to clank softly against the aluminum masts of the sailboats. Mooring lines groaned and squeaked as they pulled tight and gently released. The enchanting combination of soft sounds serenaded them as they meandered along the dock lost in their dreams.

The night was gorgeous, and Giuseppe's had become their favorite restaurant since they had rediscovered each other. They had made a custom of enjoying a couple of glasses of wine with their dinner, followed by a stroll on the dock. They leisurely made their way to the end of the dock and sat on the bench looking across Boggy Bayou. They could see the twinkling lights of cars as they slowly traveled along the winding road on the other side of the bayou. While they sat together, quietly enjoying the reflections on the water, Bill wrapped both of his hands around Anne's left hand and it felt good. She felt the embrace of his hands and turned to look at her husband. They gazed at each other for a long moment before he finally spoke.

"Remember how it felt when I had just finished school and we were starting out? It was exciting…, and scary, but we were in love. And we knew that no matter what happened, we could get through it, as long as we were together. Well, I feel that way again. We've been through so much, Anne. The joy we felt with the birth of our sons, and the pain we endured when Isaac died. The struggles we had getting Pete through high school. And then, picking up and moving halfway across the country to some little town that we had never heard of. And after all that, you didn't leave me. I never understood why, but I'm glad you didn't." Bill slid off the bench, dropped to one knee, and reached into his pocket.

Anne thought she knew what was coming and didn't know how to feel. Part of her told her that her husband was acting like a fool, but the overwhelming majority of her body and soul was as giddy and excited as the first time he had taken this pose. When she looked into his eyes, she knew that she was powerless to stop the tears that began welling up from falling down her cheeks.

Bill pulled a small box out of his pocket, opened it, and looked at his wife. "Anne Taylor, will you spend the rest of your life with me? I love you more than I ever thought possible. I want to spend forever with you, and I hope you want to spend forever with me." He was nervous because he knew how much pain he had caused her, and he truly felt unworthy of her love, but he knew he wanted and needed it. He was in love with her, and he needed her to be in love with him.

She glanced at the ring that sat glistening in the box that he held in his hand. It was a strikingly beautiful ring, but her eyes did not stay on it long. She raised her gaze and stared admiringly into her husband's eyes for a long moment before saying a word. All her concerns, pain, and heartache seemed to evaporate and she felt like she was floating on air. He was her partner again, and she was in love with him again. She felt sensations and emotions that had been absent in her life for so long. Relief, happiness, closure, and excitement coursed through her. Tears fell freely and uncontrollably. She took the box out of his hand, looked at it for a moment and then thoughtlessly set it on the bench beside them and quickly wrapped her arms around her husband and tried to squeeze him into her very core. They had been engrossed in their tight and loving embrace for a mere moment when they heard the faintest of splashes, and both of them instantly pulled away from each other and came crashing back to reality.

"OH MY GOD!" Anne quickly let go of her husband and rushed to the edge of the dock, where, kneeling over the side, she saw the little box gently bobbing in the water. A second later, she saw a flash out of the corner of her eye, and then heard a splash as Bill dove in the water. When she saw him surface a few feet away from the box, she didn't know what to do. A big smile, accompanied by a comical sense of satisfaction that she was making the poor man suffer a little more, came across her face as she directed him to the box. He was shaking his head and mumbling under his breath as he grabbed the box and looked up at his wife with his wet hair hanging over his face. Anne could stand it no more, and burst out laughing while looking at him pathetically treading water in his new clothes.

"Now what are you going to do? I don't see a ladder around here, do you? I think you're going to have to swim to shore," she said while making a feeble attempt to sound empathetic and stop laughing.

"I'm going to kill you one day, I swear to God," Bill said lightheartedly as he began the long swim to shore. As he made his way to the bank, he noticed a couple staring at him, but he was too happy to be mad, so he just waved to them and commented on the pleasantness of the weather and how it was a good night for a swim. He was caught up in the moment and loving it. When he finally reached the shore, he was greeted by his wife, who was still laughing. He climbed the small bank and stood dripping in the cool night air.

"Now what are we going to do? We have cloth seats in the car," he said to his wife while enjoying her laughter.

"I guess you're going to have to get naked in the parking lot and ride home in your birthday suit!" she said between laughs. Her laughter stopped abruptly and her eyes grew wide as Bill undid his belt and started taking off his pants.

"I was just kidding," she said while looking around the parking lot for other patrons. "You'll go to jail! Wait here. I'll go ask the waitress. I'm sure they have a towel or two they can spare." She turned and walked back into the restaurant and Bill could hear her quietly laughing as she went.

Bill made his way over to their car, and relieved to still have his keys, opened the trunk. He took off his wet shoes and socks and put them inside, and when he saw Anne emerge from the restaurant with towel in hand, he took off his shirt and put it in the trunk as well. She handed him the towel and he began drying himself. A moment later he heard a cat whistle that came from his wife. He was elated at her flattery and a crazy sudden impulse came over him. He quickly turned his head from side to side and seeing no one else in the parking lot. He gingerly walked over to the driver's side door, dancing on the rocks that hurt his bare feet, and opened the door. He gave one more look around, and satisfied that they were alone for a brief moment, dropped his pants and tossed them to his shocked wife. Bill was standing in the parking lot stark naked. He got into the car and looked back at his wife who was still standing statuesquely with a look of stunned amazement on her face.

"Well, come on, hurry up. Throw those in the trunk and let's go before I get arrested."

"I can't believe you did that. What happens if we get pulled over? You can't drive naked."

"Well, would you prefer I walk home naked?"

Anne put the pants in the trunk, closed the lid, and got in the passenger's side. Bill started the car and began the short ride home. He quietly giggled to himself, and when he saw his wife looking at him with an incredulous look on her face, he decided to share his private joke.

"You know, there are two things that could be a real bitch?"

"What, besides getting pulled over with you sitting there stark naked?"

"Yeah, well, if we do get pulled over, my license is in my pants, so I guess I'd have to get out in order to retrieve it for the officers, and that would be a lot of fun; or, we could get a flat tire, and then either you'd have to change the tire while I sat here, or I'd do it and give all the passing cars a real good show."

"Well, I guess you'd better hope that neither of those things happens, because I'm not getting out of this car until we're safely parked in our driveway. It's too bad Pete and Karen aren't at the house. Oh, I'd love it if they were. I'd make Pete bring you out some dry clothes just to see the look on his face," she said. She turned and looked at Bill. "All right, let me look at my ring. It really did look beautiful."

"What are you talking about? I'm taking it back. It's obvious that you don't want it; after all, you did throw it in the bayou, didn't you?" he asked with a sly grin on his face.

Anne looked at her naked husband driving down the road with his little belly sticking out and couldn't help but enjoy the moment. It was a classic night, and the image of her naked chauffer was engrained in her mind forever. They made the short drive home quickly, and enjoyed the ride immensely. When they pulled into the driveway, Bill was quite relieved to see that Pete was still on the river and not home. The street was quiet and dark, and not a neighbor was seen, so he shut off the car and nonchalantly walked to the back of the car and opened the trunk while Anne walked to the house. He gathered his wet clothes and made his way to the house while Anne stood at the open front door and enjoyed watching her husband make a spectacle of himself. It was quite a change from the angry, self-absorbed drunk that he'd been just a few years ago.

The house was empty and Bill walked into the laundry room, emptied his pockets, and left his wet clothes there. When he came back into the living room, he saw that the patio door was open and Anne was sitting on the lanai with a bottle of wine and two glasses. He thought about getting some clothes on, but decided against it and joined her outside, wearing nothing but his birthday suit. He handed his wife the sodden ring box, uncorked the wine, and poured two glasses while she examined the ring. It had a solid band of tiny diamonds in the center and was wrapped with etched, braided gold.

"You'll need to go into the light and put on your glasses to read the etching," Bill said.

Anne had become very serious, and started crying again as she examined the ring. She rose to her feet, picked up her glass, kissed her husband, and walked into the house. Bill watched anxiously through the glass as she put on her reading glasses and examined the detail of the ring. The solid band of diamonds was wrapped, and seemed to be held in place with three small but distinct braids of gold that held the ring together. When she looked closely at the braids, she could make out the words etched into them. On one braid was the name William, on another was Peter, and on the third she saw Isaac. She held it fondly, and kept admiring it through her teary eyes until a short time later, when she slipped it onto her finger, wiped her eyes, and rejoined her husband on the lanai.

She kissed her husband passionately, wiped her eyes again, and sat down on his naked lap with her arm around his neck.

"Thank you, Bill. I love you so much. It's beautiful," she said as she held out her hand and examined the ring on her finger once more. They drank a toast and enjoyed each other's company. After a short time, Bill looked at his wife and became serious.

"Why did you stay with me when you knew I was doing my best to drive you away?"

Anne looked at her husband and thought for a moment. It was a time to be serious and she knew it. "There are so many reasons, Bill. First off, you're my husband and I knew you were hurting. What happened to Isaac wasn't your fault. Nobody held you responsible for his death except you. We had to raise our Pete, and getting a divorce wasn't going to help him. And also, I took vows, and they meant something to me. When I said 'for better or worse, till death do us part, so help me God,' I took a vow, not just with you, but with God as well. We've been tested, tormented, and put through Hell on Earth, but I think we've made it through, and we did it together. There were times when I held you up, and there were many, many times when you held me up. And remember, you didn't leave me when I became a slobbering pile of goop parked in front of the television either."

They laughed together for a moment and then Bill engulfed his wife in a tight embrace, loving the feel and the smell of her body next to his. After another brief moment, he handed her his wine glass, put his arms underneath her, lifted her, and carried her to their bedroom, where they made love with a passion they had not known for many, many years.

CHAPTER 47

GETTING SETTLED IN

Pete barely closed his eyes that first night. He kept Joe's rifle by his side and spent most of the beautiful evening in his tent waiting for an assault from local drunk hillbillies determined to steal the barge and rape him in the swamp. He had never been alone like this before and his imagination was running wild. He had seen *Deliverance* several times and he didn't want to be Ned Beatty. Sleep avoided him again, but this time it was out of the pure fear of imaginary threats. He came out of his tent only long enough to keep a fire burning in order to make sure that everyone knew that there was someone on board, but he prayed that they didn't know that it was a scared young man who was about to pee his pants every time a coon strolled along the river bank.

While he lay in his sleeping bag staring at the ceiling of his tent, he heard every bug, bird, and animal that night. There were a few people working trot lines on the river and he could hear them talking in their boats as they went past. Most of them were amazed at the barge that had magically appeared, but they had work to do and went about their business. It was a long and chilly night and when the pre-dawn light finally began to break the night, Pete welcomed it whole heartedly. He stretched mightily as he emerged from the tent and quickly went about restarting the fire, wiping the morning dew from his utensils and everything else around him, and then he made some coffee and cooked a few eggs long before the sun rose.

Joe, Jeff, and Leroy arrived mid-morning and Pete had never been so happy to see their ugly faces, and when Joe approached the barge, Pete greeted him warmly.

"Joe, where's this cabin you talked about?" I really hope that shack isn't what you meant," he said while pointing at what could loosely be described as a cabin, but a more accurate description would be an abandoned shack. The outside had remnants of faded green paint on its walls and on the inside the sheetrock had been removed after the last flood. There was still some insulation hanging loosely from the ceilings in a few places and old mismatched pieces of paneling had been put on some of the walls to provide some privacy. The floor was off level and had planks sticking up in some places and missing in various other places, but it did have a kitchen with running water, a bathroom, and electricity.

"Yeah, that's it. Oh, come on; it isn't all that bad. It's better than a tent. We can't use it until next week though. They're having some sort of family reunion this weekend, so there might be a few people running around. I talked with Mr. Jones, who owns the place, and he said a few people might come in Friday night, but most won't get here until Saturday and they should be gone by Sunday night, and then the place is ours until we get done," Joe said.

"Oh great, and how did I get suckered into this one? Are you serious? I have to sleep in there?" Pete protested.

"Well, no, you can sleep in the dirt. I don't care, if that's where you're more comfortable, but come June and July the skeeters are probably going to get pretty ferocious out here and it might be nice to be indoors. Listen, Leroy is going to relieve you for the next couple of days, so you can go home tonight, but I need you to come back on Friday and stay until Sunday. It's going to take a couple of days to get set up; we've got to set piling along the bank and next to the ramp to tie to. I'll take you home with me tonight and bring you back on Friday."

Pete reluctantly agreed and they were soon cleaning up the barge and preparing it for work instead of travel. In the afternoon Giles delivered the Furukawa. It was a one yard loader that was big enough to move the larger rocks, and yet still small enough to maneuver around on the barge. Joe planned to rent a bigger loader to handle the loading, and to use the Furukawa to unload the rocks from the barge.

Bill meandered by in the afternoon and talked with Joe for a while, but Joe had heard every Tom, Dick, and Harry tell him how great they operated machines, so after a minute or two he told Bill to climb on the loader and move some rocks to the bank to make a ramp. Joe watched him run the machine for about an hour and was impressed with his ability to handle it. When Bill climbed down, they talked about pay and after they came to an agreement, Joe told him that they'd put him to work as soon as they got set up. The three man crew for installation was now in place; Jeff would run the boat, Pete the whaler, and Bill the loader.

Pete went home with Joe and Jeff that afternoon. He wanted to go to the dojo and see Karen, but the only thing he could get himself to do was take a long hot shower and lay down on his warm, soft bed; he was asleep immediately and slept soundly until after eight the next morning.

His father was already gone for work by the time he staggered out of bed and into the kitchen. Anne was in the kitchen enjoying a cup of coffee and getting ready to go to work.

"Morning, Mom."

"Well, good morning. I'm so glad you're home. Did you sleep well? You looked so tired and beat up when you came in last night. I heard the shower turn off, and when I went in to talk to you a half hour later, you were sound asleep. Was it a good trip?" Anne had a tone in her voice that Pete hadn't heard in a long time, since before it had happened. He almost didn't recognize her. She looked younger, happier, and quite strange to him. He'd only been gone for a week and it seemed like he had returned from a voyage to a distant planet.

"Are you all right?" He was really concerned and it showed in his voice.

"Of course I'm all right. What's the matter? Don't I look all right to you?"

"Yeah, it's just that.... Well, you seem different and you're starting to scare me. I'm not used to you being a ray of sunshine in the morning. Is there something I should know?"

"Oh, you're just being silly, that's all. Are you hungry? I can whip you up a nice breakfast. Pancakes and sausage sound good to you?" Anne hadn't finished talking before she was up and cooking her son a warm breakfast. They enjoyed each other's company and chit chatted until it was time for her to finish getting ready for work.

Pete listened as she played the radio and sang with some of the songs while doing her makeup and hair. When she left for work singing a tune, Pete felt lost and went onto the lanai to finish his coffee and smoke a joint. While enjoying his peaceful morning, he pondered what he had just witnessed and wondered what other changes were in store for him in this alternate universe that he had returned to.

While he was lounging around and enjoying the sunshine, he looked at the lanai and almost choked. There were burnt candles strategically placed around the lanai and then he saw a few candles sitting on little floats in the pool. His mind raced and the thoughts that entered his mind repulsed him. His parents had been out here and they had done this while he was gone; what else had they done out here? The thought of his parents running around naked in the pool was more than he could stand and he jumped out of the chair like there was a snake in it and went into the house. He went into the shower and tried scrubbing away the visions that were in his mind. Parents fighting and not liking each other he could deal with, but this was just too much.

He dried off and got dressed, and in the odd chance that he might find her home, he decided to call Karen. He put the phone to his ear and listened to it ring. It was answered by her mother.

"Hello, Mrs. Blake, is Karen in?"

"No. Karen's not here. She moved out over the weekend. She decided to go live with her friend Mandy. They're sharing an apartment now. I told her it was a bad idea, but what do I know. Do you want her phone number? And when are you getting into school? Summer semester's coming up soon, you know. You're a smart young man and you really should go to school."

Pete was taken aback. This was totally unexpected- Karen moving out- not the recurring lecture for him to go to school that he got every time he spoke to Mrs. Blake and Mrs. Anderson. He ignored the lecture and stammered when he answered.

"Umm... yes, sure, what is the number? Is everything all right?" he asked.

"Oh sure, it's fine; here's the number..... Now you go up to OWCC and sign up, if not for the summer, at least go this fall!" She was clearly worried about her daughter's decision making of late. She was unhappy that Karen had moved out, but even more so that she was dating- and falling in love with- an uneducated construction worker. When she was done speaking, she hung up the phone without saying goodbye.

Pete hung up the phone and stared into space for a few minutes. He must have been gone longer than nine days. Karen had talked about moving out, but this was quick. Pete dialed the number, not sure what to expect, but was relieved when Karen answered after two rings. She was bubbling over with excitement as she told him about her new place. Pete got directions and was there in half an hour.

When he arrived, she opened the door and gave him a big hug and a quick kiss and then took his hand and led him from room to room, showing off every little thing in the small apartment that made it the greatest place ever. She was very proud of herself and was astounded that they both had gotten the day off.

"Do you know what the greatest thing about this place is, Peter?" she asked.

"No, why don't you tell me."

"We're all alone until 5:30," she said with a big smile on her face. The she took Peter by the hand and led him to the one room she had yet to show him: her bedroom. They closed the door and collapsed on the bed and made love until it was time for Mandy to come home from work.

"When did you decide to move in with Mandy?" Peter asked later in the afternoon while they were snuggled on the couch and watching television.

"Well, last Tuesday, Erin, Mandy's roommate, decided to move in with her boyfriend. Mandy couldn't pay the rent by herself and I'm a working girl now, so I thought it was the right thing to do. We've known each other since high school and it was time for me to get my own place. We can finally be alone now, well, except for when Mandy's here," Karen said as she snuggled tighter to Pete.

"I've got to go back up on the river on Friday and won't be back until Sunday. It sucks, but what can I do? I promised Joe I would do the job, so I've got to keep my word. I'm so excited about camping in a swamp and sleeping on the barge. Yeah." Pete became instantly depressed. He had finally found someone he wanted to be with, she had a great apartment, and now he was going to be alone on the river.

"Maybe I can come up and visit you Friday night. You won't get in trouble, will you?" she asked.

"You want to come up there in the middle of nowhere? And just what are we supposed to do? There's nothing there but a big river and a nasty old shack," Pete complained.

"I thought you told me that there was going to be a cabin on the river," she said as she sat up and looked at Pete, surprised at the tone in his voice. He had been so excited to spend some time in the cabin.

"That place is so nasty; I'm just going to sleep in my tent on the barge. I have no clue what the hell we're going to do, but I'm damn sure that I don't want to sleep in that shack."

"Well, I like camping. So maybe I'll come up there and we can play with your fishing pole and see what comes up." She had a devious look on her face and it got Pete's emotions stirred. He wanted to be excited and to look forward to it, but deep within his soul he felt that it was too good to be true. He was frightened of, and felt undeserving of the happiness he was feeling. He quickly tempered his joy by convincing himself that some tragic event would occur, and the love that he was allowing to creep into his life would all be ripped away. When he'd eradicated any feeling of anticipation that her visit might actually occur from his mind, he forced a faux smile on his face and gave her directions to the cabin to placate her. They sat around for a while longer; she was happily snuggling with him, and he was conditioning himself for the all-too-familiar heart-wrenching pain that he was convinced would soon be returning. After Mandy got home, they ordered pizza and watched TV until Pete went home later in the evening.

Pete pulled into the driveway a little while later, and as he walked up to the front door, he was not sure what to expect. His mom had really scared him that morning. He entered the house and was surprised to see both of his parents sitting on the lanai. There were candles burning around them, the Righteous Brothers were playing softly in the background, and they both had what looked like margaritas in their hands. He looked over at the counter and his suspicions were confirmed by the open bottle of tequila.

What amazed him was that they appeared to be laughing with each other. He wanted to go out and confront them, but he felt so overwhelmed by all the changes around him that he went over to the counter and poured some salt on his hand and took a shot of tequila. He pulled up a barstool and poured himself another and sat and watched them enjoy each other's company for a while, and then quietly, and without a word to his parents, he went to bed. His mind was spinning, and emotions were overwhelming him as he lay in his bed staring at the ceiling. He wanted to be happy, to be in love, but felt that that only happened to other people. He had long ago convinced himself to be frightened of happiness. It made disappointment more tolerable.

On Friday morning, as Pete was getting ready to leave for the boatyard, his father stopped him and called him into the den. He asked Pete to sit down and that scared Pete. He knew he had not seen enough of his parents because he was spending every free moment he had with Karen. He sat and they talked for a while and after a few minutes of conversation, his father asked him for a favor that he was never expecting. When they finished the conversation and Pete left for work, he was in a daze. So much had changed so fast. His two days off had gone by so fast that he hadn't made it to the dojo, even to say hello.

A little while later he was following Joe in his truck to his new home away from home. When he arrived at Caryville, he was surprised at how much the place had changed since he'd left. They had built the ramp out of rocks, had set piling along the shoreline to keep the barge off the bank while the river rose and fell, and they had set other piling near the boat ramp to secure the barge while loading.

The plan for the day was to take the barge down to the bridge and set the dolphins that they were going to use to tie off to while they worked under the bridge. The dolphins were made up of three large piling lashed together, with one higher than the other two to set the lines on.

They set three dolphins across the front of the bridge, but it was late in the afternoon before they finished, so they decided to wait until Monday to start clearing the debris. They pushed back and secured everything for the night. When Joe was satisfied that Pete had everything under control, he told the guys to load up. In a matter of minutes, they were gone and Pete was alone again.

He sat on the barge and threw a line into the water and convinced himself that Karen wasn't coming to see him, but every time he heard a car, he couldn't help but look... just in case. He got bored and decided to make himself busy for a while by cooking some hamburgers, setting up his tent, and building a fire in the barrel. There was a light chill in the air, so he set up a chair next to the fire barrel and after everything that could be done was done, he sat in the chair and smoked a joint as the sun began to set behind the trees. There were boats returning to the ramp and even a couple leaving for a night of fishing, but it was turning into a quiet Friday night in April on the Choctawhatchee River.

It was after dark when he heard a car pull up to the gate. He quickly stood and watched as the car approached. It was hard to make out, but his heart was racing and he knew it was her. When the car came to a stop near the river bank, she got out with a big smile and a sleeping bag under her arm.

"I told you I liked camping," Karen said as she approached the barge. Pete was gleeful as he bounced down the gangplank to greet her. He took the sleeping bag from her and started leading her to the barge when he realized that he hadn't kissed her, so he stopped in his tracks, spun around, and wrapped his arms around her and kissed her passionately.

"Wow. That was a nice recovery. I started wondering when you grabbed my stuff and started walking away, but I have to give you credit, that was a good save. I brought a few treats to eat and a little something to wash it down with." She walked back to her car and reached inside. She proudly turned back towards Pete and held a couple of bottles in the air. "I hope you're in the mood for kamikazes!" she exclaimed.

They walked onto the barge and sat next to the fire, snuggled together under a blanket as the river rolled silently by and the moonlight reflected off the gently flowing water. They talked and drank a couple of kamikazes. A little while later, Pete reached into his shirt pocket and pulled out another joint. Karen had smoked with him a couple of times, but she was not one to indulge very often. Pete, on the other hand, had smoked nearly every day since he had met Jimmy and Wally on that fateful day of fishing in Wilson's stream.

"Do you want to smoke one?" he asked with a devilish little grin.

"No. I don't think I'm going to do that anymore. It's time for me to move on to the next phase of life," she replied in a soft voice as she watched the water roll past them. "You go ahead; it doesn't bother me if you do."

Pete didn't know what to think. He thought about what she had said for a moment. Her comment had caused him a great deal of concern on many levels. "Next phase;" what did that mean? How did her next phase affect him?

"What exactly do you mean, next phase?" he asked directly.

"Well, my father gave me some advice when I started high school. He said the people that seem to be the happiest the longest are those that are willing to embrace and enjoy each phase of life, without clinging onto their previous phase or trying to jump ahead to the next one too quickly. He told me to watch successful people and learn from them. The old people who are happy seem to be the ones who understand that we all go through phases. High school, college, beginning a career, the first tastes of freedom and responsibility, falling in love, starting a family, raising children, having freedom again when the children are grown, finishing our time on Earth, and then starting the next phase on the other side," she said quite peacefully and confidently.

"I like that, but what, you believe in life after death?"

"Oh, I'm quite confident. The fact is that energy can't be destroyed; it can only change forms. When these bodies wear out, I believe that the energy that makes this pile of goop a living being moves on to another form. Now, we can argue where it goes, but the energy continues to exist. And the other thing I've learned is that we just can't make something out of nothing. So, now it's time for me to move out of my college phase and into my career phase….and falling in love phase." She looked up at Pete with a warm smile and kissed him.

Pete looked at her. He was already in the falling in love phase, and no matter how hard he tried, he couldn't stop the adulation that he felt for this woman. He looked at his joint, flicked it into the river, and hugged her. They spent the evening talking about everything and nothing and just enjoyed one of the most peaceful and romantic nights of their young lives. Dew was beginning to gather on them when they decided to go into the tent for the night. They made slow passionate love before drifting into a peaceful sleep.

Pete woke first, aroused before his eyes opened. It was the first time he had spent the night with a woman, and when he looked at the beautiful young woman next to him and felt the warmth of her body next to his, he couldn't resist caressing her firm breasts and pulling her body close to him. She responded warmly to his advances and rolled over to face him. She caressed his face with her hands and brought his lips to hers. He entered her quickly and they were soon swept away with passion. Karen cried out as the waves of orgasm wracked through her body. She dug her nails into Pete's shoulders and this, along with her cries of lust, sent him over the edge. Unable to hold out any longer, he surrendered to the waves of pleasure cascading through him. They were alone in the woods and their passion had become the savage act of wild animals. He slammed his body into hers faster and faster and cried out like a beast as he released himself. He collapsed on top of her and they kissed passionately and held each other for several moments, enjoying the glow that radiated through their bodies.

Karen slid out from under him and prepared to leave the tent. She looked out the window to see what this wonderful day had in store for her. What she saw sent a bolt of lightning through her. She leapt back into Peter's arms and was truly mortified. On the river bank, not twenty feet from their tent, stood a large country woman in an old simple dress, she appeared to be in her late fifties and was happily drinking a cup of coffee and looking at the tent.

"Oh, my God! There's a woman out there. I think she watched us!" she shrieked into Pete's chest. Her mind reviewed every sound that she uttered and every nasty thought that went through her mind. Then she saw an image of her grandmother who would be horrified by what she had done and now she was near panic. She quickly decided that she wanted to die right there from humiliation, and she knew that she was never going to have sex again, ever.

"Well, I hope we put on a good show for her. Maybe we made her day," Pete said with a proud chuckle in his voice. Karen slammed her fist into his chest in mock agitation.

"You are so bad. How can we leave this tent and face them? I have to go home, but I can't leave the tent. Why don't we make a suicide pact? I really, really want to die," she cried. She slowly pulled herself away from Pete and crouched down and tried to look out the window unnoticed. She was relieved to see the woman walking back to the camp site, but as her eyes drifted past the old woman, what she saw terrified her. There had to be forty people gathered and more coming in.

Pete had forgotten to mention the family reunion to her, and when he looked out the window, he was surprised to see how many people were outside. Karen snuggled up next to him and as they peered out the window together, Karen pointed out the woman who had watched their exhibition. Pete looked at the woman and then at Karen.

"Well, it looks like she has a bunch of kids; I wonder how she got them? My guess is that she has done the nasty dance once or twice herself. Who knows, we probably brought back some happy memories," he said with a chuckle.

Karen was still mortified and it took some time, but eventually they came out of the tent and started cooking breakfast while doing their best to pretend nothing out of the ordinary had happened. A while later, three little girls from the reunion began fishing near the barge, and while they fished, they struck up a conversation with Pete and Karen. After learning all about the annual family reunion and the aunts, uncles, and cousins, the two of them were invited over to the party for lunch, and as often as they tried to decline, they found themselves unable to deter the little girls who were insistently waving their arms while holding their fishing poles.

Pete and Karen were introduced to everyone and quickly handed a big plate of food and a cold glass of sweet tea. They were surprised by how welcome they were made to feel, and how much they enjoyed the company and the food. They had a lunch of fried fish, hushpuppies, and potato salad, but to the disappointment of one of the ladies, they both declined the collard greens and okra.

Karen got over her humiliation and Pete was pleasantly surprised when he was able to convince her to stay until Sunday. They spent another primitive, but great night together holding each other tightly as they sat next to the fire and gazed at the immense sky above them. Pete knew that he was hopelessly and helplessly in love and he had reluctantly given up fighting the relentless emotion, and instead he embraced it and felt comforted by the warmth he felt, and by her. They gazed at the stars for hours and later retired to the tent where Karen enthusiastically relented on her vow of celibacy.

CHAPTER 48

THE JOB

O n Monday morning they started work in earnest. Joe, Jeff, and Leroy were on site before seven and they had the barge under the bridge and in position by 9AM. Their first task was to clear the accumulated debris from under the bridge. During numerous storms and floods over the years, trees and various types of trash had collected around the pilings, and before they could make a new river bed, they had to clean the area.

Among his other talents, Joe was a commercial diver, and because he would have to be underwater for an extended period of time, he brought his dry suit and hard hat to the site. Joe handed out assignments: Jeff in the crane, Bill and Leroy rigging. Pete had two jobs; they were simple, but important. He was to man the radio, communicating with Joe and relaying his commands to Jeff, but his most important task was to guard the air compressor and never, ever let it stop running.

Pete had never seen anyone hard hat dive before and was intrigued by what he saw as they prepared for the excursion. When all the equipment was tested and Joe was satisfied that everything was as safe as he could make it, he put on the hard hat. Pete watched Jeff screw the hat tight to his suit, and when Joe started to move into position to go overboard,

Pete decided that he looked like something out of a Jules Verne novel from a hundred years ago. He looked at the air and radio lines attached to Joe's helmet that led to coils of lines lying on the deck and wondered what would happen if they got tangled in the debris. The crew was excited to begin, but Pete was reluctant and melancholy as he watched Joe go overboard and disappear into the muddy river. He said a little prayer for Joe's safety, and knew that he could never do anything like that. The thought of being submerged and tangled at the bottom of the river made him shiver, and he knew that he'd never let his grave be the bottom of a river.

They were soon pulling debris from the bottom, and when Pete looked over at Leroy and Bill, he was happy to be on radio and compressor detail because as they wrestled with everything from large trees to washing machines, they became camouflaged with a layer of slimy muck that enshrouded everything they brought to the deck of the barge. They kept at it without complaint, and by the end of the day they had cleared more than half of their work area and were rewarded for their efforts with a barge full of pungently aromatic garbage. When Joe came back on deck, he was surprised at how much trash had been collected. He got out of his suit as quickly as he could, and they were soon on their way back to the boat ramp to unload.

Joe had brought a bed, some insulation, and paneling, and while Bill and Leroy unloaded the barge, Joe, Jeff and Pete worked on the cabin, and by the time they were finished they had the makings of a room that Pete could reluctantly sleep in. He was convinced that this was to become his new home and he didn't like it at all.

When the others left him for the night, he made his bed, walked around, and looked at his dilapidated surroundings and was extremely distressed. The air was filled with the smell of mildew and rotting wood, the floor was made up of twisted old planks, and he could see bugs flying freely through the holes in the walls. To break the silent monotony, he turned on the radio, hoping to find something to listen to. After going up and down the dial several times, the only station that he was able to hear was playing "Delilah" and her romance advice. It made him think about Karen and her new apartment with Mandy, the party animal, while he was alone in this shack in the middle of nowhere. He had a long and unpleasant night.

The second day went much like the first except that Jeff had to finish a project in Fort Walton Beach and Mike took the day off so that he could join in the adventure. Leroy and Bill were coated with slime and the barge was a mess, but they were working together as a team and making the best of a nasty situation.

About an hour after lunch, Pete heard Joe call on the radio, "There's a huge dead head down here. We might've found some real treasure. It has to be ten or twelve feet tall. It's going to take me a while to figure out how to rig this thing up."

Pete relayed the message to Mike, and several minutes later Joe gave the order to start lifting. Mike gave the crane some throttle and pulled back on his controls. The barge listed severely and the crane bogged down, but the stump didn't move. Mike eased off the levers, momentarily disengaging with the stump, and when the barge had returned to level, he took a deep breath and gave the crane full throttle. It screamed determinedly while emitting a large plume of black smoke from its exhaust. Mike pulled back on the lift controls again and this time the barge listed quickly and deeply. The crane started to slip and slide in the muck on deck, but Mike was fearless and kept pulling. He soon began pushing and pulling the house control lever as well in order to move the house from side to side in an attempt to wiggle the stump loose from the bottom.

Pete saw the crane slipping towards the edge of the barge and was overtaken with panic as he stood helplessly watching. He knew Jeff and his ability to operate the crane, and Pete had confidence in him, but he hadn't worked with Mike before, and as he watched pure determination overtake Mike, Pete was afraid that he and the crane were going over the side. Without thinking, he started running towards Mike, waving his hands frantically and yelling for him to stop. Mike saw him out of the corner of his eye and waved him off while shaking his head as he continued ripping and snorting. Pete stopped running, lowered his hands, and turned back towards the compressor. He was embarrassed for panicking and the subsequent rebuke he had received, but as he walked back to his duty-station he was still worried about Mike's safety. He had seen death on a river, and he didn't want to see again. His little brother was a tragic accident, but this was insanity. If that crane went over the side, Mike could never get out, and Joe would probably be crushed as well as it sank to the bottom.

He looked over at Bill and Leroy standing by the pile of debris. They had enjoyed the spectacle that Pete had made of himself; Leroy was laughing out loud, and Bill was just shaking his head.

He had just skulked back to the compressor and was reaching down to check the gas when he felt the barge shift violently under his feet. The stump had broken free, and when it came out of its hole, the barge popped like a cork.

Everyone was relieved, but they all knew they still had a lot of work to do before they were done. Mike pulled back on the levers and lifted it slowly from the bottom. The crane was screaming and the barge began listing dramatically again as Mike expertly worked his machine. Pete was watching him intently, still convinced that the crane was going to flip over before he could lift the massive stump on deck. He desperately wanted to run over to the crane and stop this nonsense, but he stood firm. After another moment, he decided that he could watch it no more, and turned away, concentrating on the compressors air gauges. He knew that Mike wasn't going to stop until the stump was on deck or he was on the bottom. The stump was slowly rising from the bottom, but it was taxing the limits of the machine and everyone knew it.

Bringing the stump to the surface was a slow process, and when it finally broke the surface of the water, Pete looked over toward Bill and Leroy. Bill was watching Mike closely, and it was clear that he enjoyed every moment of the epic battle; Leroy had moved over to the edge of the barge and was staring in amazement at the size of the prehistoric stump. It looked too big to fit in a dump truck and would probably require a tractor trailer to move. Mike paused for a moment to let the water and mud drain and then slowly he swung the crane around and placed it on deck.

They unrigged the stump and spent the next hour finishing their work around the pilings, and when Joe was satisfied that they had a clear work area, he came to the surface. They untied the barge and went back upriver and offloaded. Mike helped unload the giant stump with the crane, and when it was onshore, Joe was happy and convinced that he could dry it out and sell it for several thousand dollars. He didn't want to admit it to the guys- just yet - but he was also very pleased with what they had accomplished over the last couple of days.

Mike walked the crane off the barge and they repeated the process from the day before, with Leroy and Bill cleaning the barge while Mike, Joe, and Pete worked on the cabin. They made another bedroom habitable as Jeff was to become Pete's new roommate. He was going to stay for the week and return to his family on weekends. Pete was relieved when Joe told him that Bill had agreed to stay in the cabin on weekends so that he could go home and see Karen too.

On Wednesday they installed the turbidity curtain and started moving rocks. The first two thousand tons to be placed were the base rock. It took them two weeks to put in the rock and cover it with a layer of filter weave. Jeff, Pete, and Bill began to work together seamlessly. Jeff was smooth and sure with the boat and methodically backed under the bridge at a very controlled pace. Pete began to understand the currents and the effects of the wind on the movement of the barge. He started reacting by instinct and was able to put his nose boat in the right place and keep the bow where it needed to be. Bill was fearless with the loader. He scared Pete as much as Mike did, he would run it to the edge of the barge, stop on a dime, toss the rocks out of the bucket, and back up and do it again with such a relaxed and casual attitude that he looked like he could fall asleep at any moment. His tires would get so close to the edge that Pete would cringe and was forced to continuously control the urge to jump up and stop him. He eventually just stopped watching Bill altogether and looked at Jeff or searched the bank for a gator or two while they were unloading. When he heard the loader idle down, he knew it was time to go.

When they had finished installing the base rock, the DOT sent inspectors to dive on the bottom and verify the placement. Jeff and Pete assisted them, and when they were done with the inspection, they were very proud of the positive review of their work. They were gaining in confidence; the river was cooperating and they began to feel optimistic. They began talking about being able to place the seven thousand tons in the next sixty days and possibly being back in Valparaiso by the fourth of July. Pete and Bill were so confident in their success that they were already spending their bonus money in their minds. Bill needed a car, and Pete wanted to buy Karen something shiny and made of gold.

The next three weeks went wonderfully. The weather seemed to be cooperating with them and blessed them with sunshine every day. They were taking heavy loads and were meeting their quota and then some.

Joe had driven up to check on progress several times and was disturbed to see some nefarious looking people spending a little too much time checking out their operation while the barge was down river. He decided to bring Bonehead to the cabin, fix the fence, and build a gate for fear of people stealing their stuff while the cabin was unattended. Bonehead made an immediate difference. When people came too close to the perimeter, he would viciously run toward the fence with his white teeth bared, snarling and barking. He was determined to protect his territory and very quickly curbed most people's curiosity.

Pete and Jeff made the cabin livable and Pete was finally beginning to enjoy his adventure on the river. Jeff was a good roommate and a good cook. He wasn't like the other construction workers he had gotten to know; he was an intelligent man who could talk about more than sports, beer, and women. They had long conversations about everything from religion to history and politics, and Pete enjoyed learning things he had never even thought about. He was surprised and impressed with Jeff's strong conviction and faith. Their long discussions made him contemplate his future and his place in the world. He wanted to do something with his life, but he still wasn't sure what it was. He had learned one thing: nothing gave him more pleasure than operating a boat. He was getting to know and understand the river, how she moved and meandered down to the gulf. Sometimes she was in a hurry and rushed to the ocean, knocking over trees and houses and anything that got in her way. Other times, like now, she seemed to take her time and drifted lazily and peacefully.

Pete had grown to love the morning push down the river. At the corner of the first turn in the very top of an old dead tree was an eagle's nest. Joe had pointed it out to him on their first push down the river, and he had begun a morning ritual of looking towards the sky with anticipation, hoping to see her flying overhead. He had never ceased to be awed by her beauty as she glided on her morning hunt. Nature was all around him, on the riverbank or moving along the sides of the river, and he loved it. He was always able to spot a few gators lounging about and was amazed at the size of some of the prehistoric creatures. And, having grown up in Connecticut, he hadn't thought that there were as many gators on Earth as he had seen in the Choctawhatchee over the last few months.

IT WAS NOW LATE SPRING and starting to get hot during the day, with temperatures rising into the mid-eighties. The combination of heat and lack of rain had the river elevation starting to drop slowly and steadily. They started the day like every other. The barge was loaded and they were on their way down river by mid-morning. They were lazily coasting along on a straight stretch of the river, enjoying the ride and listening to Bill tell stories of the many different ways he had eaten possum, turtle, and gator, when, unexpectedly, the barge came to a quick and abrupt halt in the middle of the river. Jeff's belly went into the wheel of the *Osage* and he spilled his coffee, Bill stumbled, and the loader lurched. The abrupt halt to the forward motion of the heavily loaded barge combined with the river current caused the stern of the barge to quickly start pivoting to the side and brought the *Osage* and her props dangerously close to the river bank.

Jeff was caught off guard and instantly filled with frustration because he knew what had happened and what was in store for them. He looked at the waterline along the riverbank and was mad at himself for not realizing how much the river had dropped in elevation. Jeff looked at Pete, gave him the signal, and instantly the boat motors were screaming again; Jeff pulled and Pete pushed, and together they worked feverishly in an attempt to counter the momentum of the heavy barge. Eventually, they were able to stop its sideways motion and get it centered on the river again. They pulled and pushed with everything they had, but the barge wouldn't move off the stump.

Jeff ordered Bill to start moving rocks on deck in order to shift its weight from the bow to the stern, but after almost an hour of moving rocks, they still hadn't come loose. Jeff nervously looked around for any boats coming up or down the river and saw none.

"Over the side," he yelled towards Bill.

"What are you wantin' me to do?" Bill asked to make sure he had heard him correctly. He'd known they'd have to do it as soon as they hit the stump, but he wasn't putting anything in the river without a direct order.

"Start dumping rocks. We've got to lighten the load. Spread them out as you go; we don't want to build a pile of rocks in the middle of the river that'll chew up the props on our next trip." Jeff was nervous. He didn't want to get in trouble for dumping the rocks, but there was no other way to get off the stump and he knew it.

"All righty then; I'm on it. You just yell when you want me to stop dumpin'." Bill ran back to the loader and started dumping rocks. Jeff and Pete kept the barge moving from side to side and Bill rarely dumped in the same place twice. When Bill had put about twenty tons of rock over the side, they were relieved to feel the barge start to move. Two buckets later and they were backing off the stump.

"Mark that stump," Jeff yelled to Pete and Bill.

Joe had foreseen the very real possibility of this event happening and had stocked the barge with several buoys. Bill grabbed one and tossed it into the whaler while Jeff kept backing the barge up river. Pete quickly maneuvered his boat to the area that he thought the stump was located and felt around with his sounding rod. When he found the stump, he threw the buoy over the side. When Jeff saw the location, he put the boat in forward and slowly and carefully maneuvered around it and then resumed the trek down river.

"Bill, check the compartments and see if we poked a hole in it," Jeff yelled. He was resigned to the fact that the barge would be leaking, he was just hoping it wasn't too bad. Bill got a flashlight and lifted the hatch cover and looked inside the compartment. He popped his head up quickly and looked at Jeff.

"We got us a geyser in thar! I'm gonna start pumpin' that one before I even bother checkin' the others cause it's comin' in pretty fast." He then dragged the pump over and started pumping the water back into the river.

After Bill had inspected the other compartments and found no leaks, he went inside the leaking compartment to inspect the hole. It was hot and extremely loud inside the barge with the boats running outside and the pump echoing above him. The water was about six inches deep and rising fast. Bill quickly put a plywood patch over the hole and braced it with a 2x4. The leak continued to slowly seep water, but they would survive until the end of the day when they could patch it properly. They made their way down river and unloaded the barge without another incident. When they finished moving rock for the day, Jeff broke out his dive gear.

"Well, at least I haven't seen any gators around the boat ramp. I don't think they like all the boat traffic and the people around here," Jeff said to Bill and Pete. He was actually trying to reassure himself and build his own confidence. While he, too, enjoyed watching the gators along the bank, he was not thrilled with the idea of swimming with them.

Bill looked at Jeff for a moment while scratching his beard, and then with a sheepish look on his face, he said, "Well, I've been meanin' to tell you somethin'. You see, last weekend when I borrowed the boat and took Donna fishin', we was right over thar on the other side of the railroad tracks and there weren't nobody around. Well, I seen this big old gator just a few feet from the boat, and since I'd brought my twelve gauge to 'protect Donna,' I didn't think there was anything else I could do, so I shot him in the head. Well, I'll tell you what; that was one pissed off gator. I don't think I did more than just give 'em a damn good headache. He splashed around for a while and then went under and I lost track of him after a bit. I've been lookin' for him every day, but I ain't seen him again. I know I didn't kill 'em, so he might have just moved along somewhere else on account of this being such a bad neighborhood and all." Pete and Jeff stopped what they were doing and stared at him in amazement.

"Bill, are you telling me there's a pissed off gator wandering around with buckshot in his head, and now I have to go swimming with him?" Jeff asked.

"Well, yeah, that's kinda the long and short of it, but I wouldn't worry too much about it. Hell, it won't do no good to worry anyhow," Bill said as he held up the dive tanks for Jeff to climb into. Jeff looked at Pete, and, like a lamb to slaughter, he turned around and let Bill put the tanks on his back.

"Well, hell, why don't you just teach me how to dive and I'll go under there for ya? I always wanted to try that diving stuff. I think it'd be pretty cool to be swimmin' around with the gators, sharks, and other little sea creatures," Bill said. He looked over at Pete before continuing, "Hell, Pete, why ain't you in the water? You been working for these boys long enough, you should be under there."

"I don't dive, and I don't jump out of perfectly good airplanes either," Pete said. There was a tone of finality in his voice, but Bill couldn't leave it alone.

"Come on, now, we all got to die some time. I just can't understand it; you live in Florida, work on boats all day, and you don't dive. That's kind of like ownin' a brothel and not likin' girls, ain't it? Me, I want to learn to dive 'cause I figure this here planet's about two thirds water and that water is miles deep in places with fish at every level. There just has be a whole lot of really cool stuff swimmin' around down there that I need to take a look at. If I see somethin' that wants to eat me, I figure what the hell, I think they're delicious and they think I'm delicious. It might be fun to see who eats who first," Bill explained with a happy grin.

"You know, this conversation is not really what I want to hear when I'm about to swim blindly under this barge," Jeff interjected. He then looked at Bill and continued, "Why don't you go get your patch ready inside, and let's get this over with?"

Bill shrugged and went inside the barge while Jeff eased himself into the water and under the barge. Jeff didn't like diving on the river at all. His visibility was limited to about an inch in front of him because of the silt flowing downstream that made the river a chocolaty mess. Groping in the darkness and following the taps Bill was making, he tried to make his way to the hole. Thoughts of the mad gator kept running through his mind, and he knew that if he was attacked, the only thing he would ever see was teeth and tongue. He fought to control his emotions and continued to feel his way along the bottom of the barge as he made his way farther and farther underneath it. Claustrophobia started to set in and he wanted out, but he kept searching for the stick and the light to show him the hole. Eventually he found it, they patched the barge, and he came out from under the barge, very relieved to be done.

When he got out of the water, he saw that Bill and his car were gone. He immediately started to get mad, assuming that Bill had already gone home for the night and snapped at Pete.

"Where the hell is Bill?" he demanded.

"He went to get beer."

Jeff calmed down almost instantly. He thought about it for a moment and decided that Bill was a genius, and that it was indeed a good day to drink a few beers. He flung off his tanks and climbed up the bank and then he and Pete put away his gear. They were just finishing when Bill pulled back into the yard. When he got out of his car, Pete noticed that he was carrying two twelve packs of beer.

"Why did you buy two twelve packs, instead of just getting a case? Isn't it cheaper by the case?" he asked.

"Well, yes it is. But you Yankees don't really know that much about beer and I'm betting that you probably want it cold."

"What the hell are you talking about?" Pete asked

"All you Yankees want cold beer, right?"

"Yeah, of course I want cold beer; the colder the better," Pete said.

"Where did they invent beer?" Bill asked.

"I don't know, where?"

"In Europe; and how do they drink their beer?" Bill continued his line of reasoning.

"I don't know, Bill, how do they drink their beer in Europe?" Pete played along.

"Warm. They don't drink cold beer in Europe, and I figure if they invented it, they should know how to drink it. Yes, sir, I like warm beer and cold coffee." He paused for a moment, and then figured he should explain the cold coffee, because Jeff and Pete were looking at him kind of funny. "I got to likin' that cold coffee when I was doing that over the road truckin' with my cousin Bobby Joe. He's a crazy son of a bitch, that one is. His thermos wasn't worth a damn, and before long the coffee was cold, but we couldn't stop, so we would drink cold coffee and eat a handful of black beauties and off we'd go. We made good money, but he was dangerous as hell and I had to get out of the truck and away from him before we kilt each other. Anyways, I bought the two twelve packs, one cold for you two, and this here warm one for me," Bill finally concluded.

"You are hillbilly to the core, aren't you?" Pete asked with a laugh as he popped open a beer and handed one to Jeff.

"Well, I'm from Boonestown, Kentucky, and I bailed my momma outta jail for bootleggin'! To tell you the truth, we was way out in the woods when I was growin' up. I really didn't know how far out in the woods we were until my grandma came back from visiting my older sister in Louisville. It was the first time in her life that she left the Holler. She came back, and we was sittin' around talkin' an' such when I asked her, 'Granny, how'd you like it up there in Louisville?' She looked at me with this plum crazy look on her face and said, 'It was all right, but you know, them people is kinda disgustin'.' So I said 'Grandma, what do you mean they're disgusting?' She looked at me and said, 'They use the bathroom in the house!!!' That's when I knew for sure that we was livin' too far out into the woods."

They all laughed at his story and then Jeff asked, "How long have you been here in Caryville?"

Bill finished his beer and popped open another before answering. "Oh, a few years now; my mom's sister moved down here years ago, and finally convinced momma to come down after Granny died. My dad had died years before, and once she got down here, she kept trying to get me to come down too."

"Is that why you finally came down, to be with your mom?" Pete asked, enjoying Bill's story.

"No, not exactly; to tell you the truth, it was about three in the morning when I heard this pretty good poundin' on my door. Scared the shit out me, and I wasn't sure what the hell was goin' on, and when I opened the door, it didn't get any better, 'cause standin' on my front porch just as bright as sunshine was a couple of deputies. They came on in and made themselves right at home, and then they 'advised' me to relocate in the nice sociable way that the police do when they come to your house at that time of the mornin'. I thought about it for a very short time, and decided that they was givin' me some good advice, and so right then and there, I agreed with them and decided to see what was going on in Florida."

"What the hell did you do to piss them off so bad?"

"Hell, I was the competition. See, you got to understand, Boone County is poor. Not like these wannabe poor people around here, I mean really poor - Granny still uses the outhouse poor - so the people growin' dope and bootleggin' and such ain't doin' it to get rich. They're doin' it to eat. When my momma found my dope, it wasn't much, just a couple of pounds; she was madder than a stirred up hornet's nest, but when she found out how much money I got for it with just a few seeds and a little patch out back, she wanted in. Now Momma could grow some damn good tomatoes, so she figured what the hell, she'd get a lot more money for dope than tomatoes. So she asked me to get her some seeds. I tried to tell her how to grow it, but she told me to get on my way." Bill paused to take a long draw from his beer before continuing, "Well, several months passed; I didn't think anything more about it till one day she calls me and says she's got some dope for me to get rid of. I figured she'd grown a few plants, and I'd pick 'em up and drive to the other side of town and she'd get a couple of hundred bucks, but when I got there she had so much dope that I told her that I didn't think it'd fit in my truck. She tells me to get out of the way, and proceeds to started loading it like it was loose hay or something. She filled the back of my pickup till it was overflowin'. I mean to tell ya, she had plants ten feet long with big ol' buds hangin' out all over the place. I tried to tell her that it was illegal and we just couldn't go driving around town with a pickup truck full of dope. Well, she didn't want to hear none of it, and got all snippety like, and told me to get a tarp and cover it up if I was so worried about it. She tells me that there ain't nobody going to bother her in this town, and I'll tell you what, when she gets going, there ain't no stopping her unless you hog tie or shoot her. Well, we got a tarp over the dope, but there was still a mess of it sticking out everywhere. I told her that I really didn't want to do this, because a man could go to jail for a long time with a load like the one we had, but she told me to get in the truck and then she jumped in the other side. Now let me tell you, I wasn't sure what to do at this point, because what self-respectin' dope dealer brings his momma to the sale? But I can't stop her, and so off we go." Bill finished his beer and popped another. "Sure enough, we just get through the center of town and what do I see and hear but blue lights and sirens. I about pissed myself, and it didn't get any better when I looked in the mirror and saw that it was Sheriff Wiley G. Haines himself getting out of the car. I'm figurin' I'm screwed for sure; I'm gonna be bubba's love toy. Well, before I can do anything, Momma jumped out of the truck and went out there with old Sheriff Haines and got right up in his chest. Remember, Momma ain't but maybe 5'2 and ninety five pounds soakin' wet on a good day, and old Sheriff Haines is a big old boy over six feet tall, and she said, 'Wiley, what are you bothering me for? I changed your diapers before you could walk.' It was the funniest thing I ever saw. He looked at her all sheepishly like and said,

'I'm sorry Mrs. Price, but you can't go driving through town with this stuff just blowin' around like this. It ain't cotton. Somebody's likely to say something.' And then the damndest thing you ever seen happened: him and Momma started walking around the truck tucking in all the dope and retying the tarp! Next thing I know, she climbs back in the truck and off we go down the road again. Damndest thing I ever been a part of. Now, make no mistake, if I was by myself, I would have been in a world of shit. Well, Momma grew one more crop and then moved down here. After a couple of crops of my own and getting chased for bootleggin' enough times- they never could catch me on them back roads- they decided that they didn't like the competition anymore and gave me the choice of getting in the car with them or getting in my car and out of the holler. It seemed like a real easy decision at the time, and they were nice enough to let me take enough gas money to get here too." Bill shook his head with a smile, finished his beer, and opened another.

Pete loved the stories. He had never met a real hillbilly before and Bill was the greatest story teller he'd ever met. The day had been long and hard, the beer was cold and tasted good, and he desperately wanted to hear more, so he got another beer for Jeff and asked another question.

"Where do you go drinking around here?" Pete asked, hoping it would lead to another long tale.

"Well, I used to go to Jo Jo's, but I guess I got banned from there again for a couple of months."

"How the hell did you get banned from a redneck bar in the middle of nowhere?" Jeff asked.

"Well, it's kind of a long story," Bill said to nobody's surprise. "You see, me and Donna and Waylon went out and did some fishin' one day and we seen some baby gators swimmin' around in the water. We was pretty drunk at the time, and I looked around a bit and didn't see momma gator, so I decided to go catch one. Well, Waylon jumped in the water with me and we waded about eight or ten feet from shore, chasin' them little buggers around. I finally caught one and tossed it up to Donna, and do you know what? They make this high pitched squeal when they are in trouble. I did not know this! It didn't take long to figure out who it was a-callin', and I figured that momma was a-comin' and she was probably gonna be pissed too. Instead of throwing the screamin' little monster back in the water, Donna runs up to the truck and decides that it's her baby now. We kept yellin' for her to throw it back, but she says 'Hell, no!' This was her baby and she wasn't givin' it up. We were in water up to our armpits an' tryin' to get out as fast as we could. I may have a fat little body, but you might be surprised how fast I can move when I think a big ol' gator is comin' for me, and as you know, Jeff, what scares the tar out of ya' is that ya' can't see 'em coming in this here muddy river. I was pretty sure that I was gettin' eaten that day, but to my surprise, we got to live. Well, Donna decided she had to go down to Jo Jo's and show all her buddies her new pet." Bill once again paused to get a new beer before continuing.

"Well, she takes it into Jo Jo's and lays this little eighteen inch baby gator on the bar and says 'I'll take a beer, and one for my friend too.' Well… all them people thought it was the cutest thing they'd ever seen, and I figured if they liked that little bitty gator, then I'd really make their day. The next day I go and catch me one. Only mine is a little bit bigger. I put on my trench coat and stick the gator under it. Its head is up at my shoulder and its tail is down at my feet. I go into Jo Jo's and flop that thing on the bar and ordered a beer for the two of us…. The reaction was not quite the same as she got."

"People started fallin' backwards on chairs and stumbling around, yellin' and screamin' all kinds of shit, but they was pretty much okay until I took the strap off his snout. Then they got all pissed off, somethin' about public safety and shit like that. Ol' Big Bob the bartender decides to kick me out of the bar, so I started to leave. Then he starts yellin' at me to take the gator with me. I explained to him that he kicked me out of the bar for bein' an asshole, but the gator hadn't done nothing to be kicked out fer, so I left. They told Donna that they never wanted to see me in there again, but I'll guarantee you that the Johnson boys, who got rid of the gator for Big Bob, ate good that night. Me and Big

Bob go through this on a regular basis. I figure I should wait another month or so before I go back though; he was in a serious bad mood the last time I saw him." Bill took a breath, crumbled his can, and opened more beers for the group.

"Bill, I'm pretty sure that you've completely lost your mind, but I have to admit, you do seem to have fun and have done some crazy shit, haven't you?" Pete asked. He and Jeff were clearly enjoying the stories.

"Well, I'll tell you this. You only got one shot on this here planet and you got two choices. You can go get one of those nice safe jobs and drive to the same place every day, and eat the same food, and go to bed at the same time and have a pleasant little existence, but that's all it is… existin'. It aint livin'. Or you can throw your hat in the ring and grab the bull by the horns and go for a ride. Ya never know; you just might be able to get that eight second ride, but you won't ever know unless you're willin to get bucked off. Me, I'm goin' for the ride. I choose livin' over existin'," he said and finished another beer.

They sat around and Bill told a few more stories, and a short while later the beer was gone. Bill had finished his twelve beers in about the same time that Pete and Jeff had finished theirs and when Pete looked at Bill, he could swear that he was more sober than them. It was as if he were immune to the effects of beer. They soon said their good-byes and went to bed.

By the end of the following week, they had marked four more stumps, patched three holes, and were down to moving less than fifty tons per trip. No rain was expected for another week or two. Progress was so slow that Joe decided to pull Jeff and Pete off the job and put them to work back in Niceville. Bill agreed to move into the cabin as long as he could bring his hog dog Precious with him. He loved his dog, and since getting to know Bonehead, he had become convinced that he was the toughest and smartest little dog he'd ever met. He was convinced that Precious and Bonehead would get along really well, especially since she was going into heat.

CHAPTER 49

BACK TO WORK

The river job had been shut down for four weeks and it was now near the end of July. Joe had appealed for extra days on the contract, but was denied. Lack of water was not the state's problem and the penalties would begin September 1 as scheduled. Pete had stayed with his parents during this time, and it was hard getting used to seeing them doting over each other. He was young and in love, and his desires and behaviors were quite normal in his opinion, but his parents were old, and they hated each other. Seeing his parents looking at wedding dresses and acting like young lovers was unexpected, and it threw him for a loop. He liked it, but he didn't understand it.

They would sneak little pecks on each other's cheeks at every opportunity, and were often huddled together going over plans and ideas for the big event. They had started walking together, going to church on Sunday mornings, and Pete had even heard his father grunting and groaning while doing sit-ups in his bedroom. It was a strange environment for Pete. It was just a couple of months ago that he was wondering if his mom was having an affair. He had gone out with Leroy and Elliot and had briefly stepped into Billy's one night and saw her sitting and talking with another man. He was in and out quickly and she never saw him. He never mentioned it, because given the condition of his parent's marriage since Isaac's death, he didn't blame her and had actually been expecting them to get a divorce for years. He hadn't realized how numb and distant they had grown from each other until he now saw how close they were again.

He and his parents were embracing life, and for the first time since his little brother had died, he felt like he was part of a real family again. He was enjoying his time off the river and spent every free moment with Karen or in the dojo.

During the down time, Bill stayed at the cabin and spent most of his time running trot lines for catfish, but he had made a few trips down to Valparaiso and had gotten his diving lessons from Joe while working at the boat yard. Pete was in love and enjoyed the down time, but everyone else was tired and frustrated and ready to get back to work and finish the job. Joe was losing money every day that the job sat idle, and he grew grumpier and grumpier with every passing day.

It was a great relief to all when the storm clouds filled the sky and the rain finally came. Joe and Jeff were excitedly making plans and getting ready to go back to the river when Giles quit. He had shown up late one too many times and gotten into an argument with Joe, so they'd mutually agreed that it was time for him to get another job. They'd started to build a marina and boardwalk on base and Giles was the foreman when he left. It was a large job and his leaving put Joe and Jeff in a terrible bind and they finally decided that Jeff would stay in Niceville to complete the job and Joe would have to find some new help for the river job. Joe asked Bill if he knew anyone local that wanted to work and was relieved when Bill said he knew a boy. He warned Joe that he didn't know much, but he'd work hard and learn quickly.

Joe was relieved when Bill called a week later and informed him that the river was finally high enough to move the barge. Joe told him to have the barge ready first thing in the morning. He then informed Pete, who was very disappointed, and they left for Caryville at first light. Pete followed Joe in his truck, and by the time they got to the cabin an hour later, Bill had the barge loaded and the boats running. They had thirty days to move three thousand tons of rock. It was going to be hard, but not impossible.

Bill was standing by the cabin door with a cup of iced coffee in his hand as they drove up. He was wearing his customary ball cap, unbuttoned red flannel shirt with the sleeves cut off and old blue jeans. Bonehead and Precious almost knocked him over as they burst out of the cabin and ran past him and towards their trucks as they approached, Bonehead wagging his tail, rejoicing at seeing his friends again, and Precious barking and growling menacingly at the strangers she had yet to meet.

Precious was big and solid. She had muscular legs, short golden hair, and large white teeth. Pete instantly saw why Bill bragged that she was the best hog dog around. He pulled his truck to a stop and was looking at the dog through the window of his truck and jumped back from the door as she jumped and scratched at his door with teeth bared, determinedly trying to protect her territory. Pete got over his initial shock and was quickly convinced that this stout animal was indeed the right dog to send into the woods with an angry boar that was fighting for its life. He sat in his seat and watched the dog going nuts, amused by her behavior, but not willing to get out of his truck until Bill tied her up. Bill was enjoying the show and took his time as he approached them with his customary smile, quite proud of his dog's show of ferocity. Pete was astounded that when he finally did yell to her, she immediately stopped jumping on the truck and walked right over to Bill, wagging her tail like an innocent little puppy.

Once she was secured, Joe and Pete got out of their trucks and gathered near the cabin where Joe explained what they needed to accomplish and how much time they had to get it done. Pete and Bill quickly agreed to work seven days a week until it was finished. They finished reviewing the job and then Joe asked Bill how everything was working at the cabin. Bill hesitated for a moment and then started another story.

"Well, Joe, I guess you should know that I have a feelin' that the FPL man was rightly pissed off the other day. So you might be getting a phone call," he said.

"What did you do now, Bill?" Joe asked, not really wanting to know, but figuring he should.

"Well, I didn't do nothing! You see, the meter man came by the other day to read the meter, 'cause that's what he does. Anyways, the dogs let him in; I guess it was too hot for them to run right to him, or they was runnin' through the woods or somethin', but the foolish little man parked way over yonder," Bill said as he pointed at a spot about fifty feet from the meter. "Well, I guess they were even nice enough to let him get out of his truck and walk on over to the meter, but by the time he finished readin' the meter and turned around to go back to his truck, the dogs had kind of settled themselves between him and his truck. I guess he panicked a little bit and started backing up and that's when he stumbled into the rattlesnake cage. Well, they kind of popped up and started rattlin' the way they do, and sure enough, he found himself between the rattlers and the dogs. I'm not sure how long he was there because I was down river in the whaler checkin' on things, but when I got up to the cabin and saw him standing there, I called the dogs and they came right to me and then he made like a jack rabbit and scampered on over to his truck. He was waving his hands and yelling all kinds of nasty words, and when I started to walk over to him to make sure everything was all right, he just drove off cursing like a drunk sailor from out the window. I don't think he got bit, 'cause he was still runnin' pretty good, so I figured the dogs done their job and deserved a bonus, so I went an' got 'em each a steak. So the way I figure it, you owe me for two steaks, Joe," Bill concluded.

"Bill, where the hell did the snakes come from, and what are you doing with them?" Joe demanded. He was not as amused as Bill thought he would be, but Pete was choking himself to keep from laughing, which only caused Joe to become more enraged.

"I been out of work and the college pays decent money for a snake they can milk. I told them I'd be happy to milk 'em too. I explained that I've milked plenty of cows, but they said they didn't want me milking 'em. Too bad too, 'cause that might have been fun. I guess I've given 'em about twenty snakes by now. There's a hell of a lot of rattlers running around here if you know where to look. Anyways, that boy over there by the barge is Mark Robinson. He don't know jack shit, but he'll work hard and he's pretty damn funny."

"I don't give a shit about funny, and you get rid of those snakes when we get done today," Joe demanded, and abruptly left them and started walking in a huff towards the barge. Pete and Bill looked at each other shrugged and laughed at the situation and then followed him to the barge. Joe walked up to Mark and extended his hand. Mark was a tall and skinny young man with blonde hair and fair skin. He was in his early twenties. He had an innocent face, but mischievous blue eyes.

"I'm Joe. You'd better work hard and do what I tell you." He then turned and looked at Bill and Pete. "Pete, get on the *Osage* and get ready to back up. You two man the lines, and then Bill, you get in the whaler and do what I tell you," Joe commanded.

Mark was taken aback and didn't know if he should untie the lines or run to his truck and escape while he had the chance. He hesitated for a moment, and then decided to hang around for at least one ride and so he followed Bill and untied the lines as instructed. Joe waved for Pete to put the boat in reverse and start pulling the barge off the bank.

Pete looked towards the bow and then at the river. The barge seemed so big and the river so small from where he was standing. He had run the *Osage* many times in tight and difficult situations before, but Joe was now glaring at him and it made him nervous. But he was confident in his abilities and did what came naturally and they slowly pulled away from the ramp, pivoted, and started down the river without a hitch.

Pete looked out at the river. He could see a light blue haze already building in the air and knew that by this afternoon it would be close to a hundred degrees. He stood behind the wheel, guiding them down the river, and waited for Joe to come and take command from him, but he never did. Instead, he walked back and forth between Pete and Bill, giving them instructions and guiding them along. Pete was amazed at how calm he was. He explained everything slowly and patiently for a while. When he was satisfied that everything was under control and they were going down a straight stretch of the river, he started teaching

Bill how to move the nose boat from side to side quickly. Bill was afraid to break the little boat and kept easing up to the barge. By the third time he'd eased up to the barge, Joe blew a gasket.

"I told you to ram the damn thing. Now back up and do it again!" he bellowed. Bill shook his head and eased the boat away from the barge. When he was about fifteen feet away, Joe yelled again. "Now punch it!" Bill cringed, but obeyed. He pushed the throttle full forward and picked up speed fast. He was sure that the boat was going to shatter into little pieces upon impact, but it didn't. The bracing did its job and the boat held together when it stopped abruptly. Bill hadn't braced himself properly for the impact and slammed into the helm and wheel when he collided with the barge.

"Now, that's how I want you to do it every time! Understand?"

Bill shook the cobwebs out of his head and tried to catch his breath, but when he saw the boat and his body still in one piece and realized that his boss was encouraging him to smash into things, he was like a puppy with a new toy! He started practicing ramming into the barge and was having the time of his life when they came to the first turn and Joe told him it was time to start working and stop playing.

Pete stood behind the wheel of the *Osage*. He wanted Joe to take the wheel and get them through the turn, but knew that wasn't going to happen, so he got ready and immersed himself in his surroundings. The motors purred slowly as they made their way to the hard turn to the right. There was a sand bar on the right and an eaten out bank with trees lying in the river on the left. Joe positioned himself so that he could easily communicate with both of them and started to signal Bill to tell him where to go, but he was already in place, so he turned his attention to Pete.

"Hug the sand bar. See how deep it is right off the bank? If you stay too far out in the middle and let the current get you, it'll push you right into those trees and your whole world will turn to shit in a hurry. Starboard in reverse and port full forward," he calmly said, and Pete followed his instructions. Bill started to push on the nose and it came around and they eased through the turn like they knew what they were doing. The river was straight for a stretch and then there was a hard left turn. Once again, before Joe could signal him, Bill was already in place on the other side of the barge. It quickly became apparent that Bill had been paying attention and would do a great job on the whaler.

They came to the left turn and Pete nervously stood behind the wheel, knowing that this was where it was going to be rough. It was a left hard turn and then he had to spin the barge around and back down the river.

"Put the starboard motor ahead and the port in reverse. You're going to spin this sucker around and back under that bridge just as pretty as you please. Don't be afraid to go right into that willow tree and let the branches push you back." Joe pointed to the willow tree on the east side of the river. Pete had watched Jeff do this maneuver many times and he made it look easy. Pete soon realized that he didn't have enough forward momentum and the current caught his bow and started pushing him downriver sideways.

"Give it some throttle! What's the matter with you? Kick this stern around right now or you're going to be in the shit." Joe started to raise his voice, but never made a move to take the wheel away from Pete. Pete wanted him to in the worst way, but it was apparent that Pete was going to have to do this himself. He kicked the throttles to full forward and full reverse. The motors screamed with displeasure and Bill pushed the bow upriver as hard as he could. Water was rushing out from behind the motors and slowly, the massive barge started to respond. When the bow was sufficiently upriver, Joe instructed Pete to ease off his motors and had Bill continue to push. Eventually, the bow made it around and was in position.

"Now, put both motors in slow reverse and let it come down with the river. When you need to adjust your nose, just pop one of the motors in forward and bring it around." Joe was calm again and the barge started to slowly back down the river. They followed Joe's instructions and backed downriver for the last half mile of the trip and slipped right into place. They tied the lines off and Joe put Mark in the nose boat and told him that his job was to stand by in case of emergency. Bill climbed into the loader and quickly started dumping rocks. When the barge was empty, Bill shut down the loader and climbed back into the whaler. Pete gave the *Osage* throttle and they eased up to the dolphins and hung the lines. Joe showed Mark how to write down the draw readings from the corners of the barge to record the weight of the rocks placed, and once that was done, they headed home.

Pete was amazed at how much quicker the barge responded when it was empty. They pushed back to the boat ramp quickly and tied it off, ready for another load. When everything was secure, Joe gathered the men around him.

"All right, get it loaded for tomorrow morning and check all the compartments before you leave tonight. Pete, while he's loading, I want you to take Mark and the whaler down and do a survey of the bottom with the depth finder. From here on out, you really have to pay attention to where you're placing the rocks so that we make the bottom flat. If we build a mound down there, they won't pay me until I go down and move the rocks by hand, and if I have to do that, I'll be really unhappy. I'll be back on Friday with more fuel. Remember, be careful and take your time."

"What do you mean you'll be back on Friday? Who's going to run the boat?" Pete said in a panic. He knew the answer, but he didn't like it.

"You are," Joe said in a matter-of- fact tone.

"What are you talking about? I can't run this boat. I have no clue what I'm doing," Pete protested in vain to Joe as he was getting into his truck.

"What do you mean? You just did it," Joe said with a smile as he shut the truck door and started his engine. Pete wanted to grab him out of his truck and not let him leave, but he knew that wasn't going to happen. So he continued to protest.

"Yeah, I ran it down one time and you were right there."

"Listen, if you can do it once, you can do it a thousand times, and you really didn't need me. You know how to run a boat." He put the truck in reverse and started to back up. Bonehead and Precious followed him to the gate and Pete wanted to join them, but instead he just stood there and watched him leave.

"Well, I guess you're the new boss man. Have fun with that!" Bill said as he started walking to his loader. Pete stood motionless and just stared into space for a few minutes. He was more nervous than he had ever been and almost let doubt creep into his mind, but he reminded himself that so many people had done so much more than he was being asked to do - Mrs. Anderson, Mr. Johnson, The Old Man on the dock - and then the lessons that were pounded into him in the dojo came to him. He finally accepted what Mr. Parks and Mr. Sanders had emphasized in their classes, often with kendo sticks: that he was better and could do more than he thought he could. Finally, it hit him: it was his turn. He had earned the right to be the boss man on this job, and Joe had shown full faith in him by leaving. He came out of his stupor and grabbed Mark and the two of them did the survey.

The next morning, Bill and Mark were on site bright and early and it was already hot. Pete called them into the kitchen and showed them the survey that he had completed the night before. It laid out where the pilings were, water depths, where they had enough rocks, and where they need to place more. Pete went over every unnecessary detail of his map because he was visibly nervous and was trying to waste as much time as possible to avoid starting the trip. He rambled on about where they were placing rock, offered them more coffee, and tried every stalling trick he could think of. Bill, on the other hand, was enjoying Pete's fear and was ready to see what the boy was made of.

"Well, I think we've covered everything except your momma's blood type. Do you want to go over that too, or should we move some rocks on down that river?" Bill said, and he and Mark enjoyed a quiet chuckle at Pete's expense.

"Screw you, you hillbilly bastard; let's do this," Pete conceded and walked to the barge and boat. He hadn't asked for, nor did he want this responsibility; he was scared and questioned his own ability, but he kept his composure and kept moving forward. He walked onto his boat and set his coffee on the console and started the motors. Mark walked up to him as he was getting ready and handed him the ugliest cigar he had ever seen.

"Here, take this. You might like it," Mark said.

"What the hell is this thing?"

"That, my friend, is a 'Back Woods' cigar. I think it's kind of chocolaty and you should smoke it on your maiden voyage as captain of this vessel. Here's a lighter, and once we get this thing spun around and start down the river, light that thing up." Mark was very proud of himself and went back to the barge and got in position to cast off the lines.

Pete looked ahead and realized that the two men were standing at their positions and awaiting *his* orders. He took a deep breath, raised his hand, and gave them the signal to cast off. He then put his motors in reverse and started to pull back. The barge responded and started to ease its way from the shoreline. Pete put the motors in neutral, and before he could signal, Bill was already in place and pushing on the bow to bring the nose down river.

The barge was straightened out and Pete began his first journey as captain on the river. He took a sip off his coffee and, after contemplating for a moment, decided to take Mark up on his offer and lit the cigar. He took a draw on it and was amazed; it was like chocolate, and the combination of it and the coffee was fabulous. Pete heard the screech of the eagle and looked up to see her gliding far above them. He enjoyed his coffee and cigar for a few minutes and then looked at the men talking at the front of the barge, the pristine river surrounding him, and the eagle above him. While they were gently going down the straight stretch, his mind wandered to his parents and the tragedies they'd dealt with and the battles they'd fought, and he was inspired by, and proud of the fact that *his parents* had stayed together through it all. He knew it was and always would be a constant battle, but he decided right then and there that life was worth living and living well and that love really was worth fighting for.

They approached the first turn and Pete was brought back to the job at hand. Pete kept his speed slow and his power in reserve. He saw that Bill was in position and they slid around the sandbar without any problems. They continued down, spun around, and backed the rest of the way down the river as if they had done it a thousand times. They unloaded and made it back without an incident and were deservedly proud of themselves.

When everyone had gone home for the evening, Pete walked over to the barge and sat by the river. He watched it meander by while sipping a beer and soon began to ponder where he was in life. He began quietly talking out loud to his little brother, and really wanted to hear him respond, but he didn't. He explained to Isaac that he was sorry for what had happened, and he begged his little brother for forgiveness for failing him, and forgiveness for the happiness he was feeling. He was ashamed of his feelings and felt duty bound to cling to the belief that he should remain forever unhappy and feel guilty for his failing Isaac, but he didn't. He had spent his life evading emotional connections with people and punishing himself, but now he was in love, and so too were his parents. He was happy for them, and he wanted Isaac to be happy for them too.

Over the next two weeks the three of them began to work like a team. Pete was confident in his abilities to do the work and finish the job, but they were behind schedule because the river was still not high enough to allow them to move large loads. They knew that they had to move more rocks in less time or they were going to be killed by the fines for being late. Pete and Bill had grown to love Joe and truly cared about this company and its success.

After a successful run, they decided to let Mark load the barge for a while. Pete and Bill went into the cabin to review the latest survey and figure out a way to get the job done on time.

"Well, the way I see it, when we got back up here, we had to move a little more than three thousand tons in thirty days. That's more than a hundred tons a day. We ain't getting but eighty tons a day, and we've been workin' for fourteen days, so that means we moved about 1,120 tons and we got about nineteen hundred to go. So we need to get two loads a day and three a couple of days a week in order to get done on time and maybe a little early. So if I was you, I'd get on that telephone there and call the office and tell Joe you need some lights cause we're gonna be runnin' in the dark," Bill said with a little smug confidence.

"What the hell was that? You think you've got it all figured out, don't you…. and I guess you do. You just like to play the dumb hillbilly, but you're not that dumb at all; you're just sneaky as hell," Pete said. He thought about what Bill had said, and even though he knew Bill was right, he did the math, and sure enough, everything Bill had said was correct, and the only solution to the problem was the one he'd laid out.

"Well, I don't like attracting attention to myself. I think the Good Book says something like it's better to be underestimated than overrated. Well, it says it's better to be called to higher chair than sent down to a lower one, but the meaning's the same." Bill proudly walked out of the cabin and kicked Mark out of the loader and told him that Pete wanted to talk to him about working some extra hours.

Pete watched Bill go to work and began to appreciate the fact that without this drunk hillbilly, his job would have been a lot harder. Mark came into the cabin and Pete laid out the plan to him. He readily agreed to work as many hours as he could as his wife was going to have a baby and they needed the money.

Pete called Joe, and the next day they were hooking up the lights. In order to get three loads in one day they would have to have the barge loaded heavily in the morning when they showed up, and then they would run two smaller loads in the afternoon and at night. The first time they ran three loads they left the boat ramp at six thirty in the morning, and by the time they off loaded the loader and finished tying up it was close to 1AM. It was a paranoid custom not to leave the loader on the barge overnight, so each and every night when they came back to the boat ramp they unloaded it before they could go home, grab something to eat, and catch a few hours of sleep.

They were able to put over two hundred tons in place and decided they could do three loads every other day. They were wearing down and starting to smell bad, but they began to feel confident about their chances to pull it off and none of them complained about the work. Instead they were determined to finish on time or early.

On the next run, everything was going as planned, but when they came off the willow branch and Pete attempted to put the motors in reverse, his starboard motor made a horrific sound as the piston went through the side of the motor, and then it fell silent. Pete was now down to one motor, but his abilities had grown, and while he was scared, he didn't panic. He competently moved Bill from side to side, kept everything under control, and was able to make it under the bridge and back to the cabin without another problem.

He called Joe when they got back to the cabin, and while Joe momentarily exploded, he quickly gained control of his emotions and tried his best to help them. He called everyone he knew, but after several calls, he concluded that there was no way for him to get them another motor before the job was completed. Pete would have to finish the job with one motor. They kept working, and while Pete had to go a little slower, they were able to keep moving rocks without interruption.

On the next Friday night, by the time they got the barge loaded, it was too late to make another trip down river, so Pete sent Mike to the store to buy beer while Bill finished loading for the morning run. They had overcome many obstacles, but they believed they could finish with a couple of days to spare. When everything was secured for the night, they built a small fire to stand around and reminisce in front of the cabin. Bill opened a warm beer while Pete and Mark enjoyed a cold one. They stood around talking about what they had done and planning what they were going to do the next day. They were in good spirits, optimistic, and being rather jovial as they stood around the fire.

While Bill and Mark were talking with each other and laughing about Bill almost going over the side in the loader, Pete noticed a big, fat mosquito on Mark's chin. Its belly was distended and full of blood. Pete decided he had to act quickly and kill the blood-sucking parasite before it got away, so without thinking, he slapped the mosquito. He was surprised at how fast his hand moved, and how loud the impact was. Karate had changed his reaction time, speed, and power. Mark stumbled backwards, almost falling into the fire, and grabbed the side of his face which had turned bright red from the violent strike he'd just received. He looked at Pete with a stunned look on his face, unsure of what he had done to warrant this attack.

"What the hell was that all about?" Mark protested.

"There was a mosquito on your chin, and I didn't want him to get away!"

Bill raised his eyebrows as he went back and forth looking at the two men. "Hey, Pete, if'n ever you see a giant skeeter on my chin, let him have all the blood he wants. You damn near broke the man's jaw!"

Mark rubbed his sore jaw and twisted it around to make sure everything was still working. He was relieved that he wasn't going to fight, and somewhat amused by it all, but his face was burning red and his jaw really did hurt. Before he could say a word, Pete was apologizing through his laughter.

"I am sooo sorry. I really didn't mean to hit you that hard." He continued to laugh as he reassured Mark that it was a horrible looking mosquito and that he was trying to protect him. "I was just trying to kill the mosquito. Look at my palm and your face; that thing was so full of blood that I'm not sure if he could have flown off."

"You mean that there was a mosquito on my face that I hadn't even noticed, and he was so full that if you had waited a second later, he would have fallen off and we could have just stepped on him....without breaking my jaw!"

"Well, yeah, something like that. I am sorry, Mark. I didn't mean to hit you so hard... but, damn, your face is red."

"Lord have mercy, look at that, it's a perfect outline of your hand right there on the side of his face. Cops wouldn't even have to dust for fingerprints; they're clear as can be," Bill chimed in.

Mark was, if nothing else, a really nice guy, and he soon started laughing a little bit and turned towards Bill. "If you *ever* see him trying to help me, or rescue me again, please stop him."

"Holy Hell, I know what you mean. You might have to save me from gettin' rescued too! Might be that if we fall in the river, he'd try'n save us from drowning with a harpoon or an anvil!" Bill said with an absolutely straight face.

He then looked at his two companions and after he was satisfied that he truly liked them, he continued talking. "You know boys, this is one of the damndest situations I have ever found myself in, and I have to tell you, I've had a few good jobs in my life, and a shit load of bad ones, and the one thing that I've learned over that time is that it's not about what you're doing, or where you're doing it, it's who you're doing it with, and boys, this is a hell of a deal."

They stood around the fire for a while longer, telling stories and basking in the reassuring tranquility that is afforded good people while enjoying each other's company. They finished their beers, Mark said it was time for him to get some sleep, Pete concurred, and Bill left with a look on his face that said he was just getting started.

Bright and early the next morning, Bill showed up and was in a hurry to get downriver.

"Come on, finish that coffee or take it with you, but let's get a move on." Pete looked at him and laughed, but Bill continued to try to make him understand the urgency of the moment. "I'm serious now. Hurry up and go fire up that boat and let's get down the river," Bill said, unusually agitated.

"What's the matter, Bill? Why are you in such a hurry this morning?" Pete asked.

"Oh, it's nothin', but we should just move along and get away from here and downriver, that's all," Bill said nervously.

"Bill...you've got to tell me what's going on or we're not moving," Pete retorted.

"Well, I kind of poked a man last night and I figured there might be some people comin' around askin' questions and such, so it might be best to be out in the middle of the river where they can't bother me."

"Bill... did you stab somebody last night after you left here?"

"No, no, no. I just kind of poked a little hole in him with my pocket knife, that's all. If I was going to stab him, I'd have used a real knife, not a little pocket knife. See, they let me back into Jo Jo's, and after we got off work last night, I went in to have a beer or three and I was sittin' there talking with this feller. He seemed like a nice enough guy and we was havin' a pleasant little conversation and then I guess he decided to be funny and asked me, 'If a man and woman get divorced in Kentucky, are they still brother and sister?' Well, let me tell you what: my momma's from Kentucky and so was my granny. He was a big old boy and I asked him to apologize, but he laughed at me and that just wasn't polite. I thought about it for a minute or two, and there only seemed like one thing to do. Well, there was two, but I wasn't drunk enough to shoot his dumb ass, so I poked a little hole in him. It was only a little hole, no big deal. Now you know, so can we get down the river?" Bill said as started walking onto the barge with Mark.

Pete just shook his head and assumed his position behind the wheel. He hoped Bill was exaggerating, because he couldn't afford to lose him to a jail cell just yet. He looked at Mark as he untied the lines and then at Bill, who nervously glanced at the cars passing by. When they were ready, he put the boat in reverse and they started their work day. They successfully ran the first of three loads that day, and by the end of the night they were tired, and nobody had ever come by to question Bill. They had been able to move enough rock to have a real chance of finishing with a day or two to spare.

It was after midnight when they secured the barge back at the boat ramp. They were all dead on their feet, and when Pete looked at the two of them, he decided to be nice and allowed them to keep the loader on deck for the night. He told them to check the barge compartments for leaks while he secured the boat. When they left for the night, they were exhausted but feeling good.

Pete staggered into his bedroom and collapsed on his bed. In a span of time that felt like two minutes, the alarm was going off. It was already five thirty, and as he struggled to get out of bed he realized that he had not taken his shoes off. He staggered towards the coffee maker, still partially asleep, and put the coffee and water in the machine. He looked around, not quite sure if he was dreaming or awake while he waited for the magic brew. When there was enough in the pot, he poured a cup and started walking towards the bathroom. Something caught his eye and made him turn and look out the window. He stared out the window and prayed that he was still sleeping and having another bad dream. He silently and calmly took another sip of his coffee and then came to the conclusion that, unfortunately, he was awake and what he was looking at was real. His heart began to race, and he found it hard to catch his breath.

The front corner of the barge had sunk during the night and the loader was gone. Presumably it had rolled off and was now sitting on the bottom of the river. The boat was still tied securely to the stern of the barge and was now about five feet in the air. Pete just stood and stared; his belly started doing somersaults and his knees buckled, but he remained upright. When he regained his composure, he picked up the phone and dialed Joe's number. It was 5:45 in the morning when Joe, still sleeping, picked up the phone.

"Hello," Joe groggily answered.

"It's gone."

"Hello. What's gone?" He was more awake now.

"It's just gone. It was there last night; but now it's gone."

"What the hell are you talking about, it's gone? What's gone?" Joe was now fully awake and aggravated. He knew something bad had happened, but he couldn't make any sense of what Pete kept saying.

"The loader! It's gone. The front of the barge sank last night and it's gone." Pete finally began to make sense.

"Son of a bitch!" Joe screamed and then hung up the phone. Pete looked out the window and saw Bill and Mark standing outside staring at the barge. Rage replaced exhaustion and he wanted to run outside and knock the hell out of both of them.

"Bill, what the fuck! I told you to check the barge last night and you told me you did. What the fuck is this!" Pete screamed. It was the first time Bill had ever seen or heard Pete cursing with anger. Pete was wide awake and the blood was coursing through his veins.

Bill looked at Pete, shrugged his shoulders and replied, "We checked the ones that normally leak." He had said it in such a simple, matter-of-fact manner that Pete was staggered. He didn't know what to do. As much as he wanted to at that moment, he knew he could never hit Bill, and Bill knew it too.

"Find the damn pump, get some plastic, and start getting the water out of there," Pete said as he turned away and started back inside the cabin so that he could try to call Joe again.

"Where's the loader?" Mark asked innocently.

Bill and Pete both stopped in their tracks and looked at him. Pete was ready to hit somebody and he decided that Mark had just volunteered. Bill saw the look in Pete's eye and grabbed Mark by the arm and quickly led him onto the barge and away from Pete. Most of it was still above water, but the rake and the front left compartment were several feet below the water. Bill and Mark got the pump and put the suction hose in the hole and made a seal with the sheet of plastic. After a few attempts they had it sealed fairly well and started pumping water.

Pete tried calling Joe again, but he couldn't reach him. He went out to the barge, helped secure what was left on deck, and after about an hour there was nothing they could do but watch the pump work. After another half hour, the barge started to rise from the bottom.

A short time later they saw a cloud of dust and heard the truck coming. Joe was coming down the road hard and fast. The three of them looked at each other and waited for impact. The truck came to a sliding halt and Joe jumped out. Pete and Bill were surprised to see Jeff and Giles in the truck with him.

"What the hell have you done to my barge?" Joe demanded.

"I screwed up, Joe. I thought I had all the compartments checked, but I must have missed a leak. It was my fault. I don't know what happened," Pete stammered. Bill was listening and had expected Pete to blame everything on him, as was Joe.

"You're damn right it's your fault and your responsibility. I hope you don't expect to get paid for today," Joe said as he started pulling his dry suit and hard hat out of the back of the truck. Joe was mad as hell, but at least they hadn't tried to bullshit him and had accepted responsibility. He continued to be infuriated, but he stopped yelling and went to work. Everyone knew what needed to be done and started working without being told. Jeff walked the crane down to the water's edge, while Pete hooked up the compressor and radio and the other men stood by and waited.

Giles and Bill stood next to each other and almost looked like long lost brothers.

"I thought you went and quit this operation," Bill commented to Giles.

"Hell, I couldn't stay away and miss all this fun," Giles replied.

"Well, I know what you mean. I am convinced that there ain't nothing quite like this show anywhere on Earth," Bill agreed.

It took a couple of hours, but they got the loader back on the river bank and the barge was steadily rising out of the water. When enough water was pumped out, Bill climbed inside to find the leak. It didn't take long to find it, and when he did, he was embarrassed. The hole was on the side of the barge and it was less than the size of a quarter. He climbed out of the compartment while the others were disconnecting the loader from the crane and mixed up a batch of two part epoxy. He then jumped overboard and put the epoxy over the hole. A minute later it was patched. Bill felt horrible because he knew that had he done his job properly, they could have put the patch on the barge in ten minutes last night and avoided this calamity. As he swam back to shore, he looked over and saw everyone working frantically to get back online, and he knew that it was his lack of attention to detail that had caused this disaster.

They drained and flushed all the fluids from the machine and refilled it again. By the time they were done with fluids, filters, and grease, Joe had spent well over a thousand dollars that he didn't have and they had lost a day. The six of them worked diligently, and by four that afternoon, Bill was loading rocks.

CHAPTER 50

THE RIDE TO PETER'S SOUL

They had overcome so many obstacles and yet they were going to finish on time. Pete finally felt like all the ghosts of his past had left him. A year earlier he'd been a lost boy, but now he felt and acted like a man in control of his destiny. He had found a job that he loved, a boss that he respected, and one that respected him. He had hated living in Caryville when the job had started, but was now glad that he had accepted the challenge because he felt like he had found his calling in operating boats, and he had made a real and unique friend in Bill.

Pete watched him maneuver the loader around the deck, clearing the last few rocks, and then he looked at his watch. It was getting late in the afternoon, after two already. Since the barge sinking incident Bill had been amazing. He was diligent and serious. Bill had always been talented with the machines, but now he was working with speed and determination. When they finished this load they had one small load left on the ground, then they would push down the river and do it one last time.

It was an unreasonably hot day, a dark blue haze hung in the air, and temperatures were in excess of a hundred degrees and there was absolutely no breeze. They were long past tired, and Bill had worked himself to near exhaustion. Today had been extra hard on him because Mark hadn't come to work; a very pregnant and sick wife had taken priority. Pete was upset when Mark had called, but he understood and knew that he and Bill could do the last runs alone because they had done it once before when Mark had had to rush off to his wife. Not much changed for Pete because he ran the boat and had to remain at the wheel at all times; this left Bill to do the work of two men. He finished pushing off the last of the rocks, parked the loader, and made his way to the whaler.

Everything went flawlessly. They returned to the boat ramp, tied up the barge, and immediately started loading more rocks. Bill worked in overdrive, wanting to finish before midnight. It was hard enough to do their job in the light, but when it got dark on the river it was even worse. The mosquitoes came out in force, it was hard to see the edge of the barge with the loader, and it seemed like anything that could go wrong usually did go wrong.

Pete had the boat running and was ready to go when Bill put the last of the rocks on deck. Bill got out of the loader, cast off the lines, jumped into the whaler, and pushed the barge away from the bank. Pete could do nothing but watch him work because they were now down to one motor, and reverse had stopped working the day before.

With the barge away from the bank, Pete put the boat in gear and they headed downriver. When they came around the last turn, Pete turned the barge hard to port and into the willow tree. The barge spun around perfectly, and when the stern of the boat was downstream, Pete released the throttle and the branch sprang back and pushed them away from the bank and downriver just as Pete planned. With no reverse, they were forced to slowly drift with the current. Pete would occasionally put the motor in gear to bring the nose around one way or the other. He was in complete control of his vessel, and they drifted into position without a problem. They didn't bother tying off to the dolphins and instead free-floated under the bridge. Pete gave the boat just enough throttle to stop their motion, and then for the next hour he carefully moved the barge around the final section as Bill unloaded the rock.

When Bill dumped the last bucket over the side and shut the loader down, he climbed down and looked at Pete with a big shit-eating grin on his face. Two weeks ago they had been behind schedule and told by numerous people that they would never finish on time. They had done it, and the weight of the world was off their shoulders.

"Well, hell, that's all the rocks. Now what do we do? I just worked my way out of a job!" Bill said, half jokingly.

"You crazy assed hillbilly, get in your boat and let's go home and get drunk!"

"Now you're a-talkin' my language!"

Bill got in his little boat and Pete hit the throttle and started up the river. Bill helped get the nose pointing in the right direction and then he pulled away and tried to move the turbidity curtain they had been using out of the channel, but as he staggered around the bow of his boat wrestling with the curtain, his boat violently kicked sideways and almost knocked him into the river. He slipped and fell, and in order to keep from going over the side, he had to let go of the curtain.

Pete watched in horror. The sharp turn was coming up. He had one motor and no reverse. He didn't know if he could make it through the turn without the nose boat, but as he looked at Bill fighting to regain control of his boat, he knew he was about to find out. He idled down and kept the starboard bow as close to the bank as he dared. When the nose of the barge hit the current, he gave the motor full throttle and cut the wheel hard. The bow stopped going to the left, but was not coming around as fast as he wanted. He looked back at Bill, who was now chasing the curtain downstream.

"To Hell with it; let it go!" Pete yelled at the top of his lungs. He knew Bill couldn't hear him, but a tight knot was growing in the small of his back, so he clenched his butt cheeks as tight as he had ever felt, cursed the river, and pleaded for the nose to come around. Without a nose boat, and with less than half the normal horsepower behind it, it lumbered slowly. The nose of the barge eventually turned upriver, but unfortunately by the time it had come around, the stern was in the bank and eating tree limbs again. Pete listened in the darkness as the propeller ground on the branches, praying that it wouldn't break the propeller. It didn't and they eventually began to move upstream again. He was quickly approaching the hard turn to the left. Pete had never done it without a nose boat during the day, and now it was night and he was almost blind. He backed off the throttle, hoping to have torque in reserve that would push him through when he got into the turn. He looked back into the black night, hoping to hear the scream of Bill's motor, but he heard nothing.

He cranked the wheel hard to port and pushed the throttle all the way forward in a vain attempt to power through the turn. This time the barge did not respond. They were going into the bank on the starboard bow and there wasn't a thing Pete could do to stop it. His mind flashed a vision of losing the barge on the last run of the job; he wasn't going to let that happen, and immediately redoubled his resolve to fight until the end.

Suddenly Pete heard the whine of the little boat as it came quickly up the river. "Come on you bastard, get the hell over here," he yelled to Bill as he came zooming by trying to get to the bow before it was in the trees. Bill got between the barge and the bank, but not soon enough. Bill never made it to the bow, and where he was stopped, there was no longer room to get his boat perpendicular to the barge and push. The starboard bow of the barge had made contact with an old cypress stump and the side of the barge was being pushed against the bank by the current.

Pete was yelling at the top of his lungs when he saw that Bill was trapped between the bank and the barge. The whaler was pinned against a large tree and was in imminent danger of being crushed. Bill had nowhere to go. Pete turned white and his stomach twisted, afraid of what he might see.

"Get out of there. Come on Bill, get the fuck out," Pete yelled in panic at the top of his lungs and in a lower tone he pleaded… "Oh, Jesus Christ, please get him out of there, please. Oh, Christ, please get him out. Don't take another one from me, please."

Pete could just see the top of Bill's head as he stood in his boat and looked for an escape. Bill looked feverishly, but found none. There was a big black wall of steel in front of him and a tall steep river bank behind him. Pete continued to fight the river, but as he watched the barge continue to squeeze Bill, he knew he couldn't deal with another death on a river.

"Looks like we're gonna ride this one out, partner," Bill yelled to Pete with a smile and a strange look of acceptance on his face. The boat let out a loud and pained crack as it was squeezed between the barge and a tree, and it caused Bill to jerk his head around and refocus on the task at hand. He kept the wheel turned to port as hard as he could. He knew it was a true effort in futility, but he wasn't going to quit fighting even while he began to wonder if this wasn't the end of the road.

Pete felt lost, and was filled with fear and unsure of what to do, but an instant later a strange and reassuring calmness came over him. He didn't understand the warmth, but he accepted it and he stopped fighting the river. He reached up and backed off the throttle. The stern of the barge slowly started to move into the bank and the pressure was relieved at the bow. The barge was now moving back and the bow started to come away from the bank.

Bill almost wet his pants, he was so happy to be alive. Both men hooped and hollered when the whaler began to turn the barge into the current. The *Osage* motor was now in the trees again, but this time it was mostly small willow branches, and when the time came to give it throttle and move upriver, the motor chewed them up and spit them out without a problem.

"Thank you, dear God, oh, thank you," Pete said quietly to himself. "Thank you, Isaac." He was overcome with happiness seeing that crazy hillbilly standing in his boat.

Once they were on the last stretch of the river, Bill pulled away and moved his boat back to the *Osage* and floated next to Pete. "Now, ya see, I told ya there wasn't nothin' to it," Bill said with a smile. Pete looked at his friend and shook his head. "You crazy bastard, I thought I was going to have to clean your stain off the side of this barge. I'm buying the beer tonight!"

"Well, I won't fight you on that one," Bill answered.

The men brought the barge back up the river, unloaded it, and then tied it off without another problem. The barge sat parallel to the rip-rap protected bank with the nose of the barge upriver. Pete secured the boat and Bill checked *all* the compartments in the barge. When he opened the second compartment on the starboard side, he didn't even have to look in.

"We ain't drinkin' yet, Pete; looks like we got a geyser here. Why don't you grab the epoxy and I'll get the dive gear. How much air is left in the tank?" Bill was really bummed to have to dive on the river in the middle of the night, but he wasn't one to complain and, since he'd begged to learn how to do it, he knew that it was his job to dive under the barge when it needed patching.

Joe had told him that Pete was never to dive on the barge, but never told him why. When Bill had started diving on the barge he'd loved it, but he had grown to hate it. It was dark outside and it was going to be pure black under the barge. At first he thought diving in the river was a game, but he had found that he really didn't like swimming with the gators as much as he thought he would, and late at night wasn't a fair fight; he'd never see it coming.

He reluctantly picked up the tank and put the regulator on it. The needle moved a little, too little. There was a little over two hundred pounds of pressure. Bill shook his head and looked over at Pete.

"Aw, hell Pete, there ain't hardly enough air to last ten minutes down there. We got to do this right the first time or we're gonna be up all night with the pumps and I'm just too damn tired for that."

Pete came over to where Bill was getting set up just as a boat went downriver, casting a large wake. The barge bobbed up and down on the waves and the front of the barge bounced off a few large rocks on the bank. The area around the boat ramp was supposed to be a no wake zone where boats idled by, but some of the fishermen were working in a hurry and had no respect for No Wake Zones. Pete jumped to his feet and waved his hands in the air, cursing the operator as he by.

Bill put the regulator in his mouth, and when he was satisfied that everything was working properly, he took the equipment and walked to the water's edge. Pete followed him and helped him put the tank on his back and then returned to the deck to mix the epoxy. When he finished mixing it, he handed Bill a baseball-sized gob, the bolt, and a plate. Bill put his mask on, put the regulator in his mouth, and then disappeared under the water.

Pete climbed down the hatch and into the compartment. The hole was about the size of a silver dollar and was only about two feet from the side of the barge that was against the bank. The water rushing into the barge was loud and reminded Pete of standing near the base of a waterfall. When Pete was next to the hole, he pushed a stick through and tapped on the bottom of the barge to let Bill know he was in position. A moment later, Bill tapped back and then he inserted the bolt through the hole.

As Pete was putting his pieces into place he heard the hum of an approaching boat. He hoped that this time the operator would slow down. He listened to the pitch of noise. It changed; he was slowing down. Pete went back to work, but the boat never went to idle speed; it slowed and pushed an even larger wake than he would have if he had stayed on plane. Pete heard the waves hit the side of the barge and felt the barge rise and fall. He heard the grinding of the barge on the rocks and then he heard the pounding on the bottom of the barge. Bill was not tapping any longer; he was pounding.

Pete hesitated, and then was filled with panic. Bill was pounding and pounding. Pete was yelling to him, but all he heard in response was more pounding. There was no way to communicate with each other and Pete knew what he had to do. He shivered with a cold sweat that instantly formed on his body.

"Oh, Christ, no," Pete said to himself as he went up the ladder and out of the compartment. He looked around for help, but there was no one. He ran and dove off the side of the barge with his mind racing. He turned in the water and quickly swam to the side of the barge. "Fuck me" he angrily said aloud, and then he took a long and deep breath and forced as much air into his lungs as they could hold. He pulled himself down and went under the barge. He could hear Bill pounding on the barge, but when he opened his eyes, the only thing he could see was black. His mind raced with visions of Isaac, ice, and alligators.

He swam toward the pounding noise as fast as he could, and when he thought he was close to Bill, he opened his eyes again. He was blind. Panic began to set in and he felt his lungs burn again in their desire for air, but he fought the urge and forged ahead. He put his arms in front of him and suddenly he felt the cool, soft mud of the river bank. His mind was racing and using his air too quickly, and he was filled with an unquenchable desire to go to the surface and breathe.

He instinctively gave into the need for self-preservation, but when he started to rise to the surface, his back hit the bottom of the barge. There was nowhere to go. He opened his eyes again and frantically turned his head in all directions for light, but saw none. He reached out again and this time he felt something soft hit his hand. He was startled and quickly pulled away, but he realized it was Bill and not a gator. He felt Bill grab onto him, and suddenly time seemed to stand still while his mind raced.

He saw Isaac laughing and throwing a snow ball at him; he saw him dancing on the ice at the bottom of the hill. Then he saw Isaac again. This time his face was blue and filled with anguish and he was pleading for life. Pete was filled with emotions that were about to overcome him. He was ready to surrender and join his brother when he felt Bill pull him violently towards him and it brought him back to reality.

He opened his eyes again; he couldn't even see a shadow. He grabbed hold of Bill's arm with both hands and put his feet under him and against the bank and tried to pull him away from the bank, but Bill started flailing wildly and Pete knew he was badly hurt and pinned where he was. Bill was trapped on his back and somehow Pete had to figure out what was keeping him pinned and how he was going to free him. Pete was now out of breath and feared dying; panic was beginning to overtake him. He wanted so badly to open his mouth and take a breath of air.

He felt Bill grab hold of his arm and pull him again. Pete didn't resist and suddenly felt the rubber of the regulator hit him in the face.

He greedily grabbed it and shoved it in his mouth. He exhaled and then took in a deep breath. The air felt so cool and reinvigorating in his lungs that his mind slowed and the panic subsided. After a breath or two, he took the regulator out of his mouth and gave it back to Bill. He put his hands on Bill's torso and began to feel around in an attempt to find where he was wedged.

When Pete had worked his way down to Bill's legs, Bill moved his right leg out of the way. Pete was working quickly, knowing that they were almost out of air and that Bill was in severe pain. He reached across and found Bill's left leg. He clutched onto his shorts and began to feel down. He felt Bill's knee cap and continued to slide his hand downward. The side of his hand hit something sharp and Bill pounded wildly. Pete didn't need to see to realize that it was his bone and it was sticking out of his leg. Pete's stomach churned and he resisted the urge to vomit and jump away. Dread overtook him. He pulled his hands away momentarily, frightened and not knowing what to do. His heart was racing again and he needed more air.

He moved towards Bill's head and reached for and took the regulator from Bill and put it in his mouth and took a couple more breaths. The lessons of control that he had studied and learned in the dojo came to him. He slowed his breathing and took control of his mind and body. He returned to Bill's leg and found it grossly snapped and pinned between two rocks. The barge was sitting on top of one of the rocks, holding it in place. Pete tried to move the rock off his leg but it was futile.

Pete put his legs on the ground and his back against the barge and pushed hard in a vain attempt to lift it off the rocks, but it didn't move. His heart sank and anguish filled his soul. He tried again and again in desperation, but nothing moved. He worked his way back up to Bill and the air. He put the regulator in his mouth. There was no rush of air filling his lungs this time; he had to draw the last of the air from the tank and into his lungs. There was no more air in the tank.

He wanted to cry and swim out from under the barge and make the excuse to himself and the world that he was going to get help, when he knew in his heart that he just wanted out. He was trying his best to stay calm, but death was near him again, and again he was impotent. Peter was convinced of their doom and tempted to exhale and end his suffering.

Once again he was visited by a vision of Isaac that filled his mind. He could see him clearly. Isaac was at peace. The sense of warmth returned to him, and with it, resolve. He decided to fight on until the very end. This time he was not leaving without his partner. Pete handed the regulator to Bill and went back to the rocks.

He worked his way down Bill's body and returned to the rock that held their fate. He braced his back against the barge and pulled on the rock. It never moved; Peter was expecting a miracle, but there was none to be had. His lungs began to burn again with the need for air, and despair was quickly returning to him. He began to lose all hope when he suddenly heard a faint buzz in the water. It got louder and louder; a boat was coming up the river. He heard the hum change as the boat came off plane. There was renewed hope and he braced himself again and pushed. When the first wave hit the barge it moved a little, but the rock did not. He re-braced his legs as the second wave lifted the barge. The rock came out and Bill immediately pulled away. Peter's lungs were burning now and he wanted air badly. Bill rolled over and began scrambling for the edge of the barge and the air he so desperately needed. Peter was swimming with him, pulling his friend with his hands and kicking feverishly with his legs. He frantically swam and felt along the bottom of the barge, knowing he was so close to another chance at life.

He wanted to exhale, but knew he couldn't; after a moment that felt like an hour, he finally felt the corner of the barge and pulled himself up and out. When his face broke the surface, he refilled his lungs with fresh, life giving air. He was mentally and physically exhausted, and desperately wanted to stop for a moment and catch his breath. He reached out and grabbed hold of a tire on the side of the barge and helped Bill get a hold of it. He looked at Bill with relief in his heart, but when he saw the pain in Bill's face, he knew there was more work to be done. He wrapped his arm around Bill's chest and pulled him to the bank.

When Bill got out of the water and Pete saw his leg for the first time, he wanted to vomit, but again he controlled himself. He took off his belt and made a tourniquet, put Bill's arm around his shoulder, and carried him up the bank and put him into his truck. Pete ran around the truck and started driving like a bat out of Hell down Highway 90 to Bonifay.

"Well, shit, I guess I screwed up our plans, now didn't I? But don't think you're getting out of buying the beer. I just need a little time to get my leg put back together, and then I will be honored to drink your beer." Bill tried to laugh even though he was beginning to go into shock, "And, I have to admit to you that I am becoming soft in my old age, because this really hurts like holy Hell and has definitely ruined an otherwise good day." Bill knew he was going to be fine, but he was worried about Pete, and he couldn't help but try to make him laugh.

Pete looked over at Bill, and when their eyes met, the smile on Bill's face and the gratitude in his eyes said all that needed to be said. Pete had saved his life.

Pete got him to the hospital, and at that late hour the small town hospital was quiet and Bill got immediate attention. When he was wheeled into the back, Pete found a phone and called Joe to let him know what had happened. Joe was instantly awake, and after making sure Bill was okay, he got out of bed and was on his way to the hospital.

Pete sat alone in the waiting room while the doctors worked on Bill. He browsed a couple of magazines and then looked at a table and saw an old Bible sitting there. He didn't know why, but he remembered something Grandpa Nevers had told him years before and was surprised that he remembered the chapter and verse from so long ago. Psalms Chapter 34, verse 4. He opened the book and found it.

He sat back and smiled to himself and finally understood the people he'd met and admired, what they had done, and how they persevered. "I sought the LORD, and he heard me, and delivered me from all my fears." Mrs. Anderson had been comforted her whole life by that, and so had Grandpa Nevers. He kept reading, and after a while Joe showed up and walked into the hospital with his hair flying in all directions, his shirt untucked, and his shoes untied. It was apparent that he had wasted no time getting ready. Pete explained what had happened and was surprised when Joe remained calm and was only concerned with Bill's well-being. They talked for a few minutes until he was convinced that everything was done and Bill was going to be okay.

"Now you can take some time off to get yourself recharged, but remember, we still have to get the barge back to the boatyard. You are going to make that run with us, aren't you?" Joe asked.

"I wouldn't miss it for the world," Pete assured him.

CHAPTER 51

REDEMPTION

It was a fine Saturday morning at Grayton Beach. A gentle sea breeze was blowing and the sand looked like snow. Terns were dancing along the water's edge as waves from the Gulf lapped gently at the beach. Pete took in all that was around him while Karen stood beside him holding his hand. Pete embraced the moment and was truly free and totally at peace for the first time since that horrific day on the Housatonic so long ago and so far away.

Pete squeezed Karen's hand to reassure himself that she was really there, and then he looked out at the ocean and thought about his journey through life so far. He thought about all the people that had touched his life and helped him along the way. He thought about Isaac, Mrs. Anderson, Grandpa Nevers, and that crazy hillbilly, and then he looked up to the clouds, and though he didn't see the cross he was hoping for, he knew it was there. Mrs. Anderson had shown him that it was always there, even when you can't see it. While he was looking at the clouds, he said to Grandpa Nevers, "I think He's proud of me today."

He looked at the girl standing next to him. She was beautiful and he was in love with her, and at that moment he knew that he wanted to spend the rest of his life with her. He heard the water lapping at the beach and knew that he had come full circle. The water had almost destroyed his life, and now he wanted to spend his life working on it. If he was going to go to school, why not become Captain Peter Taylor.

He looked over at his father and fought desperately to conceal the small tear that began to well in his eye. He was so happy for the man, his father, and honored to be standing next to him on this beautiful morning. They had been through so much, and had been lost for so long, but they were still standing and they were standing together.

The music started and Karen kissed Pete on the cheek and joined the small gathering of people who'd chosen to witness this act of enduring love. Art Evens and his wife of almost fifty years watched with pride, accompanied by their son; behind them, Pete was surprised to see Joe and Jeff sitting next to Mr. Johnson in the second row. He and his father looked at the boardwalk as Anne walked over the bridge in her dress, and Pete realized that his mother was a stunning woman.

"Holy crap, Dad, that's Mom! She looks great, doesn't she?" Pete smiled at his father. "How did you ever land a woman like her? I never realized you had game."

"The old man has more game than you'll ever know, son; you just make sure you don't drop the ring in the sand."

Anne soon joined them and the ceremony began. The minister was a dedicated man who had recently become a dear friend of Bill and Anne. He proudly stood before the assembled people and began to speak.

"Before we begin, I've requested and been granted the opportunity to read a short poem that was written by a friend of mine. His niece was getting married and at the time he was flat broke. This poem was the only gift he could give her, and he hoped that through it she would understand how much he loved her. I think it may have special meaning to Bill and Anne, because this day sanctifies the fact that they remembered why they began this journey through life together."

<u>*The Beginning*</u>

It is the end of I
And the beginning of we
A change made willingly
A change made lovingly

Patiently embrace your life
Patiently embrace your love
Act with consideration
Act with cooperation

When times fill with strife
(They will, that's life)
Remember back upon this day
And the reasons for choosing this way

Remember the words, the oath and the pledge
Can you see her eyes?
Can you feel his embrace?
To find real love is rare
So, say thank you, and handle with care.

The emotional ceremony continued and when the moment came, Pete handed his father the ring and stood back and watched. He, more than anyone, knew their journey. He knew the tragedies they'd endured and the battles they'd fought and now he saw the love in their eyes and watched them embrace and remarry; he let the tear fall from his eye and didn't care what anyone thought.

Jonathan Gunger, the youngest of nine children, grew up in Shelton, Connecticut. He moved to Florida in 1984 to work with his brothers. He is a published poet, licensed building contractor, and Realtor˚. He and his wife of twenty years have five children and live in southwestern Florida.